BETWEEN
NOW AND
FOREVER

MARGARET DUARTE

Omie
PRESS

Book Cover design Yocla Designs by Clarissa

Publisher's Cataloging-in-Publication Data

Names: Duarte, Margaret, 1949- author.
Title: Between now and forever / Margaret Duarte.
Description: Elk Grove, CA : Omie Press, 2019. | Series: Enter the between, bk. 4. | Previously published in 2013 by Philophrosyne Publishing, Elk Grove, CA.
Identifiers: LCCN 2019905391 | ISBN 978-0-9860688-8-1 (paperback) | ISBN 978-0-9860688-9-8 (ebook)
Subjects: LCSH: Women--Fiction. | Self-actualization (Psychology)--Fiction. | Spiritual life--Fiction. | Quantum theory--Fiction. | Paranormal fiction. | Suspense fiction. | BISAC: FICTION / Visionary & Metaphysical. | FICTION / Occult & Supernatural. | FICTION / Women. | GSAFD: Occult fiction. | Suspense fiction.
Classification: LCC PS3604.U244 B47 2019 (print) | LCC PS3604.U244 (ebook) | DDC 813/.6--dc23.

This book is dedicated in loving memory to my father and mother, Jack and Anne van Steyn.

Winter

2001

The fourth path of initiation begins in
the North, the place of knowledge and wisdom.

You know me. I'm the sub. You've met me at least a dozen times during your days in school, stiff, alert, nose twitching like a cornered rabbit, hushing and shushing, eyes darting from student to student, looking for allies and finding none. You blushed for me and then proceeded to torment me and leave me as road kill without a second thought, except maybe: Let her get another job, if she can't handle this one.

At least that would have been my story, if I hadn't come armed.

I have a special gift, you see, an elevated mental power. Not highly refined, mind you, but something I put to good use once in a while. Use only in case of emergency, is my motto. And this was definitely an emergency.

BETWEEN
NOW AND
FOREVER

Chapter One

W E'VE GOT A NEW sub!"

The short kid with the tall voice bounded into the classroom with the exuberance of a kindergartener rather than the more guarded, image-conscious demeanor of a thirteen-year-old. His backpack hit his desk with an attitude. "Our last sub quit."

It was hard to tell if he was talking to me or just thinking out loud, because he hardly even glanced my way, too busy twitching and wiggling like a terrier pup.

"What's your name?" the kid called out, not bothering to check the whiteboard, which displayed my name in large block letters: MS. VEIL.

I pointed to it now, determined to keep an eye on the rest of the students filtering into the room—my chance to observe them before their guards went up. Nothing soft or preppy about these kids. Instead of the blues and pinks their parents had dressed them in not all that long ago, the predominant colors were now black and brown, the texture torn and frayed, accessorized by hoops and chains hanging from the most unlikely places. But their appearance, I knew, was deceiving. West Coast Middle School drew students from the millionaires' enclave of Atherton and the district of Sharon Heights, which included mansions set around Sharon Heights Golf and Country Club. The spending per pupil here nearly doubled the national average. Their outfits flashed cash, not bargain basement.

"Can I call you Ms. V?" the kid asked.

Before I could answer his question, there came another. "What's your name?" This from a girl with three inches of belly exposed between low-slung black jeans and a cropped T-shirt.

I shivered. It was January 7, and even in the paradise setting of Menlo Park, the cold still chilled my bones. How had she gotten out of the house dressed like that? Her attire—highlighted by a grinning skull medallion, black fingernails, and spiked black and red hair—was surely against school rules.

I placed a transparency of the seating chart on the overhead projector and started marking plus signs next to the names of students who were seated and quiet.

"Hey, what're the marks for?" It was the pup again. I located him on the seating chart. Time to give him a name *and* some of my attention.

"I'll tell you in a bit, Brad."

His head jerked and his eyes grew wide. "How'd you know my name?"

I pointed to my temple. "Psychic."

"She's looking at the seating chart, stupid." This from one of the quiet boys I had just awarded a plus. But the plus held. Wyatt, too, was helping me, though he didn't know it.

As I continued to dole out pluses, more students noticed and caught on, plopping into their seats and pulling out binders and pens.

"What're the marks for?" someone called from the back.

"You'll see," I said.

The tardy bell rang, which had another five kids scrambling to their seats. Those who remained standing, or were still talking, earned a minus next to their names.

"Why'd Jason get a minus?" Brad wanted to know.

"Yeah," Jason said, looking at the overhead chart and, belatedly, lowering himself onto his chair. "What's the minus for?"

I held up my hand and put my index finger to my lips. No point in explaining. Not with that loud voice blaring over the intercom. "We've designated this week *School Violence Awareness Week*. Activities include opportunities for student discussion about conflict resolution, issues of student diversity, and tolerance…"

Loudness be darned, no one seemed to be listening to the school bulletin, but since this was my first day, I let the transgression pass. My aim was to continue doling out pluses and minuses next to each student's name, for their reference and mine.

It was also a handy way to take roll.

"Good morning," I said when the bulletin finally ended. "Time for me to introduce myself and explain what the marks are for." I had just about everyone's attention now. *Use it wisely,* I told myself, or you'll lose them. "My name is Ms. Veil, and yes, as Brad asked, you may call me Ms. V, teacher, or whatever makes you comfortable, as long as you do so with respect." Their eyes were still on me, but I sensed an ebbing of interest, as if the room itself had a mood, one I could plug into, draw from, or destroy. "You wanted to know why I was marking the seating chart, right?"

"Yeah."

"Uh-huh."

"Right."

"Well, when I was in school, I hated it when we had a sub."

Mumbles and nods of agreement.

"No matter what, he or she always left a bad report, telling our teacher what a terrible class we'd been, when usually just a few students had caused all the trouble. The subs never, ever told the teacher about the students who'd been good, which was just about all of us. So" —I pointed at Wyatt's name on the seating chart— "with this method, when your teacher comes back, she'll notice that Wyatt has a plus next to his name, which means he was on task. Codi, on the other hand, has a minus next to hers. Not good."

"That's not fair, I didn't know." Codi's ignorance-of-the-law defense spun in the air like a storm cell.

"You knew you were supposed to be in your seat and quiet when the tardy bell rang. Like everyone else who now has a minus next to their name. But don't worry. You'll get a chance to make it up before the period is over. This way, you'll be judged as an individual, not as a class. Your teacher will know exactly who's been on task and who hasn't."

"How?" several kids asked at once.

"I'll keep giving out pluses for good behavior and adding or subtracting minuses until class is over."

"How come I don't have any marks at all?" Brad asked in a high-pitched whine.

"Because you've done nothing particularly good or bad. You've asked a lot of questions, and that's okay, as long as you raise your hand from now on and try not to interrupt while I'm talking."

His hand flew up and pumped up and down like a train conductor pulling a whistle chord.

"Yes, Brad."

"You look pretty good for a teacher."

After the class stopped laughing and I reined in my desire to coo and fuss over him and rub behind his puppy-dog ears, I said, "Thanks."

"Do I get a plus for that?"

"In my heart, you do."

"That sucks," he said under his breath, then added loud enough for the entire class to hear, "We're the remedial class."

Wyatt stiffened. "Shut up, Brad."

"Well, as far as I'm concerned, you're all excellent students, and I plan to treat you as such." So far, this had been easy; too easy. Something was up. My clairsentient gut was telling me so. And in the past ten months, I'd learned to trust my gut.

A brilliant white light flashed in front of my eyes. And it wasn't coming from the overhead. All sense of the world dissolved, including my body. A presence—familiar, beautiful—surrounded me. *Your light has come.*

Before I could process who or what was communicating with me, another presence forced its way into my head. *Watch out, Ms. Veil. The party's about to begin.*

The second voice had come from a female in the room.

Who was she, and what did she know that I didn't?

Chapter Two

THE OVERHEAD PROJECTOR BLINKED, then popped and blacked out, a puff of smoke leaking from its side. The fluorescent ceiling lights hummed in B-natural and dimmed to an overcast gray. A loud flapping sound had me wheeling around to see the vinyl curtains swinging back and forth, as if the windows had flown open and allowed the north wind to rush through.

"Holy crap!" It was Brad again, expressing my sentiment exactly. However, most of the students, after an initial display of excitement and laughter, were ducking beneath desks and each other. I couldn't blame them. Their secure, albeit boring, little classroom had turned into a Hollywood movie set, with the animation of inanimate objects, sound effects and all.

I closed my eyes and tried to sense where the turbulence was coming from. Instead, energy drained from me like ice melting. "Earthquake," someone yelled, but I knew better. This was no earthquake. I opened blurred eyes to more chaos. The world map above the whiteboard rattled in its moorings as if about to crash to the floor. Posters—*Mistakes are proof that you're trying; Life is tough, but so are you*—flapped like flags from the thumbtacks anchoring them to the walls. A pencil sharpener whirred in the distance.

The force was coming from the back of the room, I realized, allowing my subconscious to take over. Left side. There. Jason. Of course. He looked like a lone wolf sitting there with his bushy brown hair—and hazel eyes riveted on me. I glanced at the seating chart. Ardis. Jason Ardis. Again, I felt a drain of energy. My head ached.

My eyes felt scratchy. *Think love. Think peace. Think joy.* I smiled and sent out all the positive force I could muster.

Jason blinked, and the room became still. For a moment, it seemed the quietest place in the world—Hoh Rain Forest in Olympic National Park or Rialto Beach. Then a teacher burst through the connecting door. "What the—"

"It's Lacoste," Brad said. "We're in for it now."

Mr. Lacoste took in the classroom, his jaw pulsing to an inner script we didn't share. Apart from the acrid smell of a burnt light bulb, the room appeared normal enough. The curtains, world map, and posters were more or less positioned as before, and the florescent lights shone brightly and no longer hummed. So, I hoped Mr. Lacoste would go back to his classroom and leave the situation to me. But the likelihood of that happening was about nil. Having twenty or more vacant-eyed students huddled on the floor next to their desks didn't bode well for a substitute on her first day.

"We're okay," I said, with a confident smile.

Mr. Lacoste crossed his arms and tilted his head. "So, what's this, an earthquake drill?"

"A creative misuse of energy," I said. "But thanks for stopping by. It's good to know you're next door in case I need you."

He nodded but made no move to leave.

I turned my attention back to Jason *The Wolf* Ardis. "You must be worn out, because I sure am." Frustration radiated from him like heat from a fire, though his blank expression suggested otherwise. Poker face. Game face. Lack of communication, big time. I took a deep breath, then another. "You put on quite a show. How many minuses should I give you for that?"

Which got Brad, *Brave Puppy*, going again. "Minuses won't help."

I looked around the room. Why weren't the other students speaking up? They'd slowly gotten back into their seats and were sitting quietly. Had this happened before, or were they simply wondering what the hell I would do next?

"I'm sending for Dr. Matt," Mr. Lacoste said.

So much for any attempt of turning this into a learning experience. I wondered what part of the teacher's manual shared tips on dealing with the extraordinary. "That won't be necessary. I'll take it from here."

Lacoste's laugh sounded angry. "Need I remind you that you're a sub and I know these kids better than you do?"

The students followed our exchange with the morbid fascination of spectators at a boxing match. Arguing with Mr. Lacoste, I decided, would not only be fruitless, but unprofessional. "Then by all means, send for Dr. Matt. Maybe he'd like to listen in."

Mr. Lacoste pulled in a sharp breath, and the students came alive, shifting in their seats and whispering, probably amazed I hadn't run from the room crying by now.

"Can you help me out here, Jason?" I asked, using the little time we had left to give him a chance to explain.

"You're kidding, right?" said Codi. "After what he just did."

"And what did he just do?" I asked.

She rolled her eyes, looked away.

"He's a magician," Brad said. "But he's never been this good before."

I zeroed in on Jason, brows raised. So, his classmates thought he was an illusionist, who could move physical objects from a distance. At thirteen years old? Now, *that* was incredible.

Jason raised his brows back at me.

Wow. I'd made it a point not to let on about my powers. Whatever for? So people could distance themselves, conclude I was a freak, make excuses why they couldn't see me anymore. Why on earth was Jason taking the risk?

"That doesn't give him the right to disrupt class," Codi said. "He was showing off and that's wrong."

"I agree, but" —I turned to Jason— "were you aware that things would get so out of control?"

"I didn't know at first that—" He glanced at Mr. Lacoste and didn't finish.

But someone else did. *He didn't know at first that you had powers, too.*

I scanned the room but couldn't tell where the voice had come from, a voice with a message meant especially for me. I refocused on Jason. How had he known about my powers? I'd only recently discovered them myself. *And then you drew from them, right?*

He studied me with his yellow-brown eyes but said nothing.

I could tell Mr. Lacoste was growing impatient with my silence, but the ground had suddenly shifted here. I knew firsthand how most people reacted to the unexplainable—if my former fiancé and adoptive mother were anything to go by. So far, Jason had his classmates convinced that he knew magic, but what if they discovered he had abilities that extended beyond a talented and learnable skill?

Codi shot to her feet, arm half raised. "Admit it, Jason. You were showing off. You wanted Ms. Veil to know you're special."

"Like you?" Jason countered.

She slumped onto her seat with a look of practiced boredom. "WHAT-ehv-err."

I glanced at the door and caught Mr. Lacoste slipping out with a mobile phone pressed to his ear. "Do either one of you want to share?"

"Not particularly." Codi's moment in the spotlight where emotion overcomes self-consciousness, where the need for expression overwhelms common sense, had burnt out as suddenly as it had sparked into life. I ached for her loss.

"How about you, Jason?"

"You sure, Ms. V?"

"I wouldn't have asked if I weren't."

Jason stood, cleared his throat. "Um. Where do you want me to begin?"

I checked the clock on the wall behind me. Almost out of time. "How about the CliffsNotes version?"

He ran both hands through his hair—front and sides short, back long—as though prepping for a photo shoot, which elicited whistles and cheers from some of his peers— "Go, Jason," —and frowns from others.

"Seven members of this class are" —he paused as Mr. Lacoste stepped back into the room— "um, some people call us *Indigos* or *Children of Now*, others, well… They prefer to call us freaks and troublemakers."

"That's enough, Jason." Mr. Lacoste pulled up the waist of his pants and marched to the front of the room, kicking backpacks out of his path as though no more than roadside trash. "I'm citing you for willful disruption."

"But Ms. V—"

"I said that's enough."

Jason looked at me, and I felt a surge of resentment. He'd discovered my powers in less than thirty minutes—a record—and had reached out for help. But I'd let him down through my silence. As I'd let myself down over and over, bending, always bending.

"Wait for me outside," Mr. Lacoste said.

My insides burned with a deep sense of failure as Jason stuffed his supplies into his backpack, his eyes vacant.

Then I perceived it, a wave of resentment even more forceful than my own. It's hard to explain how a class's loyalty can suddenly turn. Kids sense fairness and the lack thereof. Though Jason had been wrong, disrupting class as he had, Mr. Lacoste's reaction—at least in the eyes of the students—had been equally wrong.

The bell was hardly perceptible over the calls of encouragement and back slaps Jason received from his peers, who, by the way, were making no move to clear the room.

"Party's over," I called over the din. I felt like a bouncer at a hosted bar where the effect of free alcohol takes a while to wear off.

Jason gave me a sassy salute and led the students out of the classroom like the Pied Piper.

Chapter Three

D R. MATT DID NOT visit my classroom. In fact, I finished my day, another four classes in all, without further mishap. With the overhead out of commission, I had to implement my point system, but that didn't matter. The kids seemed happy to humor me by putting in some effort to follow the lesson plan.

By the end of third period, I knew teaching was something I not only liked but felt inspired to do. A surprise, really, considering I'd spent the past nine years since earning my teaching credential happily doing company research for a large venture capital firm. Okay, maybe not happily. But life isn't perfect. I'd had a roof over my head and cash in the bank, which made me richer than seventy-five percent of the world's population. I was reliable, predictable, and had the right answers to just about everything.

Until my dead mother started speaking to me.

🕷 🕷 🕷

When I passed through the main office after school, Paula, administrative assistant to the principal, handed me a note from our boss. *Please see me at your earliest convenience.*

Heat worked its way up my neck, across my face, and through my hair; the way it's supposed to in a sauna but is unpleasant when you're dressed up and trying to look your best. Being summoned to the principal's office after my first day on the job struck me as a bad sign.

"Dr. Matt," I said, peering through his open office door. "You wanted to see me?"

His smile was instant and appeared to be genuine. "Hello, Marjorie." He rose from his chair and approached me with an outstretched hand.

I tried to smile in return but only managed a grimace before shaking his hand. He closed the door and directed me to one of the upholstered armchairs facing his desk. I sat and looked around. This was my first time in a principal's office, which said a lot about my stellar performance while in school—strict adherence to the rules, manageable.

File cabinets and bookshelves loaded with binders and school trophies took up most of the wall to my left. Framed diplomas and school banners—*Go Buffaloes!*—lined the wall to my right. Nothing surprising, except for the resin paperweight—embedded with a furry taxidermy spider the size of my palm—prominently displayed on the desk in front of me.

"I'd like to get your impression of the classes you taught today," he said.

Was he interested in my overall subbing experience, or was this a "he said, she said" inquiry into what did or did not happen during first period?

I glanced at the paperweight, which served no purpose, as far as I could tell—other than freak me out. It weighed nothing down, unless you considered my thoughts, which should have been on Dr. Matt instead of an arachnid with eight eyes and two sharp fangs. "Things started out a bit hairy—" *Oh Jeez, did I just say that?* "—but improved over time. Actually, the day went better than I'd expected."

"Heard you experienced a bit of excitement during first period."

"Yes." Little did he know that what I had experienced during first period was nothing compared to what I'd experienced in the past ten months. What would he say if I told him I heard the voice of my dead mother, a Native American who'd died only weeks after my birth, and that I communicated with animals, particularly a scrawny cat named Gabriel, and that sometimes I saw the dead?

11

Dr. Matt sat on the chair next to mine and leaned forward, hands clasped on his knees. His perfectly tailored suit had the sheen of a wool/silk blend, the kind Cliff, my former fiancé, often wore. "How about clueing me in to what happened."

"I found some of the students...interesting." How could I share what I had discovered about these kids without risking them being classified as mentally ill or written off as frauds? "Two or three showed promise in unexpected ways, and I wondered why they'd been placed in a remedial class."

Dr. Matt pursed his lips but said nothing.

Was he reflecting on what I'd said, or was his silence a ploy to keep me talking and over share? With the adage, "He who speaks first, loses," in the back of my mind, I said, "One of the students exhibited a creative misuse of energy as if desperate to prove himself in some way, and I'd hoped to—"

"What are your aspirations as a teacher?"

His abrupt change of subject put me on edge. Too much self-disclosure without room for clarification could lead to misunderstanding. Too little could come across as evasion. "I'd like to contribute in a way that matters. Open doors for students who feel muted or suppressed, help them heal through inclusion. Schools work so hard on educating our youth and training them to improve their circumstances, they neglect to give them the keys to success."

"Which are?"

"Resolution and self-reliance."

At Dr. Matt's questioning look, I added, "Students need purpose in their lives and the will to accomplish that purpose. They need training in improving themselves, as well as their minds."

"On what do you base your teaching philosophy?"

"Much of it comes from what I learned working alongside my sister Maya at a treatment facility for substance abuse. The facility provided support for the newly sober, helped them feel heard, accepted, and loved."

Dr. Matt eyed me as if I were an exotic new animal at the zoo, or

12

better yet, a new circus act. I pictured myself in a turban, with bejeweled fingers. *Abracadabra.* "You're comparing students to addicts?"

"We're all addicts in some way. The trick is to learn from our addictions, about who we are and what makes us tick."

"Go on," he said.

"In working with my sister, I realized that all of us, not only those addicted to drugs and alcohol, need to feel heard, accepted, and loved. Which includes our youth. Especially our youth. The rest of my teaching philosophy is based on life experience. I've learned that we need to take responsibility for our own choices, stand up for ourselves, try new things."

"Aren't these matters best left to a life coach?"

"Life coaching should be part of a teacher's training."

"Sounds ambitious."

"Playing small doesn't serve the world."

In the silence that followed, I wondered if I'd blown what had morphed into an impromptu job interview. I should have been prepared, but was not. Especially without knowing Dr. Matt's motivations and what he was looking for. The type of education I envisioned—a form of classroom-based cognitive-behavioral therapy—was not part of mainstream education. Was Dr. Matt enough of a visionary to understand what I was trying to say and give me a chance?

"How does one teach resolution, responsibility, and self-reliance?" he asked softly, as if talking to himself.

"I'm not sure. Touching base with the students' experiences would be a start. They would need a safe, nurturing environment to stretch their abilities, fail, dust themselves off, and try again."

Dr. Matt straightened in his chair and tugged at his right ear, bringing to mind a baseball coach signaling one of his players.

I hovered over a vocational precipice like a cursor marking the key to my future. Left click, tasks ahead and a life worth living. Right click, hidden options and more of the same.

"On your substitute application, you stated your plan to marry soon. How would that affect—"

"My aim is to control my own narrative. Until then marriage is out."

Dr. Matt's nod implied that the force of my answer had surprised him less than it surprised me. "And in the process, I assume, you plan to encourage students to control their own narratives as well."

Darn, he was connecting dots I hadn't been aware of. "With 'help' being the operative word, I can open doors but can't force students to step through them."

Dr. Matt pursed his lips and squinted at me.

With a sinking feeling, I figured I might as well plan on subbing for a while. No way would he hire a rookie with such an unconventional approach to teaching for a position in his traditional school.

"I'd like for you to take on a special class," he said.

Blood rushed in my ears. *He must be desperate.*

Then came another thought not meant to be spoken out loud. "But you don't even know me."

Chapter Four

D R. MATT STOOD AND walked to the window overlooking the front parking lot, currently clogged with vehicles picking up students after school. "You come highly recommended."

One minute I was focused on what he was saying and the next on what my psychiatrist, Dr. Tony Mendez, had suggested ten months before. "You need to push past your perimeter of comfort and safety, follow some blind alleys, celebrate the turn in the road." To comfort me on the day of my sister Maya's funeral, Morgan, my fiancé, had delivered a message from Dr. Mendez about an opening for a part-time teaching position at West Coast Middle School. An opening I would consider only after giving substituting a try. The reason I was here today.

"You mean, by Dr. Tony Mendez?"

"Actually, yes." Dr. Matt swung from the window and aimed his gaze at me. "Tony's a good friend of mine, and he recommended you as an ideal candidate for the job. Which counts for a lot, because he doesn't give out endorsements lightly. But I'm talking about someone else whose opinion I value."

Someone else?

"My nephew was in your first period class today."

Damn.

"And he had a different take on what happened than Charles Lacoste did."

That meant *two* cracks in my cocoon. "Is his name Jason by any chance?"

"Oh no, people usually don't take notice of my nephew. He can fade into the background to the point where you don't even know he's there. He'd make a good spy."

"A good spy, maybe, but I think that's sad. We all have special talents, even if it's just fading into the background, and we need recognition for such."

Dr. Max tugged at his ear again as if trying to tell me something I couldn't hear.

Okay, that also eliminated Brad and Wyatt. I searched my memory bank, trying to picture a kid so cloaked in unimportance that I hadn't noticed him.

"What counts here is that Shawn is impressed with you," Dr. Max said. "He claims you have psychic abilities."

Double damn. What I'd meant to keep hidden had surfaced. As closet skeletons usually do. How had his nephew discovered this about me?

"To see Shawn and kids like him happy again, to hear them ask questions and show enough interest to seek the answers, would be the culmination of my career."

Kids like Shawn? Was Dr. Matt's nephew one of the seven special children Jason had talked about called *Indigos* or *Children of Now*?

"We could attempt to improve things," he said.

We? I felt an ache in my belly, a painful yearning, similar to how I'd felt when I met my sister Maya for the first time, my duplicate, except for the wine-colored stain covering half her face. Maya, who died before we'd had a chance to renew the bond broken at our birth.

"Shawn is an Indigo."

I heard a buzzing in my ears.

"Indigos, if you believe they exist, have special needs, even more so than the general school population. And the needs of my nephew are not being met, not here and not at home." Dr. Matt rubbed the palms of his hands together like a cartoon villain, except with a frown instead of a smile. "Indigos are unusually sensitive to taste, touch, sound, and smell. They also share intuitive enhancements, if you know what I mean."

I knew what he meant all right. Jason, for instance, had a problem with overhead projectors and florescent lighting.

"If Shawn continues at the rate he's going, by the time he reaches college age, he'll either drop out of school or drop out of life. I suspect he and others like him are on the verge of experimenting with drugs and alcohol. If they haven't started already. Anyway, I hate seeing him so unfulfilled. He needs a little dreamtime, some loose, unstructured down time, to explore himself and his world."

Apparently, my unconventional approach to teaching hadn't put Dr. Matt off after all.

He took a seat behind his formidable desk, leaned back, and folded his arms over his chest. "Shawn's future is at stake here, Marjorie, as are the futures of at least six other students inappropriately assigned to the remedial class you taught today. I also met with Jason and Codi, who backed up everything Shawn said."

"What about Charles Lacoste's version of the situation?"

My question brought a shift in Dr. Matt's expression, from pliant to tight and focused. I was amazed at the transformation. It was like watching molten lava solidify.

"Charles is highly qualified in his particular discipline and is doing an admirable job of teaching our students. But to ask him to serve as a bridge to higher consciousness would be like asking him to fly to the moon."

Bridge to higher consciousness?

"The usual classes are put together based on such things as IQ tests, nationality, and income level" —Dr. Matt gripped the arms of his chair and the leather buckled beneath his fingers— "but we have the opportunity to do something new here, create a class based on consciousness of body, mind, and spirit."

Right up my alley. Though the life I was living was far from abundant and balanced. You can't give from an empty cup.

Dr. Matt leaned forward and folded his hands on the desk. But his thumbs did not still. They massaged each other as if to relieve pain. "Shawn felt the energy you poured into the classroom, and when he, Jason, and Codi added their energy to yours—"

"Oh no," I said, thinking about the damage they could have caused.

"Their energy is powerful, but undefined, so they must learn to control it at all times."

"Thank goodness they realize that," I said, though they hadn't done a very good job in the control department this morning.

Dr. Matt nodded before swiveling his chair to face the window again, a window that revealed little more now than it had the last time he'd turned to face it. "Shawn thinks this energy can be used in a group situation to uplift others."

"I agree, since the energy fields surrounding our bodies play an important part in our physical health and influence how we interact with our environment and others. When harmonized—"

Dr. Matt spun back to face me. "Are you an Indigo, Marjorie?"

"I—"

"You're about the right age for the second wave called Generators. The positive energy they generate affects everyone they contact. They're also called Antennas and Channelers."

Generator? Antenna? Channeler? Whoa. He was way ahead of me. "Sorry, I—"

"Indigos exist all over the world, yet the world is deaf and blind to them."

I nodded, let him talk. This man was on a mission, and he… Well, he was scaring me. Did he plan to accomplish single handedly what the rest of the world had failed to do until now, recognize and nurture a group of kids with unique abilities and special needs?

He looked into my eyes with such laser-sharp intensity that I thought maybe he, too, could read minds, but then he shook his head and said, "Shawn tried to re-circuit my brain telepathically without success. Psychic talent is lost to me, I'm afraid. And these kids will lose it, too, if they aren't encouraged to keep the circuits open."

"What about their parents?" Were they using their kids' special gifts as an excuse for bad behavior? I shivered at the thought. It would be hard enough to deal with seven gifted, unruly students, let alone their protective parents.

"They'll be on their knees in gratitude for what I'm attempting to do," Dr. Matt said. "Can you imagine what they're going through trying to raise children who, for the most part, are considered freaks?"

My heart did an impressive flip-flop. *All too well.*

"All seven of these kids have been diagnosed with either ADHD or some other form of brain disorder, so I've been planning to add an after-school class for some time now, run from three to five, Monday through Thursday, using one of our vacant facilities. It'll be an alternative educational model that won't compete with the rest of our school or cause our teachers to feel personally threatened or challenged. The students will still get their basics from teachers like Charles Lacoste, who are trained for, and capable of doing, just that. If all goes well, our Indigos will do better in academics as they gain a more solid emotional foundation. You see, it all works together. I've just been waiting for the right teacher, one qualified in ways that can't be taught in a credential program or learned through classroom experience, if you know what I mean."

I pictured seven Jasons vying for my attention, which had me searching for something to fan myself with. I noticed a paperback on Dr. Matt's desk, titled *Being and Vibration.* I'd read the book several times. Joseph Rael, otherwise known as *Beautiful Painted Arrow,* wrote about entering one's own life more courageously, trusting one's own truth, and daring to live it.

"And that's where you come in…" Dr. Matt's voice sounded soft and confident like the voice of a psychiatrist or close friend trying to convince me of my inner potential.

I grabbed the paperback and fanned myself. The floral scent of my deodorant was making me woozy. I put the book down and shrugged off my blazer.

"I'm talking about kids who thought and spoke like adults at age nine," Dr. Matt said, "born with knowledge and wisdom independent of age or experience. They're way beyond what we're teaching them in school. Yet, as you mentioned earlier, they lack the keys to succeed. Which leads to confusion and restless impatience simmering just below the surface or, in a worst-case scenario, explosive anger and aggression."

I sensed doubt in him. Though his eyes sparkled with a fervent light, his hand and body movements told a different story. Plus, he was talking too much, as if trying to convince himself, as well as me, of the value of this class. Was he a deluded mad man or a courageous visionary who dared to step forward, break with tradition, and stand up for what he believed?

"I'm calling it an after-school learning lab, so it won't sound too foreign for the mainstream."

First Light said a voice in my head.

"First Light," I repeated.

The words floated between us like soap bubbles, iridescent, distracting. I had no way of knowing if the message had come from my birth mother or my sister Maya. Voices from the beyond sound alike, in the line of a bad telephone connection or static on TV—irritating and hard to ignore. "It signals the dawn of a new day. Better than 'learning lab,' don't you think?"

Dr. Matt's lips curved into a "gotcha" smile. "So, you're in?"

An internal voice—my own this time—screamed, *No, no, no. Better to start with a regular class, start out small.* But then I thought of Jason and how I'd let him down. I sensed his helplessness, and a surge of protectiveness ran through me. Who besides Dr. Matt would speak up for these kids? No one, it seemed, but me.

"Yes," I said.

He leaned forward, hands flat on the desk. "Great. I'll give you two weeks to prepare."

"Two weeks?" My brain numbed at the thought.

"Meanwhile, you can check out the building on the perimeter of our campus that I've reserved for this class. It's next to a nature area, which I'm sure you can put to better use than we have during the past several years. Currently, it looks like a jungle." He came from behind his desk and offered his hand, a good thing because I was having difficulty getting out of my chair. "The classroom is in the old art wing and hasn't been used for a while. But don't worry. The building is sound and in two weeks we can have it up to par."

You're not alone, said a voice in my head.

Ha. I'd heard those words before.

Right before my world had turned from bad to worse, and I'd nearly lost my life.

Chapter Five

TWO WEEKS TO PREPARE. After just one day of substituting. My only references Dr. Tony Mendez and a thirteen-year-old, so unobtrusive, so unremarkable, he could virtually disappear into his surroundings. What had Dr. Matt been thinking asking me to take on this experimental class? What had I been thinking by accepting?

Actually, I'd been thinking about Jason and kids like him, how lonely and afraid they must feel. As I had, until I'd learned to accept rather than fear my psychic abilities. But I'd been lucky. I'd had help. From my psychiatrist, Dr. Tony Mendez, and my sister Maya.

Who would help these Indigos if not me?

Showing up at West Coast Middle School as a substitute teacher confirmed my intention to control my own narrative and contribute in a meaningful way. Agreeing to take on an after-school class of Indigos clarified that intention. Now, it was time to put up or shut up, trust I was the right teacher for the job.

I'd give myself one day to fret over my decision before getting to work. Because *work* it would be. To come up with a way to implement my teaching objective. Maybe I could call on Dr. Matt's nephew, Shawn, for help. He seemed to have full confidence in my abilities. Maybe *he* had a plan.

So, here I was back at Bayfront Park. My last visit had been in June with Truus, my adoptive mother, the day she'd called me a pagan squaw. She'd been referring to my Native American background—Esselen, to be exact, a Bay Area tribelet that had nearly dropped out of modern consciousness. Something she'd planned to keep secret; along with the fact that she'd adopted me. Which had seemed easy enough at the time. After all, my hair was blonde, my eyes blue, and my *real* mother had died after giving birth to me. But secrets have a way of wiggling free, like babies who have just learned to crawl. It's only a matter of time.

As before, I headed for *The Great Spirit Path* sculpture, intending to reread this visual poem of rock clusters for inspiration. The four stanzas of the poem, conceived by Menlo Park artist S.C. Dunlap, stretched over a three-quarter-mile trail. So, I had some walking to do. I took a brochure from the box installed along the path and scanned the numbered illustrations for the section of the poem that had inspired me most. Then I walked past the first forty-one rock clusters to number forty-two: *Rest here.*

I sat in a lotus position, eyes closed, and took a deep breath, asking for nothing, expecting nothing. A cool breeze circulated around me, and yes, even in January with cloudy skies, the air currents felt comforting as they lapped at my face and ruffled my hair.

I stood with the reluctance of someone leaving a holiday dinner, sated and ready for a nap, then walked to the next stone cluster: *Talk here.* And talk I did. Or rather, I prayed. "Send me your guidance, oh Lord, because I may be in way over my head."

I moved on to the next cluster, then the next, until I stood in the center of a large Medicine Wheel. *To the Great Spirit everywhere.*

That's when, just like in June, a hawk screeched from above. No gift of great wisdom. No directions from my dead mother (She was good at getting me into trouble not out of it). But one thing I'd learned over the past ten months was to pay attention. Messages come at the most unexpected times in the most unexpected ways.

"Ms. Veil?"

A voice after all; one I hadn't heard before.

"Excuse me, Ms. Veil."

I opened my eyes and twisted toward the sound.

"Are you okay?" A young boy stood nearby with a bike balanced between his legs. Black hair, no expression besides calm awareness.

I didn't recognize him, yet he knew my name. "Yes. I'm fine. How about you?"

"Fine, thanks."

"Are you here by yourself?"

The boy eyed me through what appeared to be a yellow glow. "My uncle fell back to meditate." He fiddled with the handlebars of his bike as if he had something else on his mind.

"Sorry. My brain's in a fog this morning. I—"

"You subbed in my first period class yesterday."

My mind scrambled for a name but came up blank.

"You know, when the overhead blew."

I slapped the dirt off my jeans. "Yeah, that's one for the memory books all right." I stepped toward him and reached out my grimy hand. "Sorry, but with all the commotion, I don't remember your name."

"No problem. If I'd wanted your attention, I would've gotten it." He let go of the handlebars long enough to shake my hand. "The name's Shawn."

Great. The principal's nephew; how was that for a sign? "Nice to meet you."

He turned and glanced behind him. "My uncle and I come here a lot. It's pretty cool, especially now that the winter bird population is at its peak. The bay is the most important west coast stop on the Pacific Flyway."

The kid sounded more like a monitor for the San Francisco Bay Bird Observatory than a potential school dropout.

"This used to be a landfill," he said.

I scanned the hills covered with grasses, bushes, eucalyptus, and pine, marveling at the transformation. "A good conversion of resources, I'd say."

He didn't respond, just looked at me as if thinking about what I'd said. Which blew me away, of course. I wasn't used to thirteen-year-olds thinking about what I said. Listening would have been nice, but even that was asking a lot. In fact, listening was a talent even I hadn't mastered. Which was inexcusable, considering dead people talked to me all the time.

"I hear you're going to be our after-school teacher," he said. "If you need any help" —he looked back over his shoulder— "um…"

I didn't know my number one fan well enough to confide that I had no clue where to begin.

"That's easy," Shawn said. "Just show up."

Had he read my mind?

He laughed at the expression on my face. "We need a place to hang out, you know, with fellow minds, away from the others."

Just show up? I shook my head. If only it were that easy.

"It is," he said.

If he was reading my mind, I was in more trouble than I'd realized. How many of my future students could do that?

"Usually only me," he said. "And Codi, but not all the time. It's easier out here, where there's less interference. In school, there's energy shooting in all directions, so it's hard to concentrate. Take Jason, for example. He's an energy robber."

"Energy robber?"

"I tried to help when he started drawing on all that energy you were sending out yesterday, but things kind of backfired."

"The overhead." I said.

"And the world map and posters. We have this problem with control." He spun the pedal on the bike with the toe of his sneaker. "You can block it, you know."

"Block what?"

"People getting into your head."

I nearly choked on all the breath I'd inhaled at his disclosure. "How?"

"I can teach you," he said, "but it'll take time."

"How much time? There are only five months till June."

He laughed. "Here's Uncle Matt now."

Chapter Six

SHAWN'S ADVICE ABOUT JUST showing up should have been a comfort, allowing me to relax, take my time. Instead, it energized me into action. Now more than ever, I felt the need for a plan. For starters, I wanted to know more about *Indigos* and *Children of Now*. Who or what were they, and why hadn't I heard of them before? A trip to the bookstore was in order, followed by some research on the Internet. No problem. That would be the easy part. Figuring out how to handle these kids would be the challenge.

Finding Indigos shelved under *New Age/Parenting* at the bookstore came as no surprise but was discouraging just the same. Such labeling would make it difficult, if not impossible, to confer about Indigos with folks in the mainstream, people who believed only in what they could see, hear, taste, and touch, the stuff backed by science. Unless safely locked between the pages of the Bible, the unexplainable didn't exist for them. Then again, the beleaguered parents of these Indigos would likely be open to any reasonable explanation as long as it helped their kids navigate the school system—and life.

Over the sound of the bookstore's gurgling and steaming espresso machine, I discovered there were three waves of Indigos: *Wayshowers*, born during the late 1950s to '60s, *Generators*, born during the 1970s to '80s, and *Children of Now*, born during the 1990s to the present, which included my future class of thirteen-year-olds. Heck, it included the whole school. How did Dr. Matt differentiate between kids who were and were not Indigos? By their psychic abilities alone?

I scanned the pages for suggestions on what to teach these kids, which included anger management, honesty codes, yoga, meditation, and creativity. "Train the brain to respond intelligently to sensory impressions." "Train the mind to hear promptings of the heart and unfold the spiritual self, so it may emerge." This was *Celestine Prophecy* stuff, great in theory, but hard to apply. Where would I begin?

If Dr. Matt were a true believer in this after-school class, wouldn't he have come up with more than vague references to providing an open environment, multitasking, and exposure to nature? He said all could be up and running in two weeks. All *what* could be up and running? A classroom, a nature area, seven troubled kids, and a greenhorn teacher?

On my way to the register, I heard someone call my name. "Marjorie?"

My muscles tensed. *Damn.*

I turned to face my ex-fiancé.

"You look good," Cliff said, the surprise on his face disconcerting. Was he surprised to see me or surprised I looked good? Our last meeting ten months ago had been rather traumatic, as breakup scenes usually are.

"You look good, too." His looks had never been a problem. He was handsome, no doubt about it; wavy blond hair, gray eyes, sculpted nose and lips, model-perfect body. What more could a woman ask for? Indeed. How could someone so physically attractive be missing what I needed most, that one, essential ingredient—a loving, understanding heart?

"Your mother said…" he began, then seemed to think better of it. "How've you been?"

"I'm doing research for a class I'm about to teach."

His brows rose in the way I knew so well, a run-up to him saying something derogatory. "*You?* Teaching a class?"

I evaded his question and the wisecrack sure to follow with a question of my own, "New hobby?"

He followed my glance to the book he was holding, featuring the muscle cars of yesteryear. "Have to do something with my free time."

Free time? During our two-year engagement, he'd barely had time to take me out to lunch.

He eyed the books cradled in my arms. My first impulse was to hide them behind my back, but that would only fuel his curiosity. Anyway, I was a big girl now, no longer beholden to the likes of Cliff. I held up the books for his inspection.

"Indigo Children? What kind of New Age hogwash are you into this time?"

I shrugged. Not bothering to explain. He hadn't responded well when I'd told him about my auditory hallucinations (his words, not mine); a wake-up call—or head-slap warning—that something was terribly wrong with our relationship. He glanced at the checkout counter and shifted his weight. "Your mother said you have a sister…"

"Two, actually." Cliff was behind on the news, which meant he and my adoptive mother weren't as tight as they once were. "I found out I was adopted and that I'm one of three, a triplet. Veronica's the oldest. She's staying in Carmel Valley, waiting to hear if she's been accepted into the DEA basic training program at Quantico. The youngest was Maya. She died four weeks ago and… I can't talk about this anymore."

To my surprise, Cliff folded me into his arms and patted my back, his Burberry Brit Eau de Cologne—smoky, leathery—conjuring up a sense of luxury and elegance. The Cliff I used to know and love was sleek, cool, and unfeeling, like the Mercedes he drove. "I understand," he said, kissing my cheek. Then he added, "Heard you met someone."

I stepped out of his embrace. So, he knew about Morgan. *Thanks, Mom.* "Yes."

"A dairy farmer."

"Yes."

A tightening of his lips; otherwise no sign of emotion. "You left me for a farmer?"

"No. I left you. And then I met a farmer."

A smirk which, as usual, evoked a sinking feeling inside of me. "Heard he has a kid."

No comment.

"Okay, I get it. None of my business, right?"

My answer, a sigh. Just thinking about Morgan made my eyes burn. I missed him and wondered if I was doing the right thing, trying my hand at teaching instead of marrying him and moving to the farm. But I had to know if I could make it on my own before choosing marriage. I had to know if I could align my personal growth with Morgan's rather than lose myself in a relationship, as my birth mother and my sister Maya had. And I'd almost done with Cliff.

"What you need is a strong hand," Cliff said, mistaking my tears for regret, "not encouragement to follow paths to who knows where." He paused and barked a laugh. "What have you accomplished since our breakup, besides quitting a good job and strapping yourself to a farmer and a kid?"

I smiled, forced myself to look normal, carefree. "Following paths to who knows where."

Chapter Seven

AT ELEVEN THE FOLLOWING morning, I sat in a lounge chair on the back deck of my Menlo Park home with a mug of black coffee cradled in my hands. I still wore my fleece robe and furry slippers, adequate protection against the lingering chill. A low-branched fig tree stood nearby. At night, strategically placed up-lights illuminated its gnarled trunk, but even by daylight, it possessed a wizened charm. Rose-colored buds filled the flowering quince adorning my backyard fence, the first shrub to bloom each year on leafless stems with needle-sharp thorns. Later, hard and astringent fruit the size of golf balls would load its branches and release an apple-pineapple scent rivaling any chemical air freshener. I'd already clipped a branch to display on my kitchen table where the tight buds would soon break into bloom.

I loved my home, proud that I'd purchased, decorated, and landscaped it on my own. Outside, it appeared simple and unassuming, set in a suburban neighborhood of look-alike, single-family homes from the 1940s and '50s. But thanks to the help of my now deceased adoptive father, Gerardo, the inside had a personality of its own. We'd removed most of the interior walls but left the ceiling heights varied, preserving each living area's own defined and sheltered space.

Coffee gone, I got up and opened the patio door for Gabriel, my backyard stray, to enter for his pre-noon snack. So far, no show. Nothing new. The cat directed his own life via his own schedule. He'd spent time on the farm with Joshua and Morgan during my six-month stay in Big Sur and Pacific Grove, adapting to what would soon become his new home. On my return to Menlo Park, Joshua had lent him back to me. "You're going to need him," he said. And since he often knows more about me than I do, I believed him.

My attention strayed to the phone on the kitchen counter, wondering what my sister Veronica was up to, a woman so determined to achieve success with the DEA that all her behavior was directed toward that aim. She had completed a written assessment and panel interview at the San Francisco Recruitment Office and was now clearing the rest of the multi-step hiring process. Which could take another six months! After finishing DEA basic training at Quantico, she planned to go back to school for instruction in mental health nursing. Yeah, in addition to long and odd hours as an agent. Her goal? To team up with another special agent and help people in need of medication and treatment instead of or in addition to jail. Thanks to Maya, Veronica now viewed many drug-related problems as mental health issues that, if caught and treated early, could prevent criminal acts. "Sometimes more is needed to fight the war on drugs than a badge and a gun," she'd said over Thanksgiving dinner, over a month and a half ago.

I'd assumed that Veronica's kick-ass personality would rub off on me during our nine-month acquaintance, but, as I'd quickly discovered, I'd assumed wrong. There was no way of implanting her confident, aggressive, and sarcastic self into passive-aggressive me. What I could do, however, was line her up as a guest speaker to deliver some gut-wrenching facts to my students about the use of alcohol and drugs. I grabbed the phone, slid into the cushioned seat of my breakfast nook, and punched in her number.

"Hey, Sis," she said after five rings. "How's it going?"

"I miss you," I said.

A chuckle. "It's only been five weeks since our last meet up."

"Seems longer. And it'll be longer still when you get accepted with the DEA."

"*If* I get accepted."

31

"Which means weeks of training, followed by long hours as an agent, assigned to who knows where."

"Mobility is a condition of employment—"

"That doesn't mean I have to like it."

Silence. Just enough to scold myself for trying to lay a guilt trip on Veronica for doing exactly what I intended to do—control my own narrative. The very qualities I admired in her—her power, her strength, her independence—guaranteed to keep us apart. "Veronica…"

"Yeah?"

"I also miss Maya."

"Me, too…"

Jeez. Quit longing for something Veronica can't give you and Maya took with her to the grave. Getting reassurance and approval from Veronica was like squeezing water from a rock. For crucial decisions, commitments, and action, however, she had my back. She'd proved that during our stay in the Los Padres National Forest when she'd risked her life to save mine. "I got a part-time job at West Coast Middle School."

"That's great…I think. You sound kind of glum."

"I'll be teaching a class of seven students with special needs."

"Disabled?"

"The opposite, really. They're extremely capable and talented, which creates its own set of problems."

"Gifted, then."

"They're Indigos. Maybe you've heard of them."

"You're one up on me, girl. Gen Y, Nexters, Boomlets, Baby Busters, the Millennials, kids with ADD, ADHD, junkies, crackheads, crackpots, yes. Indigos, no."

"According to the school principal, they're highly susceptible to alcohol and drugs."

"Most middle school kids are. So, let me guess. You want me to drop by and provide your students with some research-based alcohol, tobacco, and drug prevention tips."

I ran my fingers over the soft buds of the thorny branch on my table and smiled. Tender and spiky, just like Veronica. "Uh-huh. Since you plan on getting into mental health nursing and are applying with the Drug Enforcement Agency—"

"Administration, Sis."

"And you know so much more than I do about—"

"Practically everything, except generosity and love. When do you want me to come?"

"The second week in March. And I was hoping you could bring Ben along. To introduce my students to the Native American Medicine Wheel, as he did for me."

I thought back to my first meeting with Ben *Gentle Bear* Mendoza, eighth-generation descendant of the Esselen tribe. His name certainly fit, with his long, black hair held back by a bandana headband and the way his chest expanded like Paul Bunyan's beneath the black tee he wore with jeans and beat-up cowboy boots. His casual manner contrasted sharply with that of the men I knew in Menlo Park. Try as I might, I couldn't picture any of them in the wilds of the Los Padres National Forest, nor would I trust a single one as my spiritual guide. Ben had helped me appreciate the gifts of nature and had encouraged rather than ridiculed my quest for self-worth and meaning. Once Veronica's fate with the DEA was decided, Ben would become my brother-in-law. Unlike me, however, Veronica had no qualms about choosing a career over life as a stay-at-home wife and mother. Granted, she wouldn't be entering marriage with a built-in child. But working for the DEA meant committing way into the future. How would this affect Ben and any upcoming children?

"If I haven't heard back yet about my acceptance into basic training, I'll be happy to meet with your students," Veronica said. "And I can probably convince Ben to come along, too." A pause. "Are you sure you won't get into trouble for including Native American spirituality in your curriculum? Some people might accuse you of promoting the occult."

Gabriel rubbed his head against my legs, and the vibrations of his soft purr traveled through the fabric of my jeans. "Hey, fella.

Welcome home." I scratched his back, something he wouldn't have allowed only nine and a half months ago. He'd hiss and run away whenever I ventured too close.

"Marjorie?" Veronica said.

"Umm… This will be an alternative education model," I said, quoting Dr. Matt, "that won't compete with the rest of the school or cause the teachers to feel personally threatened or challenged. Dr. Matt gave me free rein, and… Everything works in circles, Veronica, the earth orbiting the sun, the annual cycle of the seasons, the liturgical year, the Medicine Wheel—"

"I'm not the one who needs convincing, Sis. It'll be the parents arguing that the course you're offering is religiously based and that you're not a licensed mental health professional. Ben's been there, done that, and sometimes the results aren't pretty. Make sure you have the parents' written consent before you step too far over the line."

"Dr. Matt's taking care of all that," I assured her, despite my unease over the possible ramifications of the project. What if I failed? Who, besides me, would suffer in the process? "Anyway, the school's mascot is a buffalo, the totem animal associated with the North. Isn't that a wonderful coincidence?"

"You sound hyped, that's for sure."

"Actually, I'm scared."

"We all are," she said.

"Not you."

"If you say so."

"Your presentations may take more than a day."

"Which means you'll be setting us up at Marjorie's Comfort Inn, right?"

"It'll give us a chance to catch up.

Was catching up even possible after twenty-eight-years of separation? We were adults now—strangers—with different life histories, different expectations. Maybe strong, independent Veronica didn't need catching up to feel complete. Maybe we were destined to go our separate ways. Again.

Chapter Eight

IT WAS TIME TO call Morgan, the love of my life. Our future home was under construction on a corner lot of the farm, a ranch-style house, which I'd helped plan. It would be a comfortable, spacious home, backed by fields of corn in the summer, oats in the winter, and bare dirt in between. However, each time I tried to imagine life in the country instead of here in Menlo Park, I drew a blank; as if my mind refused to go there. From freeways, high rises, and crowded streets, to pastures, barns, and cows. Could I handle the transition? As if to muddy the waters, a picture of my former fiancé, Cliff, would come to mind, his handsome face, his trim body, his designer suits—his spiteful comments. "What have you accomplished since our breakup besides quitting a good job and strapping yourself to a farmer and a kid?"

Peering through the kitchen window at the darkening scene outside—blacktop and sidewalks, streetlights and manicured yards—I assured myself that my love for Morgan would carry me through. Seeing him prosper in his own environment would only add to the respect and admiration I already felt for him. We first met when I was eighteen and he was twenty-one, but we hadn't come to know each other until ten years later. Even then, I'd seen little of him. Just enough to fall in love.

His nephew and our soon-to-be-adoptive son, Joshua, would also help me adjust. I'd met him in Dr. Mendez's office, back when the poor child couldn't speak. He was seven at the time compared to my advanced age of twenty-eight, and we'd ended up going through a lot together.

It was 6:00 p.m., which meant Morgan would be home. Yes, even on a Friday night. Cows don't know about clocks and schedules, weekends and vacations. They give birth in their own due time, often in the middle of the night and during holiday meals. They require twice-a-day feeding and milking. Though a crew of employees carries out these duties, the "boss" is called in when the cows get sick, the milk barn equipment fails, or the tractor needs servicing. There are also electrical failures when the generator has to be fired up to keep the whole process going. Add to that the evening phone calls and paperwork. Then comes spring harvest, when the oat crop is converted into silage as feed for the cows, followed by the disking of fields and planting of corn for harvest in the fall.

There would be benefits to farm life, however. I would always know where to find my husband in case of an emergency, within walking distance, only a Nextel call away. Plus, I would have a built-in babysitter. Morgan's mother had already volunteered for the job, her two-story ranch house and spacious back yard providing plenty of room for future children to play.

Anyway, I'd committed weekends to Morgan and Joshua, the reason for my call.

"Van Dyke residence," Joshua said after only two rings.

"Hey, sweetie, it's me."

"Marjorie!"

"Tell her Morgan's in the shower," my future mother-in-law called in the background.

"Morgan's in the shower."

A charge ran through me at the mention of Morgan, all showered and clean, smelling of soap and Gillette aftershave instead of Burberry Brit Eau de Cologne.

"How are you, sweetie?" I pictured Morgan's nephew as I'd first seen him in Dr. Mendez's office, with his intense brown eyes and straight black hair. He'd been alert and observant and had spoken to me without saying a word.

Instead of answering my question, he asked, "Are you coming over?"

"Yep, Gabriel and me, first thing in the morning. We miss you"

"I know."

Of course, he did. His telepathic powers exceeded my own, though his family acted as if this is no big deal. On a farm, so close to nature, telepathic intelligence comes in handy.

"Here's Morgan," he said.

"Marjorie?"

My heart took on the special rhythm it always did when I spoke to Morgan, a powerful churning. This man, and only this man, loved me in the way I need to be loved, unconditionally.

Could he say the same about me? "I miss you."

He grunted. "Not as much as I miss you. Can't wait to—"

"Watch it. Joshua and your parents are listening."

"My parents? You should hear them when *they* get going."

"Morgan. Stop."

The charge of his laughter circled the length of my spine. "Okay, I'll keep my feelings for you a secret. My family will never know that I love you beyond reason and think about you to the point of distraction."

"Yeah," his father said in the background, "that's why this place is going to hell."

I felt a wave of unease. I loved Morgan and I missed him, but I didn't think about him to the point of distraction. Love didn't require that, did it? "Keep the place running smoothly until I get there, so you'll have a little time left for me."

"Will do," he said. "Love you. Drive safe."

Thinking of the class I was about to teach brought a sense of expectation—and guilt. For me, the months ahead would fly by, while our wedding and the resulting transition in my life remained on hold. I promised myself not to burden Morgan with ideals and desires he couldn't fulfill, as he was doing for me. When we joined in marriage, we would love and hold each other gently. "Love you, too, Morgan. See you tomorrow."

Chapter Nine

IT SEEMED LIKE A good idea to take an alternate route to Morgan's farm, passing through Rio Vista and taking the levee roads to the I-5 overpass and on to Elk Grove. This would allow me glimpses of the Sacramento River, with fishing boats and barges floating at an easy pace and speed boats slicing through the water, creating wakes like strokes of a wizard's wand only to disappear like dreams on waking.

Too bad about the fog.

I could barely see ten feet ahead of me let alone take in views of the river. And this on a winding levee road, with traffic coming from the opposite direction just as blinded by the fog as I was. My entire concentration focused on staying on the road, except for occasional musings of plunging into the river below. I mentally rehearsed what I knew about escaping the car while sinking into the murky waters, which, sad to say, wasn't much. Something about waiting for the water to stabilize before opening the window and climbing out. I shivered at the thought.

My Jeep crawled forward, windshield wipers slapping, while I used the faint yellow lines on the center of the road as a guide. I prayed that any other drivers stupid enough to be on the road under these conditions would at least be smart enough to drive slowly. Every few yards, I saw images in the fog, some shaped like animals, some like people, others like cars, when in fact, they were only mirages created by my busy mind. I hunched over the steering wheel like a myopic old lady, teeth clenched, breath coming out in spurts.

What a way to start my reprieve, surrounded by debilitating fog. I would be a nervous wreck by the time I reached Morgan and my future family, if I reached them at all. In no shape to combat my doubts about marriage and life on the farm. What I needed was the sun, darn it, a guiding light, not a misty veil to further confuse me. But since when did life ever go according to plan? I should have known by now that its lessons never come easily.

The road passed through the small town of Isleton, but before I could relax into the temporary release from the fog, I was out of town again, back on the levee road, back into the murk. Crossing the narrow metal bridge over the river nearly did me in. I imagined meeting a semi—head on—meaning one of us, namely me, would have to back up, something that would stump me even under normal conditions.

I made it over the bridge without mishap, but before I knew it, there came another, shorter and wider this time, leading into the small town of Walnut Grove, crouched and withdrawn in the soupy mist. I checked the time: 9:15 a.m.

I'd been on the road for nearly three hours.

When I pulled into the van Dyke Dairy, which also looked rather crouched and withdrawn in the fog, I wanted to slide out of the Jeep and kiss the ground. Instead, I planted my feet on the paved parking space, took Gabriel out of his carrier, and aimed my weak-kneed self toward the light streaming from the ranch house windows.

Even before reaching the door, the heavy, sweet scent of maple syrup, fried bacon, and butter made me realize I was hungry for food as well as a warm place to settle in. Though many conditions were uncertain on the van Dyke farm, the Saturday morning menu never changed. Dutch pancakes with all the trimmings. My mouth watered as I lifted the knocker and tapped three times. The response was deafening. Dogs barked. Joshua shouted, "It's Marjorie." Racing feet on linoleum.

After flinging open the door, Joshua circled my waist with both arms and pressed against me with the enthusiasm and innocence that make eight-year-olds so lovable. "You're taller," I said, unable to express the elation I felt. Okay, so his head fit higher against my chest than last time he'd given me such a selfless hug, but was this all I could say? *You're taller.*

Joshua straightened and gave me a gap-toothed smile. That's how it was with him. No matter what I said or did, I was his hero. Only a major screw up on my part would diminish his admiration and love. My only consolation was that my intentions were good, screw-ups and all.

"Hi Gabriel." Joshua stroked the cat struggling to escape my grasp.

Though he preferred not to be held, Gabriel went limp and purred when I released him into Joshua's arms.

I'd felt Morgan's presence the moment I entered the house and knew he was as eager I was for a kiss and hug. Yet he held back, allowing Joshua to bask in my attention. "Hi, Morgan," I said, once the cat had claimed ownership of Joshua's world. Then I stepped into his arms for that long-awaited greeting. He smelled like home.

"We were worried about you driving in the fog," he said, still holding me tight.

Not half as worried as he would have been had he known I'd taken the levee roads in.

"Sit down, dear, before your pancakes get cold," Morgan's mother called from the front of the stove.

Morgan kissed my cheek and ushered me through the large open dining room to the kitchen table. Actually, it was more of a booth, like in a restaurant, a leather bench curved around a kidney-shaped table. I scooted in and Morgan slid in next to me. Joshua crawled in from the opposite side. Morgan's father grinned over his newspaper from one of the captain's chairs at the open end of the table, as though accustomed to the role of silent observer. Two Border collies rested at his feet.

"Maple syrup, blackberry syrup, or sugar?" Carla asked as she set a plate of crepe-like pancakes in front of me.

I smiled at my future mother-in-law, feeling as though I'd just been wrapped in a warm blanket. "Maple syrup will be fine."

🕷 🕷 🕷

Carla refused my help with the dishes, suggesting instead that I go check out the progress of our future home. "See if all is going according to plan," she said, as though I'd even think of voicing my opinion. My position as Morgan's future wife and newest member of the van Dyke clan was still too precarious for that. Her blonde hair was styled in a short bob that required only a quick comb through to look neat and stylish. Her face was free of makeup, rosy with good health. She wore jeans and a chambray shirt, her body fit and trim. She had to be in her mid-fifties but looked more like forty. Farm life agreed with her. A good sign.

"We have a surprise for you," Morgan said as we headed out the door.

The fog had lifted like a curtain on a stage, and the sun felt warm on my skin. I took in a deep breath, appreciating the earthy farm smell.

"We're sleeping in the new house tonight," Joshua blurted, "and looking at the stars."

I hardly considered a slab foundation with rough framing a house, though the solidness of this load-bearing portion of the structure had transformed a blueprint of confusing lines, symbols, and numbers into reality.

"Like it?" Morgan asked as we neared the stark frame of my future home.

It was hard visualizing the completed house, considering it currently looked like a bunch of Popsicle sticks glued together. "Love it." When we'd picked out the plan, I found the project generous to the extreme. According to Morgan, dairy farming was not the most lucrative of businesses, considering most of the profits were reinvested in land, equipment, and repairs. The house under construction resulted from much sacrifice, not only on Morgan's part, but that of his parents, brother, and sister-in-law. This project would set the business back for years, and I vowed to make it up to them someday.

Morgan pulled me into an embrace and kissed the top of my head. "A dream come true."

I returned his kiss. "For both of us."

Joshua squeezed in between us. "How about me?"

"You," I said, "are the center."

"You," Morgan added, "are the king." He tousled Joshua's hair. "But even kings get tired, so how about rolling out the sleeping bag in *your* tent, so all is ready in case you conk out during our stargazing?"

I laughed, noticing two tents separated by vertical two-by-fours. "Bedrooms without walls." There would be no privacy for us tonight.

Morgan held up a canvas tarp. "Wall."

Confining. Freeing. "Guess beggars can't be choosers."

He twitched his brows like Groucho Marx, though sexier. "When there's a will, there's a way." And when I took in his green eyes, full lips, and the dimples in his cheeks, I sensed a definite will on my part to put a temporary wall, no matter how flimsy, between one small eight-year-old and his adult companions.

But that wouldn't be for a while.

I looked up at the sky and wondered if the fog would descend again and obscure our nighttime view. But I said nothing, not about to destroy the moment.

Chapter Ten

WE HAVE ANOTHER SURPRISE, don't we, Morgan?" Joshua said, his eyes glimmering like brown orbs. "Can I tell her?"

"Might as well." Morgan waved at his brother David who'd just driven up to the farmhouse in his white Ford pickup. I'd met David when he was studying at Saint Patrick's Seminary in Menlo Park. Morgan and his family made regular trips from Elk Grove to visit him and often celebrated Mass at the Church of the Nativity, which I also attended. Eventually, David left the seminary and his younger brother, John Phillip, became the priest instead. The priest who would officiate at our upcoming wedding.

"We're going to ride horses to the woods so you can see the Cosumnes River," Joshua said, a bundle of energy that fueled me. "The water makes lots of noise, like a water fall."

On a previous visit, Morgan had told me about the woods that stretched for miles behind their property, land left undisturbed since the time of the Native American. The owners, an elderly couple in San Francisco, planned to donate it to the Nature Conservancy after their death. Until then, Morgan's family and a few neighbors had sole access.

"Last summer, I got to swim in the river," Joshua said. "Without a life jacket."

In response to my inquiring gaze, Morgan explained, "During the summer months, the river runs low and the current is practically nonexistent, just strong enough to keep the water from going stagnant. There's an ideal spot for swimming with its own little beach."

"Where we swing from ropes and jump from trees," Joshua added.

Although this was exactly what my Indigo students needed, open space, freedom, and fresh air, I gasped at the thought of Joshua swinging from ropes and jumping from trees.

"Uh, Joshua," Morgan said. "We weren't supposed to share that bit of information with Marjorie, remember?"

"Sorry," Joshua said.

Before I could complain about their antics, Carla called from the house. "Wait up. I packed you a lunch." That meant she'd been in on the surprise, too. The van Dykes were one big happy family, and part of their intimacy came from sharing. Too much emphasis placed on privacy and self-protection, by their way of thinking, built walls that led to mistrust and misunderstanding.

"Thanks, Mom." Morgan took the insulated lunch tote from her and handed it to me. "Time's a wasting, Josh. We'd better saddle up if we want to get back before dark."

Carla scooped up Gabriel with both hands, his butt facing forward in a football carry, a sign of her familiarity with cats and their need for a secure hold. "Better leave Gabriel with me. He disappears on long excursions, which upsets Joshua to no end."

I shook my head. *Some things never change.*

🕷 🕷 🕷

I wasn't prepared for the silence.

Not on land between two major freeways and two growing towns. Morgan called it the *Cosumnes River Preserve*. I dubbed it the *Land in Between*.

We entered the woods using the winding dirt road that connected it to Morgan's farm and experienced complete and utter silence. Sure, we heard the *clip-clop-clip-clop* of horses' hooves, along with the occasional squawks and songs of birds (over 200 species according to Morgan) and the sporadic movement of animals concealed behind bushes and trees. Otherwise, it was so quiet I could hear myself breathing.

No one spoke, deciding by some unvoiced agreement to advance as if on sacred ground. As we wove through the canopy of valley oaks, I inhaled the musty air with the greed of someone long deprived of oxygen, recalling the time we'd spent together in the Los Padres National Forest. It had been peaceful there, too, until a lightning storm had triggered events I hoped never to repeat.

The sound of rushing water broke the silence.

"We're almost there," Joshua said.

We guided our horses down an inclined path to the edge of the swiftly moving river. Morgan pitched his voice to be heard above the water's roar. "The Cosumnes is the last undammed river running from the Sierras into the Central Valley. The sandy beach I told you about is a side arm of the river, dry in the summer but now covered with water. Swimming here can be dangerous this time of year. The water looks calm on top, but the undercurrent has enough power to tow even a strong swimmer along for miles, totally at its mercy."

Like my new job, I thought before I could suppress it.

"There's whirlpools," Joshua said.

I felt my own undercurrent, that of fear, and wondered if we should back our horses up a bit. As if sensing my concern, Morgan turned his mount and headed back up the incline. I was about to do the same when I glimpsed someone standing on the opposite bank of the river. "Morgan. I think I see one of your neighbors."

He twisted in his saddle. "It's usually just us…"

I pointed toward the man with long black hair, naked, except for a loin cloth of grass or bark fiber and an animal pelt over his shoulder. He held a stick in one hand and what appeared to be a dead jackrabbit in the other.

Morgan looked in the direction I was pointing. "I don't see anyone."

The man was short, five-foot-four tops, with dark, deep-set eyes and a wide nose. "There," I said, jabbing my finger at the solitary figure. "Looks like he's been skinny dipping."

"Do you see anyone, Joshua?" Morgan asked.

Joshua sat on his mount, head erect, eyes wide, as he'd appeared when I first met him in Dr. Mendez's office, engrossed, even amused. "He's from before."

A shiver shot through me. I should have been accustomed to my intuitive gifts by now, but my logical mind rejected what I saw. "An Indian?"

"Probably a Miwok," Morgan said. He'd grown accustomed to Joshua and my psychic abilities by then without understanding or trying to change them. "Of the Cos-os tribe that once lived in this area. They gave the Cosumnes River its name. One of their burial mounds was discovered near here in the sixties."

"They may be our ancestors, Joshua," I said before realizing this was unlikely. Though we were both half Native American, my mother and Joshua's father were descendants of the Esselen tribe, otherwise known as the Ohlone/Costanoan Esselen Nation, located in Carmel Valley and Big Sur. The Miwok and Esselen were distinct tribes, therefore didn't mingle.

"He sees us," Joshua said.

"And we're probably a scary sight sitting on horseback, especially me with my blonde hair flapping in the breeze. You'd think he'd be running for cover."

"He thinks he's dreaming," Joshua said. "To him, we're like spirits. Let's sing a song, so he'll remember us when he goes back to where he came from."

"Good idea. Like a healing incantation. What do you suggest?"

"Something easy, like *Row, Row, Row Your Boat.*"

Little did Joshua know the symbolic significance of the song he'd chosen: the boat representing our lives, with ourselves at the oar; the stream representing the stretch of time; *Merrily, merrily* indicating it's all about attitude; and *Life is but a dream* suggesting we don't see what we see, but what we want to see.

I turned to Morgan.

He chuckled. "Let's do it."

We repeated the song three times, while the slack-shouldered Miwok listened in silence.

I glanced at Joshua. His face beamed with an inner glow.

When I turned back to the Miwok, he was gone.

"We were looking into the past," Joshua said, "and the Miwok was looking into the future. It's all mixed up, isn't it, yesterday, today, and tomorrow?"

Mixed up? Hell, yes. So many unanswerable questions: Do we exist in time, or does time exist in us? "I think so."

"Ready to go?" Though Morgan had accepted the reality of Joshua and my psychic gifts, he kept his feet firmly planted on the ground. "I know of a great spot to eat lunch. Under a giant oak over eight hundred years old."

I winked at Joshua. "Might as well picnic under a tree that spans the past, present, and future and once provided our Miwok friend with acorns and shelter."

"We're family," Joshua said with such conviction I believed him.

🕷 🕷 🕷

We returned to the ranch house for dinner—steak, mixed green salad, and baked potatoes. But this time Carla had help: David, his wife, Linda, and their sons, Todd and Jon. All pitched in to lighten her load. David and Morgan's father, Leonard, sat at his usual place at the kitchen table with the two Border collies at his side. He looked up and smiled. "Have a good time?"

"Wonderful," I said.

Morgan glanced at Joshua and winked, the Miwok sighting remaining our secret.

Linda put her hands on her jean-clad hips with an exaggerated sigh. "Well, Todd and Jon were fit to be tied when you slipped away without inviting them. Next time they'll be watching."

"Next time, they can come, too," Joshua said. He and his cousins exchanged a high five.

Linda's cropped hair, pert nose, and saucer-sized eyes made her look like a pixie. But there was nothing pixie about the way she took to the role of mother and farmer's wife. She drove tractors and trucks, fed calves, even milked cows in a pinch. "Marjorie has to put up with a bunch of clowns like you when she returns to Menlo Park. Don't you think she needs a break?"

"No," Todd and Jon said as one. They also had farm duties. On weekends and during school breaks, they helped feed calves and herd cows for milking. Plus, they assisted their mother and grandmother with household chores when needed.

"Marjorie likes kids," Joshua said.

Linda glanced at Morgan and laughed, her sense of humor refreshing.

David slid his thumb and index finger across his mouth in a my-lips-are-sealed gesture, as if he knew what lay ahead for Morgan.

Todd and Jon followed the exchange wide-eyed. As far as I could tell, they were polite and attentive to Joshua. They called him "cuz" and taught him everything about farm life from the perspective of a kid, like how to vault over baled hay in the field and build forts once the bales were stacked in the barn.

After dinner, Morgan, Joshua, Gabriel, and I headed for our future home to camp beneath the stars. Once we'd settled onto blankets on the plywood floor, framed by wall studs and roof rafters and warmed by a pagoda fireplace, I told them about my future class of Indigos and their special talents.

Seeing Morgan frown, I asked, "Is something wrong?"

"Could Joshua be an Indigo, too?"

"It's possible," I said, having wondered the same myself. "I'll know more by June. Meanwhile, why not treat him as such?"

"Which is how?"

I smiled at Morgan's look of concern. What a kind and loving father he'd make for Joshua and our future children. "Exactly, as you're treating him now."

Joshua bundled next to me with Gabriel curled at his feet. No sooner had Morgan pointed out Orion, *The Hunter,* and Taurus, *The Bull,* then the child's head dropped to its side.

Morgan's eyes glistened with a promise of what lay ahead.

🕷 🕷 🕷

With only Popsicle sticks and a tent separating us from the outside world, the following morning started early—2:00 a.m. to be exact—with the milker herding cows to the barn, whistling and calling "Ándale! Ándale!" Bulls blared in protest of the disruption to their harem, followed by the steady hum of milking equipment, which lulled me back to sleep. The next sound to wake me was the tractor loading grain, silage, and hay into the box of the feed truck, followed by the grinding of truck augers. On and on came the reassuring sounds of a dairy farm coming to life.

Morgan had been awake since five, the normal start to his day. "Sleeping when your body's programmed for action takes some getting used to," he said. "I'm alert to the cows' *moos,* which tell me what's going on. Happy cows are quiet cows. But when their *moos* get loud and high-pitched, something's wrong. If a cow escapes the corral, her herdmates *moo* as if singing in a choir before following her out. And if a cow is in trouble, the herd makes a different sound, like blares of sympathy, recognizable to any dairyman worth his salt."

Joshua slept through it all.

"He's used to it," Morgan said. "Plus, he knows he's safe and surrounded by people he loves."

If Joshua was an Indigo, he was getting exactly what he needed—love and a solid emotional foundation. The farm and its occupants had a similar effect on me, but I wasn't yet ready to commit to that kind of security. Morgan visualized me as a butterfly, beautiful and fully formed, while I saw myself as only emerging from my cocoon. I needed time to integrate the changes going on inside of me, which meant more time in Menlo Park to prepare for my *first flight.*

Chapter Eleven

MY MOTHER WAS WAITING for me when I got back from the farm, the woman who had adopted me, raised me, and couldn't stop telling me what to do. She'd entered my house using the keys I'd given her before my retreat to Carmel Valley nine and a half months ago. I'd forgotten to ask for them back, and now I regretted it. She took the overnight bag from my hand and shooed me to the kitchen. "Hurry and wash up. I made you some *stamppot met boerenkool en rookworst.*"

I sniffed with appreciation. Mashed potatoes and kale with smoked sausage, a recipe straight from the Netherlands. Mom's ancestors were Dutch, just like Morgan's. I had hoped this would work in his favor. Fat chance.

On entering the kitchen, I stopped and caught my breath. Mom had exchanged my *Autumn Sunset* tablecloth for one in deep scarlet, accompanied by rainbow-striped place mats and yellow napkins. She'd even swapped my classic white dinnerware with shamrock Fiestaware. In honor of Saint Patrick's Day, I assumed, still two months away.

"I figured you could use a little cheering up after your trip to the fa-arm," she said.

Something about the way she drew out the word "farm" rubbed me the wrong way, but I let it pass. How could a woman otherwise so rigid and subdued favor dinnerware with such in-your-face cheerfulness? There was no reconciling the two.

No sooner had I washed my hands than she ushered me to my

usual spot at the breakfast nook facing the front window. "You must be starving." I sank onto my seat and tolerated her ministrations, though I would have preferred being alone. A soak in the tub would have been nice, followed by a cup of hot apple cider. But that was not to be. Apparently, my mother hadn't learned a thing during my nine-and-a-half-month absence. But I had. I'd learned there was no harm in accepting her love and attempts at control, as long as I didn't allow them to imprison me. My comfort zone and safety zone no longer occupied the same space. The riskiest thing I could do now was continue to allow her to copyedit my world.

Mom brought the *stamppot* to the table, and my mouth watered. The part of me I couldn't control, the part conditioned and trained by years of nurturing, was under her spell. Comfort food was on the way.

She scooped a generous helping of mashed potatoes and kale onto my plate, followed by a topping of smoked sausage. "Well, I hope you got *that* nonsense off your chest."

Shamrock was all wrong. Sunflower yellow would have contrasted better with the kale.

"Your visit to the farm," she clarified when I didn't respond.

Mom made a point of voicing her disapproval of Morgan as husband material whenever she got the chance, but this was the first time she'd brought up the farm. "I'm sure you've given some thought to what it would be like living with the dust, dirt, and smell. And that you'd be in the middle of nowhere with cows and flies as neighbors."

Of course, I'd given it some thought, but coming from her, the suggestion made me mad.

"And you'd have to give up that teaching position at the school, which wouldn't be such a bad thing, since it's a poor substitute for the job you already had."

I shrugged. Different subject, same outcome. Mom never gave in. It was her way or no way. "Dinner's getting cold," I said.

She picked up her fork, then set it back down. "Go back to Cliff, hon. Go back to your old job. You have the opportunity for a secure future and nice things."

I forced a piece of kale into my mouth, closed my eyes, and waved my fork in the air. "Yummm."

"Please listen, Marjorie. I'm telling you this for your own good."

I repeated my performance with a slice of sausage this time, then pointed at her plate, nodding, smiling.

She took the hint and started to eat. But barely had she swallowed her first bite when she said, "You're going backwards, Marjorie, to the premodern."

I knew what she was referring to, though she was way off base. The farm was hardly premodern. "There's a dark side to modernity," I said, because to defend the farm in any other way wouldn't compute with her. She hadn't been to the country in years, so I understood that she pictured it as many city people did, backwards and behind the times. "Plus, being with the man I love counts for something."

"It won't be enough."

I'd read somewhere that some people were nouns and some people verbs, and I knew which one my mother wanted me to be. But the small part of me she loved and wanted to protect was emerging into something larger, and the more she pressed, the more excited I became by the unlimited possibilities that lay ahead. I was finally breaking free of my cocoon, and with a little practice, my butterfly wings would serve me well.

"Cliff says you won't last a month as a teacher, and I agree."

When my mother didn't get her way, she resorted to put downs, her take on tough love. It had worked so many times in the past to prevent me from taking a risk and exploring new possibilities that she wasn't about to give up on me now. She'd talked to Cliff since our meeting at the book store, which meant they were still chums. Heck, Dr. Matt and his nephew Shawn were rooting for me on one side and my mother and ex-fiancé heckling me from the other, in what threatened to become a life-altering battle of minds.

Okay, if I failed at teaching, I would still have Morgan. He would continue to love and support and spoil me to no end. In fact, he preferred I become a stay-at-home wife and mother like his sister-in-law. But Linda had *chosen* her path; I'd seen it in her eyes. Being immersed in family and farm life brought her satisfaction and, as a result, made her a success. I, on the other hand, felt teaching was the right path for me. And I wanted to prove—to myself at least—that I could make it a go.

The phone rang. "Let the machine get it," Mom said.

I got up and grabbed the receiver. "Hello."

"Marjorie? Dr. Matt Lee, here. Your classroom will be available first thing tomorrow morning."

I heard dishes being stacked in the kitchen. Running water. Long sighs. "That's great."

"Go ahead and get a feel of the place. I'll meet up with you as soon as I'm free." A beat missed. A small rush of air. "I have great confidence in you."

Chapter Twelve

"WHAT DO YOU THINK?" Dr. Matt asked after meeting me in my classroom on Monday.

He smiled at my expression, which I assume was similar to when I'd stepped through the archway of the Sleeping Beauty Castle into Fantasyland as a child or the colossal portico doors of the St Joseph Cathedral in San Jose years later. The entire east wall of the classroom—from the waist-high counter running the length of the room to the lofty ceiling—consisted of windows. They were old, single-paned, and hardly crystal-clear, but sunlight streamed through just the same. "Oh, my God. They don't make classrooms like this anymore."

We stood in silence and watched the bare elms wave their branches as if trying to lure us outdoors. Black birds swooped like kamikazes, coming so close to the windows they appeared to be looking inside.

"Very distracting," Dr. Matt said. "I suppose we could put in retractable blinds."

"Are you kidding? My lessons will just have to play second fiddle for a while."

"What if you want to use the overhead," he said, failing to hold back a smile.

I recalled the disastrous overhead incident during my short-lived stint as a sub and shuddered. "We'll find other things to do."

Something flickered across Dr. Matt's face and disappeared. He pulled at his ear, didn't meet my eyes. "Let's move on to the nature area, shall we?"

We entered a small foyer intersected by three doors in the southeastern corner of the classroom. Dr. Matt pointed to the door on our right— "Restroom" —then the door up ahead— "Home Ec room. Outdated but functional" —before opening the door to our left. We stepped onto a sidewalk that ran the length of the building, separating a landscaping of succulents and trees from the school's east parking lot. We took a right and, after no more than forty feet, entered a refuge of indeterminate size and shape that had the feel of an ecological island.

What I noticed first was the breeze, chilly but invigorating, and then the dank, musty smell. The fenced-in grounds looked like an overgrown thicket of weeds with long grasses growing along dirt paths. Most of the trees were bare, waving their boney branches against hazy gray skies, encouraged by the currents in the air.

"The maintenance crew is itching to fix the place up," Dr. Matt said.

"You won't let them, will you?" I pictured future class sessions here, the students running free, observing bugs and insects, even building a Medicine Wheel. Like the one Ben *Gentle Bear* Mendoza had introduced me to in the Los Padres National Forest; to impart knowledge of the vital energy and power inherent in nature—and in myself. "I doubt Maintenance understands the healing value of a natural setting. Please tell them that landscape money would be better spent elsewhere."

"Embrace the messy," he said with an encompassing wave of his hand. "I'll take that into consideration."

"I hope so," I huffed, "since you're asking me to take on a project without guidelines and with few restrictions."

A brief silence before he said, "Within limits."

I followed Dr. Matt back to the classroom. "Okay, I promise not to abuse the kids or burn down the school." He knew I was kidding. Then again, the part about missing guidelines and few restrictions was true. Twenty-nine years of my life had revolved around rules and regulations. This would be a new experience for me and likely the students as well.

Dr. Matt opened the door to the foyer, and we stepped inside. "It's not about control but management," he said. "On your first day here, you weren't in control, but you managed quite well. Trying to constrain a group of Indigos is like trying to constrain the weather. A far wiser use of energy is to allow for what comes and have fun with it, direct your energies toward enjoying the show."

The euphoric sense of escape and freedom I'd experienced in the green space outdoors gave the classroom the sudden feel of confinement. "What about lesson plans and ways to measure the students' progress?" I only had seven days left to pull it all together.

"'Knowledge which is acquired under compulsion obtains no hold on the mind,'" Dr. Matt said. "Plato shared that advice 347 BC, and it still holds true today."

I blinked, focused on his face.

He took a seat on one of the tables scattered helter-skelter throughout the room. The only available chairs were stacked in untidy piles against the cabinets on the west wall. "Let me make a suggestion."

Suggestions were welcome, especially from my boss.

"Have you ever done slip-casting with ceramic molds?"

I thought back to my friend Anne's ceramic studio in Monterey and how she'd introduced me to the basics of working with clay. "Few materials respond to a sculptor's hands and tools as clay," she'd said. "It's plastic when moist and yields to the slightest pressure. But once it's fired, it can never become fluid again."

"Sort of, I mean, yes, under the direction of an artist."

"After getting acquainted with your students," he said, eyes bright as a wizard's, "why not introduce them to the art room and have them select a plaster mold?"

I sank onto the table next to him, noticing for the first time that all the furniture in the room could use a good scrubbing. "Art room?"

"Oh, I forgot to tell you." Dr. Matt motioned toward the door in the north wall. Another entrance into the classroom which, including the doors leading to the main corridor, kitchen, and nature area amounted to four. How would I keep track of them all? "There's an art room connected to this one that you're welcome to use. It's full of supplies from before we dropped vocational education from the curriculum. Selecting a mold will take time, since your students will do a lot of searching, rejecting, and choosing, but no rush. The lesson will be worth it. Next, you can ask them to visualize the molds they've chosen as the form of their thoughts."

"Thought equals form," I said, so he'd know I was following him.

"Exactly. While pouring ceramic slip into the molds, you can explain that like slip, the mind is plastic and receptive, and, just as the slip takes the form of the mold, the mind solidifies into the form of one's thoughts."

I visualized my mind taking the form of my thoughts, and the result wasn't pretty. Though I looked forward to helping the students find purpose in their lives—and the will to accomplish that purpose—my mind threatened to solidify into the form of failure. Who was I to present myself as an advocate for resolution and self-reliance when I hadn't yet succeeded in speaking and living my own convictions? If I could 'think' my way into discovering and following my life's purpose, I would have done so already. As far as I knew, finding one's truth, one's inner power, could only be achieved by taking action toward one's dreams. Which would also apply to my students.

"Think always and only about what you want and believe it will happen," Dr. Matt said. "Then, like a magnet, you'll attract the conditions you want."

"You sound like a philosopher."

"Principal, philosopher, same difference."

The art project he suggested would take at least five days to complete: one day to select and pour slip into the molds, another to disassemble the molds and witness the solidified clay inside, then time to cut away and even out the seams, adding a new lesson with each step. During the process of firing and glazing, we could focus on what we wanted to achieve in our lives.

Dr. Matt rose and headed for the door to the outside corridor.

I slid from the edge of the table and followed him, trying to block my thoughts from their downward spiral. *What if I failed?* "All this, you, me… It's all so experimental, so—"

"'That which has been believed by everyone, always and everywhere, has every chance of being false.'"

I waited to hear the source of this wisdom.

"Al Valery, French poet and philosopher."

I laughed. "Positive thoughts—"

"—become the mold into which the mind can pour itself," he finished.

Energy surged through me as though someone had thrown a switch. I was a string of blinking Christmas lights. "There won't be enough time in the day to do all we need to do."

"Your job is to groom, monitor, and inspire. The rest is up to the kids."

Non-interference, benign neglect, there had to be more.

"You've got the rest of the week to set up," Dr. Matt said. "Let me know what you need in the way of supplies and equipment, and I'll do my best to provide them."

"How about lining up some parent volunteers?" I asked. "They'd make excellent chaperones for field trips."

"Field trips?" He dropped his gaze and tugged at his ear.

Maybe this wasn't a good time to approach him about the excursion to the James Lick Observatory I envisioned. "About those parent volunteers…"

His face cleared. "I'm sure some of the parents will take on any reasonable project."

"You mean they're desperate."

Dr. Matt's shoulders squared. "More like ready for change. Their children are traumatized by education as soldiers are traumatized by war."

I thought that an exaggeration but said nothing.

He opened the door and stepped into the corridor packed with students circulating between classes like traffic on a freeway. "Enjoy."

Chapter Thirteen

IT WAS PAST ELEVEN by the time I'd finished cleaning and arranging the classroom to my satisfaction. I'd read that Indigos were uncomfortable with the sharp corners and angles of traditional row seating, so I'd positioned three rectangular tables horseshoe fashion, with seven chairs lining the perimeter and my desk facing the top. As far as decorating with construction paper and posters, I declined either. The outdoor view would provide all the décor we needed for now. I'd let the students decide if they wanted to display anything on the walls as time went on. I'd bring in some live plants, though, some spider, Boston, and maidenhair ferns and possibly Christmas cactus and mother-in-law's tongue—plants that thrived on *benign neglect*. While debating whether to use an aromatic diffuser with essential oils to eliminate the room's musty odor or pry open some windows, I heard a rap on the door jamb.

Charles Lacoste. I gave him a welcoming smile, willing to start fresh, let bygones, be bygones. "Come on in."

He didn't smile in return, just strode in like a guest speaker heading for the podium. He halted in front of the wall of windows and clasped his hands behind his back. "You've got quite a set up here."

I couldn't tell by the tone of his voice if he approved of my 'set up' or was being sarcastic, so I waited for him to clue me in.

He turned to face me. "Excuse me for saying so, but I was surprised to hear you were hired after last week's fiasco, let alone be offered this." He crossed his arms and peered at me over the rims of heavy, out-of-date glasses. His bow tie—a muddy forest green—appeared crooked and sad. "I understand you've never taught before."

"That's right, except for a year of student teaching."

"Yet you've convinced Dr. Matt that you can take on seven impatient, resistant, tuned-out brats."

"Actually, hiring me was his idea. He believes I'm suited for the job."

Lacoste pivoted toward the windows, turning his back on me—again.

Not about to let the burning in my chest escalate into anger, I followed his lead and faced the windows, smiling at the antics of the birds outside. They rode the wind like surfers riding the waves. "You don't have a very high opinion of my teaching ability."

His reply; quick, impatient. "What teaching ability?"

To my surprise, a giggle bubbled to the surface. "Some people are naturals, I guess. You know, born with skills that solidify with experience."

He swung around, his eyes twitching as if taking on a life of their own. "You think this is funny, that all these kids need is some flower child with her head in the clouds to whip them into shape?"

Flower child? Hippies and flower children were of my mother's generation—and likely his, by the looks of him—though I doubted either of them had been active participants. I held out my hand. "I understand your reservations, Mr. Lacoste, but maybe lack of experience is a prerequisite for the job. I don't know enough to be scared."

He gave my hand a half-hearted shake and dropped it. "You *are* very inexperienced."

"You bet I am, and I'd appreciate your help, if you've come to offer."

His gaze locked onto the ancient linoleum floor, which had plenty of defects if he cared to look. But his mind seemed focused on mine. "I hardly have time…"

"That's okay, I understand. This type of class will be a new one, so I'll be reinventing the wheel, so to speak. But if you come up with something to help the kids, I'm open to suggestions. You're seasoned and well-respected, and I appreciate that."

He met my eyes for the first time since entering the room. "I know these kids. They're easily distracted. They refuse to follow directions. In other words, they're tough."

"Yeah, I got that impression on my first day."

"You need to tow them into line, show them who's boss. You're not here to be their friend, but to teach them the body of knowledge they need to prepare for high school, college, and future jobs."

I thought back to my conversation with Dr. Matt and realized I needed to choose my words with care. Apparently, Charles Lacoste wasn't aware of the Indigos' special gifts, and it wasn't my place to tell him. "Well…not exactly. Mine will be an after-school session to help these kids gain a more solid emotional foundation, which is also a prerequisite for success in high school and beyond."

Lacoste snorted. "Most of the students you're referring to have been diagnosed with ADHD. Best leave their emotional foundation to mental health professionals."

"Consider me a supplement to—"

"The only supplement they need is prescribed medication for focus and control."

"Prescribed medication?" I heard the pound of foot soldiers in my ears. "Just because they're unable to conform?" I was going into battle mode and tried to rein myself in. When angry, I often say things I regret later. In fact, I was regretting this conversation already.

"These kids don't have the mental maturity to know what's best for them," he said, "and you'd better come to grips with that, or you'll be in for more of what you experienced on your first day."

He pulled something from the pocket of his jacket and held it up between his thumb and index finger. "See this? It's a two-and-a-half-dollar Indian Head gold piece."

"It sure is small," I said.

"It was minted in 1929, the year my grandfather came to this country from France. He gave it to me when I was thirteen, four years before he died."

"You're lucky," I said. "I never knew my grandfather."

"Grandpa was a good, honest man, who believed he had immigrated to the *Promised Land*. But he was unschooled and overly influenced by anyone with a high school diploma and the gift of charisma. In other words, he was gullible and lived with his head in the clouds."

Like me, I suppose.

Lacoste palmed the coin and raised his fist like a salute. "I carry this coin as a reminder of my grandfather's love…and failure."

"'And what if they eat clouds and drink wind,'" I said, quoting Emerson. "'They have not been without service to the race of man.'"

But Lacoste wasn't in the listening mood. "Do you know what Lacoste means in French, Ms. Veil?"

Do you know what Veil means in English, Mr. Lacoste?

"It means coast, and I've made it my mission here at West Coast Middle School to convince the students that education opens doors and saves lives."

And I will make it my mission here to lift some veils and rattle some cages.

I wondered if Mr. Lacoste, aka *Mr. Coast*, knew that surface learning was a key reason Emerson left teaching in the formal classroom. He knew the difference between memorizing and reproducing data and deep learning. "Students need to understand ideas for themselves and apply that understanding to their lives."

A muscle twitched under Lacoste's right cheek and his breathing sounded labored. "These kids need structure, not encouragement to fantasize about a perfect world."

At this point, I could have told him not to worry, that I'd only be here until June and, though I'd like his support and to be friends, in reality, I could do without either. Negativity was such a drag, and I sensed truckloads in this man. As talented as he might be in his particular subject, his attitude was one of lost hope, the very thing we would be fighting against in this classroom.

At least, if I had anything to say about it.

Anyway, it was time for lunch, and I was hungry. Bending like a willow was, in my opinion, highly overrated. "I have a job to do," I said, "and I plan on doing it. If you have a problem with that, take it up with Dr. Matt."

Lacoste's smile was so hostile, it would have made my ex-fiancé proud. "I already did."

Chapter Fourteen

AFTER A QUICK LUNCH in the school cafeteria, something I swore I'd never repeat (pizza and coke not being my favorite menu items and mass hysteria not conducive to digestion), I checked out the art room through the door at the north end of my classroom. Slabs of clay sealed in plastic bags lay under a long Formica countertop. Gallon jugs of ceramic slip stood waiting to be poured into myriad molds housed on the wooden shelves. I located sanding pads, carving tools, and paintbrushes in rubber trays, plus glazes, banding wheels, and a large kiln.

Something jarred loose inside of me. For the second time that day, I thought of my friend Anne's ceramic studio in Monterey. During one of my visits there, she'd taken a mass of pottery clay and, while cutting it into pieces with a wire, explained how to knead it into a workable state. She lifted a piece of the clay to the height of her shoulder and slammed it onto the piece below, impressing me with the violence of it. Then she handed me a chunk of what felt like damp mud and told me to go into the wilderness of my intuition. "But first you need to relax," she said, "so creativity can flow. Make a mess. Let the clay get under your nails."

"Hello," a female now called from my classroom next door.

"In here," I said.

A fifty-something woman dressed in a bulky red sweater, navy slacks, and brown loafers entered through the doorway. "I'm glad this building is being put to good use again," she said without a hint of malice.

Unable to see her eyes behind the dark aviator sunglasses she wore, I stepped forward and reached out my hand. "Hi. I'm Marjorie."

She clasped my hand in both of hers. "Maxine."

An outrageously funny Hallmark cartoon character came to mind. "Anyone ever call you Max?"

"Just about everyone, my dear, except for the kids, they call me Granny Max, but I wanted to make a good first impression."

"Well, you certainly did." I enjoyed the firm grip of her hands and the way she punctuated her sentences with commas instead of periods. "And I could sure use your support about now."

"I'm not called Granny Max for nothing." She gave my hand a final squeeze before releasing it, a gesture so full of good will that I felt like the malleable clay in my friend's art studio. "Give me access to one of those old but still functional kitchens next door, and I'll whip up a batch of oatmeal raisin cookies, my forte, besides teaching math, that is. In my opinion, the two best ways to respond to the students' unanswerable questions are with 'I don't know' and cookies. The first promotes quiet reflection, and the second stimulates the reward center of the brain. It takes about five cookies to erase a negative thought, a bit fattening, but fewer cookies are needed once the kids realize that most of their problems are only in their minds."

I laughed. This woman was unreal, in a refreshing way, the elderly Good Witch of the North. "We'll be open for business starting Tuesday next week and, after that, Monday through Thursday, three to five. So, feel free."

I led the way back to the classroom with reluctance. I wanted to stay in the art room a bit longer, savor the memories of cool, wet clay and the exhilaration of molding it with bare hands. I'd felt comfort and love in my friend's Monterey studio, so much so that my hands had developed a mind of their own, molding, tearing, pressing, and pulling. All had just flowed together.

"Good Lord," Granny Max said, halting in front of the wall of windows, "what a view."

I chuckled, wondering once again why classrooms of old had windows that embraced the outside world, while modern classroom windows were draped and shuttered, if they existed at all. I thought of cages full of tamed, sensory-deprived animals, learning tricks that had little to do with the here and now, then stopped my mind from lingering there, the analogy too depressing.

Granny Max slid her sunglasses onto her graying brown hair, revealing eyes the color of Bordeaux chocolates. "This may sound crazy coming from an old-school math teacher, but I believe I'm spending way too much time squelching the very capabilities you'll be encouraging here. Kids who don't fit the mold throw traditional classrooms out of whack, if you know what I mean, so we reduce imagination and self-awareness to a minimum, in favor of technical proficiency."

Her comment surprised me, and I wanted to press her for more.

Granny Max must have noticed the lighthouse beam in my eyes, because she went on as though glad for a listening ear. "Dr. Matt has a friend with a doctorate in transpersonal psychology, specializing in mind-body dynamics, all that Deepak Chopra-manifesting-the-life-you-want stuff. The concept of integrating western psychology and eastern spiritual traditions lit the fire beneath Dr. Matt's feet, if you know what I mean, and now he's really into all that spiritual development stuff, due to his nephew and all. Quite a character, Shawn is, quiet, but deep. Anyway, all kids need work on their social and emotional skills to become more responsible citizens. Too bad your class will be limited to just a few."

"For now," I said, with a confidence I had no right to feel, not yet, maybe never. "Who knows where an option like this might lead, especially if people like Charles Lacoste can be won over. He's not a fan of what I'm being asked to do."

"I'm no busybody gossip," Granny Max said, then grinned as though being labeled as such wouldn't bother her in the least. "But there are a few things you should know about the undercurrents in this school."

I said nothing, figured even bad news was better than maneuvering blind. Plus, I hadn't yet decided if she was an ally or another detractor in disguise.

"At least ten of the fifty-four teachers here think Dr. Matt is way out of line, giving special treatment to a bunch of disorderly students. This after-school class will cost money that, according to them, would be better spent elsewhere and will take precious time away from extracurricular activities, plus, it's hardly foolproof, so" —Granny Max paused then finished like a boxer throwing a jab punch— "why not modify the students instead? A little pharmaceutical intervention for focus and impulse control would do the trick."

Her jab made contact, as had a similar suggestion by Charles Lacoste only an hour before. I felt my blood pressure rise.

Granny Max shook her head and frowned, an unnatural gesture for someone as upbeat as Mrs. Claus. "That's not me talking, mind you, just passing on what I've heard."

I blew out my breath. "That's crazy."

"Did you know Einstein, Churchill, and Edison did poorly in school?" she asked.

I didn't answer, still stuck on *pharmaceutical intervention.*

She tut-tutted. "Silly me, of course you do, which serves as a reminder that we should never stop looking for geniuses among the unlikely. Anyway, Edison was disruptive, and Einstein's parents thought he was mentally disabled. Good thing they didn't medicate kids back then."

"Lacoste is among those who think hiring me was a bad idea," I said.

Granny Max gave a what's-the-world-coming-to sigh. "You need to see it from his point of view. The entire school staff is trying to make every day a teachable one, mainly by standing in front of the students, presenting them with data, and then testing them to see what they remember, while you get the luxury of doing something new, something Charles knows in his heart could make a big difference in their lives. He doesn't think it fair that he's rated according to student achievement on standardized tests while you'll be getting off scot-free."

The sudden pause in conversation seemed to rest on a question that made my mouth go dry and my adoptive mother's words sprout like thistles in my head. "Go back to Cliff, hon. Go back to your old job. You have the opportunity for a secure future with nice things."

"At least the rest of the staff has a target with a big bull's eye in the middle," I said, my old job and secure future a bull's eye no longer within reach. "My target is vapor thin with no place for an arrow to stick."

"You've got a point there," Granny Max said with an 'excuse-my-pun' grin, "but it's about as useless as your vapor thin target for converting some of the other teachers to your way of thinking. They're overworked, underpaid, and exhausted. Anyway, I'll be rooting for you. You have my backing one hundred percent. I'm only one building away, trying to convince a bunch of 'Nexters' that algebra and geometry are fun and exciting, but it's an uphill battle."

Algebra and geometry fun and exciting? I could hardly suppress a shudder. Math had been a struggle for me in school, too structured, too black and white, too step-by-step. "Yeah, that would be a tough sell."

"Not you, too," she cried. "We need to talk."

"If you can convince me that math is fun and exciting, I'll owe you big time."

"Are you kidding me? There's math all around us, built into the very fabric of the universe. It's spoken and understood by nearly all the world's population. Some say there's even a mathematical basis for psychic abilities and spiritual phenomena. Right up your alley, if I may say so myself. We use math to explain life's mysteries, discover cures for diseases, and" —she snorted, slid her shades back over her eyes, and headed for the door— "bake oatmeal raisin cookies."

Soon I realized I'd met my only faculty ally besides Dr. Matt. Before another hour passed, four more detractors walked through the door, all teachers, all limited in scope and horizon. Look up, look around, look deeply, I wanted to say, but by the looks on their faces and the stiffness of their gaits, I knew they were beyond convincing. In fact, as far as I could tell, they considered me a threat. Good grief, if I succeeded here, they'd take it as a personal slight, a blow to their worldview.

After each one's departure, I stared out the window to calm myself, making me realize that my students would soon need similar calming experiences. The bank of windows with all that natural light would be a start, but they would need more.

Chapter Fifteen

SUNLIGHT DID NOT STREAM into my classroom as I had imagined it would on my first day. Instead, wind-driven rain pelted and rattled the single-pane windows, an icy chill seeping through. Bare tree branches undulated in the wind as though pleading for something I couldn't provide. No amount of potted plants, beeswax votives, and aromatic oils could change the room's mood, and I wanted to shout in frustration.

Oddly, on getting up that morning, I had opted to wear Maya's brown bomber jacket, well-worn jeans, and boots instead of my favored blazer, slacks, and pumps, as if expecting a combat rather than a meeting of minds.

You're not in control of the weather, I reminded myself. *So, work with the cards you've been dealt.* Wasn't that what I'd planned to tell the students today, that there was hope and possibility in every circumstance? It was only a matter of visualizing the clouds, the rain, and the heaviness in the air as opportunities instead of excuses to fail.

I checked my watch. It was early yet, just past one. My class didn't start until three. I wanted an inviting, secure place for my students to gather, a place where they'd feel comfortable, where they'd want to share. The home economics room next door stood idle and unappreciated, like a grandmother with myriad gifts to share waiting to be recognized.

Time to bake cookies.

🕷 🕷 🕷

All seven students entered the classroom in silence, their faces expressionless, their bodies bent. Heaven forbid, they reminded me of martyrs heading for execution. This, I decided, had nothing to do with the atmosphere of the room, which had improved significantly since my arrival. The rain and wind had died, and the scent of baked cookies mixed with myrrh and sandalwood wafted in the air. Even the sun was making an effort, its light, though weak and sporadic, penetrating the windowed wall.

"Take any chair around the tables," I told them. "You can always move later."

They sat. Backpacks dropped to the floor.

I eased from behind my desk and stood at the head of the tables forming the U. "What's wrong?"

Their power was off, big time. *Out of service; game over.* They didn't even have the energy—or inclination—to answer me.

"Shawn?" I hated putting him on the spot, but only two weeks ago, he'd offered his help.

He shrugged and looked at his hands.

I'd planned to save the chocolate chip cookies until later, after we'd had a chance to get to know one another. But as I was quickly discovering, my plan needed major adjustment. Jason *The Wolf* Ardis leaned back in his chair at the base of the U and focused on the wall of windows. I sensed a quality in him that saddened me, a sympathetic, congenial energy muted by despair. You'd think these kids would be happy to be in a class created just for them, a class based on consciousness of body, mind, and spirit, where they could be free to be themselves. Dr. Matt had stuck his neck out for them. Where was the gratitude? Maybe these kids were impatient, resistant, tuned-out brats after all.

Stay loose. Stay flexible. I headed for the kitchen. *Give them a chance to explain.*

After distributing the treats, I took roll, a formality really, since all seven students were present and I already knew three of them. But it gave me a chance to note the silent messages in the air. Jason bit into his cookie, but the other six simply sat there, waiting. I tried to enter their silent dialogue, but they weren't giving themselves away. Not a blink, not a twitch, empty eyes. How could I get them to voice their insecurities without turning them off altogether?

Work with the cards you've been dealt. Seven students; lucky seven; magic seven. Seven planets; seven wonders of the ancient world; seven days of the week; seven days of creation; seven sacraments; seven virtues; Snow White and the Seven Dwarfs. It felt as if I were playing a game of solitaire: Twenty-one cards face down; seven cards face up. It helps if you start with a king or a queen for a base. That is, if you plan to win.

"What's wrong?" I repeated, then positioned myself in front of Codi, seated on the west end of the U to the right of Jason. Her last name was Baad. No kidding. What would it be like to be shackled with a name like that? No wonder she dressed like vampy Morticia Addams. "And no shrugs, please. You look like a bunch of zombies sitting there. What's the deal?" I concentrated on Codi's forehead, just below all that spiked black and red hair. *Woodpecker, ambitious and determined.*

"We feel like test rats," Jason said.

My first instinct was to laugh, but I suppressed the urge. "In a way, you're right. This class is an experiment, but if it works, the plan is to—"

"You're going to try out a bunch of psychological mumbo jumbo on us," he said.

I repositioned myself in front of my desk and threw up my hands. Psychological mumbo jumbo just about summed up the day's lesson. "Right again. But who knows? Maybe we'll stumble onto something significant while we're fumbling around in the lab, like Einstein or Ben Franklin. Why not consider ourselves lucky volunteers?"

"Volunteers," Codi cried. "I'm no candy striper."

"I thought you wanted to be here." *And that you, Jason, and Shawn had recommended me as your teacher.*

"You weren't counting on threats from our parents." This from a student new to me who'd claimed the seat left of Jason. Red hair, thick glasses, Luke Quin.

Their parents? Okay, at least I had *them* on my side.

"Let's face it, Ms. V," Jason said. "We're just a bunch of guinea pigs."

I shook my head. "Well, if you're guinea pigs, so am I."

"But you came into this by choice," Angelina Souza piped in from the seat to my right. Long brown hair, milk-white skin; the word Angel came to mind.

"Yeah, you can walk out any time," Codi added.

A shiver as pleasurable, as it was involuntary, shot through me as the sky lit up and sunshine filled the room.

"Dr. Matt's treating us like a bunch of underachievers," Codi said.

"We *are* underachievers," Jason said softly.

Silence.

Okay, back to solitaire. Twenty-four cards in hand, Jack of Diamonds and six low cards face up on the table. Low numbers present a problem, except for aces. You need an Ace to start a discard pile. Count three cards, turn over, third card on top. Come on king.

"Before we continue, I'd like to share a few rules based on the teachings of Emma Curtis Hopkins, who, in my opinion, was one of the most effective teachers in the world."

"Of course." This from Jason, elbows on table, chin propped on palms.

I sensed a trace of amusement in him, a turquoise glow. *King of Hearts: sympathetic, congenial, and engaging, acknowledges any true call for help, sometimes provocative and condescending.*

"Don't worry. I won't test you on them, at least, not on paper and not for grades. Hopefully, over time, these rules will become second nature to you."

"If we won't be tested on them, we probably won't bother to learn them," Shawn said from the table to my left. *Jack of Diamonds: perceptive, alert, and shrewd, inquisitive, original thinker.*

"Rule number one," I said, my heart lifting. So far, five students had spoken up, two to go. "No complaining."

"This whole thing sucks," said the student sitting next to Shawn. Ethan Stein, a small kid with a large head and what appeared to be a perennial scowl. *Ace of Spades: solves problems through doubtful means, source of illumination for others, key to the profound secret of life.* Assort according to suit, color, and rank. No room on the table for the king to serve as a base.

I raised a second finger. "Don't condemn or criticize."

"This is crap," said Codi. *Queen of Spades: joint-ruler with high influence, level headed, and right judge of values.*

"Three: What upsets you tells a lot about you."

Unified laughter at Codi's expense. "That's not a rule," she said under her breath.

"Four: Be happy about the success of others."

This time Codi laughed.

"Five and six: Embrace criticism as an opportunity to learn and grow. And handle change with grace and ease."

No more comments. The kids probably thought I was using them as inspiration for my rules, and they didn't want to be part of the script.

"Seven: Know that flaws and mistakes are part of the grand scheme of things."

"Cool," said Angelina. "I'll remember that one." She wore a Pandora bracelet with beads and charms made of silver, gold, and glass, reflecting her own particular symbolism. *Ten of Clubs: warm hearted with genuine desire to be of service to others without personal benefit.* Ranks below Jack of Diamonds; space now open for King of Hearts.

"Eight and nine: Be happy with yourself and consider yourself creative."

No comments, but at least they no longer looked spooked.

"And lastly: Be grateful."

"Those don't sound like rules to me," Luke said. *Nine of Diamonds: charitable, kind-hearted, companionable.* Ranks below Ten of Clubs.

"That's because this class will differ from any class you've ever experienced. For some reason, call it synchronicity or luck of the draw, we're all in this together. Something about each of us is special, or Dr. Matt wouldn't have selected us."

"Yeah, right," Jason said, casting a long look out the window.

"If you're nervous about this, you're not alone. I'm nervous, too. The biggest obstacle to this class's success is thinking things impossible." Jeez, what a hypocrite I was.

"What are you going to teach us?" Angelina asked. Lord, she was pretty, my *Ten of Clubs*. Enormous brown eyes, thick brows, Audrey Hepburn stare.

I pointed at the door behind me. "Let's check out the art room for starters."

Seven Indigos, including Tessa Lambe, who hadn't spoken a word, got to their feet. Pinched noses, crossed arms, clenched fists. I felt the mood in the air. *We've been had.*

"We're going to learn about ceramic molds and how when slip is poured into them, it takes on the shape of the mold," I said.

No wonder solitaire was sometimes referred to as patience. This job was going to be even harder than I'd expected.

Chapter Sixteen

ACCORDING TO WHAT I'D read thus far, Indigos were particularly sensitive to taste, light, texture, smell, and sound. So, while setting up for class the next day, I decided that, besides potted plants, votive candles, and aromatic diffusers, I would add background music to keep the atmosphere calm and balanced. Instrumentals and the sounds of nature would be nice. Maybe some Bruce Springsteen.

"Hello."

I turned, surprised. I hadn't heard anyone enter the room.

"My son, Jason, is in your after-school class," my visitor said by way of introduction, "and I came to ask you to be careful."

Jeez, not more negativity.

"The decisions Jason makes in the next few years will affect the rest of his life, and it won't take much to turn him in the wrong direction." My visitor coughed, cleared his throat, and I braced myself for more unsolicited advice. "Excuse me if I come across as a bit overanxious, but…to be quite honest, my wife and I are at our wits' end."

He was wearing a *Cal Bears* navy fleece jacket over a white dress shirt, an easy blend of football enthusiast and professional. His erect posture and firmness of jaw suggested a man who would have no trouble in the boardroom or at the helm of a ship. But in dealing with his son, it seemed, he was powerless.

"You're certainly not alone," I said.

"That's what I'm here to tell you. I'm not the only parent who feels this way." He sat on the edge of a table and shook his head. "Education has not been a friend to our kids."

"I'll do my best, Mr.—"

"Ardis. Ron Ardis." He held out his hand with an almost desperate eagerness as if he'd come to Oz seeking solutions to the unsolvable. His hand felt cold; a surprise. I'd expected warmth coming from this man. "Old-style parenting isn't working," he said. "I need to be more open, do more listening, give my son choices." He chuckled. "But knowing and doing isn't the same thing now is it? I end up falling back on 'because-I-say-so' parenting more often than I care to admit."

Unlike previous visitors to my classroom, Ron ignored the windows spanning the classroom wall and put the full weight of his attention on me. "I don't know how Dr. Matt located you, but like an idiot at a slot machine, knowing I'm betting against the house and the odds are stacked against me, I'm feeding the machine in hopes of a win. Each push of the button, each spin of the wheel, gives me hope that this time will be different."

He stood, followed by another shake of his head. "I'm sorry. You must have a million things to do."

"It's okay. This conversation is an important one." Without the advantage of smoke, wheels, and levers and a booming voice with empty promises, I wished I could assure him I had what it took to accomplish the win he was seeking; that by focusing on the attributes he sought in me as a teacher, they would somehow manifest.

"Do you think there's any truth to the theory that my son isn't the result of some freak combination of my wife's genes and mine, but a leap in human evolution?"

"My awareness of reality has been stretched a bit lately," I said.

"By Jason, I assume."

"Meeting Jason only confirmed what I already suspected, that we're looking for the right things in the wrong places. We can't keep talents like Jason's suppressed or hidden. My aim is to help him and others like him gain control of their own narratives and share their gifts with the world."

"I swear to God, if you help my son, I'll provide moral and financial support to the addition of more classes like this one, so more students can benefit."

"The world needs people like Jason."

"You could've fooled me," Ron said, his voice hoarse. "Jason's in pain and there's nothing I can do about it. He turns everything I say into an insult and judgment. I can't handle seeing him this way. The wall between us is so thick, you'd think I was his enemy instead of his father. 'Quit judging me and telling me what to do,' he says. 'Just listen.' But when I listen, he wonders why I'm not saying anything and misreads my silence as disapproval. I thought of getting him counseling with someone who knows what to say and when to say it, but that would only confirm his suspicion that I think he's a loser. I've given him everything, yet he isn't happy. How does one handle that?"

I didn't answer because I had no answer. Instead, I followed Ron's gaze to the ancient acoustic tiles fitted into the metal grid suspended from the high ceiling. Tiny holes dotted the tiles as though someone had used a ballpoint pen as a punching tool. They reminded me of the *Lite-Brite* peg screen I'd played with as a child. I would insert plastic glow pegs into the holes to create pictures and watch them light up like constellations against a black sky. "What would *you* teach them?" I asked.

"Cosmology."

His answer surprised me. Schools don't usually stress the study of the universe and its origins.

"Newton's and Darwin's cosmic perspective makes the universe sound meaningless, blind, and purposeless," he said, "but we have to believe there's more. Cosmology allows us to ask big questions, like where we come from, who we are, and where we're going. I'd teach them about how the universe started as a tiny speck and unfolded over time to become galaxies and stars, eagles and butterflies, music and all of us alive today. I would teach them that the universe is not only a place, but a story they take part in, belong in, and out of which they arose. When the universe arrives at a fork in the road, it transmutes into something new, teaching us to break apart aspects of ourselves for ongoing creativity to continue."

"You sound like Carl Sagan," I said. "What makes you such a purveyor of the cosmos?"

He grinned. "My company develops software for computer-controlled telescopes that hunt supernovae. I also teach astronomy at UC Berkeley. If you need my expertise, all you have to do is name the place and time. Maybe in a classroom context, Jason would listen to what I have to say."

Just the person I needed to chaperone the trip I'd envisioned to the James Lick Observatory. My spirits lifted as they always do when I think of the cosmos and how it goes beyond personal predicaments and locates us into larger stories. "Where would you start?"

"I would expose them to nature."

I smiled and gestured for him to follow me.

When we entered the nature area, the wind blew my hair in all directions, covering and uncovering my eyes like someone playing *Surprise!* The birdsong was so raucous I had to raise my voice to be heard. "I want to teach them how to 'make silence' as Maria Montessori did in her schools, plus teach them meditation and yoga."

Ron faced the wind, either unaware or unconcerned that his hair stood on end. He stretched, unkinked his neck, and closed his eyes. "Nature is speaking to us. Do you hear it?"

I wondered if he was testing me to see if I was loony enough to handle seven Indigos with inexplicable powers. Though at this point, being a bit loony would be an asset. "Mr. Ardis, I want to caution you—"

"I know." He blinked like someone waking from a dream. "You think I'm being overly optimistic, but if optimism works in business and science, and believe me it does, why can't it work in school? I'm too old to be embarrassed by my enthusiasm, Ms. Veil. I'll volunteer to help in any way I can."

"I'll only be here until June," I said, with an uneasy ache beneath my ribs.

"Then let's pray for a miracle."

Chapter Seventeen

THE STUDENTS FILED INTO the classroom with an eagerness that contrasted sharply with their entry the day before. I gave the mouse totem I always carry with me a final squeeze before slipping it back into the leather pouch belted around my waist.

Jason, who'd been balancing his backpack on his head, dropped it to the floor. "Let's check out our greenware."

I'd taught the students the previous day that after ceramic slip hardens and separates from the mold, it's called greenware and is extremely fragile. "You'll need to remove the rubber bands holding your molds together and gently pull the molds apart to see if the casted pieces are ready to come out."

"Are we going to wipe away the seam lines and clean the greenware for firing?" Luke asked. He peered at me over the rim of his glasses like a stereotypical librarian—protector of books, facts, and order.

"Casting the slip into molds was meant to be a symbolic lesson," I ventured. "To remind us that our thoughts take the form of the molds they're poured into. I'm not sure how to proceed from there, especially the firing part. Something about using specific cones, numbered according to the necessary temperatures to be reached…"

"They're called pyrometric witness cones," Luke said. "To gauge the heat during firing. You put them into the kiln sitter. No problem. When the kiln reaches the cone's set temperature, it'll turn off. I saw boxes of them in the art room. Plus, fettling knives and sponges and jars of glazes and stains. It would be a shame not to put them to use."

I'd already figured there would be advantages to seeing this project through, and it seemed Luke had a handle on the firing process. A little more research on my part and we could probably get the job done. "You seem to know a lot about ceramics."

"My mom was way into it when I was a kid. She still has a kiln and stuff out in the garage. She used to let me mess around with her rejects, which could've filled a warehouse when she first got started. Later, when she got better at it, the pickings got slim. I bet she'd come help."

Excitement was as palatable in the air as the scent of cookies, myrrh, and sandalwood had been the day before. We opened the molds to seven pieces of greenware, fully formed: a brown bear, a German shepherd, a duck, a goose, an owl, a crow, and a teardrop vase. We stood back and stared at the molded clay. Luke was right. We couldn't leave the project unfinished. Ethan traced the outline of his owl with the tip of his finger, wide-eyed wonder replacing the usual scowl on his face.

"Let me know what your mother decides, Luke. If she can't make it, we'll wing it on our own."

🕷 🕷 🕷

Luke's mother showed up the following afternoon, hefting a cardboard box with shredded newspaper spilling over its sides. "Hi. I'm Jenny. Heard you could use a little help with your ceramics project." Her hair was the color of pumpkin spice, her skin flecked parchment. She spotted her son and waved. The sudden flush of Luke's cheeks reminded me of ripe pomegranates, blending nicely with his copper-colored hair.

"Then let's get started," I said.

Jenny presented the students with scraps of greenware on which to practice until they felt ready to tackle their own casted clay. There were plenty of cleaning tools, sponges, and water bowls from the stock room to go around, and I marveled at how each student took to the task of sanding and cleaning. Fingers, faces, and hair covered in ceramic dust and smeared with murky water, they scraped and sponged with the absorption of plastic surgeons. What was it about Indigos refusing to follow directions and being easily distracted? There was no sign of this now.

I held my breath, fearing a breakage and the resulting bad behavior Charles Lacoste had warned me about. Then, of course, there was one. Jason's German shepherd lost its paw.

"Damn," he said, eyeing the severed foot with the intensity of a nurse in triage.

Jenny rushed over. "No problem. I brought ceramic glue." She moistened the broken tips with water, brushed on the glue, and pieced the dog and paw back together.

Jason stared at his dog for several seconds before responding. "Thought Ralph would end up a misfit like me."

"Wait for it to dry, then sand around the seam," Jenny said, sounding like a veterinarian discussing an injured pet. "Once fired, he'll be as good as new."

My throat swelled when I saw pink light sweep over Jason like the pulsating blush of a winter sunrise. How could he feel such attachment to a piece of clay? In fact, all seven students seemed to feel the same, the entire force of their concentration aimed at the molded pieces in their hands. Not a single impatient, resistant, tuned-out brat among them.

※ ※ ※

It took one more class session for Jenny to instruct the kids on how to load the greenware into the kiln and fire it, then another for them to glaze the bisque pieces for re-fire. It didn't matter that it rained and the wind blew at twenty miles an hour. It didn't matter that the room was often dark and dreary, lit only by votive candles and fluorescent lighting. I sensed no pressure to hurry on to other lessons. The experience wasn't over until it was over, and a lot was going on here.

For one thing, the kids weren't complaining or condemning. They were also handling Jenny's corrective criticism without a trace of resistance. In fact, they seemed to thrive on her gentle evaluations of their work. They fettled away the seam scars of their pieces with cleaning knives and wiped them smooth with damp sponges as if they were fettling away their own scars and wiping them smooth. "Help, Ms. Quin, I think I've messed up. Ms. Quin, how come this side looks weird?"

"Mistakes are part of the process," she told them. "Some of the best discoveries and inventions come from failures."

I wanted to hug her and say, *hear, hear*, for depicting stumbles and screwups as simple and natural parts of learning.

Another advantage of this lesson was that the students were being creative—testing out various decorating techniques and experimenting with color, while bringing their creations to life. Though not perfect, the animals and vase turned out remarkably well.

On her last day, Jenny showed a reluctance to leave. She blotted her eyes with the tail of her T-shirt. "Thanks for letting me help. I haven't seen Luke this involved in anything outside a book for a long time. In fact, I haven't felt this involved in a while either."

I gave her two thumbs up. "You saved the day, and you have my sincere gratitude."

🕷 🕷 🕷

All but Ethan chose to display their creations on shelves and windowsills throughout the classroom after we unloaded them from the kiln the next day. He opted instead to keep his owl on the table in front of him where he could handle it at any time. "You'll have to move your owl sooner or later," I told him. "Someone could accidently knock it over, and it would meet an early demise."

His eyes shone like copper pennies, reminding me of my soon-to-be-adoptive-son, Joshua. Upsetting him had not been my intention. I searched for a solution and noticed a display case on the west wall. "How about putting it up there?" I said, pointing at the glass-fronted cabinet. "It'll be safe and open to view."

The creases on his forehead eased, but he made no move to release his owl.

"Your totem," I said.

"Totem?" A spark of interest at last.

"Yes," I said, making a sudden decision, "the subject of tomorrow's lesson."

Ethan picked up his owl and handed it to me. My chest expanded at this sign of trust. Before he could change his mind, I placed his treasure in the display case and secured the doors. He smiled, and I smiled back, feeling as if I'd crossed a great divide. Lord, he was intense.

Though all my students were labeled Indigos, each was unique in his or her own way. How had they been selected and by whom? Jason, Shawn, and Codi had telekinetic and telepathic powers, but what distinguished the other four? They all seemed perfectly normal to me. "So, what have you learned in the past few days?" I asked.

Jason laughed. "That you're trying to brainwash us."

"True," I said, "though I consider my methods a rewiring rather than brainwashing. All I ask is that you think about what I say before you accept or reject it."

"Can you fit that on a bumper sticker?" Jason asked.

Smartass.

Codi, with her black and red hair standing on end like a surprise, raised her hand. "I still don't get how our thoughts mold reality?" She had a teacher's nightmare face, minus the nose ring and tattoo, testimony to the deep currents running below the surface—currents that were my responsibility to tap into and understand. In six months! Ron Ardis was right. I needed a miracle.

"Does anyone have an answer for Codi?"

Shawn was the first to respond. "It's like the day you taught in our remedial class. Ms. Goldsberry is one of our favorite teachers, and we're always upset when she's gone. So, things didn't go too well."

"It was a disaster," I agreed.

"Nah. You kept your cool instead of freaking out. That's why we're here. So, I guess your thoughts molded reality."

As had theirs, with some powerful results.

"You mean our thoughts can affect others?" Codi asked, as if she didn't know.

"That's one meaning, yes. Your thoughts are like well-ordered light."

This pulled red-headed and bespectacled Luke back into the fray. "They're like cosmic lighthouses, so beware of what you think."

"We all have control over our experiences," I said. "And therefore—"

"We control our happiness," Luke finished for me.

"Success and failure, my fellow classmates, exist only in your mind," Jason *The Wolf* Ardis imparted like a self-elected sage.

Codi booed. Jason shrugged.

"It has to do with biophotons and light," Luke said, "our body's communication system."

Jason rubbed his forehead. "Unbelievable."

"So are your powers, Harry Potter," Codi said.

"*Our* powers, Hermione," he reminded her.

Finally, we had approached the subject of what set us apart.

Chapter Eighteen

THE PLAN WAS TO discuss totems; I had promised Ethan we would. But within minutes after our class session started on this last day of January, the plan veered off course.

"Ms. V," Jason said from his seat at the table. "What happens if this after-school class sets us apart, I mean, really sets us apart? Being in a remedial class is one thing. Even top students need a kick in the rear once in a while. But this…"

"I would discuss the situation with Dr. Matt." I was still at my desk, performing the logistical tasks that better be finished before the office aide arrived, or class would come to a complete halt while he or she waited with impatient sighs. "From what I understand, you're free to be here or not. You have a choice."

"Yeah right," Codi said.

I glanced up in time to catch her eyes orbiting in their sockets. Her way of telling me to "kiss off" in that passive-aggressive manner common to thirteen-year-old girls—upped to the nth degree! Our gazes met and held. Kohl eyes. Woodpecker eyes. Apparently, my opinion carried about as much weight as the school dress code no one bothered to enforce. Except for her slightly flushed face, she didn't appear the least bit apologetic about her remark. In fact, the tilt of her chin and tightness of her jaw gave the impression she was begging for a fight.

"You're not a victim," I said.

I'd known from day one that she had an attitude. Her clothes alone were a dead giveaway. Dress code be darned, her T-shirts often spoke for her. Today, emblazoned across her chest was the message, *Rock Me!* If something got in her way, she'd whack her way past it, no apologies. So, what was it with the anger? She bit her lip but remained silent.

After attaching the attendance form to the clip next to the corridor door, I stood in front of the class and continued my exchange with Codi. "Unless, of course, you insist on sabotaging your life. Your mind can do so easily enough. If you let it."

Her response, a deep, shaky sigh.

She was suffering. I glanced at the flickering votive candles spaced along the tables and took in their honey scent. *God give me strength.*

"Um... Ms. Veil?"

All attention focused on the speaker, and rightly so. Angelina, like Shawn, seldom spoke. Everything about her said "angel," from her porcelain-doll skin to her shiny brown hair, with bangs feathered around perfectly arched brows. In contrast to Codi's punk style, Angelina was all lace and embroidery and pastel flowers. "Can you give an example of choosing in an impossible situation? Like, what if you know someone who's sick and might die? What choices does he or she have?"

My sister Maya's face filled all the space in my mind, her blue eyes brilliant with inner fire. She'd known she was going to die yet had remained serene, even joyful, until the end. I now drew from a lesson I'd learned from her. "The idea is to send this person your love and—"

A blast of cold air struck me from somewhere in the room before Luke cut in. "People who've died and lived to talk about it say they passed through a tunnel leading to a warm white light. That doesn't sound so bad."

"Omigod," Codi said, aiming her eyes toward the ceiling.

Angelina licked her lips and gave Luke a wobbly smile.

"How about we send out our—" I began, only to be cut off by Luke again.

"And then there's the life review. When you see your whole lifetime flashing in front of your eyes. It's important to do good deeds before you die so your life review won't be too incriminating."

I was missing something here. What had prompted Angelina's question about choice during an impossible situation, and why was Luke blocking my replies? If she was sick, the school would surely have informed me.

Jason, *King of Hearts*, stared out the window, his eyes fixed on something stationary and far away. Codi, *Queen of Spades*, fiddled with the skeleton-face ring perched on her hand like a bloated bug. Ethan, *Ace of Spades*, frowned at his ceramic owl in the trophy case, and Shawn, *Jack of Diamonds*, shook his head. Only Angelina, *Ten of Clubs*, and Luke, *Nine of Diamonds*, met my gaze; Angelina with her doe brown eyes and Luke with eyes a fathomless green.

I'm going to die.

If I hadn't already been familiar with the disembodied messages coming from my mother and sister, this eerie whisper would have frightened me. Still, the words caused shivers to swell over me like a starling flock maneuver wave.

Interference followed—the fret buzz of a four-string guitar.

A blackbird smacked into the window with a painful thud that rattled the glass. The ancient classroom clock started to tick.

"Ms. Veil?" Ethan said after a short silence, which by middle school standards marks a lifetime. "What about the totems?"

It took me a moment to answer, *I'm going to die* echoing in my head like a cruel commercial jingle. "You're right. Time for a change of pace. Let's get our ceramic pieces and bring them to the tables."

All but Ethan were slow to comply—lethargic, wary.

Codi mumbled, "What the hell?" loud enough for me to hear.

Ethan slid a chair up to the trophy case and reclaimed his owl.

After the students had gathered their ceramic projects and settled back into their seats, I said, "Now, ask yourself why you picked the particular mold you did. Why, for instance, did Ethan pick an owl and Jason a dog?"

"German shepherd," Jason corrected. "Thought equals form, remember?"

"Yeah, I remember." My tone suggested he was a smart aleck, but I liked him anyway. The students looked at me, eyes blank. The wind blew; the clock ticked; the heater kicked in, forcing warm air smelling of mildew through the vents along the east wall. Why were they so slow on the uptake?

"Codi," I said. "Any idea why you picked the crow mold?"

Another eye roll, a gesture I was getting used to and beginning to like. "Because you didn't have a woodpecker mold."

The class laughed.

"No seriously. I like woodpeckers."

"Do you have any idea why?"

"I've liked them since I was a kid. Wanted one for Christmas but got a parakeet instead."

"So, for now, we'll call the woodpecker your lifelong animal totem."

"Holy crap." She poked her crow with the blackened tip of her index finger.

"I don't care much for German shepherds," Jason injected into the discussion. He scratched his jaw and furrowed his brow. "But I do like coyotes. I hear them yowling when we're on camping trips. They scare the crap out of me but get me interested just the same."

"The first time we met, you reminded me of a wolf," I said.

He snorted and gazed out the window with dog-like stillness.

Beware of stillness, I thought, unable to decide if his intent stare and outward calm resulted from inner tranquility or a tense emotional state.

"What about me?" Codi asked.

"You reminded me of a woodpecker, still do."

She poked her crow again as if to elicit some kind of response. "You're just saying that."

"Those with the woodpecker totem don't always conform to society's standards."

"Cool," she said, with a now-we're-talking grin.

"The woodpecker is also one of my animal spirit totems," I said. Her grin turned into a frown.

"Can you have more than one totem?" Ethan wanted to know.

I nodded. "Jason, for example, said coyotes scare him during camping trips. That could mean the coyote is his shadow totem, which will test him until he overcomes his fear."

"Of coyotes?" Ethan asked.

I laughed. Couldn't help it. At times Ethan looked exactly like the thirteen-year-old he was, brow furrowed with curiosity rather than internal demons. "More likely something he's not aware of. The shadow totem forces you to bring this fear to light and overcome it."

"Jason's not afraid of anything," Angelina said.

"Wanna bet." Jason threw me a look of challenge. "What's your shadow totem, Ms. V?"

I thought of Gabriel, my backyard stray. Could he be my shadow totem? If so, what fear could an abandoned cat force me to bring to light and overcome? "Okay, I think you might be getting the message."

"But I picked a vase!" Angelina cried. "Does that mean I don't have a totem?"

"I was only using your mold choices as an example. A totem can be any animal, plant, or natural object you believe has spiritual significance. There are many ways to discover the totems in your life."

"Like what?"

"Have you noticed an animal or natural object lately that you've never noticed before?"

She fingered the beads and charms on her Pandora bracelet, her face contorted as if she were about to cry.

"Have you dreamed of a special bird, plant, or animal?"

Again, she shook her head.

"I have," Luke called out.

"Good, Luke. Hold that thought." Besides signifying *Nine of*

Diamonds in my mind, he was also taking on the persona of *Mr. Detail.* He had something interesting and over-the-top to contribute on just about any subject, quite an asset in a group situation but of limited value in his personal life. Back to Angelina. "How about something that startled or entranced you lately?"

She shook her head, but then her face brightened. "On the way to school today, a vulture almost hit the windshield of Mom's car."

Jason's laugh was mocking. "You mean a buzzard?"

Angelina's bottom lip trembled.

"No worse than Jason's coyotes." To Angelina, this wasn't a laughing matter.

"Is it my shadow totem?" she asked, now toying with the rainbow of silk flowers clipped to her hair.

"Actually, it may be your message totem. The vulture is resourceful and patient and teaches us to use all our senses to pursue our highest goals. It also symbolizes renewal."

"You think it was trying to tell me something?"

"Possibly."

Ethan gazed at his owl, his lips puckered like a toothless old man.

"If you've been attracted to a new animal lately or are dreaming or thinking about one, it might be your journey animal totem." I clapped my hands, startling some of the students out of their blank-faced stares. "Time for some research." I pointed at the set of encyclopedias in the bookshelf on the west wall.

Ethan sneered. "People don't use encyclopedias anymore."

"Some of us still prefer the color and texture of books," I said.

Angelina pulled a laptop computer from her backpack that carried a price tag most students, let alone adults, could ill afford.

"I thought EMF emissions from electronics and other equipment made you guys uncomfortable," I said. My reward? A where-do-you-get-this-stuff stare. Was my research a bunch of New Age mumbo jumbo, or had these kids built up a resistance to such irritants? Anyway, electronics were here to stay. Might as well use them.

"Electronics interfere with intuition," Luke said. "They block alpha, theta, and delta brain waves."

"*Brilliance* interferes with intuition," Codi said, tapping her temple. "Paralysis by analysis." She eyed the encyclopedias collecting dust on the bookshelves. "You want us to look up our favorite animal, right, Ms. Veil?"

"Or a plant or natural object you're interested in."

"Hey, Codi, let's work as a team," Luke said, "the old-fashioned way. You know, challenge our regressed interpersonal skills."

She gave him the finger. I pretended not to notice—non-interference, benign neglect—and pulled my treasured stone mouse from the leather pouch cinched at my waist. "This is one of my animal totems. Someone special gave it to me. Who received it from someone special, who" —I wiped my eyes, which had started to tear— "found it someplace special." My words came out shaky, making it hard to go on. "I then gave the totem to someone I loved, and he gave it to someone he loved and, after she died, the totem came back to me."

The room became quiet. Even the wind seemed to subside. Only the clock persisted in its rhythmic ticking. I closed my eyes and swallowed what tasted like salt in the back of my mouth. *Don't leave me, Maya. Please, Maya, don't leave me now.*

Someone took my hand. It was Shawn "Are you okay?"

"Yes, hon." I forced my thoughts back to the present. *Get real. Maya's dead.*

Six students, plus the one now holding my hand, waited for me to continue. "Maybe someday I'll tell you about it."

Chapter Nineteen

A LL WEEKEND I WORRIED that I'd revealed too much of myself to the kids and that maybe they hadn't been ready for my lesson about totems. What if they thought I was pushing some kind of pagan superstition, as Veronica had suggested, when my sole purpose had been to help them adopt a personal spiritual helper; a symbol to capture their imagination, aid them in self-discovery, help them cope? Admittedly, the lesson leaned toward the mystical, but so did music, art, and poetry, all bridges between the earthy stuff around us and the spiritual stuff inside. These Indigos, with their developed sixth sense, already walked between worlds. Why not give them a few more tools for the journey? On the other hand, they were smart, way ahead of me. Maybe it was their parents I should worry about. What if *they* objected, called the school, insist I be fired? I dreamed of an angry mob on a witch-hunt—me burning at the stake.

What I hadn't expected, though, were the rumors flying about campus when I got back to school. This I discovered from an unlikely source soon after my arrival. It was the short kid I'd likened to a terrier pup during my brief stint subbing in Ms. Goldsberry's remedial class. He stood waiting in the corridor outside my classroom door. I'd been disappointed on finding he wasn't an Indigo, though looking at him now, I couldn't fathom what differentiated him from my kids. He was smart and perceptive. Plus, I liked him.

"I heard about your class," Brad said, in that straightforward manner of his, "about you running some kind of weird experiments."

It bothered me to hear this from a kid I felt partial to. I reminded myself that he wasn't being malicious, only repeating what he'd heard. I hesitated before responding, my mind in knots. Was this what Jason meant when he'd asked if our after-school class would set them apart? If so, the true test was about to begin. Not only for me, but for my students as well.

"There's one way to find out," I said, forcing a smile.

Brad tilted his head and squinted at me as if I were too bright for his eyes.

"Why don't you come visit our class sometime?"

The way he stared at me, you'd think I was Rod Serling delivering his prelude to the Twilight Zone. *There is a fifth dimension beyond that which is known to man.*

His chest expanded. "Me?"

I bit my lip, suppressing the urge to hug him, *Brave Puppy*, all wiggles and joy and innocence. "You were the first student to catch my attention while subbing in Ms. Goldsberry's class, which makes you special. To me, anyway."

"When?" he asked.

"As soon as you get permission."

"I'll call my mom."

"You'll need to ask Dr. Matt first."

"She heard about your class, too."

Already? I'd been here less than two weeks. "From you, I presume."

He yanked the straps to his backpack and balanced the heavy burden between his shoulders.

"So why not ask her to come along?" What the hell. Invite the critics in.

"Mr. Lacoste said your class is secretive and highly controversial."

Darn that man. Since when did teachers talk about other teachers with their students? Or had Brad overheard him discussing me with another faculty member? Either scenario spelled trouble. Best way to stop a rumor was to nip it in the bud.

I checked my watch; time to get moving. I had materials to prepare before the students arrived at three. We were doing a mask-making session today, a way for the students to explore various aspects of themselves. I'd facilitated with masks as art therapy before, at the alcohol rehab center in Pacific Grove where Maya had worked. And I'd learned a thing or two about how we hide from the world. "See ya, Brad. Gotta go."

Brad pulled a cell phone from the cargo pocket of his jeans. "Later, Ms. Veil."

🕷 🕷 🕷

"But it isn't even Halloween," Luke said, peering at me through his heavy-rimmed glasses. This surprised me. I would have thought he'd come up with some line of trivia about the purpose and meaning of masks instead of questioning the timing of my lesson.

"Come on, Luke," I said from my usual spot in front of the classroom at the introduction of a new lesson. Later, depending on the assigned tasks, I would take up a less conspicuous location— accessible, but unobtrusive, that fine balance between control and neglect. "There's more to masks than costumes at Halloween."

He took his time to answer, left hand cupped over his chin, fingers scratching his cheek. "They're used for protection, like gas masks and catcher's masks."

"Go on." He was doing a fine job of initiating the discussion, in a reluctant way.

"They're ceremonial."

"We wear masks every day, Ms. Veil," Shawn said, "to hide behind."

Dr. Matt had shared that Shawn could fade into the background to the point where you didn't even know he was there. How could anyone ignore this child, with his kind Buddha face and thick black hair?

I got the sudden impression that someone was probing my mind. *Shawn?*

He looked down at his hands.

"Makeup can be a mask," Codi said, her voice pitched low.

"You should know," Jason said from his seat to her right.

Codi gave him her signature glare, intensified by the Cleopatra liner above and below her eyes.

"They're all for protection, one way or another" —Luke was warming to the subject now that he had an audience— "except when used for plays or in ritual. I saw on PBS once how in West Africa masks are used to communicate with spirits."

"Some people use *research* for protection, Luke," Codi said.

"So, what are you getting at, Ms. V?" Jason asked.

I crossed my arms, giving him time to figure out the answer without being told.

"Let me guess…" He watched me with bird-dog stillness. "Something about masks being casts of our inner selves… Ha, don't tell me…"

"Jason, you're such a turd," Codi said.

"Thought equals form," he said.

All expression disappeared from Codi's face as if she feared what might reveal itself there. "Are you saying our inner selves show up on our faces?"

And the clothes you wear, I wanted to say but held back. That she found comfort in cropped T-shirts and low-slung jeans during the chill of late winter, so be it. For me, comfort consisted of slacks and blazers; for Veronica, black leather and animal prints; for Maya, dear Maya, raggedy jeans and a brown bomber jacket.

"That means homely people can look beautiful and beautiful people can look homely, depending on their thoughts," Angelina said, studying her classmates one by one. Her mention of sickness and dying during last week's discussion about choice had triggered my concern. Was she ill? After school, I would make it my number one priority to find out.

"Our faces include twenty-three surface landmarks," Luke said, "and have twenty-eight bones."

I thought of the skull medallion dangling from Codi's neck and the equally morbid skull ring on her finger, certain this information hadn't crossed her mind. My guess was that to her the skull symbolized something poles apart from the role it played in facial expressions.

"Jeez, Luke, where do you come up with this stuff?" Jason asked.

"The Internet. Six muscles have to cooperate to move our eyeballs."

"The face is mighty," Codi said, using her said muscles to perform an eye roll. "So, are we going to make masks today or what?" She opened her compact, checked her makeup, seemed satisfied, and looked up for my answer.

"That's the plan, though they won't be fancy. We're just using construction paper."

I thought back to the tables at the Guidepost alcoholic recovery center where Maya had led a group of men and women in making masks. She'd worked the room like a butterfly, settling here and there, spreading the pollen of inspiration and enthusiasm before moving on. She clapped when she saw the two masks I'd made. "Witches. One for you and one for me."

"Not just witches, but healers," I said.

She picked up a mask and held it to her face. "And we'll look exactly alike."

"Externally, yes." We would never be alike within. I could never give of myself the way Maya did. She was too good to be true, too good for this world.

"Ms. Veil," Ethan said. "Ummm, Mssss. Veil."

I blinked, reluctant to leave my sister behind.

Ethan eyed me with what appeared to be suspicion. "What kind of masks?"

His question put me on edge. I didn't look forward to another night worrying about all the ramifications of my lesson. "How about a mask of the totem you researched yesterday?" He'd been okay with the totem exercise, actually seemed to enjoy it. But, as I was beginning to suspect, his feelings were as mercurial as the weather.

"I have something else in mind," Jason said.

About to respond, I heard a knock on the door. Then in walked Brad and a woman I assumed to be his mother. "Hey, Ms. Veil," he said, waving both hands. "Hey class."

"What's *he* doing here?" Luke asked, red-faced.

I hadn't expected Brad and his mother so soon. How had they gotten Dr. Matt's permission this fast? "I invited him. And he invited his mother, as you did last week."

"Oh," Luke said, surrounded by a brownish yellow glow.

Brad seemed oblivious to Luke's strained reception. His mother, however, appeared less at ease. "Brad said it would be okay…" Although her son reached no higher than four-foot-ten, she only topped him by a few inches. Her intelligent brown eyes pleaded for acceptance. Not for herself, but for her son.

I pulled up two chairs. "We were about to do a mask project. Want to join us?"

"Cool," Brad said. "And it isn't even Halloween."

I extended my hand to Brad's mother. "I'm Marjorie."

"Vicki," she said, her hand moist and trembling. "Let me know how I can help."

🕷 🕷 🕷

Dr. Matt was not pleased with me.

I'd arrived at his office after class to ask if there was anything about Angelina's health that I should be privy to, but before I could raise my question, he'd started in. "I wish you hadn't invited outside guests into your classroom at this early stage of the game."

Game? Apparently, Brad and his mother hadn't asked his permission before their visit, which, in my opinion, was no big deal. I defended myself the best I could, with comments like, "They enjoyed themselves," and "Brad's mother thanked me for setting the rumors straight," but Dr. Matt wasn't having it. He tapped his pen on the desk. "What's the problem?" I asked.

"The problem is that Mrs. Johnson came to see me after leaving your classroom. In fact, you just missed her."

I nodded, thinking, *So?*

"She asked why a course such as yours wasn't being extended to all needy students at West Coast Middle School. She also wanted a list of prerequisites for admittance."

Both legitimate requests. I'd had similar ones myself. I eased forward in my chair and placed my hands on the edge of his desk, suddenly upset with him for being upset with me. Then one of my class rules hit me with the force of a slap: *What upsets you tells a lot about you.* "You knew questions like this would surface, so why the surprise?"

His former optimism and humor had vanished, and my attitude wasn't bringing them back. "You may have opened a can of worms, Ms. Veil."

Great, now he was calling me Ms. Veil. "I was trying to stop the rumors about me running weird experiments in the classroom. Which would never have surfaced with a little advance planning." I caught myself—*Don't condemn or criticize*—and softened my tone. "You can't keep what's going on here a secret, Dr. Matt. Call it Montessori education if you like or transformative learning, but call it something people will understand." Maybe *First Light* hadn't been such a good moniker after all, even if the suggestion had come from the beyond. "Sure, you might want to omit the part about the Indigos' psychic abilities, but hopefully, someday, you can share that information, too, without fear that people will misunderstand or abuse. If you don't believe in what we're doing, your disbelief will appear to the jury of our peers and this trial class will become your disbelief." I was relying on Emerson again, but darn it, last time we met, Dr. Matt seemed to thrive on aphorisms, so it was one way to communicate with him at least. "Be the class, don't just talk about it."

"The rumors I can deal with, but not demands for other students to enter the class."

Okay, so Emerson wasn't working; maybe Nietzsche or Valery

next time. Anyway, I found it hard to believe that many parents, let alone students, would demand entry to a class that involved extra hours after school and, as Jason had put it, set students apart. As far as I knew, only Brad's mother had asked thus far, and as my students had made clear on our first day, even they weren't thrilled about being included. "Ignorance breeds fear, Dr. Matt, and, believe me, fear breeds its own can of worms."

He dropped his pen on the desk and leaned back in his chair, but made no comment.

What had brought about this change in him? It felt as if I were doing a free fall without a parachute. *Handle change with grace and ease.* "If you fold after only a few questions from a woman with a legitimate cause, there's no chance for this class." *Know that flaws and mistakes are part of the grand scheme of things.* "I'm proud of what we've accomplished so far. Why don't you ask the kids what they think?"

"I have."

Blood surged to my face and pumped in my ears. What had the kids told him about me? *Be happy with yourself and consider yourself creative.* "And?"

"Why don't *you* ask them?"

"Okay," I said, standing. *Embrace criticism as an opportunity to learn and grow.* "And afterwards, I'd appreciate it if you let me know what you expect of me. Because, to be quite honest, I don't have a clue."

No complaining.

So much for class rules. I'd flunked them all.

Be grateful. Ha!

After exiting Dr. Matt's office, I realized I'd forgotten to ask about Angelina's health. Going back was the last thing I wanted to do, but for Angelina I'd do it. I re-entered without knocking. A mistake. Dr. Matt was talking on the phone with his back to me. "She just started, Charles. Give her time."

I backed out the door.

"She came highly recommended. No need for concern."

Questions about Angelina would have to wait, until I found out what my students were saying about me.

100

Chapter Twenty

AS SOON AS JASON, *King of Hearts*, took a seat at his table the next afternoon, I questioned him, not bothering to seek the privacy of a separate room. If the other students listened in, so be it. All would come out in the wash, anyway. I tried to keep my expression neutral, my voice steady. "What did you tell Dr. Matt about me?"

He dropped his backpack to the floor and rummaged inside. "Damn. I could've sworn I put it in here last period."

I folded my arms and waited.

He halted his search and looked up as though surprised I was still standing there. "Uh? Oh. I told him your pep talks were nice." He grinned then mimicked, "'Know that flaws and mistakes are part of the grand scheme of things.'"

Pep talks?

"And that we like you," he added before holding up his pencil. "Found it." His air of triumph turned to one of concern when he saw the expression on my face. "It's not that you're doing anything wrong, Ms. V." He glanced at Shawn, who gave him two thumbs up. "Just that there's a lot going on here you don't know about."

"It takes time," I said. "And that's good, because there are many paths—"

Jason held up his hand. "You aren't listening, Ms. V."

I felt defensive, combative. Listening was the last thing I wanted to do. I stared at his upraised hand, wanting to slap it away and remind its smart-assed owner who the authority was here. But then

I realized my pride was getting in the way. I wasn't here to suppress these kids but help set them free.

If Jason sensed my discomfort, he wasn't letting on. "We're not sharing ourselves. We're not sharing our stories."

"The mask project was a prelude to that."

"I know," he said with a shake of his head. "But we're still wearing masks…for you."

"For me?"

"And for this class. Even though it keeps us after school and is more talk than action, we don't want it to fail."

More talk than action? I must have looked pretty silly standing there with my mouth hanging open, because the way Jason was eyeballing me, it seemed he wanted to shake me. "I know some things can't be rushed, Ms. V, but we don't have much time."

All was silent, except for Bruce Springsteen singing from the CD player in the background. "Trouble in Paradise," of all things. Why was everyone in such a damn hurry? "Next year someone will come in to replace me. Hopefully, someone more experienced and—"

"Is that why you won't allow yourself to care?"

"Care? What are you talking about? Of course, I care. I'm putting my life on hold for you." Jeez! I turned and took several deep breaths, embarrassed at my outburst and the silence that followed.

"The road to hell is paved with good intentions," Luke said.

Road to hell? Good intentions?

Jason observed me as a teacher observes a dense student. "You need to enter our world."

My eyes ached the way they always do when my brain tries to absorb more than it can handle. They floated in their sockets like blue marbles in zero gravity. Enter their world? No way. Theirs was a world I meant to avoid—the constant fear of having a serious mental illness, of losing one's mind. Maybe we could join forces and escape together.

"What upsets you says a lot about you," Luke said, throwing one of my class rules back at me. Currently a sore subject. *Be the rules, don't just talk about them.*

I turned back to the students and took a deep breath. "Okay, time for me to shut up and for you to explain what's going on."

"We need to deal with some *real* problems, *now,*" Jason said.

I'd agreed to keep my mouth shut but couldn't help asking, "Like what?"

"Angelina's dying."

Dying? I gasped like a chain smoker after years of abuse. "How do you know?"

He rubbed his temples with the fingertips of both hands. "I just do."

Bubbles rose in my airways and made a crackling sound in my throat when I realized Angelina wasn't in the room.

"And then there's Tessa Lambe," Jason said.

I grabbed the edge of the table in front of me for support.

"Someone you've ignored until now."

Jason might as well have punched me in the gut. I felt like the loser in a round of amateur boxing.

"It's not all your fault, though. She did a number on you."

I looked at Tessa, really looked at her, for what seemed like the first time. She sat like a rag doll, hands folded on the table, her face expressionless, her aura a bright emerald green. The word apathetic came to mind, and I realized apathy was worse than hate. Her apathy and mine. She'd asked for nothing, and I'd given her nothing. We hadn't engaged at all. I smiled at her. She did not smile back. You can't play the game if you're missing a card. *Eight of Spades, healer, enormous spiritual energy.*

"How about you, Jason? Did you do a number on me, too?"

The look he gave me was that of a fifty-year-old. I should know. My birth father had given me a similar look when he'd admitted to being an alcoholic, a look of pity for the clueless. "We just don't want to screw up," Jason said.

"Okay. As I told you before, we're all in this together. Guess it's time for you to share."

Jason's gaze followed my hands, which had crept to my chest. "Remember what you said the day you started telling us about your mouse totem and we waited for you to tell us more?"

When I didn't answer, he answered for me. "You said, 'Maybe someday I'll tell you about it.'"

"Wait a minute. This isn't about me."

"Are you afraid that if you share *your* story, we'll lose respect for you?"

Again, I didn't need to answer. He already knew. My story, like the stories of all the others in the room, was one not easily shared. On the one hand, it was too unbelievable. On the other, I wasn't proud of my role in it—a reactor, instead of an actor, a walk-on, a placeholder. I was performing a bit part in my own life story.

"So, what makes it different for us?" he asked, nostrils flared. "What do we risk when we spill our guts in front of the class? More than loss of respect, Ms. V. Much more. Anyway, Shawn reads you like a book."

"And you?"

"I mostly sense things, like that you're healthy and Angelina's not."

"How about Codi?" I asked, aware she was listening and could speak for herself. "Does she have problems, too?"

Jason gave her a lopsided smile. "She's a different kettle of fish, but, yeah, I'd say so."

"How about Ethan?"

After studying my face for what seemed a full minute, Jason said, "Do you really want to know about us?" When I nodded, he asked, "Are you sure?"

"You mean, I have a choice?"

"Oh, you have a choice all right, but choosing means upsetting some apple carts, especially your own."

Before I could react, Jason turned to Luke, who nodded and said, "As you told Codi during our lesson about totems, 'You are not a victim, unless, of course, you insist on sabotaging your life. Your mind can do that easily enough, if you let it.'"

Luke was a walking, talking video camera, recording and replaying what I'd said with complete accuracy, down to my smallest gestures and expressions. I responded to the words as Codi had, with a deep shaky breath.

Jason stood, guided me to his seat at the base of the U, and turned to the rest of the class. "Show time."

Shoot! Sitting in the direct path of a tornado-force storm, I was truly starting to wonder about choice and consequences.

Jason took on the role of class spokesperson as if born to it, and none of his peers seemed to mind. Maybe they'd discussed this beforehand, or maybe they shared a psychic connection.

"We'll start with Tessa," he said.

She rose from her seat next to Codi like a shadow—gray, featureless. Then, like a Polaroid picture, she sharpened and took on color. The girl I'd hardly noticed until now had blonde hair, a thin pointy chin, a small nose, and blue eyes. She wore faded denim jeans and a hooded gray sweater. I recalled how upset I'd been when Dr. Matt told me that Shawn could fade into the background to the point where you didn't even know he was there. It wasn't like me to ignore a child, especially one who'd been in my class for nine days.

"During our lesson on masks," she said, "we had a visitor." Her little girl voice was soft, yet forceful, like the storm I imagined headed my way.

I thought of our class guest, Brad, *Brave Puppy,* and the memory brought a smile to my face. He and his mother had so loved the lesson on masks they'd precipitated a reprimand from Dr. Matt. But his tongue-lashing had been worth it. I would do it again in a heartbeat. In fact, I would invite the entire school to take part if they could fit into the classroom. I relaxed my grip on the seat of my chair.

"Not Brad," Shawn said softly.

I blinked. *Not Brad?*

"She looked just like you," Tessa said, "except for the birthmark on her face."

105

"Oh God." I stood and my chair tipped on its side. "Oh God." I dropped my face into my hands and started to shake. *Maya.*

Someone straightened my chair and eased me back onto it. "It's okay, Ms. Veil."

I eyed the door leading to the outside corridor, fighting the urge to escape.

"Trust me," Shawn said. "It'll be okay."

Trust?

"Only Angelina and I could see her," Tessa said.

This ghost of a girl, this chameleon, had seen my sister, when I had not. Her voice sounded like it was coming through a long, narrow tunnel, distorted by the loud pumping of my heart. Why hadn't I sensed Maya's presence? I'd been able to do so before.

"She said you're no longer open to her messages. Or to your mother's."

I thought I heard accusation in Tessa's voice, but her next words proved me wrong.

"Which, in my opinion, isn't so bad. Why should dead people be telling us what to do, anyway? They had their chance while they were alive and should leave us alone to live ours. That's how we learn. Right?"

I nodded, wracking my brain for a reason why I'd lost contact with my sister. The consciousness that had survived her death would know of my attempt to help others and that I needed her now more than ever.

"What I'm trying to say is that Angelina and I sometimes hear and see the dead. We thought you should know this as our teacher."

"Thanks, Tessa." Jason turned to Ethan. "You're on."

The smoky white aura swirling around Ethan's body indicated a lack of harmony in mind and body, possibly some kind of artificial stimulation. "I can see into the future, but usually, I don't know it's the future until it's already happened and it's too late to do anything about it. Maybe what's going to happen is set. Or maybe there are a bunch of outcomes, like in one of those pick-your-own-ending books." He eyed the cabinet holding his ceramic totem. "My vision, or whatever you want to call it, tells me that my owl's going to crash and burn, and I can't stop it, because" —he grimaced as if there were a sudden bad taste in his mouth— "I don't know which ending to choose."

I looked at the trophy case, where his owl stood safe and protected, then back at Ethan.

He gave me a smile accompanied by drooped shoulders and the shake of his head. "The cabinet won't help."

"You can make another," I said.

He sat down. "That's not the point now, is it?"

"Codi," Jason said, moving things right along.

She stood slowly and leaned on the table in front of her like an eighty-year-old granny with a weak heart. "I get into people's heads." Her aura was confusing, a bright lemon yellow with pockets of violet, as though she were struggling to maintain power and control in a relationship.

"Like in Ms. Goldsberry's class," I said. "You were the one who warned me, right? 'Watch out Ms. Veil, the party's about to begin.'"

She shrugged and dropped back into her seat. "Yep, that was me."

"Not so fast." Jason frowned as though he were her teacher instead of a peer. "Codi can plant thoughts into your head, Ms. V, and influence what you do. Sometimes I feel like wearing a bicycle helmet when she's around to keep her from messing with my mind."

Codi's smile vanished, and her posture straightened from granny pose to superhero. "I don't mess with people's minds unless it's important. It makes my head hurt."

"Good." Jason turned to Shawn. "Shawn reads minds, but he can't mess with them like Codi can."

Shawn didn't agree or disagree, just shrugged, his demeanor so calm you'd think he lived in a monastery under a vow of silence.

"Luke's specialty is trivia," Jason said. "Like Sherlock Holmes and inspector Nash Bridges, he has near perfect recall. Except he's alive and breathing instead of a fictional character. They call his talent eidetic memory, which more or less makes him a walking, talking encyclopedia. I'd go nuts if I remembered everything, but there you have it."

Luke hung his head. "A lot of good it does. Crowds out all the important stuff."

"Tessa is our healer," Jason said. "She's trying to—"

"You promised not to tell," Tessa said, her voice a plaintive kitten meow. "I don't work miracles and you know it."

"Depends on what you call a miracle, but, okay, I promised not to tell. As Tessa said, she and Angelina can sometimes see and hear the dead. And you already know about me. I move stuff with my mind. Usually not very well."

"Show her," Codi said. "Show her what you can do."

He gave her a sour look then held up a pencil. With the flair of a stage magician, he flicked open his fingers and the pencil disappeared.

"Where did it go?" I asked, finding it hard to believe what I'd just seen.

"I don't know," Jason said.

"Magic?" I asked.

"Not magic, but real. I let my mind go blank, so it doesn't interfere with my hands, and then things just disappear. I don't see the openings they disappear into, but my hands know there're there. It's kind of like breathing. You do it without thinking. Sometimes I pull weird things out of the pockets surrounding me. Things I don't want and can't return. Like a bad purchase."

I shook my head, gaining a new understanding of why Jason's father expressed concern. For now, Jason could masquerade as a magician, but at some point, if only for his own mental health, he would have to reveal his abilities. And then what? How would people react if they knew the extent of his powers?

"It's sort of like the hidden portals in Earth's magnetic field called X-points," Luke said, "that open and close to other dimensions dozens of times a day. They're located thousands of kilometers from Earth, but Jason discovered something similar here, like the Bermuda Triangle, except smaller, and found the invisible entry points."

"My God, Luke, do you have a scientific explanation for everything?" Codi asked.

"In this case, NASA does," he said, unperturbed by Codi's question. In fact, he seemed to thrive on her attention, as though aware that his knowledge secretly impressed her.

"Sometimes I hide my hands in my pockets," Jason said, "so it's hard to get things done, especially at school. It's at the point where I'm afraid to touch anyone, and I don't like to be touched. This bugs Mom and Dad to no end, makes them worry I'll never get married and have kids. As if that would be the end of the world."

The ache of imagining his pain settled deep in the walls of my chest. I wished I could fly away like those crazy, dive-bombing birds on the other side of the windows. These kids didn't need me; they needed a frigging miracle worker. I could be married to Morgan right now, my biggest concern what to fix for dinner and pack in Joshua's school lunch. Morgan would take care of my every want and need, provide peace and security, but...

How long before boredom set in?

I could get a job as a regular teacher and hand over this assignment to someone else. But who? If I with my emerging psychic abilities had zilch to offer, who would?

God, I felt helpless. Just like the kids.

"Um, Ms. V?" It was Jason again. "What mold are you pouring your thoughts into?"

I shook my head, rolled my eyes.

He grinned. "Now might be a good time to practice what you preach."

Smartass!

Chapter Twenty-one

NOW MIGHT BE A good time to practice what you preach." Jason's words raced through my mind long after the students had left for the day. I sat, elbows on table, forehead cupped in hands, unable to dispel images of Angelina sick, maybe dying, and Jason living his life afraid to touch or be touched.

As if to mock me, Bruce Springsteen crooned the lyrics to, "The Price You Pay," from the CD in the distance. Damn. Why was it so cold in here?

The warmth of someone's hand seeped through the yoke of my blazer and traveled to my heart, which felt like a bruised fist. Instead of tensing at the intrusion, I relaxed into it. The warmth was more than physical; it exuded care and concern.

"Bad day?"

I nodded, wondering how Granny Max had entered the room without notice.

"I brought all the fixings for oatmeal raisin cookies, dear, thought I'd give one of the old kitchens a try."

When I didn't respond, she withdrew her hand. "Are you okay with that?"

I twisted around and studied Granny Max's face, glad her aviator sunglasses were propped on her head instead of covering the serenity of her brown eyes. "Sure, why not?"

"Let's go then. I preach better with my hands busy."

I followed—comfort food, like the warmth of a hand, an irresistible draw.

"Sit," she said when we reached one of the dated but fully functional kitchens. "No assistance required."

I sank onto a chair at the small table in the kitchen's dining area, tempted to lay my head down and take a nap.

"Looks like you need some refueling. Consider this your pit stop." Granny Max pulled bowls, measuring spoons, and cookie sheets out of cabinets and drawers as if this were her kitchen instead of one in a chilly old classroom. "Maybe we should give this place a modern twist by calling it a 'food lab' where kids can learn some basic life skills… Like how to put out a kitchen fire."

While she measured butter and sugar into a large plastic bowl and creamed them together, I watched mesmerized, as if this were the first time I'd ever seen someone bake cookies. And when she beat in the eggs and vanilla and started singing, "Shake, Rattle, and Roll," she could have been waving a magic wand and singing "Bibbidy Bobbidy Boo" as far as I was concerned. She blended in the dry ingredients and, when done, lifted the wooden spoon to her lips, microphone style, and swayed her hips. "Baby, let's shake, rattle, and roll." Then finally, while stirring in the oats and raisins, her voice quivering with the effort, she said, "Your kids may be unique because of their Indigo status, but basically all kids are alike. Could you handle another thousand?"

"Dear God, no."

Granny Max dropped mounds of dough onto the cookie sheet. "Don't look so glum. Most of our students will grow up to become well-adjusted and content citizens despite what we do, or do not, teach them, to which I say, 'Thank the Lord,' or I wouldn't be able to stand the guilt."

My back and shoulders slumped, and I couldn't manage to straighten them.

After she'd put the sheet of cookies into the oven, Granny Max pulled out two mugs, dropped in tea bags, and put water to boil. "Once we've had our fill, you can give the rest of the cookies to the kids, you know, to stimulate their reward centers." She frowned. "Hang in there, hon."

I rested my chin on my hands and sighed.

"Cream? Sugar?"

"Black, thanks."

She puckered her lips as if tasting something nasty. "Never could figure out how some women get all the brains, good looks, *and* self-control, doesn't seem fair, somehow." A pause. "Sorry for pointing this out, my dear, but women like you" —she glanced at the acoustic ceiling tiles as though deliberating a connect-the-dots puzzle for the outline of her response to be revealed— "how to put it, let me see now… I don't think people with special gifts know what they've got, if you know what I mean. Since it's just been handed to them, they, well…they take it for granted."

If her aim had been to snap me out of my funk, she'd succeeded. Plus, the aroma of warm butter and vanilla created such a mind-numbing turbulence in my taste buds and stomach that her words turned into white noise. She brought two mugs of steaming tea to the table and winked before adding three heaping teaspoons of sugar and at least an eighth cup of milk to hers. Then she headed back to the oven, pulled out the sheet of cookies, put in another, and returned with a platter of mouthwatering delights. "Are you catching on?"

My mind was as mushy as the warm cookies.

"It's all about distraction." She edged the oatmeal raisin treats my way. "Part of your job as a teacher is to distract the students from the mundane and open their eyes to possibilities."

The sugary, buttery concoction tasted heavenly as it melted in my mouth. "Dr. Matt should've picked you to take on this class."

"Dear God no, you're better qualified by far; your youth alone a definite asset. Those kids can wear a person out, if you know what I mean, and I've heard you've got other talents, as well."

"More like curses."

Granny Max's face showed neither surprise nor disapproval. "My guess is that extrasensory abilities are like any other aptitude or skill. If not feared or abused, they can lead to great things. It would be sinful not to use them, think of the good you can do."

How had she heard about my psychic abilities? If she knew, so did others, which could lead to trouble—if past experience was anything to go by. "Hope you're right."

"I know I'm right, and I'm not even psychic."

"I wouldn't be too sure about that."

In what seemed like no time, she shoved back her chair and made for the oven, just as the alarm beeped.

"See what I mean?" I said as she took out the cookies and put in the last batch.

"Only a matter of much practice." She reset the timer and winked— "Just in case…" —before returning to her seat at the table.

I rolled my eyes, Codi style.

"Don't get too cheeky, hon, you've got dish duty when we're done."

"My forte, cleaning up."

Granny Max stared at the single cookie left on the platter as though it were imparting its own particular wisdom. "What do you want, Marjorie? I mean, here at West Coast. What do you hope to accomplish?"

When I didn't answer, she said, "If you don't believe in the outcome, it won't come to pass."

She was giving me a dose of my own medicine, making me realize what a hypocrite I was. "I'm trying to think big."

"What do you want," Granny Max repeated.

Words didn't come. At least not right away. But Granny Max's kind expression suggested there was no rush, that sometimes talking just got in the way. *Enjoy the company,* she seemed to say, *relax into the topic. Moments of insight need time to sink in.*

"For the kids and me…" I started, then regrouped and started again. "For the kids and me to step into our own life stories." It came as a surprise that I'd included myself, though I'd suggested something similar during my interview with Dr. Matt. The need to control my own narrative. "And for me that isn't easy, because… To tell you the truth, I'm a follower, a wuss, can't even stand on my own two feet."

Granny Max stood, headed for the stove, and right on cue, the alarm went off. She grabbed the oven mitt and pulled out the cookies, then closed her eyes, as though, she, too, needed a measure of silence for insight to sink in. "You have a special light, Marjorie, and it pulls things out of the darkness towards itself. Believe me. I don't bake cookies for just anyone."

"Did I pull *you* out of the darkness?" I asked, chuckling at the very idea.

"You're helping me express and utilize my energies in altruistic love and service."

"Does that mean you'll do the dishes?"

She threw the oven mitt at me, actually threw it. "I wouldn't think of depriving you of the chance to utilize *your* energies in altruistic love and service."

I caught the mitt, tempted to throw it back, but didn't. Which seemed wrong somehow, as though I weren't playing my part in the game. Then it struck me; commitment meant involvement, which meant going solo wasn't an option. I wasn't playing solitaire but bridge, drawn into the game by seven thirteen-year-old slight-of-hand artists. Jason was right. It was time to forgo the affirmations and crafts. These kids were beyond that.

What card was *I* in the new game we were playing? *Two of Spades: Tendency to willfulness with consequent self-undoing. Wants home roots, but often obliged to work away from home. Looker after lost souls.*

"Your Indigos need training to face the unknown and give voice to their inexplicable experiences," Granny Max said. "They need to learn to live in the world in a spiritual way, integrate and open their hearts for the deepest kind of freedom."

Give voice to their inexplicable experiences? Isn't that what they'd done today? As far as opening their hearts, how did one teach that?

Granny Max took the oven mitt and put it back in the kitchen drawer, giving me time to formulate a response to her comment.

Reorder cards by suit and rank. Set terms of the hand.

"That's what I meant, I think, when I said I wanted my students to step into their own life stories." I'd been concentrating so hard on providing them with a safe, nurturing environment that I'd neglected to allow them to fail, dust themselves off, and try again. Starting tomorrow, I would urge them to hone the psychic skills in the part of their brains that had been allowed, if not encouraged, to atrophy; the part of their brains that was dying.

"Now that you've put your intentions into words, put them into action," Granny Max said on her return to the table. "Sounds like you're being put to the test, so you need to prepare."

"I think I'm getting the picture."

"I'm sure there's a fancier way of saying this, but I'm tired, so I'll give it to you straight. Follow your gut and use your damn powers."

Was this what Jason and my class of Indigos had been trying to tell me? "You're as bad as the kids," I threw back at her.

"Yeah, and proud of it. Maybe you should take a lesson from me and step out of that ivory tower you've erected for yourself. Ivory towers are built from the brittle bones of the past." She pointed to the kitchen counter. "You have work to do, because, to be quite honest, it's late and, even though I like you and all, I don't plan on spending the night here."

I nodded and stood. *Ivory towers are built from the brittle bones of the past.* Had I, in an attempt to feel safe, stable, and secure, erected an ivory tower from the bones of my dead sister? Had I been using her death as an excuse for avoiding what it was in me to do?

"Don't take yourself too seriously, Marjorie, or you won't last another month here, let alone four. The kids need you. Their behavior can be outrageous, but seen from a different perspective, well, there's almost something sacred about it."

"I'll keep that in mind." Energy coursed through me as if I were about to run a marathon. Step out of the ivory tower? What a relief that would be.

Chapter Twenty-two

IT WAS WEDNESDAY, FEBRUARY sixth, and my seven charges sat in their usual positions around the tables: Shawn and Ethan to my left, Angelina, Tessa, and Codi to my right, and Luke and Jason straight ahead at the base of the U. Only Tessa, however, looked my way. Jason was digging through his backpack with the enthusiasm of an archaeologist on the verge of a great find. Codi's find appeared to be locked in her compact, Shawn's on the other side of the window, Angelina's and Luke's in the books they were reading, and Ethan's in the design he was drawing on the back of his hand with a black marker. Votives flickered on the tables. The background music was Rascal Flatts this time, singing about a candle in a hurricane.

I handed out Granny Max's oatmeal raisin cookies, thinking back to her words. "Sounds like you're being put to the test, my dear, so you need to prepare." How could I help these kids give voice to their inexplicable experiences and, as Granny Max put it, express and utilize their energies in altruistic love and service? Maybe in the process of stepping out of my ivory tower, I needed to take some risks. With or without Dr. Matt's consent. No doubt, the answer to my questions would come. But if the past was anything to go by, they would sidestep any attempt at control and ignore any demands that the students and lessons proceed my way.

So, where should I go from here? My charges were running out of patience. And out of time.

I leaned against my desk and waited.

Jason dropped his backpack to the floor, hands empty. Codi exchanged her compact for a cookie. Angelina ear-tagged her book and set it aside. Luke, Shawn, and Ethan carried on with what they'd been doing, and Tessa, sweet Tessa, continued looking at me with a faint smile.

"We need shifters," I said.

Jason scrunched his face. Otherwise no response.

More waiting, which caught Codi's attention. She wasn't used to me being quiet. "What'd you say?"

"We need shifters."

"Uh?"

"Aides. Helpers."

Ethan scowled, eyeing the tattoo-like drawing he'd sketched on his left hand. "You mean totems?"

I strolled to the back of his table and paused behind him. He'd drawn an owl. "Sort of."

I moved on, peering over each student's shoulders until Luke put his book down and I had Shawn's attention. "What, for instance, can we use besides cookies to turn things around when we're in the dumps?"

Codi passed her cookie over a candle until it smoked, then blew on it and put it down. She wore blue lipstick today, and her brows were black and heavily arched. This, along with her ghostly pallor, made for a look of dark drama—Vampire Goth. It was hard to look away.

"Music works for me," Jason said, while Rascal Flatts crooned in the background about tasting what you're made of.

"Music is definitely mood altering," I said, "though some types can make you melancholy."

Jason feigned a gag. "Like Country."

"I've been meaning to ask you to bring in your own music," I said, "on condition that you point out its mood and theme."

Codi picked up her charred cookie and sniffed it. "You can bet it won't be Country."

"Mom always tells me to go watch the grass grow when I'm bored or cranky," Luke said. "She says sometimes it's good to do nothing."

"I like to read," Angelina said. Her skin appeared rosy today, her eyes clear and bright. Maybe Jason had been wrong about her critical condition.

Codi reached for a second cookie, having gouged the first like a sacrifice. "I talk to my friends. They don't mind my whining."

Jason coughed into his hand to hide a grin. "What's the point, Ms. V?" He wore a tweed jacket, black T-shirt, khakis, and brown loafers, dressy for a day at school. Heck, he dressed better than many of the teachers.

I returned to my usual position at the foot of my desk. "I'm talking about replacements for the bad stuff."

"She means instead of drugs and alcohol," Shawn said, his eyes flat as they peered from beneath rounded upper lids.

"Yes, alternatives less harmful than nicotine, alcohol, and—"

"Like peanut butter and love," Jason said.

"Ha." *Wise guy.*

"I heard that squeezable honey works," Luke said. "It processes similar to—"

"Get real, Luke." Codi's hand fisted as if of its own accord and chunks of the cookie dropped onto the table.

"Talk about getting real…" I eyed the smushed cookie Codi was wiping from her hand and wondered if it had prompted unanticipated therapeutic benefits. "I wasn't planning on sharing this yet, but…what the heck. I invited my sister to talk to you about alcohol, tobacco, and drug prevention tips."

"Your sis-ter?" Jason's voice rose on "sis" and dropping on "ter" with such a tone of disbelief, you'd think I'd just announced the sky was falling. "No offense, but if she's anything like you, um—"

"She's waiting to hear if she's been accepted into the DEA basic agent training program in Quantico, Virginia."

Jason's brows shot up; his eyes widened.

"A lecture from a narc," Codi said. "What the hell for?"

Good question. The answer to which I couldn't share. At least not yet. Straight out honesty would, in this case, do more harm than good. They wouldn't take kindly to hearing that Dr. Matt suspected one or more of them of experimenting with drugs. "It's never too early to talk about prevention. Like wearing a seat belt to avoid injury and death."

"That's a stretch." Codi's attention lingered on the remains of the ravaged cookie in her hand, which, to my relief, meant she wasn't probing my mind.

"It'll also give you a chance to meet my sister. Her name is Veronica, and she provides barf bags with her presentation."

Tessa's face contorted as though she'd just bitten into a slug instead of an oatmeal cookie. "Barf bags! Ugh."

Jason scratched his jaw, which appeared rough, like fine-grade sandpaper.

"I understand her presentation can be quite upsetting," I said.

Codi looked suddenly cheerful. "I can take it."

"Do you and Veronica look alike, too?" Tessa asked, her expression wistful.

"Exactly, except her hair is black."

"That makes you, Maya, and Veronica triplets." She clapped her hands and bounced in her seat like a game show contestant. "When's she coming?"

At the mention of Maya, my throat closed up, making it hard to swallow, let alone speak. "Not until mid-March. I still have to okay it with Dr. Matt."

Tessa slumped in her chair. "That's a long time."

"By then it'll…" Codi coughed, then clammed up.

"What's *your* shifter when you feel bad?" Ethan asked.

I looked at Jason. He looked away. "Well, yesterday my shifter was an oatmeal cookie."

"What's your shifter on other days?" Ethan asked.

I pulled the stone mouse from the leather pouch I wore around my waist as often as fashion allowed. "On most days, this does the trick." I set the totem on the table in front of him. "It has seen many places and has had many owners besides me."

Luke shoved his glasses up the bridge of his nose and leaning forward with laser focus. "Where'd you get it?"

"Initially, my soon-to-be-adoptive son gave it to me. His name is Joshua."

"Tell us about him," Tessa said.

With these kids, you never knew where a subject might lead, from shifters to drugs, barf bags to Joshua. I hesitated, knowing I should share but unwilling to do so. "Maybe someday."

"Why not today?" Tessa was persistent now that she was no longer impersonating a gray ghost.

"Because this isn't about me."

"Sure, it is," Jason said. "You're our teacher."

"And that makes your story our story," Tessa said.

"Maybe someday," I repeated.

I pulled five stones out of my pouch and set them on the table in front of Luke. "I use these to mark the five directions of my Medicine Wheel, which, by the way, is another one of my shifters." I positioned four of the stones in a circle, yellow for the East, red for the South, black for the West, and white for the North. Then I placed the green stone in the center. "When I feel the need to conquer some critical self-attacks or seek answers to seemingly unanswerable questions, I construct a big circle, sit inside, and meditate."

"A magic circle?" Luke asked.

"Only if by 'magic circle' you mean a place to bring out desired changes. The Medicine Wheel is more like a circle of knowledge. When my sister's fiancé, Ben *Gentle Bear* Mendoza, comes with her in March, he'll explain."

The room grew quiet, and I wondered at the cause, until Dr. Matt cleared his throat. "I hope you planned to run that by me first."

He'd come in unannounced, which was fine. He had every right as principal to observe my interaction with the class unrehearsed.

But for him to interrupt a lesson to enquire about guest-speaker logistics was another matter.

At my tight-lipped silence, Dr. Matt added, "I came by to check on your progress."

"So far, so good," I said.

Dr. Matt frowned.

"Our purpose today, Uncle Matt, is to find our shifters," Shawn said.

At the lift of Dr. Matt's brows, Shawn hurried on. "We're going to find out what we can use to pull our energy from a frequency of negativity to one of happiness. We're going to find out what we want and believe we deserve it. Then use that information to dig ourselves out of some deep, black holes. In other words" —Shawn took a shaky breath— "apply the knowledge to circumstances outside ourselves and beyond this room."

I was reduced to putty by Shawn's comment. As, it seemed, was Dr. Matt. His eyes welled up and his chest expanded. Smart as Shawn was, the words hadn't come from him. Not by a long shot. Someone else had planted them, and the thought that Shawn had allowed it, warmed my heart. "I have this field trip planned…" Might as well leap into the breach and seize the opportunity while Dr. Matt was in a receptive mood. "To the James Lick Observatory on Mt. Hamilton."

Dr. Matt nodded. I could have announced a trip to Mars and he probably would have reacted the same; with a nod and a blank stare.

I pressed on. "And another to the Winchester Mystery House. I think a little inspiration is called for."

"Mom won't take me to the Winchester Mystery House," Angelina said. "She says it's haunted by Mrs. Winchester's ghost."

Angelina's words brought Dr. Matt out of his daze. "Well, we'll see about that."

On gathering up my stones, I noticed that my mouse was missing. My heart did a clumsy flip. "Has anyone seen my totem?"

Heads shook. Tessa scrambled to the floor. "Maybe it fell off the table somewhere."

Nope. Someone had taken it, and I had a pretty good idea who it was.

But I said nothing.

For now.

※ ※ ※

I knocked on the door frame of Dr. Matt's office the next afternoon before class. "Hi. Do you have a minute?"

"What's on your mind?"

"The field trip to the James Lick Observatory."

The blank look on Dr. Matt's face was not encouraging. He gestured for me to sit across from him at his desk.

"Since this is all new to me, I don't know the proper procedure to follow. There must be permission slips to fill out—"

His raised hand stopped me dead. "Sorry, no field trips."

"But—"

"This after-school option is still in its infancy, and I'd prefer not to put it in jeopardy."

Jeopardy? "But you said I had your complete backing and there'd be volunteers for—"

"It's early yet, and a few issues have come up since then that I need to check into."

I sank into the same chair I'd occupied during my first visit to his office. What had caused the optimistic philosopher who'd hired me to turn into Mr. Caution? "What issues?"

"Issues I can't discuss with you at this time."

Okay, I could understand his restraint due to possible litigation in case of a field trip emergency. He would have to plan for an assortment of eventualities, which was nothing to scoff at. But to outright say no... "If they limit my ability to lead the class, I should at least know what they are."

He picked up a pen and started doodling on a legal pad. It was a Mont Blanc, a *Boheme Bleu*. I knew because I owned one just like it, a gift from my parents on my graduation from San Jose State. But I'd never considered bringing it to school.

"You'll know in time." He eyed me with what appeared to be regret, then rose from his chair and turned to face the parking lot, still free of the parade of cars that would soon pass through to pick up students after school. His back was ramrod straight, rather impressive with the Armani suit that looked sculpted rather than tailored to fit his body. Taking his silence as a dismissal, I stood and headed for the door.

I sensed rather than saw him turn from the window.

"I'm sorry," he said.

I shrugged and walked out of his office.

Funny thing, it sounded like he meant it.

※ ※ ※

"What do you mean, he won't let us go on the field trip?" Jason's disappointment came as a surprise. I hadn't realized the school outing meant that much to him.

"Dr. Matt said no."

"But my dad was going to volunteer to help supervise."

His dad? Wait. I thought they weren't getting along.

"I know what you're thinking, Ms. V. That me and my dad have issues. But he's a cosmologist…" He frowned at Codi, who had gone wide-eyed at the news. "Cosmologist, not cosmetologist."

"Oh, I get it," Codi said. "You had me going there for a second."

Jason shook his head and continued, "Anyway, Dad gets to apply for observation time on the Lick Observatory 3-m Shane telescope. It's nearly impossible for kids like us to get anywhere near an instrument like that. But, if he's able to pull some strings… I mean, think about how awesome that would be."

Frustration filled my chest like toxic fumes. The field trip would have been an opportunity for father and son to bond, let alone serve as a learning experience for the rest of class. "I don't know what to say, Jason. My powers are limited here."

Instead of sulking, he gave me a sly smile. "Don't worry, Ms. V, I have a plan." He looked more wolf-like than ever.

Codi came alive at the news. Until then, she'd seemed to be

having a bad day. Her hair was stringy and lifeless instead of jelled into its usual high peaks. "Guess we're going then, cause when Jason puts his mind to something, watch out."

Angelina leapt up on tiptoes and spiraled like a ballerina who'd been practicing for just such an occasion. "Go, Jason."

He grinned. "I'll update you on Monday if my plan pays off."

Whatever he had in mind, I was all for it. Dr. Matt had been wrong in denying us this small excursion. Plus, I appreciated the way Jason was taking a stand on the class's behalf. "In that case, why not conduct a little research on the Lick Observatory?"

I didn't have to mention it twice. Luke and Codi headed for the encyclopedias that were rapidly becoming time capsules filled with information meticulously researched, edited, and losing value with the mainstream. The rest of the students dug into their pockets and backpacks for their BlackBerries and notebook computers.

No further instructions required.

Chapter Twenty-three

EACH DAY AT WEST Coast had so far been, and would likely continue to be, a struggle, so it was only natural that I needed a break. It wasn't about being physically tired. I only taught one two-hour class, four times a week, and in the afternoon at that. I could sleep until noon if so desired. I could run errands, go shopping, visit my mother (heaven forbid), but emotionally I felt drained. I also missed the two people I loved most in the world. So, on Friday, it was off to the farm, over a three-hour drive, not quite with my tail between my legs, but close.

My search for freedom to follow my own truth had ruled my life for months now. But if I were truly seeking freedom, would I have allowed seven students with special needs to pull me into their world? The fact that I'd even considered doing so was more of an indicator of who I was than all the doubts floating around in my mind. It's difficult to say no when you see yourself reflected in someone else's eyes.

I pressed on the gas. Morgan was waiting.

❋ ❋ ❋

Morgan was waiting all right, with Joshua at Methodist Hospital in ER.

When I arrived at the van Dyke farm, Morgan's mother informed me that Joshua had experienced an allergic reaction to an insect bite. His leg had swollen, followed by puffy eyes, lips, and tongue. He'd complained of abdominal pain and started wheezing and finding it hard to breathe. The skin on my scalp quivered at the news, as if under siege by a thousand such insects. "Morgan meant to call you," Carla said, "but decided against it. He figured you had enough on your plate without adding more."

Talk about stepping out of my ivory tower. What kind of mother would I be for Joshua if my priorities remained focused elsewhere? I'd broken free of the suppressive protectiveness of my adoptive mother and ex-fiancé, refusing to surrender my freedom for the security of having someone else telling me what to do. But for what, to what, or to whom was I now responsible? Apparently, freedom was only part of the story and half of the truth. How would I exercise my capacity for choice?

Methodist Hospital is only a thirty-minute drive from the farm, but the trip seemed to take twice as long. I counted five stop signs and fifteen traffic lights on the way, with farmers moving equipment on two-lane roads at the beginning of my journey and delivery trucks clogging multiple lanes near the end. I broke out in a sweat. "Please, God, let Joshua be okay."

Shell-shocked patients awaiting triage crammed the emergency waiting room. No Morgan. No Joshua. The receptionist asked if I was family. I said yes. She directed me to the emergency ward nurse's station. The on-duty nurse led me to a curtained area where Joshua was receiving acute short-term treatment. Though the pounding of my heart seemed loud enough to announce my arrival to the entire hospital floor, I entered the small space undetected.

Morgan sat in a chair next to Joshua's bed, dozing. Joshua, too, appeared to be asleep. An IV bag hung from a pole with a line taped to his hand. Monitors clicked and beeped.

A nurse whisked into the partitioned space with no qualms about waking the sleeping patient. She adjusted his bed. "How're you feeling, young man?"

Joshua opened his eyes and blinked.

She checked his eyes with a flashlight, then checked the EKG monitor and wrote something on the clipboard dangling from the foot of his bed.

Machines. Buttons. Cords. I looked for a place to sit.

Morgan, awake now, motioned for me to take his chair.

"Once the antivenin takes hold," the nurse said, "you'll be as good as new."

Morgan winked at me, and I made a choking sound.

Joshua jerked and tried to sit up.

"Oh, no you don't, kiddo." The nurse eased him back onto the bed and re-adjusted his blanket. "Any shortness of breath?"

Joshua shook his head, his eyes fixed on mine, as though I were a hero in his story instead of a bit player.

"How's the throat when you swallow?" the nurse asked.

"Better."

I smiled at Joshua. He smiled back.

"Stay put," the nurse said. "Got it?"

"Got it."

When I turned to hug Morgan, he drew my attention to his stained work shirt, wranglers, and boots. I leaned in and kissed him, anyway.

"I got stung by a bug," Joshua said, his voice groggy.

The nurse tidied the bed, rechecked the monitor, and left the room.

"Morgan brought me here, and he didn't even take a shower."

"He must've been in quite a hurry," I said, drawing closer to his bed.

"His hands were shaking. I thought he was going to pass out."

I touched the place where the IV entered Joshua's hand. "How are you feeling?"

"Good," he said, before veering to a subject of apparent more interest. "How's Gabriel?"

My heart softened at the mention of my backyard stray. "Up to his feral ways, running off to who knows where and showing up whenever he's hungry or needs a rest."

"He'll be there when you need him," Joshua said.

"How about when *you* need him?"

Joshua gave me a smile that spoke of love and trust and the security of a supportive family. "I've got Morgan and" —he touched the opal ring hanging from the chain around his neck— "the totem you gave me."

"I'm surprised the hospital staff didn't make you take it off."

He glanced at Morgan then whispered, "They tried."

"I wish I could've been here to see that," I said filled with gratitude for Morgan's strong devotion to his nephew and our future son. I reached for my mouse totem, intending to press it against Joshua's fire opal in a gesture of approval, then remembered it was missing. I offered him a fist bump instead.

Joshua gave me an ominous look I knew too well. "Don't worry, Marjorie you'll know what to do."

I shivered, not knowing what he meant and opting not to ask. "How's school?"

"I'm catching up fast."

Catching up? My insides tightened. It had taken Dr. Mendez; it had taken me; and it had taken near tragedy for Joshua to regain his voice after witnessing the death of his parents. It's amazing he'd adjusted at all. "Any new friends?"

"Lots," he said before veering off course again. "The doctor said I'm allergic to whatever stung me, probably a bee."

I tousled his hair and leaned back into Morgan, who now stood behind me. The sudden caress of his arms—yes, despite the smell of diesel and farm work—brought relief; followed by guilt for a list of unintended offenses. "I'm not spending enough time with you and Joshua." Morgan kissed the top of my head, sending heat down to my toes. "They can find someone to replace me." Even as I said it, I knew this wasn't true. Not now. Not anymore. I was invested, broken in, determined to follow it through.

Morgan's chuckle vibrated through my shirt to the inner wall of my chest. "Why would you do that? You just got started."

"But you and Joshua are doing all the giving, and I'm doing all the taking."

"One thing you learn fast on a farm is that nothing worth having comes easily. No short cuts, no quick fixes." Morgan's caress turned into a full embrace. "I'd tie you to my side if I could, selfish brute that I am. But isn't that your biggest complaint? That I'd make you a passive figure in my dreams, instead of a partner in dreams we share?"

"Yes," I said, amazed at the breadth of his understanding. He'd spent four years in college before returning to the farm, but that didn't account for the full span of his knowledge. It was probably due to all the hours he spent immersed in nature. The greatest teacher of all.

"Has anything changed?" he asked.

"I'd go nuts if you tied me to your side." It hadn't worked being tied to my mother; it hadn't worked being tied to my ex-fiancé; and it wouldn't work being tied to Morgan, no matter how much I loved him. I planned to give of myself freely, but I would not be bound—or limited—ever again.

"And you'd go mad if you had to spend more than an hour confined in the same room with this little guy." Morgan winked at Joshua. "He needs outdoor time. Even Mom and Dad say so, and they love him to distraction."

"Marjorie could play outdoors with me," Joshua said, reminding me of Shawn, with his straight black hair, enormous brown eyes, and serene, caring face. Morgan was right to suspect that Joshua, too, was an Indigo. Maybe while mentoring seven Indigos at West Coast Middle School, I'd become a more informed and effective mother. The thought gave me hope.

"And get eaten alive by venomous bugs," Morgan said. "I don't think so."

"But Marjorie likes to play with me."

I leaned closer to Morgan, felt him stir in response. He knew my heart was torn. But he also knew I couldn't leave my cocoon too early. Not if I intended to fly.

Jason *The Wolf* Ardis's words came to me as clearly as the

haunting voices of my mother and sister. "Is that why you won't allow yourself to care?"

Maybe all the things I believed the world was withholding from me, I was, instead, withholding from the world. Could it be that while Morgan was building a house with strong walls and a solid foundation, I was building a house of cards with a shallow deck from which to draw? By walking as an individual, did I risk walking incomplete?

"You *do* like to play with me, don't you?" Joshua asked, sounding less sure of himself.

"Of course, I do, my precious. Morgan's just teasing."

Chapter Twenty-four

O N MONDAY, JASON CAME to class with an
announcement. "Pop talked to Dr. Matt and the field trip's
a go." After his six classmates stopped jumping and clapping like
crazed monkeys, he added, "And Pop's arranging the whole thing.
He has his work cut out for him, though. The only time slot
available this month for observing the 3-m Shane telescope is this
Thursday."

Thursday? How had Ron Ardis gotten Dr. Matt's approval that
fast? And why hadn't Dr. Matt briefed me about the sudden change
in plans when I passed by his office on my arrival at school? Would
the permission forms get sent out in time? How about signatures for
excused absences? "Did your father mention how we'd get to the
observatory and back?" It seemed all the field trip formalities had
been taken out of my hands.

"In a rented minibus. On his dime."

The class hurrahed and spent the rest of that and the following
afternoon researching the Lick Observatory like mad scientists with
little or no input from me, taking the concept of self-motivation to
a new level. "This is how education is supposed to be," I said. Not
that anyone was listening.

Wednesday was a repeat of Monday and Tuesday, at least for the
kids. For me, it marked the day I'd first heard the voice of my dead
mother. One year ago, at the site of the Lone Cypress near Pebble
Beach, I heard her whisper, *Sunwalker, you have come at last.* And so
had begun the journey that took me to Carmel Valley, Big Sur,

Pacific Grove, and back to Menlo Park. Full circle, Ash Wednesday to Ash Wednesday, blustery winds time.

※ ※ ※

On February fourteenth came the big day.

Be it a holiday of romantic love, commercialized with flowers and chocolates; be it an offshoot of a pagan Roman feast to avert evil spirits and purify the city; be it the celebration of one or more Christian martyrs named Valentine; the students didn't seem to notice or care. They aimed their full concentration on the trip ahead.

Because the Lick Observatory was located over twenty miles from downtown San Jose along narrow and twisty Mt. Hamilton Road, we had to get an early start. We needed at least an hour and a half to reach our destination. No problem. Ron Ardis had arranged the whole thing, including passes out of core classes.

Charles Lacoste would not be pleased.

There was no snow on Mount Hamilton (a miracle, since the year before it had experienced blizzard like conditions, with the biggest snowfall in twenty-five years), so the road, though strenuous, was open.

Watching Codi, Tessa, Angelina, Luke, Jason, Shawn, and Ethan talk, laugh, and jostle in the seats behind me brought hot salty tears to my eyes. And when I caught the barely concealed smile on Jason's face as he observed his father behind the wheel, I thought, *Life is good.*

"This has got to be the crookedest road I've ever been on," Codi said. "One more turn and I think I'll puke."

Luke pressed his nose against the window in his eagerness to take in every twist and turn of the long and narrow route. "Three-hundred and sixty-five curves. Designed for horse-drawn wagons, not minibuses."

"Thank goodness, it's covered in asphalt now," I said. "Do you want us to stop for some fresh air?"

Shawn dumped the contents of his lunch bag and handed it to Codi. "Barf in this."

"Gee, thanks." She glowered at the flimsy brown bag as if doubting it would hold up under siege. "Guess I can hold out bit longer. Anyway, it's freezing out there, and I don't see any guardrails."

By the time we passed the Grant Ranch Park entrance, the mood in the minibus was electrifying.

"I've been wanting to come here for a long time," Ethan said.

"Me, too," Luke said.

"Will we be tested on this later?" Jason asked.

"Absolutely not. I want you to notice how the universe is not only a place, but a story you take part in, belong in, and out of which you arose," I said, rephrasing Ron Ardis's words in my classroom over three weeks before. "This trip is meant to be fun. We need to keep our brain cells fired up for all the other data bombarding us each day."

"Good thinking," Codi said. "Like when we go to the Winchester Mystery House. Mrs. Winchester was crazy, you know, and her ghost haunts the place."

"Let's not get ahead of ourselves," I warned as we pulled onto the observatory grounds. "We may not get this lucky twice."

Codi didn't reply, her attention diverted by the scene outside. "Omigod."

Chapter Twenty-five

THEIR GIFTS WERE EXTRAORDINARY. But, as usual, it seemed my students had no clue what to do with them. "This isn't what I expected," Angelina said, her shoulders slumped. We were in the warm and well-lit control room next to the 3-m Shane Telescope, with its racks of electronic equipment and flocks of computer terminals. Quite a privilege since it wasn't on public tour. "This place looks messy and old," she said, "like the computers and monitors at recycling centers, and there are so many wires and dials and stuff."

Tessa echoed Angelina's disappointment. "I thought we'd be able to see through the telescope, but it's bigger than a dinosaur, and we can't even get to it from here."

So much for my take on how the lesson should unfold.

"When the universe arrives at a fork in the road," Ron Ardis had said on our first meeting, "it transmutes into something new, teaching us to break apart aspects of ourselves for ongoing creativity to continue." What aspect of ourselves did my students and I need to break apart for our creativity to continue?

"If you'd done more research," Luke said, "you'd know that almost all observation is done from here and through remote links from other locations." He scoped the control room, otherwise known as the Readout Room, with camera-sharp focus as if documenting every nook and cranny for future reference. "It searches for planets and spectra of supernovae."

Codi was chewing gum, something I'd asked the students not to do on this trip. She worked the synthetic wad of rubber, her teeth, jaw, and tongue twisting, pulling, *smack, smack, pop, pop.* "Uh, for the sake of those less inclined" —she gestured toward Angelina and Tessa— "would you mind defining supernovae, please?"

Luke paused from his fevered inspection of the room long enough to appeal to Ron Ardis for help. "Your call."

"I'm sure your definition would top mine," Ron said, observing Luke with the pleasure of someone who'd recognized a like mind. "Want to give it a try?"

Luke re-positioned his glasses on the bridge of his nose. "Even you might find this interesting, Angelina."

She shrugged, gaze fixed on the floor. "I doubt it."

"A supernova is when a star dies."

Tessa wailed. "That's awful."

Codi rolled her eyes. "Some scientist you'd make, Tessa."

"I don't want to be a scientist which sort of makes this trip a waste for me."

Luke hurried on. "Just like with people, stars are born, live, and die, except a star's death is faster, more violent, and more beautiful."

Another wail from Tessa. "Jeez, Luke. You call death beautiful?"

"Consider it a form of recycling. We were born from all the explosive material that comes from supernovae."

Codi snorted. "Tessa was born because her mom and dad got it on, Luke. What's the matter, you flunk Sex Ed?"

Luke's gaze darted to Ron Ardis, then to me. I shrugged, enjoying the show.

"The elements Tessa and her parents are made up of were born from all that explosive material," he said.

"Oh, I get it." Codi's customary tortured look took on one of near pleasure. "You mean, even before we were sea creatures and creepy crawlers."

Luke closed his eyes and heaved a long sigh.

"I knew you'd do fine without my input," Ron said, his grin similar to that of his son.

But Luke wasn't ready to give up the floor. "Supernovae explosions are rare in our own galaxy. The last one exploded about four hundred years ago, but they've been seen in other galaxies, like the one in 1987."

Though aware of Luke's capacity for processing incredible amounts of information, his grasp of the universe still amazed me.

Angelina held up both hands, fingers spread, to inspect the glittery pink polish on her nails. "So, we're made of stardust."

Luke's glasses slid to the tip of his nose. "If you're thinking of the fairy dust Tinker Bell spreads around, you better think again."

Tessa directed her attention to me. "Do we have to stay with the group, Ms. Veil, or can we go to the gift shop to browse?"

"The gift shop is quite a distance from here," I warned. "And it's cold outside, so—"

"Hey!" Codi jabbed a finger at Luke. "Just because these dinosaur telescopes don't turn Angelina and Tessa on, doesn't mean they're stupid little girls."

Angelina brightened at the compliment. I, on the other hand, felt stunned. I hadn't pictured Codi as a defender of her own sex.

"Tell them, Angelina," Codi said.

I didn't expect Angelina to comply but was again surprised. "I want to study ways to cure illness and disease, so don't think I'm a starry-eyed fool."

Jason laughed so hard I thought he would lose his footing, while Luke looked like he might implode. Ethan and Shawn said nothing, only stared at Angelina as if she'd metamorphosed from angel to earthbound human in front of their eyes.

"Off to the gift shop," I said, nodding to Ron Ardis. "Anyone besides Angelina and Tessa want to come along? It's at least a ten-minute walk…"

"I'm good," Codi said. "I like this place."

I liked the place, too, but my job was to allow each student to follow his or her own motivation—minus the gum. I pointed at Codi's mouth and held out my hand. Our eyes locked. Then she did something she hadn't done since my first day subbing in Ms. Goldsberry's class—tweeted my brain. *Gum rules suck and you know it.*

I tweeted back. *Humor me.*

Ms. Veil, I really, really need something to chew on. For stress.

I hesitated. Gum was a better tension reliever than many other choices available to her. Was she truly stressed or just using that as a rule-breaking excuse?

Before I could decide yea or nay, she moved deeper into my head and provided me with a little demo of the mood she was in. Sadness struck with such force that my first thought was to curl into a ball and cry. That not being an option, I craved another form of relief, anything to remove this dizzying, dark weight of despair. Afraid to close my eyes, afraid of what I might see, I refocused on Codi through my tears. *I'm so very sorry.*

She wadded up her gum and dropped it into my hand. *It wasn't helping much, anyway.*

The sadness evaporated, and I nearly cried out in relief. *Is there anything I can do?*

She smiled. *It helps that you know.*

I wanted to cradle her in my arms, rock her, comfort her.

She took a step back. *Thanks, but no thanks.*

While processing my new respect for this brave, stoic girl, I pressed her gum into a piece of paper from inside my leather pouch and gestured for Angelina and Tessa to follow me to the door.

Luke turned to Ron Ardis with a question about black holes. No doubt, they'd soon be discussing parallel universes and the harmonic relationships between planets.

"The stars and planets are all so far away," Angelina said in her defense as we headed for the exit of the domed building housing the Shane telescope.

Once again, I recalled something Ron Ardis's had said the day he'd visited my classroom. "Newton and Darwin's cosmic perspective sounds meaningless, blind, and purposeless. We have to believe there's more."

The intensity of Angelina's sigh revealed deep emotion. "The observatory makes me wonder about God and about where we go after we die. And I just don't want to think about that right now."

"I read that they buried James Lick at the base of the Great Lick Refractor," Tessa said, following Angelina like a shadow.

Angelina halted, and Tessa nearly collided into her. "You mean, the refractor in the main observatory where we're headed?"

Before Tessa could answer, Angelina dashed out the door.

"Me and my big mouth," Tessa said before hurrying after her.

I quickened my pace and followed the girls. It was freezing outside at 4,200 feet. Windy. Nasty. The dome emitted an eerie groan as it rotated to keep its opening centered above the slowly moving telescope inside.

"Angelina," I called, trying to divert her attention from James Lick's gravesite. "I'm sure there are some really cool things in the gift shop."

She continued as though running a marathon, with me following, huffing and puffing like an old lady with limited heart and lung capacity.

She and Tessa reached the main observatory before I did, but waited long enough to hold the door for me before sprinting through the center hall into the east vestibule and veering to the right. I followed at a more leisurely pace, noting the observatory office next to the center hall before following the two budding athletes into the long southern corridor. We passed celestial pictures on the walls and a series of interconnecting doorways before reaching the south dome. Angelina signaled for me to follow, then tripped lightly down a staircase leading to a basement. She'd definitely done her floor-plan research before our trip.

When I finally caught up to my charges, they stood in front of a placard that read: *Here lies the body of James Lick.* A soft light shone from above, with a bouquet of fresh flowers underneath. I experienced a moment of vertigo as I stared at the inscription, hoping Angelina would tire soon and concede to our original plan.

Instead, she began to shake.

"Oh, oh," Tessa said. "She's tuning in."

I nodded, knowing what Tessa meant. I'd been there myself, encountering a reality only a thin veil beyond our own. But it felt weird standing on the outside looking in.

"So far in life, I have borne my yoke patiently," Angelina said in a voice that sounded strange, as if she were playacting on stage, "and I will not shirk my duty now."

"She's quoting James Lick," Tessa said.

"She probably looked it up on the Internet."

"Nope. She hears him."

The surrounding space turned refrigerator cold, and I shivered. Angelina would need my support when she re-entered the world of the ordinary, currently a dreary place, over the bones of the observatory's dead benefactor.

I will not shirk my duty now. A good reminder that I was responsible for the well-being and safety of the students I had accompanied here.

I waited for Angelina to turn for my help in case of dizziness or confusion. Instead, she slumped at our feet.

"Damn." I dropped to my knees and reached for her wrist to check her pulse.

Tessa blocked my hand. "Not yet."

She turned Angelina onto her back and knelt next to her, then floated her hands over her friend's throat, chest, and belly, pausing a few seconds after each position change.

Taut with uncertainty, I reined in my urge to react in some way. It was my job, not Tessa's, to keep Angelina safe. Yet here I sat, butt on heels, hands on thighs, allowing a thirteen-year-old to take charge.

"Don't worry," Tessa whispered. "She's going to be okay."

I couldn't decide if responding with calm instead of reacting out of fear was the best way to go, or just a plain cop-out. My gut told me to have faith in Tessa, my mind told me otherwise. The option that made most sense was to call 911 from the observatory office. I stood. Dear God, what if they didn't have ambulance service way up here? Even so, with narrow and twisty Mt. Hamilton Road, it could take hours for the responders to arrive. Maybe they had on-site emergency staff.

"Ms. Veil," Tessa said.

Figuring it was okay to touch Angelina now, I bent down to check her pulse and breathing. Both seemed normal.

"Ms. Veil," Tessa repeated.

I looked at her, eyes blurred with worry. "Yes."

"If you're serious about us believing in ourselves and applying what we know, you have to believe in us, too."

Damn. Another student reminding me to practice what I preached. "Jason said Angelina was" —I halted as if voicing the word *dying* would make it true. "This could be a medical emergency, Tessa. We can't treat it as a minor incident unless we're certain there's no underlying cause."

"Does that mean you don't trust me, Ms. Veil?"

Trust? I was beginning to hate that word. It was one thing to entrust the students with tasks and responsibilities that had minimal consequences, quite another when it came to the big stuff. Dared I have faith in Tessa's assessment that Angelina would be okay? Dared I believe that somehow this thirteen-year-old could channel energy into her friend by touch and activate some kind of natural healing? How could I practice and inspire trust while focused on its limitations? How could I find the right balance?

"Do you trust Maya?" Tessa asked.

"What?"

"Maya says Angelina will be okay."

Maya? The mention of my sister's name caused my breathing to became labored. Mucus built up in my nose and throat, making it hard to swallow. "I tried to trust Maya. I tried to believe she'd do the right thing. And you know what? She died. Instead of listening to me, she died."

"Angelina fainted because of overstimulation and dehydration," Tessa said. "Look, she's coming to."

"Thank God."

Tessa helped Angelina rise into a sitting position, then asked, "Do you mind if I head for the gift shop?"

I shook my head, wondering why she was abandoning us.

Until I saw her tears.

"I'll buy Angelina some bottled water," she said. Then before heading for the stairs to the long hall, she added, "Maya's life wasn't yours to live."

No sooner had Tessa disappeared than Angelina asked, "What happened?"

"You passed out."

She rubbed her forehead and shivered.

"Are you okay to stand?"

She gave me a faraway look as if caught between worlds. "I went to the stars, Ms. Veil. They were inside of me, and I was inside of them, glowing in billions of galaxies. It was better than seeing them through a telescope. Much better. I didn't want to come back, but Tessa..." She looked around and blinked, then reached for my hand.

With more effort on my part than hers, she rose to her feet. "Do you feel well enough to make it to the gift shop?" I asked. "Tessa went to buy you some water."

"We never die," she said.

I hugged her. It was time to face an uncomfortable truth. Trust would cost my gifted students and me in unforeseen ways. But without it, we'd continue to avoid risks and question our decisions. We had to accept our fallibility and the fallibility of others, which meant letting go of control and allowing for mistakes.

Trust is a journey. It doesn't come easily. And it doesn't come free.

Chapter Twenty-six

B Y THE TIME RON Ardis, Codi, and the boys met us at the gift shop, Angelina had made what appeared to be a full recovery from her fainting spell. Hydrated by the bottle of water Tessa had provided, her face glowed and her eyes sparkled. Only Shawn, who'd been markedly quiet during the trip, looked at Angelina with a frown. She giggled and held up a T-shirt with an imprint of the Lick Observatory on front. "This would be perfect for Luke, don't you think?" Shawn glanced at me and gave a slight nod. He knew something was up. Of course, he did.

Meanwhile, Codi, Luke, and Ethan were inundating Tessa with information about the Shane telescope she'd missed due to her early departure.

"It's a reflector, not a refractor," Codi snapped during Ethan's animated discourse about how the Shane telescope helped discover planets outside our solar system.

"Yeah," Ethan said, nodding like a bobble-head doll.

In the seconds it took Tessa to puff air through her lips as if to say, *No one gets that I don't care*, Ethan's attention switched to an assortment of astronomical photographs stacked on a table nearby. He picked up a picture of a supernova and checked the back for a price.

The next aisle over, Jason and his father were examining a chart featuring the many posters available for sale. I favored the one depicting before and after images of the Supernova 1987A. Jason, however, chose one titled *Crab Supernova Remnant*. "I can see why you like this cosmic stuff, Dad. It sort of gives you a wider perspective." What was going on here? Father reaching out to son? Son reaching out to father? A little of both? Had they dodged the emotional and attitudinal hot buttons that undermined their relationship via a common interest in cosmology? If so, for how long?

Aware that I had witnessed the father and son moment, Ron winked at me. I gave him a thumbs up and turned my attention back to the rest of the students.

After locating Luke, Shawn, and Ethan at the cash register with their merchandise, I discovered that the girls had taken off without notice. It only took seconds for me to deduce where they'd gone. I informed Ron of where I was headed and, after a few stops to catch my breath, found the delinquents in the basement huddled around the placard commemorating James Lick. Fearing a repeat performance of earlier, I hurried forward.

On my approach, Codi said, "Angelina's cured."

The word *cured* stopped me dead.

"Tessa's got the touch," Codi said, pulling her leather moto jacket more tightly around her.

I glanced at Tessa and felt an odd pain in my chest, unable to determine if this was good news or bad.

"If my cancer's gone," Angelina said, "I'm going to become an oncologist."

Cancer? The sound of footsteps and male voices coming from the stairs to the basement kept me from asking why no one had notified me of her disease.

"What're you guys doing?" Jason called from a short distance away.

Angelina rubbed her forehead and quoted James Lick as she had earlier. "'So far in life, I have borne my yoke patiently, and I will not shirk my duty now.'"

Ron halted on hearing her words.

"Angelina hears stuff," Jason told him.

"Probably a quote she read somewhere," he said.

"Nope." Jason looked at Angelina with the pride of being friends with such an extraordinary human being. "She sees and hears dead people."

After a quick glance at me, Ron looked away, probably struck by the compassion in my eyes. No matter how hard you try, it's almost impossible to comprehend that some people can see and hear things you can't.

"How about you?" he asked his son.

Jason waved his hands as if warding off flies. "Nah."

Ron closed his eyes and released his breath.

🕷 🕷 🕷

I lagged during our walk back to the minivan, giving my students time and space to absorb and share what they'd experienced during our first and likely last excursion from the classroom. Tessa giggled and Codi jabbed her in the side as they tottered along, oblivious to the frigid temperature that had me longing for the protection of wool socks, snow pants, and full-finger gloves. Shawn walked alongside the girls, observing them in silence.

"I figured out what I want to be when I grow up," Angelina said, skipping backwards in front of her friends. She looked more the angel than ever, rosy cheeks, full lips, plaited hair. All she lacked were the wings.

Though out pacing his classmates by at least six feet, Luke had no difficulty following their conversation. "I hope it has nothing to do with astronomy or cosmology," he called over his shoulder.

Codi snickered.

Luke turned and gave her a reproving look.

"What?" she asked, all innocence.

"How'd you decide?" Luke asked, ignoring Codi.

Shawn's focus on Angelina sharpened.

"A little help from a friend," Angelina said, pulling the Pandora bracelet from her wrist and tossing it to Tessa.

Tessa caught the bracelet before swinging her gaze to Angelina. "You're going to tell?"

144

"Shush," Codi said.

"Tell what?" Somehow Ethan had kept pace with his friends without lifting his gaze from the astronomical photos he held.

"We better get a move on," Ron said on reaching the minivan. "We've been darn lucky with the weather, but the road still gets treacherous after dark."

Getting out of here before nightfall was an excellent idea. My bones had turned into ice, not only due to the fifty-degree temperature and wind gusts but also the strange happenings beneath the Lick Observatory telescope.

Had Angelina communicated with James Lick or had she picked up thoughts left behind from another time by someone long dead— thoughts now part of the web surrounding the living?

More importantly, and just as incomprehensible, had she been cured?

Chapter Twenty-seven

MONDAY WOULD BE PRESIDENTS' Day, followed by mid-term break, so I had ten guilt-free days to spend with Morgan and Joshua. When I arrived at the farm, however, Morgan's broad chest and capable hands were covered with manure and blood. He beamed at me from behind a calving cow. "She's having trouble, so I'm helping her along."

I looked on, feeling frustrated and neglected. Then, somewhere between the cow's blares and Morgan's encouraging words—"Come on girl, push. You're doing fine" —I heard a chant in my head. *Thought equals form, mind manifests through form.* Frustration turned into pride. My sweet, erotic lover was a cow doctor, a self-taught vet, and he was comforting this large animal with his gentle hands and softly spoken words, "It's okay, girl, you can do it."

While the cow pushed and blared, relaxed and shivered, my eyes burned. Five minutes, ten. "Come on girl," I whispered. A nose. The head. "Good girl, good girl."

The calf slid from its mother's birth canal in a warm, steamy gush and landed on a soft bed of straw.

"Oh my God." I couldn't look away. Instead of feeling revulsion at the afterbirth dangling from the cow's behind and seeing her turn and lick the birth fluids from her calf, I realized I was witnessing a miracle. The calf shook its head, wet ears slapping, then gave a little kick.

"In thirty minutes, he'll be licked clean," Morgan said. "Then he'll try to stand."

"So soon?"

"He needs to nurse within the first four hours after birth. That's when his mother produces colostrum with a heavy dose of antibodies to protect him from disease."

"Poor thing."

Morgan laughed. "After a few tries, encouraged by his mother's licking, he'll find his feet and you'll see him switching his tail in contentment." Morgan stripped off his elbow-length synthetic gloves and dropped them into a bucket. "You okay?"

I wiped my eyes with the sleeve of my jacket, thinking about the great effort needed for a butterfly to pass through the tiny opening of its cocoon, pushing fluid from its body into its wings. Without struggle, it wouldn't be able to fly. "That was beautiful."

"Kind of bloody and smelly," he said, looking at his hands.

"It smells of the earth, natural and therefore beautiful."

He grinned. "Tell me that in a year."

"I won't change my mind."

"Wait until it's time to wash my coveralls." He picked up the bucket and exited the maternity corral through a steel gate.

"That's what the heavy-duty washer in our utility room will be for. Drop the dirty clothes in, and it'll take care of the rest."

"Greenhorn."

"I may be a city girl, but I know what I like."

He peered at me from below the bill of his John Deere logo cap, then shook his head and walked to an outdoor faucet where he stripped off his coveralls and rinsed his hands. "How about a hug?"

I stepped into his embrace, but before the quick squeeze could turn into a full-fledged cuddle, small hands clasped me from behind. "Marjorie, Marjorie."

The tightening of Morgan's arms revealed a reluctance to let me go, but the choice wasn't his. Or mine. Joshua tugged on my sleeve, impatient with my slow response to his cuteness. "Marjorie!"

I backed out of Morgan's arms and turned. "Sweetie. I swear, you've grown another inch since I last saw you." It had only been a week. And he'd been in a hospital bed, but still…

Joshua stretched to his full height, all four feet, nine inches. I thought of Ethan, who was small for his age. "You're only seven and you're almost as tall as one of the thirteen-year-olds in my class."

He hugged my middle.

Ten days. Ten days of this. And then?

"Oma says breakfast is waiting," he said.

Dutch pancakes. Bacon. Sausage. My stomach grumbled at the thought of Carla's, aka Oma's, hearty breakfast.

"Go on while I finish up," Morgan said.

Gabriel, who'd dashed out of his carrier on our arrival, appeared at our feet as if he'd slipped through one of those invisible portals Jason had access to. He twined himself around Joshua's legs and purred. Joshua bent down to pet him— "Hey there, buddy" — before peering at the maternity corral with a frown. "Was it a heifer or bull calf?"

"Bull calf, fourth one this week," Morgan said.

Joshua shook his head. "Another one for sale."

"Sale? When?" I asked, hurting for the calf and its mother.

Morgan exchanged a glance with Joshua. "Some parts of farming aren't pretty."

"When?" I repeated, knowing the news wouldn't be to my liking.

Morgan's dimples deepened to where I could slip dimes into them and they'd hold. "If I kept every bull calf born on this farm, we'd be out of business in no time. They're expensive to feed and serve no purpose."

"How about for breeding?" I asked.

"I buy sires from outside the herd to prevent interbreeding." Morgan was kind enough not to mention this should have been a no-brainer. He smiled at my look of embarrassment. "The question gets asked a lot."

"So, bull calves don't earn their keep," I said, stating the obvious and wishing it weren't so.

Morgan shifted his feet as though expecting the next question most greenhorns ask: "What happens to them after they're sold?"

Instead, I turned to Joshua. "Come on, kiddo, breakfast is waiting."

Some aspects of farming, like nature, aren't pretty. I would have to accept the good and adjust to what I couldn't change, or marry someone else.

And that was unthinkable.

🕷 🕷 🕷

Our future home was taking form. The plumbing was in and the walls had been sheet-rocked, textured, and were ready to prime. During breaks between chores, Morgan, Joshua, and I drove to the hardware store for supplies. The rest of the time, we sanded, vacuumed, and painted. "Getting tired?" Morgan asked Wednesday afternoon.

"It's giving us a chance to catch up," I said, withholding the part about it also giving me a chance to keep thoughts of my West Coast students at bay.

By the look in Morgan's eyes, I sensed he craved some alone time to fuel the passion that had been simmering between us for days. "We need an outing," he said.

Joshua dropped his paint brush and clapped his hands. White paint streaked his face, clothes, and hair. Gabriel, on the other hand, appeared paint free and impeccably groomed.

A wink from Morgan before he suggested a trip to the woods for a picnic the following day. "But tonight, I'm taking Marjorie out to dinner."

"Someplace fancy?" Joshua wanted to know.

I met Morgan's intimate green gaze; one that spoke an inclusive language I'd come to understand and hold close to my heart. "You bet. She'll have to get all gussied up."

"In a dress and high heels?" Joshua asked, his eyes wide as a fawn's.

"I hope so."

And gussy up I did. At least the best I could, considering I was using someone else's facilities. Fortunately, Carla didn't begrudge me the time and privacy needed to accomplish the task. "Go make yourself gorgeous," she said with a wistful look in her eyes.

One would have to be blind to miss the flirtation between Morgan's parents each day: a pat on the rear; a quick peck on the cheek; a hug; a kiss blown into the air. Which bode well for Morgan and me. Kids learn from their parents.

Morgan's hands clung to my behind like magnets after I entered the kitchen in my little black dress and spiked heels. Yes, even in front of his family. I, on the other hand, showed about as much passion as a fish, uncomfortable with displaying my ardor in front of an audience. But later, when we were alone, I would prove that some fish have warm blood and can reach some high body temperatures.

After that, when Morgan and I were in a more talkative mood, I would tell him about my struggles at West Coast Middle School. He would hold me tight and tell me to resign, that I needn't go through such heartache and he'd take care of me. I would answer no, as he knew I would, and he'd say he loved me. I'd tell him I loved him back. Then we would kiss, secure in each other's arms. That's what lay ahead once we were married, and that's what I wanted. But first I had a job to complete. Struggle was a natural part of growth. It would help strengthen my wings.

🕷 🕷 🕷

I took a trip to the woods for a picnic all right. Alone.

Morgan had an emergency in the milk barn, involving something as trivial as a worn-out bolt. That's how it is on a farm. Minor break downs often turn major and take hours to repair. Morgan called it putting out fires.

Joshua received a last-minute invitation to join his cousins for youth hockey practice.

Did their desertion upset me? Sure. But it also eased the guilt I felt at being absent from their lives for weeks at a time. I turned down Morgan's offer to saddle a horse for me, not about to be caught alone with such a large animal, regardless of how docile Morgan claimed her to be. I also turned down the use of the farm pickup truck and ATV. I preferred walking the four miles to the woods, where I would hang out for a while, get back on track.

My first thought on entering the woods was: *It's alive.* I saw squirrels and cottontails and an occasional deer. I saw blackbirds and hawks, vultures and crows. I heard harsh *checks* and high *tee-eeks*, emphatic *kee-uks* and loud descending *caws*. I smelled musty vegetation and damp soil. My second thought was: *I'm part of this. My root. My anchor.*

When I reached the eight-hundred-year-old oak Morgan had introduced me to on my last visit, I sat below its massive branches and relaxed into a yoga pose that felt as natural as the setting. I closed my eyes and took deep breaths, absorbing the positive vibes rippling around me in rotating columns like the tame tornado that had whisked Dorothy to Oz. After what could have been minutes or could have been hours, in that altered state where the perception of time is malleable and illusive, I opened my eyes. Time to get real, admit I was mad.

Not at Morgan and Joshua, but at Dr. Matt and Charles Lacoste. For withholding their support from the gifted students who needed it. Dr. Matt had put me in charge of seven fragile, thirteen-year-olds, grappling with chaos and pain. He'd claimed that I came highly recommended by two people whose opinions he valued, that he'd been waiting for the right teacher—me—qualified in ways not taught in a credential program or learned through classroom experience. I'd accepted the challenge, jumped right in with both feet. And then… Nothing. A black hole so dense even light couldn't escape its gravitational pull. Okay, so maybe that was an exaggeration. I would only be at West Coast until June, so Dr. Matt wasn't likely to fire me. But still… Seven kids and their futures were at stake here. While prodding them onto paths unknown, I had no guarantee they'd find their way home.

Where should I go from here? Whom could I call on for advice?

Granny Max? What for? To bake more cookies? Ron Ardis? Hell no. From what I'd observed during our field trip to the James Lick Observatory, his son's gifts, and those of his fellow students, scared the bejesus out of him. Cosmologist or not, he was still a scientist with a reputation to uphold. How about Dr. Tony Mendez? Ha. I could already predict the outcome. "Trust your gut," he'd say.

I picked up the insulated bag containing my uneaten lunch and squared my shoulders, decision made.

No more playing it safe.

Chapter Twenty-eight

ON MY FIRST DAY back at school, I had a visitor. And it wasn't Dr. Matt.

After my initial shock at finding Charles Lacoste wandering about in my classroom, I asked, "How'd you get in here?"

He eyed me in a way I thought rather predatory, making me wonder what I had that he wanted. A classroom with a view? "Manuel let me in."

I shook my head.

"The custodian," he said.

"I know who Manuel is. The question is why?"

"Because I asked him to."

"I figured that much." I tried not to let my impatience show. "Why did you want to come in?"

"It was cold outside."

"Why didn't you wait until you knew I'd be here?"

"Because I wanted to talk to you before you became distracted."

He handled the students' ceramic pieces and navigated the classroom as if it were his instead of mine. I wondered how he'd feel if the situation were reversed. Not happy, was my guess. I dropped my briefcase onto my desk and walked to the thermostat to turn up the heat. "I'd offer you refreshments, but you caught me by surprise, coming in unannounced and all."

"That's all right." He hiked up his pants, adjusted his shirt, and said no more.

I took a seat behind my desk. Lacoste walked to the window and looked out. I removed papers from my briefcase and sorted them into neat piles.

He turned. "I'm here to warn you."

His small unblinking eyes reminded me of *Snake Eyes*, the outcome of rolling a single pip on each die, the lowest possible roll, winner or loser depending on the game. But dice weren't part of this game and his opinion was not my law.

"I filed a complaint with Dr. Matt about your incompetence for the job."

Okaay. At least he hadn't insisted on anonymity which meant no lying-in-wait for the enemy. The enemy resided within the school gates. "Thank you for letting me know."

The disappointment on Lacoste's face nearly made me smile. He probably thought I'd be more upset or deluge him with questions, but I wasn't about to ask him for one tiny detail. Deprived of this victory, he said, "As to the reason for my complaint" —he paused and, right on cue, my heart started hammering in my chest, a dead giveaway that I was falling right into his hands— "there are schools that cater to teachers like you, but this isn't one of them."

Something about me rubbed him the wrong way, but I didn't have the time or inclination to figure out what it was. "Oh?"

"That's it? Oh?" Lacoste regarded me in silence, his snake eyes probing.

About to tell him to march his pompous ass out of here and mind his own damn business, I heard a whisper. *Treat him with care.* Maya, back to haunt me, in her kind, thoughtful way. "I'd like to hear you out before I respond," I said.

He turned his back to me—again. "No offense, but the students in your care have the potential to become future scientists, doctors, lawyers, and leaders of this country. Therefore, they need prepping for the finest colleges. What you're doing here is taking precious time away from their studies. Menlo Park is the heart of Silicon Valley, headquarters of SRI International, home to software startups, biotech companies, venture capital companies, and high-tech workers. We smash atoms at SLAC. What more proof do you need that these kids must develop their mental skills to the max?"

"Much of what makes Silicon Valley a success involves the holistic thinking of the whole brain, not just left-brain skills," I said, sticking to my guns, though this was starting to sound more like a lecture than a debate. "I'm talking about intuition, creativity, and the power of the unconscious for breakthrough insights."

"These kids need to learn the cold, hard fact that they're not special. Encouraging them to play their way to success will land them in the unemployment line."

"Monetary security isn't everything," I said.

"Tell that to the poor."

Damn, I wished he'd turn around. "What about probing the deeper questions in life?"

"That's the job of their parents and the church."

"Many of their parents don't know the answers themselves."

"Do you?"

I heard a buzzing in my ears, as if something mean and angry were stuck inside. But to my surprise, a Novocain numbness came over me, not necessarily bad, not good either. Where does one draw the line between bending and fighting back? "No, but maybe through community and mutual need, we can learn to be comfortable in our own skins."

"You can't teach that."

Tempted to throw up my arms in frustration, I realized he might see my reflection in the window. *Hey, Maya. How long do I have to play nice?* She didn't answer. Never does when I'm being a smartass. Veronica, alive and well and never around, would encourage me to express my emotions, expose my wild side, the tactic I preferred about now. Revenge, or maybe just a good catfight, would be a lot more fun.

When Lacoste finally turned to face me, I gestured for him to continue. For one thing, I was still hearing that annoying buzzing in my ears, which meant Maya was still hanging around. For another, unless my shoulder angel—aka Maya—put words into my mouth, I had no idea how to proceed in my defense. How could I explain to him something I couldn't explain to myself? Should I tell him that all the knowledge in the world doesn't guarantee success and happiness, that I'd gotten the good grades and the resulting dream job, only to give it up to teach for a pittance, because dream jobs that offer nothing to live for, add up to nothing? Or would sparring with him do more harm than good?

My blank look must have egged him on, because Lacoste proceeded to berate me for the sake of the kids. "Dr. Matt took seven of our brightest and most indulged and troublesome students and put them into your care, which not only has me confused, but has the entire faculty fired up as well."

Not entire. Granny Max likes me.

"By your own admission, you're inexperienced, and, as I mentioned, you're unqualified as well."

The pencil sharpener started to whir, which put me on the alert. This was not Maya's doing. Not her style.

Lacoste ignored the wayward sharpener, so intense his concentration on taking me down. "Why don't you do the right thing and release these kids from this hairbrained experiment? I know Dr. Matt regrets having started the whole thing. He practically admitted as much at the staff meeting before term break when we voiced our concerns. Your contract doesn't end until June. However, if you quit, you can save yourself, Dr. Matt, and the kids a lot of trouble."

We voiced our concerns? How many faculty members had he turned against me? And why? What I offered was a little testing and allowance for mistakes, preparedness rather than prediction, and serendipitous exposure in a world that conspired against it.

Tables and chairs scraped and tapped on the linoleum floor. Books fell from the shelves.

"Earthquake!" Lacoste dropped to his knees and crawled under a table.

"No earthquake," I said.

"Duck! Cover! Hold!"

I couldn't help but chuckle. Some messages are so engrained in our psyche, they bypass common sense. If this were an earthquake, a lot more would be shifting and rolling than a few tables and chairs, and it would make more sense to skedaddle outdoors than duck, cover, and hold.

The tables and chairs stilled, as did the pencil sharpener, leaving the room eerily quiet. I waited for Lacoste to compose himself and come out from under the table. "My class is about to begin," I said, hearing screeches and laughter coming from the outside corridor.

Lacoste hit his head on the edge of the table before climbing to his feet. "Don't let them in!"

Too late. Jason and Shawn entered, their attention immediately zeroing in on the disheveled teacher. "Hey Mr. Lacoste," Jason said. "You don't look too good."

"Earthquake," he said, rubbing his head.

Jason and Shawn exchanged glances, and the table nearest Lacoste slid sideways like a walker on wheels. He jerked back and cursed. A chair lifted off the floor and held—one second, two—then dropped with a loud *thwack*. Lacoste looked at me, eyes wide. I felt sorry for him. Stuff like this isn't supposed to happen. It weakens our hold on sanity.

"Watch out," Shawn said just before a potted fern flew within a foot of Lacoste's head and crashed to the floor.

Lacoste screeched, "What the hell's going on?"

"Earthquake," Jason said before sitting down. He looked exhausted. The demonstration had cost him.

I smelled wet soil interspersed with melted beeswax, sad for the destroyed fern, sad for Lacoste, and sad for the kids and me. Lashing out would do nothing to help the situation. We needed to put our egos aside and make room for inspiration, creativity, and possibility.

"You're going to clean this mess up, I assume," I said to Jason.

"Sure, Ms. V, just for you."

Lacoste turned to Shawn as though deeming the principal's

nephew the only trustworthy person in the room. "What was that all about?"

"A lesson in metaphysics," Shawn said, straight-faced. "No offense, sir, but you have no idea what's going on here. And until you do" —he hesitated, likely aware there would be reprisals for what he was about to say— "I think you should leave Ms. Veil alone."

"Shawn," he said, with what appeared to be great restraint. "Your uncle agrees that Ms. Veil has to go, for your good and the good of the school."

"I doubt it," Shawn said.

Lacoste brushed the legs of his trousers and straightened to his full height, which didn't give him much over the kids.

Maya spoke again. *Treat him with care.*

Jason and Shawn swung toward me, eyes wide, mouths ajar, their gestures in perfect sync. *Who was that?*

Lacoste was oblivious to the silent interchange, still intent on pulling himself together.

Later, I mouthed, which seemed to satisfy them, though my guess was that Jason preferred to do the disheveled teacher—and his ego—more damage.

Codi breezed into the room and swung her backpack onto her table, unaware of what had just occurred. That is, until she saw the books and fern on the floor. "Whoa. What have we here?"

Shawn gestured toward Lacoste and grinned.

Lacoste noticed their exchange; a shame, because it made him mad. "If you think this is funny, you have another think coming."

Codi's eye roll came as no surprise. Jason dismissed him altogether. "What's on the agenda, Ms. Veil?"

Before Lacoste could say or do anything further, Ethan, Tessa, and Luke walked in.

"Where's Angelina?" I asked, feeling as though I'd just pulled on a jacket of ice.

"H-home," Tessa said, not meeting my eyes, gray little Tessa, back to being a shadow without her friend. After what happened at the Lick Observatory, this wasn't good news, but I dared not question her with Lacoste still hanging around, geared up to use anything I said or did against me.

It was time to start class. Surely, *now* he'd leave.

"I better go," he said, regarding the wall clock as if it kept some kind of mystical time. He glanced at Shawn on his way out. "I'll be seeing *you* in your uncle's office."

"I wouldn't count on it," Shawn said under his breath.

With Lacoste gone, I sank into my chair.

"What's with him?" Luke asked, his glasses askew.

Jason dumped the contents of his backpack onto the floor, looking for a pencil no doubt. "Dad says he's a pompous ass."

No one responded, so Luke said, "Oh," and dropped onto his seat. "What's up, Ms. Veil?"

I got up and closed the door. "First, I'd like to know where Angelina is, and then I want to talk to you about Maya."

Chapter Twenty-nine

"MAYA?" LUKE TOOK OFF his glasses and cleaned them with the tip of his multi-plaid shirt, the type of shirt made of carefully brushed flannel that won't scratch your lenses.

I stood in front of my desk and crossed my arms. "First Angelina. Then we'll get to Maya."

"I-I'm sorry," Tessa said.

"Sorry for what?" Bad news was coming at me so fast and from so many directions, I risked wrenching my neck in my attempts to dodge it.

Tessa began to cry. I handed her a tissue from the box on my desk. "Angelina told her parents t-that she was c-cured and t-that she wanted to go in for tests, and they're p-planning to-to call Dr. Matt to complain."

I'd sensed something like this would happen, so why the surprise? Had I expected Angelina's parents to wait for another round of test results before jumping to conclusions, or had I hoped for a miracle? "You were only trying to help a friend, which is what this class is all about, so there's nothing to be sorry for."

Tessa blew her nose then dropped her head onto the table, her hair spilling out like a platinum veil. "I d-don't want t-to get you f-fi-red."

Chest burning, I figured getting fired might not be such a bad thing.

"Uncle Matt shouldn't be disappointed in you," Shawn said. "You didn't do anything wrong. I told him so, but he wouldn't listen." Shawn's jaw jutted out in such an adult manner, he resembled the very man he was discussing. I half expected him to tug at his ear. "He listens to Mr. Lacoste, who's always talking crap about you."

"We want to help," Codi said. Black lips today. Kohl eyes. Spiked hair.

"I know." These kids were proving to be more than extraordinary. They'd become my helpers, my friends. One of my greatest fears was that I'd let them down. Instead of giving in to the urge to whimper like a child, I said, "How would you like to get to know my sister?"

"If you're t-talking about Maya, Angelina and I already have," Tessa said. "She's here practically every day. Sometimes, she…she even puts her hand on your shoulder."

The thought of Maya being in this room visible only to Angelina and Tessa hurt, as if the votive candles I'd placed on the tables for their consoling light were burning inside of me, consuming me like a sacrifice. "She started talking to me again," I said, "and today Jason and Shawn heard her, too."

All attention turned to Jason and Shawn. "You did?" Codi asked.

Jason cracked his knuckles. "I think so."

Shawn said nothing, only stared at the votives flickering on the tabletops.

"What do you mean, you think so?" Codi said. "Either you heard her or you didn't."

"I don't know if it was Maya," Jason said.

"What did she say," Ethan asked.

"To treat Mr. Lacoste with care."

Codi peered out the window as though seeking wisdom from the trees; their branches, boughs, and twigs twisting and swaying as if trying to speak. "Next, they'll be blaming us for all the bad stuff."

"Like the witches in Salem." Luke's eyes appeared huge, magnified by the thick lenses of his glasses.

"It's sort of h-happening already," Tessa said. "Like Angelina's p-parents blaming Ms. Veil for telling us to think things as possible,

161

when they, of all people, sh-should know better. Angelina's one of us, but…but they still believe we're—"

"Freaks," Jason finished for her.

"And witches," Codi said. "So, quit ticking them off, Jason."

"Okay, I get the point," he said, "So what *can* we do with our powers besides get into trouble?"

"Help others," I said.

"How?" This from Shawn, who'd faded into his surroundings again.

"Like Tessa did with Angelina, but subtler."

"You mean less sneaky?" Jason asked, wolf eyes squinting.

"She means unnoticed," Codi said. "Tessa should've cured Angelina slowly instead of all at once."

Tessa looked offended, and I couldn't blame her. She'd done what she had out of concern for a friend. "I couldn't help it," she wailed. "When I-I get like that, I lose control."

"Cork it," Jason said, then backtracked when he saw her mouth drop. "I didn't mean for you to shut up, Tessa, but to control your powers."

"Like you do?" Codi asked. Beneath all that pasty makeup, her skin had an olive tone, what my mother called a natural tan. What a shame she went to so much trouble to cover it up.

No answer from Jason, distracted as he was by the smile on Tessa's face, a radiant combination of gratitude and renewed confidence—wallflower to sunflower.

"You need to cork it, too," Codi said, regaining Jason's attention.

"How about you?" he rallied.

"I cork my abilities all the time. Otherwise, I'd go crazy."

Sensing an argument brewing, I said. "We need an expert. Sort of like a trainer."

"I thought that was your job," Ethan said.

"I'm still learning, like you. In fact, I only discovered my powers during the past eleven months, and I'm willing to bet you discovered yours long before."

"Lot of good it's done us," Ethan grumbled.

"If your experience is like mine, you're probably lonely and scared and trying to cover up your gifts. What we need is someone to teach us what to do."

"Like who?" Jason asked.

The lesson had veered off course again, therefore so did my plan. "A dear friend."

"Your sister's dead." Ethan's head bobbed as though attached to his shoulders by a spring. "She wouldn't understand."

"You'd be surprised. But I wasn't talking about Maya."

They waited for me to continue, eyes flat, as though doubting anyone could help them. And who could blame them? With all our scientific discoveries, the human mind still remains a mystery and psychic abilities are still delegated to charlatans and writers of fantasy.

"I have this friend who's a transpersonal psychologist. He's also a friend of Dr. Matt's, which means I might be able get his permission to—"

"So, you admit we're crazy," Jason said.

Before I could answer, Luke popped in. "I've already been to a psychologist. He said I have ADHD, and he referred me to a psychiatrist, who put me on Ritalin, which numbed me out, big time. I couldn't sleep at night, and my skin got all swollen and itchy. When I found out Ritalin decreases blood flow to the brain, I told my parents and they took me off. Who knows how many of my brain cells were killed? Mom finally bought me a small ball to squeeze to help me concentrate, but Mr. Lacoste swiped it and sent me to the guidance office for disruption."

"You've still got plenty of brain cells," Codi said, "but I get what you mean. Psychiatrists mess with your head. Mine put me on Cylert. My teachers loved it."

"Getting professional help means you're smart, not crazy," Shawn said. "At least that's what my mother says. She's been trying to get Dad to go for years." He grimaced as though regretting what he'd just revealed.

"Dr. Mendez doesn't prescribe medication," I said.

"What makes you so sure?" Luke asked.

"Because he's a psychologist, not a psychiatrist, and sees altered states of consciousness as spiritual emergencies rather than manifestations of illness."

An embarrassing silence descended over the room.

"I agree with Shawn's mom," I said. "Getting help is smart, as long as you're careful which doctor you choose. In our case, that means someone trained in metaphysics as well as human behavior. Dr. Mendez believes in supporting rather than suppressing non-ordinary states of consciousness. He considers them spiritual openings."

More silence.

I leaned against my desk. "Okay, I get it." We would have to continue doing things on our own, which I had hoped to avoid.

The lights dimmed and the tables began to shake.

"Jason," Codi snapped. "Cut it out."

He looked confused, even frightened. "It wasn't me."

"Then who?" she asked.

Me.

"Maya," I whispered.

For the first time since she'd died, I saw my sister as she'd appeared when we first met: arms outstretched in welcome, face the mirror image of mine—except for the puckered red skin disfiguring her right cheek.

"Oh, dear God," I said. And then instead of bursting into tears, I got mad. "Don't you dare fade out on me again."

Maya smiled and did just that.

"Maya!"

"She s-says you know what to do," Tessa said.

"But I don't."

The way the six Indigos stared at me you'd think I was trying to beat a traffic ticket.

"What?" I asked

"T-tell us about Maya," Tessa urged.

"It can't be all that easy for her spirit to keep hanging around," Luke said. "She must have a good reason. Did you have unfinished business before she died?"

"Well, yeah," I said, *like twenty-nine-years-worth*. "Maya told me she would reach out to me after she was gone."

"Did you believe her?"

With my mother haunting me from the grave, I knew it was possible, but I didn't know if Maya could break through. "Yes."

"What was the last thing she said to you before she died?"

"What is this, an inquisition?"

"Just answer the question, please." Luke sounded like the prosecutor in a criminal trial accusing me of breaking the law.

"She said to love him."

"Love who?"

"The plastic surgeon who removed the birthmark on her face. The birthmark she treasured, the birthmark that gave her the power to heal herself and others, the birthmark that gave her life meaning. She wanted me to get in touch with my anger, rage, and hate, so I could be whole again. She said that when the time was right, I'd know what to do."

"Maybe the right time is now," Luke suggested.

"She told me to cry every time I experienced a little death in my life," I said, finding it hard to stop venting now that I'd cracked open the door to my past.

"Like now?" Luke asked.

"Sorry, my friend, I never cry."

"I think she wants to teach you about forgiveness and trust," Tessa said.

"You know what the priest said at her funeral?" My voice vibrated with pent up emotion. "That Maya's contribution to society took humility, inner strength, and surrender. He said she was humble enough to know that one needn't be perfect to make a difference and that her deepest demonstration of inner strength was her love.

'Look at love long enough,' he said, 'and you will become lovely.' Then he told us that when Maya was stuck, when nothing seemed to be moving along, when people weren't doing what she wanted, she took herself out of the way, and miracle of miracles, things always seemed to work out fine. 'The goal of life is not to win,' he said, 'but to play the game with love.' I'd been searching for Monarchs since my arrival in Pacific Grove and, at Maya's funeral, there they were, clouds of them, veiling the setting sun, their wings quivering and reflecting the fading light like precious jewels. They'd escaped their cocoons, just like Maya."

"I thought you never cried," Jason said.

"Shut up," I said.

Chapter Thirty

STARTING THE NEXT DAY, instead of concentrating on the outcome of my work, which I couldn't measure anyway, I would concentrate on the work itself. And today that meant visiting the nature area.

"You're kidding, right," Codi said, eyeing the span of windows that revealed bare trees swaying under overcast skies. She clasped both arms over her thinly clad body and shivered. "It's frigging cold out there." I took in her *Alice in Chains* T-shirt—cut to hang off her right shoulder—her pinstriped cotton pants, and black canvas sneakers. Though stylish, in a gothic way, her outfit offered no thermal protection for a cold February afternoon.

I pointed to the rack of coats I'd set up for such an occasion. "Ugh," she squealed, her face contorting dramatically. She had the facial structure and skin texture of a model, from the apples and hollows of her cheeks to the tip of her perfectly rounded chin. With the right makeup, she could melt seamlessly into an incarnation of myriad characters from Snow White to Elvira. Today, however, she looked more like one of the walking dead, with charcoal shadow and black liner accentuating her eyes. "Are they from *Goodwill?* I'm no homeless person."

"Go out there without a coat and you'll feel like one," I said.

"Codi, Codi," Jason tutted. "You're so out of touch. Second-hand stores stock some great funeral vintage."

She regarded his J. Crew jacket, linen shirt, and broken-in chinos with the mouth-pursed disdain of a fashion critic. "As if *you'd* know."

"Pretend you're dressing up for Halloween," I said.

She sorted through the coats with outstretched hands as if staving off the cooties she imagined inhabited there. She squinted, stepped closer, sniffed the fabric. "Hey, these aren't half bad."

Thinning out my closet had felt good, and my mother, believing she was helping to clothe the poor, had been equally generous.

Codi squealed and held up a black trench coat. "I've been wanting one of these."

Giggles followed as Tessa joined in the search.

"Look," Tessa said, holding up a yellow anorak. "It's from the Gap."

Yellow didn't suit her, not with her light blonde hair and pale blue eyes, but who was I to spoil her fun? I draped both of my female charges with a wool scarf—black for Codi, blue for Tessa—as my mother had when I was their age. Unlike me, however, they didn't seem to mind. The boys waited, arms crossed, heaving impatient sighs. Cold wasn't an issue for them. They wore so many layers they were more likely to burn up from the heat.

When we stepped through what to me had become the door to the magic kingdom, we were welcomed by a blast of cold air.

"Explore," I said. "Hands on. Hands dirty."

Codi and Tessa scurried off, screeching like banshees. Jason and Shawn followed at a more leisurely pace. Luke and Ethan, however, stayed put, eyeing their surroundings like astronauts on the moon's surface.

"Go," I said, shooing them with both hands. "Nature is full of missing information. Find it."

Ethan blinked and said something under his breath before venturing forth. Luke, however, stood firm. "Contact with the natural is called the eighth intelligence."

Impressed, as usual, by his encyclopedic knowledge on just about any subject, my thoughts wandered to my future adoptive son, Joshua, petting a newborn calf, swinging from trees into the Cosumnes River, vaulting over hay bales. Luke needed to experience life outside of his know-it-all state of mind and learn to trust his inner guidance.

"Being out here is like being in a giant Wi-Fi zone," he said, "where you can plug into nature."

"Right, kiddo. So, plug in with both hands and feet. Nature is alive. Become part of it."

A smile. A salute. "Your wish is my command."

The nature area was wet and by most standards a mess. The paths were crude and uneven, not a manicured shrub in sight. Yet, the students acted like visitors to a foreign land, peeking behind bushes, scavenging anything that appeared remotely interesting, and climbing some of the sturdier trees. I let them play, yes play, something neglected these days by most teens and adults. Tessa scooped up pebble-sized rocks from a gravel path, held them to the light, and pocketed those that passed her inspection. Codi retrieved a small branch and twirled it like a baton. Shawn and Jason chose larger branches to use as swords. Luke appeared to be inspecting the variety in flora and fauna, and Ethan wandered about talking to himself.

Half an hour later I waved them in and instructed them to form a circle in a paved alcove between the brick wall of the classroom and a thicket of overgrown bottlebrush and pine. My charges breathed hard, and with every breath, clouds of moisture formed in front of their faces.

"Look what I found," Tessa said. She wore leather engineer boots today with her jeans tucked in, very Maya-like, except Maya would have worn a beaten-up military jacket instead of a yellow anorak. Tessa held five colored stones in her open palm. When I leaned in to inspect them, she closed her hand and snatched it away. "Guess what colors."

I started to answer but changed my mind. Though these kids weren't all capable of probing minds, they *could* communicate telepathically by sending out their thoughts. It was time they started using their gifts. *Yellow, white, black, and rust,* I said silently.

Tessa smiled.

My skin tingled. She'd heard me.

After dropping the pebbles into the pocket of her anorak, she held out her right hand. Scissor-sharp pain sliced through me when I saw the strawberry hemangiomas birthmark on her palm. The same shape and color of the birthmark that had disfigured Maya's face.

"Mom wants to have it removed," Tessa said.

Words couldn't pass the blockage in my throat. I wanted to kiss her hand and plead that she not allow it. *No. No. Look what happened to Maya when Dr. Shane Donovan tried to remove hers.*

But Tessa was way ahead of me. "Maya said we all have a right to our own beauty."

I swallowed hard and rubbed my eyes. Then why hadn't she practiced what she preached?

I knew you'd get around to the important stuff sooner or later, someone said.

Which of the six had spoken? Shawn sat, hands spread on knees. *You?* I asked, brows raised.

He gave nothing away, other than his silent response. *Good call.*

Birds gathered in the surrounding bushes and pines as if eager to witness the show. Their chatter took on a loud, serious bent, their chirps becoming shrieks. Even traffic sounds from the nearby street grew in intensity, horns honking, tires hissing. Clouds gathered; the sky darkened.

I'd know if I were an Indigo, wouldn't I? I asked silently.

The narrowing of Shawn's eyes. A surge of heat.

Most people don't realize they're Indigos, someone said. *Only that they don't fit into a nice neat box.*

Luke! I could tell by the way his words came out in lecture mode. *Grandstander!*

Ah, Codi. I closed my eyes, no longer concerned about who was speaking. I wanted to join in their experience, figure out how to help. Three and a half months until the end of my tenure here. *Three and a half months, three and a half months*, I repeated like a mantra, until I sensed a pull in my head. Colored squares formed inside my lids and shifted like pieces of glass in a kaleidoscope. I was light as air, floating through what appeared to be the warps and wefts of a cloth on a loom. I was the size of a molecule, the open weaves as large as doors. Soft pinks, blues, lavenders, and pale yellows swirled and shifted around me. Everything existed where it should be. No questions. Just right.

I'd experienced something similar last April while listening to Native American chants around a campfire in the Los Padres National Forest. Guided by the music, I'd entered a serene state of stillness with no separation between my physical and spiritual reality. I followed the drumbeat and journeyed out of my body, expanding and becoming less dense like warm air rising. The heavens and earth merged into a nacreous-like cloud, curling and uncurling in the semi-darkness, an iridescent gap appearing like a ladder between. As if drugged, I floated toward the thin white opening. The drumming stopped; the flute and chanting continued. And just as I was about to pass through the shimmering portal, I sensed a tug on my arm. I resisted. Another tug. *No!* Someone was blocking the closest I'd ever come to complete and total freedom. I opened my eyes, irritated, angry.

Joshua knelt next to me, his face the manifestation of love.

Now, again, I'd entered another dimension, and I didn't want to return. Everything was good. I was good. I loved and felt loved. Why couldn't real life be like this?

He's hurting my sister.

Damn!

My focus snapped back from my escape into the realm of imagination.

Birds. Wind. Distant traffic. Otherwise silence.

I longed for background music. Even a song parodying the situation—Springsteen's "Wages of Sin" or Rascal Flatts "My Wish"—would have been preferable to this. The words, *He's hurting my sister*, could have come from me. My biological father had hurt Veronica through his drunken rages and empty promises. Dr. Shane

171

Donovan had hurt Maya by removing the birthmark on her face. Two men mistaking love as the permission to overpower and suppress.

Not physically or anything, the voice said, *but with yelling and put-downs. Dad's really messing her up, and I don't know what to do.*

Someone was cracking open his heart.

Jason cleared his throat but responded silently. *I know what you mean, Ethan. My dad calls me a loser and good-for-nothing freeloader at least once a week. It gets to you after a while. You think you're adjusting, when, actually, you start believing it.*

A loser and good-for-nothing freeloader? Could this be the same man who had visited my classroom and expressed his sincere love for his son, the same man who had organized and chaperoned our trip to the Lick Observatory and procured rare observation time on the 3-m Shane telescope? How could Ron say such painful things one moment, yet act so loving the next? Were his actions the result of a brain-heart disconnect, a slip into irrationality, or suppressed fear for his son bubbling to the surface?

Mom says he's high strung and doesn't express himself well, Jason said. *Maybe the same goes for your dad.*

Geniuses aren't known for their patience and common sense. This from Luke, his words magnanimous, since he bordered on genius himself.

That doesn't make it any easier on my sister.

A lull. A rush of energy.

Ethan sat up straighter.

"Your sister can choose what she wants to experience," Tessa said out loud, looking like a doll child, all hope and innocence.

"She can shield herself with her thoughts," Jason clarified.

Ethan's stubby hands tightened into fists. "How? How? How?"

"She can ask herself what he's trying to say," Tessa said.

A shake of Ethan's head, Tessa's suggestion apparently too hard for him to swallow.

"What can your sister learn from him?" she asked. Was that a Pandora bracelet peeking from the cuff of her anorak?

"How not to treat your kids," Ethan said.

"What else?" she asked.

Ethan looked at her blankly.

That sometimes your parents want to help, but don't know how. This from Angelina. Yes, the child who was still absent from school. No one besides me seemed surprised that she had joined us remotely. Something left unsaid clung to her words like a shadow. But like a shadow, that something was elusive. I recalled how she had talked about death and dying and sensed an added chill riding on the wind. *Ten of Clubs, moon card, elegant, dramatic.*

In the silence that followed, I marveled at how well the Indigos had interacted as a group, searching for and finding Ethan's higher self and then sending him their energy and love. The whole process had pretty much proceeded without me. I'd served as a catalyst, sure, but they'd taken it from there.

The power of eight minds—seven students and one teacher—working together.

Chapter Thirty-one

THE CLASS FUNCTIONED IN relative peace for two days. Day one, some of the kids caught up on work for other classes, the rest listened to CDs. Not mine, mind you. They'd had enough of Bruce Springsteen and Rascal Flatts and had brought in selections of their own. Tessa, bless her heart, selected organ music in honor of Angelina, who, she claimed, liked church music. Johann Sebastian Bach's *Toccata and Fugue in D minor* wasn't exactly what I'd call church music, but Tessa meant well.

"Best organ music ever made," Codi said, eyes dilated as though in a music-induced trance.

"Of the haunted mansion variety," Jason added.

Day two, we talked about judgment, freedom, and security. I started by saying, "Let's treat this classroom as the poet Rumi described a field where he wanted to meet a friend, '…beyond ideas of wrongdoing and rightdoing…' In other words, as a place without judgment. Judgment sets parameters. It's limiting. It locks us in." I, in particular, needed addressing on this issue, since I found myself judging Ethan, who'd taken my mouse totem, though he knew how much it meant to me. "Did you ever like someone, regardless of his or her faults?"

Ethan, the kid who could look into the future, squinted at me as if aware I'd been thinking about him. "My sister. She's mean and selfish, but I love her." He'd taken his ceramic owl out of the cabinet and held it as though saying goodbye to a dear friend.

"How does it feel, loving her no matter what?" I asked.

He didn't take his eyes off the owl. "Good, I guess."

"How do you think it makes your sister feel?"

"Probably good."

"And free, I suspect. Free to be herself. Because she knows you'll love her anyway."

He looked up, forehead creased, mouth pinched. I'd hoped he would be beyond the scowls and sneers by now, but they appeared to be back in full force. *Too much black bile. My Ace of Spades.* "So, in this classroom, let's not encumber ourselves with judgment. Let's allow our souls to meet here in freedom and oneness."

Ethan regarded me with the wisdom of an ancient but said nothing.

"You mean love each other?" Codi asked. "Like Tessa? Her love has medicine in it."

"Yep."

"That means Codi has to love me, too." Jason's grin was that of a confident flirt.

Codi, however, appeared immune to his cheeky self-assurance. "Impossible," she said under her breath.

"If you knew you were loved, regardless," I pressed on, "and no one would hurt your most tender self, wouldn't you take off the armor and feel free?" Who the hell was I to preach about taking off one's armor? Me, who had built impenetrable barriers against love in the name of freedom. Me, who considered love synonymous with sacrifice and guilt? *There are different kinds of freedom,* I reminded myself, *freedom from and freedom to.* I wanted freedom *from* the restrictions preventing me from being free *to* follow my own heart. Sometimes it was just hard to tell the difference.

As with my birth mother, who'd given her life for a man who claimed to love her while being married to someone else. Had she been free? And Maya, who'd died because the man she loved insisted on removing the birthmark on her face. Had she been free? The answer to both, I realized, was yes. Freedom is choice, and their choices, not their lack of freedom, had led to their deaths.

"I'd feel a lot lighter if I took off my armor," Jason said. "And naked."

Codi groaned. "You're such a goon."

"I-I'd feel free to discover more" —Tessa's words revealed themselves slowly— "knowing I c-could make mistakes and...and you'd still like me."

I walked to the window and tapped my fingers on the glass, disturbed by Tessa's continued stuttering. "Okay, let's talk about some boundaries we've created to keep ourselves separate from one another."

"I like my boundaries," Codi said, cinching the belt of the trench coat she'd claimed as her own. A gothic vintage version with a hood would have been more her style, but apparently mine sufficed in a pinch. "They tell people to keep out."

"You mean, hands off," Jason said.

Codi jabbed her index finger at him. "My boundaries say who I am."

Jason laughed. "Gamma Girl."

"Hardly, but at least I'm no follower."

"As long as your personal boundaries don't alienate you." I thought of my relationship with Morgan. Was I alienating myself from the man I loved? "All things in moderation."

"Are you t-talking about compromise?" Tessa asked.

I nodded and headed back to the front of the room. "Like choosing *the between*."

"You mean sitting on the fence?" This from Luke. His hair stood on end, a result of combing his hands through the dense red mass at least five times during our conversation thus far.

"No, I don't mean choosing inaction, only knowing when to let down your guard."

"At ease, Igor," Jason said.

"Then again, you also need to know when to snap to attention and protect yourself. If you're in a secure environment, as I hope you are here, then you're free to be your true self and get lost in the learning." When no one commented, I went on. "How do you talk to babies, for instance?"

Tessa laughed. "I m-make faces at them."

"How do the babies know you aren't going to hurt them?"

"I talk softly and...and don't make sudden noises, and s-sometimes I tickle them on the cheek and...and keep at it...u-until they smile and laugh."

"So, you repeat your behavior because it works."

"Yeah." Deprived of her sidekick, Tessa had taken Angelina's seat at the head of the table on the west side of the U near where I stood. She smelled of lavender.

"Until you find a common language," I said.

"I guess."

"On the other hand, when someone you don't trust walks into the room—"

"Like Mr. Lacoste," Codi said.

Ethan became suddenly alert. "What's wrong with Mr. Lacoste?"

"His diet," Luke said. "He needs to cut out acid-forming foods and work in more alkaline to balance his pH."

"We set boundaries," I said.

Codi rose from her seat and leaned against the table in front of her. "Like you should do, Ms. Veil. Don't trust that man."

"Why?" Ethan wanted to know.

"He needs to add grapefruit and lemons to his diet," Luke said, "or he'll start to decompose like a corpse."

"With that attitude, things will only get worse," I cautioned, ignoring Luke, who was apparently clearing his brain of mental plaque. "If I'm feeling negative toward someone, my language, my gestures, and my facial expressions will be divisive right from the start."

"The unspoken will speak for you." Luke was back to finger combing his hair, which now reminded me of a California poppy field.

"Exactly, and the person will sense it."

"Maybe that's why Maya told us to treat Mr. Lacoste gently," Jason said.

"You want us to…to look p-past people's outward behavior?" Tessa asked.

I thought of Cliff, my ex-fiancé, and Charles Lacoste and Dr. Matt. "Or consider their actions as an expression of, or a call for, love."

"Please tell me you're not going where I think you're going." Codi pressed her fingers to the table to keep them from trembling. "Please, please, please, don't tell me you want us to look past the behaviors of people who hurt us, because I can't. I've tried and I can't. They just keep at it. It never stops." She dropped back into her seat and burst into tears. "Dammit. Now look what you made me do."

"You let down your mask," I said gently.

Jason leapt to his feet and draped his arms over her shoulders, a gesture so protective it brought tears to my eyes. "No. She just stripped herself naked."

I didn't put my thoughts into words because I didn't want to destroy the moment, but he'd just told her he loved her in the language of oneness. "Case closed," I whispered.

🕷 🕷 🕷

On Monday, March 4, the other shoe finally dropped. Knowing Dr. Matt and some staff members weren't pleased with me, I'd been avoiding the main office and central quad, which meant arriving at odd hours to check in and pick up my mail and then rushing to my room to put my head in the sand. But I couldn't hide forever.

After my class had ended for the day, Dr. Matt stopped by for a visit. He sat in one of the student's bum-numbing, bucket-shaped chairs and grimaced, as though wondering how anyone could tolerate the discomfort of sitting on such an instrument of torture all day. "I've been meaning to talk to you." His designer suit appeared even more extravagant and out of place in this remodeled room with its hand-me-down furniture.

I hadn't realized until then that the room's furnishings consisted of rejects from the rest of the school. It hadn't seemed important before to think about how hastily all of this had been organized and put together. My last days here at West Coast would likely be the same, hastily organized and put together.

"Good," I said. "Because I'd like to know why I've lost your support. Why, for instance, did you refuse my request for a field trip, only to change your mind when Ron Ardis entered the picture, and why haven't you told me about Angelina's cancer?"

He blinked then tugged at his ear, a gesture as familiar now as Codi's eye rolls.

"What have I done to account for this?"

It was only a matter of time before he'd rise from his chair and walk to the window, a tactic the men around here seemed to use rather than look me in the eye.

"You gave me a job to do, and I'm doing it," I continued, since Dr. Matt seemed at a temporary loss for words. "All of my students, including your nephew, are responding positively, and I've heard nothing but praise from their parents. Sure, Charles Lacoste is unhappy with me" —*and Angelina's mom and dad*— "but we both expected that from the start."

"I have it from a reliable source that you have issues that may disqualify you from teaching our youth," he said calmly.

You'd think we were discussing a migraine or toothache. "Oh, please. Who would say such a thing about me?" *Besides Charles Lacoste.*

"My source says you talk to dead people."

Was this the same man who'd hired me two months ago? "So?"

"You, you…" Dr. Matt stopped, started again. "You don't deny it?"

"What's to deny? Some of the Indigos you're so intent on helping can see and hear the dead. One moves objects through telekinesis, another can heal, another claims to see into the future. Do you need a demonstration to refresh your memory, or are you suddenly afraid of what you don't understand?"

"My source also says you're pushing cult-like behavior," Dr. Matt continued as though more impressed with my opponent's argument than mine, a reminder that pro se defendants typically lose.

I laughed. "The closest we've come to cult-like behavior is having a common goal. A goal you not only agreed to but instigated."

"Paganism then," Dr. Matt said.

I thought of how my adoptive mother had called me a pagan squaw when I told her I wanted to discover more about my Native American ancestry. And *this* from someone who loved me. My self-image should have been in shambles. Instead, I'd felt alive, expanded. By becoming less, I'd become more. Which was how I was beginning to feel now. "I admit to incorporating spiritual practices that may seem taboo from a Christian perspective, especially regarding Mother Earth. Call my ideas postmodern, if you will, like my teaching philosophy, which you endorsed enough to hire me. I also plan to introduce yoga, meditation, and visualization to help these kids use their powers constructively."

After a slow shake of his head, Dr. Matt continued, "I'd hoped you would encourage them to rely on their mental powers, not pagan activities."

Okay, Dr. Matt, you're not even making sense now. What were meditation and visualization if not mental powers? Maybe if I used terms he would recognize from our previous conversations? "How about considering what I'm teaching as casting the oldest of thoughts into the mold of our times?"

He scowled at me. "Parents and faculty have expressed concerns about you."

My face grew hot. "About me or the class?"

"The way you're handling the class."

There was something Dr. Matt wasn't telling me. The excuses he was using for withholding his support were unconvincing. I'd been living up to my end of the bargain, while he was reneging on his. There had to be a reason important enough for him to go back on his word, but I was running out of time and the motivation to discover what it was. "Does the fact that *you* approached *me* and promised your full support enter the equation and that you gave me full rein and offered no guidance or lesson plans?"

"I admit I was a bit hasty."

"No, Dr. Matt. You weren't hasty. You showed wisdom and foresight and should start doing so again. These kids need someone with my abilities, and we don't have much time."

He stared at me, silent.

I remembered what I'd told the kids about judgment, how it sets parameters and locks us in. My freedom depended on my decision to forgive and to love. Only through forgiveness and love could I cut the chains that bound me. I wasn't about to spend the rest of my life a model prisoner, waiting for a release that would never come. My only escape was my own permission to fail.

"Dr. Matt, I liked you from the start. I respected you for the love and concern you have for your nephew, and I believed, and still do, that you meant what you said about helping him and kids like him. You said Shawn's opinion was enough for you and that I bore the truths he needed to hear. You also said I brought soul into the classroom. Remember that before throwing me under the bus."

With that I got up and walked out the door.

If I didn't hear back from him that I'd been fired, I would continue to follow the path I was on. With or without his permission.

Chapter Thirty-two

"WHY ON EARTH…" I began the following afternoon. The words caught in my throat. The previous day's conversation with Dr. Matt had been an in-the-face lesson about the power of choice. I could either play the victim and pass the blame or use this as an opportunity to fulfill Dr. Matt's original expectation of me: "Imagine a class of seven students concentrating on the potential energy levels they can attain and then, within the safety of a group, learning how to control and master this energy without repressing or fearing it."

Paganism, my foot; it was time to bring a little *soul* into the classroom.

"Why on earth," I repeated, "don't we, the luckiest, richest people in the world, feel free to be who we truly are? I don't get it. Why are we so afraid of failure?"

I might as well have been talking to an empty classroom with six mannequins propped in front of me, mannequins with fiberglass bodies and vacant stares. The wind sent twigs and leaves slapping against the windows. All eyes were turned in that direction, all but Ethan's and mine. Fortunately, I'd lit the votive candles before class. Their flickering light and honey scent helped dispel the depressing scene outside—and within.

Dr. Matt had given me zilch to work with, and he'd made it clear that he frowned on field trips. Lack of computers didn't concern me. I considered their value in the classroom over-rated, anyway. But the chalk-and-talk method I'd been resorting to hadn't accomplished much either. These kids had powers too hot to handle for their age and experience, like a bunch of thirteen-year-olds owning Lamborghini Diablos, worthless until their owners were old enough and skilled enough to drive them. Yet, my job was to help put these very thirteen-year-olds into the driver's seat, someone who'd never even seen such a car up close, let alone driven one. Ethan squinted at me, his head at an angle. I wondered if anyone else was listening or if the rest of my students were caught up in their own worlds. Either was fine with me. Sometimes I talked too much when silence was what they needed.

Silence. Peace. Release. Death. I shivered at where my thoughts were headed but allowed them to flow unimpeded, eager to see where they would lead. *A spark. Rebirth. Participation. Chaos.* And there it was, my mind's message shrunk down to size. Life means participation, which means sticking out one's neck, which leads to chaos, which, in turn, leads to change. Nothing peaceful about it. My students would have to learn this on their own. And with Charles Lacoste and Dr. Matt's current attitudes, they would likely speed the process along.

"Sounds like this class isn't about learning, but unlearning," Luke said at last.

My entry into the world of silence and release had been so complete I didn't reply.

"I could get my parents really worked up with that one," Jason added.

Codi jerked in her seat, her words woodpecker sharp. "If enough of us go blabbing to our parents about things they don't understand, this class is doomed."

Why did her remark sound like a foreshadowing of things to come?

"Dr. Matt hired me in part to help you get in touch with your special gifts and teach you how to direct them, so I think it's time to do just that. Your energy is powerful but undefined and undirected. In other words, you don't know what it is or what to do with it."

"And *you're* going to teach us?" Jason asked with bird-dog stillness.

He had every right to doubt my capability. I doubted it, too. But I came closer to understanding their unique powers than most of the teachers on campus, which counted for something. "I'm going to try."

"How?"

"Through meditation, for starters."

A raised eyebrow this time.

Ethan straightened in his chair as though sensing something foreign in the air. "You mean prayer?" I could imagine the wheels in his head turning. *We can't pray in school.*

I reached out my hand than dropped it, trying to keep my voice neutral. "Prayer and meditation both use the mind. They're both concentrated thoughts, but their goals are different."

"How?"

"Well, the best way I can put it is that with prayer you send your thoughts to a being outside of yourself, who can affect change in your world. With meditation you focus within to reach a heightened level of spiritual awareness. In a way, prayer is talking and meditation is listening, where you sit in silence so the force of whatever's out there can pour into you."

"And through you," Tessa added. "Sometimes it...p-passes through you."

"And into someone else," Codi said, "like with Angelina."

"Are you talking about God?" Ethan asked.

Luke pushed up his glasses and rubbed both eyes. "Give it up, Ethan." His flaming hair was spiked this morning. A new hairstyle? Or neglect? With his nearly constant blush and thick distorting glasses, he didn't stand a chance with females of his age, a shame, because his enthusiastic attention to life's details and the optimism that fueled him shone like a healing, orange-yellow light.

"I didn't say—" Ethan began.

But Luke cut him off. "Since we're breaking a lot of other rules

184

around here, and since it's hard to talk about our talents without allowing for some kind of higher power, why not talk about God if we want to?"

Wow. I could have used that argument with Dr. Matt yesterday.

"I just want…" Ethan eyed the ceramic owl behind the glass doors of the cabinet.

"To stop h-urting," Tessa finished for him. The words were spoken with difficulty, thus painful to hear, her crystal blue eyes mesmerizing, her pain visible for all to see. She, above all the others, was extremely sensitive to her environment, which meant she felt things deeply. She was compassionate, generous, and giving, a peacemaker who couldn't abide conflict. No wonder she preferred to hide and hope no one noticed. Being a wallflower feels safe, but it also guarantees missed opportunities and the enrichment that comes through connection. As I was slowly discovering, pain comes when we take part in life, suffering when we resist. Thank goodness she'd chosen to engage instead of hide.

During the silence that followed, accompanied, of course, by wind and rain knocking at the classroom windows, I again wondered what was causing Tessa to stutter. She had selected a goose as her ceramic totem. Geese work together when they fly. They encourage one another by honking and rotating leadership position, using the wind to go long distances. *Show us how to go with the flow*, I said silently. *Show us how to work together.*

"I believe meditation can help ease our pain." I eyed each student, searching for a point of entry. They sat around the tables poised in boneless, droop-lidded concentration, but at least I sensed no hopelessness or dejection as I had on our first day.

"I'm in, Ms. V," Jason said, straightening in his chair.

My spirits lifted. "We can take a chunk of time, let's say twenty minutes a day."

"Ms. Veil?"

"Yes, Codi."

"What do you know about meditation? Are you an expert or something?"

An expert? Jeez, I was an expert at nothing. But that didn't mean I didn't care and couldn't try. "Not much and no."

"Then how?"

"It doesn't take a nuclear scientist to know how to sit cross-legged, take deep breaths, and say 'Ummmm'," Luke pointed out from his seat next to Jason.

"Is it that simple?" Codi asked.

"Yes and no," I said.

"You say that a lot, Ms. Veil," Ethan mumbled.

Jason's fingers fluttering in the air as if he were conjuring up a portal to a parallel dimension. "It's like there's always a middle ground, *a between.*"

"Thanks, Jason. It's good to know I can count on you to sum things up." He was not only likeable and funny but also able to grasp almost any concept and put it into words. The world needed people like him, and I hoped he'd find his place in it. "As I said, meditation isn't hard to learn, but you can't master it overnight either."

"Of course," Codi muttered.

"Meditation can help stabilize your emotions and teach you to depend on yourselves for fulfillment," I said, focusing on Ethan. "It helps you recognize that you're spiritual beings." He flushed under my gaze, then looked up at what I knew to be his owl. His attachment to the ceramic figure disturbed me. Something about it felt wrong. Sure, I valued my totem, but this was different. Rather than serve as a helper, his owl appeared to fill him with dread. "Meditation helps you replace anger and fear with empathy and compassion for those in need."

Jason chuckled. "A tall order."

I gestured toward the wall of windows. The rain had stopped and the wind had stilled, leaving a cleansing calm. "We're nearly cut off from the rest of the campus here, like being on our own private planet, reasonably safe from judgmental eyes and gossip." And isolated and unprotected, but I kept that thought to myself.

"What if meditation makes us lose control?" Codi asked.

"I don't think that'll happen."

"Maybe yes, maybe no." Ethan was speaking up more and more. I couldn't decide if this was good or bad.

"We're all here to help one another," I said, "so no matter what, the experience should be positive for each one of us."

"How do you know?" Codi asked.

I glanced at Ethan, his look a challenge, his smile a sneer. "I don't."

Silence; and into the silence, I said, "Author Victor Davich defines meditation as 'an opening to each moment with calm awareness.'"

"I'm all for that," Luke said. And so, our lesson began.

Chapter Thirty-three

GIGGLING AND WISE CRACKS aside, our daily meditation sessions went more or less according to plan. First, we concentrated on prepping our meditation muscles, so to speak. We began by sitting on beach towels—which work just fine in a pinch—then took whatever postures we could comfortably hold. Codi lay on her back, her trench coat wrapped around her Dracula style. Ethan crouched, head bowed over bent knees. The rest of us sat cross-legged in makeshift lotus positions as though sitting around a campfire.

Next, we worked on our breathing, and yes, it was work. Being aware of one's breath—the gaps between the exhalations and inhalations—without aiming for control isn't easy. We concentrated on the doubts that popped up like weeds in our heads, beginning with Ethan's. He raised his head just long enough to ask, "Is this a religion, because if so, you can get in real trouble, Ms. Veil."

After I assured him meditation was not a religion, Tessa asked, "Is it hypnotism?"

"During meditation, you'll feel relaxed, but that's not the goal," I said. "Remember Victor Davich's definition, 'It's the art of opening to each moment with calm awareness.'"

Luke, *Nine of Diamonds, Mr. Total Recall,* couldn't resist contributing his reflection of the truth. "Seems like an escape from reality."

Then Jason added his two cents of wisdom. "Why not leave this nonsense to monks?"

"I think it's weird," Codi said from her prostrate position on the floor.

I understood their misgivings. I'd felt—and fought—them myself over the past eleven and a half months. So many misconceptions are generated by our rational, left-brain against anything intuitive and right-brained. One of my jobs as mentor, however, was to help six fidgety skeptics dissolve the walls that limited their ability to understand opposing views—and one way to do that was to help them overcome their resistance to meditation. "How about we at least give it a try? Let's say two weeks. Then you can take it or leave it, no questions asked."

Jason eyed his peers. "Fair enough."

All nodded, except Ethan, his forehead still facing his knees.

"Would you like to be excused from this exercise, Ethan?" I asked.

"No," he said, without raising his head.

I sighed, at a loss for words. The votives flickered on the tables. Their wicks were running low. I would need to replace them soon. Flute music played in the background, Mary Youngblood's poetry of the heart, its notes touching, haunting, persistent, like the wind rushing through the trees outside.

"Let's sit like flowers, our spines the stems, our heads the blossoms," Jason suggested, which made me wonder if he'd been reading up on the subject.

"Will we have a mantra?" Luke asked.

That made two students more familiar with yoga than they were letting on. No surprise. From what I understood, more people on the planet meditated than not, and most people in the West had at least heard of the practice. "Sure, what do you suggest?"

He closed his eyes and drew out the words, "Om ah hum."

Codi spoke up, eyes closed, arms crossed over her chest. "That's so boring."

"Well I...I... How about saying, 'L-let go, let God'?" Tessa's stuttering had been going on for over a week now, ever since our trip to the Lick Observatory and Angelina's supposed cure. Was there a connection?

189

"Let's think up our own," Jason said.

"Good idea." Codi conceded.

Jason grinned. "Well, I'll be."

"Oh, shut up," she said.

※ ※ ※

Monday brought a new surprise.

While rain poured outside and wind lashed at the classroom windows, we practiced Tibetan visualization. In other words, we focused our attention on something we wanted to realize for ourselves. Sitting on our towels in lotus positions, we started by visualizing our bodies and minds filled with total darkness, a blank slate.

"Feel the sadness without becoming lost in it," I murmured to help them navigate their meditation as it evolved.

Ethan whimpered and Tessa began to cry, which had me shifting to the suggestion that we imagine a healing light coming from a source of power within, warm and joyful. In the brief silence that followed, Tessa gasped. "Angelina's here."

My eyes shot open.

The rest of the students kept their meditative poses.

"She says she's healed," Tessa said, "but her parents won't let her come back to school."

Healed or cured?

Shawn's sigh came from deep within, like the sigh that follows news of a miracle: The Virgin Mary appearing to the children of Fatima, or a woman lifting a car with her bare hands to save the child trapped underneath. "She says she's going to be okay, Ms. Veil."

Codi looked pretty, with her long lashes against the olive skin not fully masked by layers of makeup. "She misses us."

"Luke. Jason. Do you hear her, too?" I'd seen and heard nothing. Had I lost my abilities, or were they being inconveniently selective?

"Sure do, Ms. V," Jason said.

Luke's eyes moved behind his closed lids as if he were watching a fast-action movie. "Yep."

Ethan still had his head down. He could have been sleeping for all I knew.

"She says she likes the meditation we're doing." This from Tessa. Without a stutter. "She can talk to us without actually being here."

They'd found one way, at least, to direct their energy constructively, and I, as observer rather than participant, felt wowed to the bone.

🕷 🕷 🕷

It was the kids' turn to be wowed, the next day, by my sister.

Veronica sat on the edge of a table facing the door as the students filed in, her hand raised in welcome. Three steps into the classroom, Codi jerked to a halt; Ethan bumped into her from behind; Jason peered over her shoulder; Tessa, Luke, and Shawn edged around her. But no one said a word.

"I'm Veronica," my sister said, her face set in what she referred to as her 'resting bitch face.' But there was nothing bitchy about the glint of compassion in her eyes. "Just so you don't think I'm your teacher in disguise."

Jason, the first to recover, pressed forward, propelling Codi along. "You look like Cher, but younger."

"So I've heard." She stretched out her legs. All gazes traveled to her black leather pants and spiked boots, which brought to mind my friend Anne's comment on first meeting her. "She dresses like a vamp, for God's sake."

Clothing that screamed "vamp" fit right in with Codi's sense of style. She shoved her hands into the pockets of her trench coat and tilted her head with a look that said: *You are beyond cool.* "I like your outfit."

Veronica gave me a triumphant glance. "It's what I wear when I'm undercover."

I managed not to laugh from my seat at the back of the room, my attempt—so far successful—at emulating a fly on the wall. Veronica was trying to protect me. Bringing an ex-undercover operative into the classroom was one thing, bringing in someone who dressed like a hooker on a regular basis was quite another. Dr. Matt hadn't okayed Veronica and Ben as guest speakers, but he'd heard me mention them coming and hadn't gotten back with a refusal. If questioned, I would point out that Veronica worked with the DEA, which should ease his concern about one or more of the Indigos being on the verge of experimenting with alcohol and drugs. My argument in Ben's defense would be more in line with something else Dr. Matt had said about the Indigos before hiring me. "They're way beyond what we're teaching them in school. Yet they lack the keys to succeed. Which leads to confusion and restless impatience simmering just below the surface or, in a worst-case scenario, explosive anger and aggression." What better *key* than the Medicine Wheel to lead my students to illumination and clarity rather than confusion and restless impatience, explosive anger and aggression?

"Are you and Ms. Veil really twins?" Ethan asked, looking back and forth between us.

Veronica focused on him with the precision of a laser. "Triplets, actually."

I thought Ethan would shy away from her piercing scrutiny, as he shied away from anything unfamiliar, but he seemed to expand under her intense blue gaze.

Veronica grabbed a tissue from the box on my desk and handed it to him. "Got a cold?"

He shook his head no but took the tissue and wiped his nose, anyway. I hadn't noticed it was running.

Tessa edged toward my sister as if she were an exotic bird that would fly away if disturbed. "Are you our teacher for the day?"

"No, sweetie. Not today."

Tessa's aura grayed. It was like watching a flower wilt from lack of sun and water. When Veronica was around, you wanted to become part of her, or at least, bask in the circle of her energy and strength. There are people who, through no conscious effort, draw the eye, the will, the soul. Such power can be dangerous if misused, but with Veronica, I wasn't worried. She stood on the right side of the law and used her power only for good. She touched Tessa's hand with the lightness of a butterfly. "All in good time, dear."

"That sounds like something Ms. Veil would say," Tessa said, her tone petulant.

Veronica winked at me before replying, "I learned this from my *other* sister."

"You mean Maya?" Tessa asked. "I like her."

Veronica, master of the poker face, rarely shows surprise, but the way her brows lifted and her hands formed into fists, she was displaying just that. Or maybe shock would be a better word. "Maya's dead, honey."

"I know."

Veronica opened her mouth to say something, then closed it before giving me a wide-eyed stare. I shook my head and shrugged. Maybe now she would understand what I was dealing with here, a helplessness bordering on fear.

"So, what's up, Ms. V?" Jason asked, turning his attention to me.

His yellow-brown gaze reminded me of Veronica's blue one. They both had a way of slicing through me and demanding my full attention, an attention I gave freely, no questions asked, because to question requires self-confidence, determination, and mission, which I often lacked. Anyway, I was accustomed to playing second fiddle to my sister and enjoyed every minute.

"Today, we're going to spend time in the nature area, with Ben *Gentle Bear* Mendoza, Veronica's fiancé," I said. "He'll introduce you to a circle of knowledge used as a form of meditation by the Native American."

"Cool," Luke said.

Jason walked up to the window and peered out. "It's wet out there." Codi, Luke, and Shawn joined him, exchanged glances, and shrugged. Only Tessa and Ethan remained at Veronica's side, staring at her as if expecting her to conjure up a miracle. She smiled at Ethan, and to my surprise, he smiled back. *He's lonely*, I thought, *lonely and scared*. It had taken Veronica only minutes to discover what I'd missed until now.

"Let's go outside and meet Ben, shall we?" Veronica suggested.

Tessa and Ethan nodded, and I wondered if Veronica could pry herself loose from her new friends anytime soon. Then again, judging by the smile on her face, prying herself loose wasn't one of her current priorities.

※ ※ ※

In his own way, Ben was as striking as my sister. His thick black hair was pulled into a ponytail, his Paul Bunyan bulk covered only by a black T-shirt and Wrangler jeans. I zipped my parka to ward off the chill, but Ben didn't seem the least bit bothered by the cold. He'd arranged a circular tarp over a patch of grass in the nature area. At our approach, he said, "Had to improvise, since the ground is soggy from yesterday's rain."

My sneakers sank into the grass, absorbing its moisture. The musty scent of wet dirt and vegetation filled the air, reminding me of Anne's backyard in Pacific Grove, where I'd discovered a labyrinth and all the mysteries it offered. I drew in the heavy earth scent with pleasure. "Ben. Meet my students."

One by one, they introduced themselves.

"Ben will acquaint you with a meditation circle called The Medicine Wheel, where you can center your power and re-energize yourself spiritually." I glanced at Ethan to see if my alluding to spirituality had bothered him, but he seemed perfectly content standing next to Veronica.

"Did you bring your marker stones, Marjorie?" Ben asked.

I reached into my pouch for my treasured stones. All rested inside, except the mouse totem. Ethan glanced at me, then looked away, his face flushed. Ben motioned for us to step onto the waterproofed cloth. The tarred hemp fiber stretched and groaned under our feet, causing startled birds to shoot from the trees in a loud screeching mass.

"Today, I'll show you how to set up a Medicine Wheel," Ben said. "Then I'll introduce you to the four primary directions or paths to discovering your own truths."

Chapter Thirty-four

THE TEMPERATURE WAS A chill fifty-seven degrees, and the sun barely had enough strength to penetrate the clouds, yet we stood in the circle compliant and uncomplaining, expectation flooding our senses to the point of numbness to any discomfort.

After taking my five stones, Ben said, "These are Ms. Veil's personal markers. She spent hours searching for them. They had to feel right to her before she could accept them. They also had to be the right colors, white, yellow, red, and black, to represent the four primary races of mankind and green to mark the center."

I remembered the day Ben had directed me to find my markers. The air had been chilly and the sky overcast, hinting at showers, like today, except then we were in the north-eastern edge of the Los Padres National Forest instead of an overgrown nature area in the middle of a city. He'd cautioned that the stones I'd be searching for would be my helpers in the Medicine Wheel, so I'd have to choose them with care. Then he'd left me alone, on the edge of a mixed hardwood forest, surrounded by grassland and patches of flowering chaparral. I walked for close to an hour through tall grasses, picking up stone after stone, only to discard them, while using a massive oak tree and a compass to keep from getting lost. Funny, how the first stone I'd felt drawn to was white to represent the north, the direction of my present journey on the Medicine Wheel, a journey that had started in the direction of the east nearly twelve months ago. Ben now took that stone and placed it at the north point of the cloth circle. "North is the direction of the mind and of receiving."

After a short pause, he made a quarter turn to the right and put the yellow stone—clear as topaz, bright as a diamond—on the eastern edge of the circle. I'd found this stone by accident after watching a doe and her fawn shoot in and out of the underbrush near where I was sitting. It rested on a rockslide of pebbles that had gathered at my feet.

"East is the direction of spirit and of determining," Ben said before taking another quarter turn and placing my red stone at the southern point of the circle. This stone had been my second find that day, a stone that looked like a turtle and changed from brick red to red-violet to magenta when I held it up to the sun. "South is the direction of emotion and giving."

Ben marked the western boundary of the circle with the black stone, my Apache Tear. "West is the direction of the body and of holding." The Apache Tear had eluded my search in the Los Padres National Forest. I'd found it the next day at the Carmel Mission wedged in the knot of a pepper tree next to the gravesite of my Native American ancestor, Margarita Butron.

Ben rose to his full height, towering over the six transfixed students grouped on the edge of the circular tarp, and closed his eyes. All was quiet, except for the tree branches creaking like arthritic fingers, birds chirping, traffic humming, and wind whispering a foreign yet familiar refrain. We stood cocooned in our own little world, surrounded by nature, and for now, nothing else mattered. "White is also the color of decisiveness and penetration," Ben said, opening his eyes and fixing his gaze on the white stone marking the North.

We did likewise, staring at the stone as if it were a priceless work of art.

"Yellow is the color of optimism and stimulation," Ben said, turning to concentrate on the stone marking the East this time.

We changed our focus, stared in silence, and I regretted that I'd forbidden the chewing of gum. I could have used the taste of spearmint to displace the dryness in my throat. I'd met my sister,

Veronica, for the first time during my journey through the eastern portion of the Medicine Wheel. Her cold blue eyes had looked at me as if I were her worst nightmare come to life.

The scent of wet dirt and fermenting leaves reminded me of how I'd heard my birth mother crying during my first encounter with the Medicine Wheel. Though I hadn't known it at the time, she'd been crying for Veronica, for Maya, and for me. Her voice had grown stronger and more frequent over the following weeks, and I'd longed for her to shut up, leave me alone, and stay dead.

Now I missed her.

Was she finally at peace, or had I just quit listening?

"Red," Ben said, then paused.

I snapped back to attention and stared at the stone marking the South. An emotion I couldn't name swelled in my chest as I remembered my time in Big Sur, how much I'd endured, how much I'd learned.

"Red," Ben repeated, the timbre of his voice so low it sounded like a drum roll coming from inside his chest, "is the color of energy, strength, and courage."

It had indeed taken energy, strength, and courage to seek out my dead mother and bury my past so I could step into my future. More courage than I'd called on in twenty-nine years.

Ben picked up the stone that marked the West and held it up so it reflected the light like a black tear. "Black is the color of solidity and endurance." During my journey in the western portion of the Medicine Wheel, I'd met my second sister Maya and was forced to embrace the pain of her death, which nearly decimated my world.

The students' stillness amazed me. Sure, Shawn, Ethan, and Tessa usually kept their comments to a minimum, but Jason, Luke, and Codi were not ones to keep silent for long. After motioning for them to take positions on the circumference of the Medicine Wheel, Ben placed the green stone in the center, the stone I'd found under a rippling stream of water, my little green frog. "Green marks the center, the place of the soul." Ben took time to look each student in the eye, and not one of them looked away. "In the center of your Medicine Wheel, you take full responsibility for your life and take charge of your own destiny."

I shifted my feet, afraid the kids would become restless with this talk of endurance, responsibility, and destiny and misuse their powers as they had on my first and last day of substituting.

Ben clapped his hands, a lightning crack—a tear. "But before you can do any work with your Medicine Wheel, you need to perform a cleansing called 'smudging,' sort of like washing your hands before a meal."

Veronica handed him a large seashell from outside the circle. He set it next to the green stone at the center, then lifted a smudge stick from the shell and lit it with a match. "You burn a bundle of herbs containing sage, cedar, and sweetgrass and use the smoke to clear away negative energies from your surroundings." The herb bundle began to smolder, sending off a trail of writhing, curling smoke. "Smudging ensures that you'll begin your meditation with a clean heart and a clear mind."

I pulled the scent of burning herbs through my nose and mouth; cold, wet, foreign, yet soothing, in a mind-numbing way.

"It's all symbolic, isn't it?" Ethan asked. "Not religious."

Ben fanned the smoke throughout the circle and then smudged the four directions. "Native American spirituality contains no dogma."

Ethan turned and peered at Veronica standing outside the circle. She winked and waited for him to refocus on Ben before reverting her attention to Codi.

If Ben was aware of Veronica's keen interest in Codi, he didn't show it. His concentration remained focused, like a scout leading his followers through tricky landscape and uneven trails. "The four stones represent the four directions, but also the four winds and the four seasons. Winter is represented by the direction of the cold north winds." He motioned for us to sit at points around the circle facing north. "I understand your school mascot is the buffalo, totem of the north. The buffalo gave its all so others might live and therefore has much to teach us.

"The North is also the direction of knowledge, and wisdom. I'm not talking about useless information, but wisdom, which is knowledge applied with love. How do you handle life's challenges and emergencies? What is your philosophy of life? These are questions to think about and answer while meditating in the Medicine Wheel. In the North, you learn to turn ideas into action and bring desirable changes into your life."

Ben opened his eyes and smiled. Dear Lord, what a transformation. No wonder Veronica loved him. The kids must have been equally impressed, because they continued to sit without saying a word. I wondered if he had hypnotized them. Entranced more likely.

"We are nearing the end of the third cycle of the North called 'The Blustery Winds Time,'" he said. "Its totem is the wolf."

Jason jerked at the mention of *wolf*.

"This is a time of rapid changes and anticipation, purification and renewal. I call it the 'in-between time,' where you can draw in energy and lessons and refine them before bursting forth into your new life, a time when your new story begins."

Did my students understand the significance of Ben's words? So much applied to what I'd been trying to get across during our talks and meditative sessions. Would some of it take hold and send out roots? Likely, I would never know.

"Now, rest your hands on your knees and close your eyes," Ben said. Then instead of leading us through a meditation as I'd expected, he sat, closed his eyes, and took deep, steady breaths. He remained silent for at least ten minutes, yet the students made no sound. No restless shifting. No giggles. No wisecracks.

"Face the death of who you think you are," Ben said finally, jerking me out of a somnolent daze. "Throw out the garbage."

I heard sighs but didn't open my eyes to identify the sources. I would allow my students the solitude of their thoughts.

"Think about all the experiences you've had that science or accepted reality can't explain," Ben said. "What do they mean? Honor your own inner knowing."

"Holy crap," Jason said, then relapsed into silence.

In a voice so hypnotic I felt as if I were rising into the air, Ben said, "Then consider ways you can share your experiences with others."

Again silence, broken only by the inroads of nature and traffic and the occasional shouts of students still hanging around after school. We were at the door between worlds.

Another ten minutes passed before Ben's deep voice brought us back from our separate journeys. "Gifted Indigos, seers, and healers, embrace the center point within you with open hearts. Don't be afraid of what you feel and see or have felt and seen. Don't let the wounds of the past influence the present moment. Move forward."

I opened my eyes and marveled at the calm on the Indigos' faces. No frowns, no smiles, no tears, only the appearance of heart-wrenching innocence—and surrender.

I glanced at Ben, and he nodded. The session was over.

🕷 🕷 🕷

Next afternoon was Veronica's turn to face the class, but her message was to be less palatable than Ben's. Whereas he had introduced them to a tool capable of turning them on *without* destroying their health, Veronica's job was to discuss something capable of turning them on *by* destroying their health. Fortunately, she already had two adoring fans, and by the rapt look on Jason, Codi, Luke, and Shawn's faces, she would soon have four more.

"I need not tell you that drugs and alcohol are bad for you," she began. "You've heard it before."

What about the barf bags? Had Veronica, during her short acquaintance with the kids, decided they didn't need the lesson called *Shock and Awe*? Part of me was disappointed, the other part relieved.

"And I need not tell you that drugs and underage drinking are illegal. You know that, too. So, does this mean I have nothing to say to you, that I'll just head out of here for the DEA basic agent training program at Quantico? Of course not. I'm here to tell you that you are good."

She paused and rested her gaze on each student in such a loving way, you'd think she was shapeshifting into Granny Max. "You are a blessing, a mystery, and a wonder. Let no one tell you different. You don't need to rebel, drop out, or turn to drugs to affirm your existence. You don't need to hurt your precious bodies and minds with Snot balls, Uppers, or Pot. Anyone who tries to convince you otherwise is not your friend."

Veronica looked like she might cry. My cool, tough sister had a soft spot for animals and children. She glanced at Ben and me, positioned at the back of the room but no less enthralled than the students by her magnetic presence. "Ms. Veil, Ben, and I are here to help you through any difficulties you may have concerning alcohol and drugs. You don't need warnings. You need someone who cares." She looked at Ethan for what seemed a long time. "Any questions?"

"Isn't meth less harmful than crack?" Jason asked.

Veronica shook her head, her eyes deep blue pools of sadness, as though she'd heard this question many times before. "Meth is often made from battery acid, drain cleaner, and antifreeze." She paused to let her words sink in. "With meth, you stand a greater chance of suffering a heart attack, stroke, or brain damage than with crack. You can also get hooked the first time you use it. Meth leads to poor judgment, agitation, confusion, anxiety, and stealing. Some addicts become so desperate they'll fry their own urine to extract the meth crystals."

"But grass is safe and better than cigarettes, right?" Jason said.

Again, Veronica shook her head. "Early marijuana use lessens white matter in the brain, which can affect how the brain learns and functions." She looked at Ethan and smiled. "It can also trigger panic attacks and paranoia."

"What about fake weed?" Luke asked. "It's—"

Veronica's gaze struck Luke with the quick kick of a Taser. "Fake weed, like KZ and Spice, is made of herbs sprayed with synthetic chemicals that not only cause hallucinations, seizures, and addiction, but can also kill you."

Luke sat in red-faced silence.

"Don't let the easy availability and pretty packaging of synthetic marijuana fool you. Moon Rocks, Genie, Ninja, Panama Red Bull, and Voodoo Spice are catchy names for stupid."

Ethan's knee bounced up and down. He glanced at the owl in the glass cabinet, then asked, "What about prescribed medication?"

Veronica closed her eyes for a moment before answering. "Stuff you can get at the grocery store or from the medicine cabinet with innocent nicknames like Skittles, Cotton, and Skippy are not a safe way to get high. Hallucinations, seizures, coma, and death can result from accidental overdoses, especially when you down them with fruit-flavored, caffeinated drinks, which often contain alcohol. Prescribed medications are also addictive."

"So, what *can* make you feel better besides drugs?" Ethan asked.

Veronica glanced at Ben. "You mean other than the Medicine Wheel?"

Ethan nodded.

"Service."

"Service?" Tessa said, as though she, of all people, were unfamiliar with the concept.

"I can think of no greater happiness than helping your fellow man."

"Even if they don't want your help?" Tessa asked.

"I'm sure you've heard of karma."

Tessa nodded.

"True happiness kicks in when you quit thinking of yourself as separate from others and think of all as one. Pick a cause, any cause, that takes you outside of yourself. It'll give you a high no drug can."

"Not always," Codi blurted. "Sometimes helping others is not enough." She rested her forehead on the table and stifled a sob.

Veronica caught my eye and frowned. I shrugged, unable to offer help. I'd experienced Codi's debilitating sadness at the Lick Observatory, and it had settled over me like a lead apron.

Veronica stilled, and the students followed suit. Minutes passed, apparently no one in a hurry to continue. I glanced at Ben. He leaned against the wall next to me, observing the proceedings through hooded eyes. I become aware of the ticking clock, the beating of my heart. *Veronica, Codi, are you okay?*

Codi sat up and her hand crept to head-level before dropping to the table. "So, what's so bad about alcohol?" Her voice sounded pained, yet defiant.

"The pain of addiction and recovery is beyond most people's comprehension," Veronica said. "I've seen it first hand in my personal and professional life, and I wouldn't wish it on my worst enemy."

Codi fingered the lapels of her trench coat and released a raspy breath.

"If you are the victim of drugs or alcohol, don't let guilt or depression take you down. Instead, get the hell out of the house and out of yourself. When helping others, you'll forget about yourself. It works. I can vouch for it."

One last concentrated look at each student and Veronica closed her presentation. "And if that doesn't work, be smart and reach out to people like Ms. Veil, Ben, and me. We're only a phone call or text message away. I also have a nifty presentation called *Shock and Awe* I can share with you in case you need extra persuading. I don't use it often because, to be quite honest, it makes me sick to my stomach each time I do."

Veronica caught my eye. Mission accomplished.

For her anyway.

Mine was about to begin.

Chapter Thirty-five

B EFORE VERONICA LEFT ON Thursday, she suggested it might be a good time for me to step aside for a while and let the kids show their stuff. I understood what she meant. I'd been trying to do just that—and failing. Dr. Matt wanted me to help them use their special talents to become who they truly were. The question was how?

When I arrived at school the following Monday, I was no closer to an answer.

"Okay, Maya," I said as I stepped through the classroom door. "Help me out here."

I headed for the thermostat to turn up the heat. With the sun's rays streaming through clouds and reflecting off buildings and streets, the outdoor temperature had felt almost warm, but inside it was downright chilly. I wondered, not for the first time, if it had been Maya's suggestion to call this class *First Light*? Not half-bad compared to 'after-school learning lab,' but open to misinterpretation and hard to live up to. I sat on the floor facing the wall of windows and closed my eyes. "I'm waiting, Sis."

No sound from Maya. But a series of watercolor images flashed across my inner eyelids like templates in a PowerPoint presentation; evocative images meant to conjure strong emotional responses like the ones Maya had used to assist alcoholics and drug abusers on their road to recovery. I jumped to a stand, and by the time my six students arrived for class that afternoon, I'd purchased a deck of *SoulCards* from the downtown bookstore and formulated a plan.

"Off to the nature area," I said as the kids filed in. "We have some exploring to do."

No sooner had we stepped into spring's exploding pinks and greens than Jason *The Wolf* Ardis balked. "Nah, we've done this already."

Shawn, Ethan, and Luke massed around him with conflicting expressions: puzzlement, detachment—yearning.

Tessa, who had darted ahead with Codi, skidded to a halt, blonde locks flying like Medusa hair. "Jason, we don't have to *do* anything."

"I saw some St John's wort last time we were out here," Luke said, eyeing his surroundings through fogged-up glasses. "And a cat."

"A cat?" Dr. Matt hadn't mentioned any animals inhabiting the nature area, though it would be easy enough for one to bypass the aging chain-link fence.

"Yeah, a Mackerel tabby with an M pattern on its forehead. It must be feral, because when I tried to catch it, it hissed at me."

Codi peered at him as if he'd just turned into *Dexter's Laboratory's* red-haired and bespectacled boy-genius. "You tried to catch a mutt cat full of diseases? That's crazy, Luke."

Not crazy. I would have done the same. Actually, I did, with Gabriel, my backyard stray. He was also a Mackerel tabby with an M pattern on his forehead. If I didn't know better, I'd think it was him, but my home was two-and-a-half miles away.

"Go," I said, waving my arms as if shooing cattle. "Explore."

Forty-five minutes later, I had difficulty herding them in.

After we'd formed a circle in our outdoor cove, I held up the *SoulCards* and waited until I had everyone's attention. "I'm going to pass this deck around, and when it gets to you, I want you to shuffle it and pick a card, face down. No peeking till I tell you to."

I handed the deck to Tessa, who shifted the cards from back to front in an overhand shuffle. She then made her choice and passed the cards on to Codi. Codi repeated the process and handed the deck to Luke. "According to math," he said, "you'd have to overhand shuffle ten thousand times to get a random card distribution. With the 'riffle method,' you only have to shuffle—"

"Not now, Luke," I said. "Move it along."

Jason was next, and with the finesse of a magician, he bowed halves of the deck and got the cards falling and interlacing so fast, I couldn't keep track. He gave Luke a high-five before making his *random* selection and passing the rest on. Ethan declined to shuffle, probably figuring Jason's masterful card redistribution need not be repeated. Instead, he took a deep breath and drew from the collection. Shawn, the last member of the circle, shot me a look I could only define as wary while shuffling and making his pick.

"Your energy is powerful but undefined," I said once everyone held a *SoulCard*, "and you need to learn to control it at all times."

Shawn exchanged a glance with Jason before focusing on his hands.

"Dr. Matt believes we can use this energy in a group situation to uplift others, and since you communicate telepathically more easily than most people do with words, today you'll do just that."

Silence. Even the birds and late afternoon breeze drew into it and took up residence there. Codi pressed her face into her coat sleeve. The remaining Indigos sat in rigid expectation, their reluctance a jet of cold air. A chill settled over me like a netting of ice, but I wouldn't back down now. I was about to carry out not only what I'd been hired to do but was destined to do. I sensed it in my ice-cold bones. "Think of an issue in life you'd like to get in touch with, then flip over your card." I wrapped my arms over my chest to quell my trembling. "Don't think too hard about the picture's meaning. Just pick a theme or pattern it presents and how it relates to the issue you're exploring."

I stopped talking, not only to allow the kids time to follow my instructions but also to pull myself together. The shaking had grown so intense that my insides hurt. I feared what I might learn about these kids—and about myself. That I was a coward, for instance. And the reason I always buckled under authority was because I didn't have the stomach to take life head on or deal with the disillusionment of failure in case I chose wrong. *Help me, Maya, help me, Mother, wherever you are.*

Six intelligent but insecure Indigos looked at me through narrowed eyes, puffing out cloudy bursts of air like chain smokers.

"Look at the images on your cards and receive their messages from a knowing beyond your consciousness." I pulled a card out of the deck and before looking at it said, "Quiet your mind. Open to the stillness." I flipped the card and felt a rush of relief. It showed seven figures locked arm in arm, with serene facial expressions.

Seven?

A jolt zipped up my spine. Who'd been excluded? Angelina, or me?

By this time, I was a trembling mess. In contrast, my students appeared calm and in control. "Okay, now we'll share what our pictures bring to mind." I expected a string of complaints, but not a word or gesture to clue me in to what they were thinking or feeling. "You can start with 'Once upon a time,' if you like, as long as some kind of story emerges. Let your picture speak. Does it present a question? Does it offer a gift?"

While all six students waited for further instruction, I sensed myself drifting into my own private space. Tessa took my hand and warmth seeped into my veins as if her blood were transfusing into mine. God, how she reminded me of Maya. I closed my eyes and the netting of ice melted.

I'll start, Ms. V.

I opened my eyes and smiled. Jason was communicating telepathically. He held up a card showing a figure crouched next to a bare tree. Branches twisted in the wind, debris swirled, and a what appeared to be a coyote peered from its hiding place nearby. *When my father comes into my room, the air shifts and the walls close in on me. I hold my breath and wait, the way birds do before a storm, afraid to move, not wanting to set things off. Vibrations build up around me like an ocean of energy to the point where I can hardly stand or breathe. And when my father talks to me, I don't answer, and he gets mad.*

Is that why you steal people's energy? Codi cut in.

Sometimes I borrow it.

Use your own!

Sometimes he shares, Tessa said. *If it weren't for him sharing his energy with Ms. Veil in Ms. Goldsberry's class, we wouldn't be here today.*

True, though I would have preferred that he'd directed his sharing in a more constructive manner than burning up an overhead light bulb and disrupting class.

Can you believe Dad wants me to play football? Jason asked. *I can't kick or throw a ball to save my life. I'd get squashed like an October bug during my first game. That is, if I ever made it off the bench. Dad has no talent for sports either, so why put his hopes on me? Does he think I inherited the sport gene from my mom, Miss Universe?*

Our parents don't mean to hurt us, Shawn added to the silent conversation. *It helps to know that.*

Tessa held up a card of a woman with blonde hair, hands stretched in front of her, light streaming from her fingertips like garden hose spray. *I have a trick I use when I get too close to someone else's pain,* she said, minus the stutter. *I usually don't talk about it because people think I'm joking or telling a lie. I put my hands where it hurts and concentrate on the heat coming from my fingertips and palms. I relax and absorb the heat, then slowly lift my hands, pulling the heat back out again. The pain follows the heat, attached to my hands like a magnet.*

Codi cut in, with no other direction than intuition that the time was right. *Like Tessa, I'm sensitive to other people's pain to the point I take on the pain myself. You name it, chest pain, stomach pain, cramps in my legs, headaches, nausea.* Codi's *SoulCard* depicted a woman with her belly on fire. She had her arm draped over a child who, untouched by the flames, was reaching for a bird flying above. *When people say something feels like the stab of a knife, they're right on. Sometimes, when I hold babies, I close my eyes and send them my love, you know, tell them silently that I love them. They get sleepy and hold on to me and don't let go. I also attract birds. They circle around me, and sometimes I tell them where to land. Mom thinks I do black magic. She thinks I'm in a coven and wander around at night doing bad stuff.*

The person in my card is crying, Ethan said without raising his card. *There's gray light around him and what looks like leaves and twigs. I don't know what it means, and that's all I have to say.*

Luke held the face of his *SoulCard* up close to his glasses and studied it like a lab specimen. *Mine's of a person with the top of his head missing. I hope it doesn't mean what I think it does or I'm in big trouble. I don't know if the card holds a gift or a question, but since you're always telling us that what we think becomes reality, Ms. Veil, I guess I'll consider it a gift. I just don't know what the gift is. My parents say I get downloads from the universe because I know stuff I didn't learn in books or at school. Oh, and I'm gay. Figured I'd throw that in for Ms. Veil's sake, since the rest of you already know. No secrets in this class, right?* Luke looked at me with a blend of pleading and relief in his eyes. *In fact, I'd like to say it out loud.* "I'm gay. I'm gay. I'm gay." He dropped his head and said no more.

I managed a smile. There was so much about the students I didn't, nor would ever, know, but at least this was progress. "We accept, support, and love you, Luke. Live as your true self."

My turn.

I twisted toward the voice but saw nothing except for swooshing branches and open sky. All the Indigos, except Shawn, sat perfectly still, eyes closed. Shawn picked up the deck, reshuffled it, and drew out a card of an angel holding a harp. *This one's for Angelina.*

"I'm sorry, Angelina," Tessa said out loud.

"Hang in there, girl," Codi added.

Luke pushed his glasses up to the bridge of his nose, out of habit, it seemed, because his eyes remained closed. "Tell the doctor to look into positive thinking and how it acts on brain neurons to—"

Let her talk! Jason said, the only one, besides Angelina, still using his telepathic powers.

I love organ music, Angelina said, her voice faint, as though our mental dials weren't set to the right frequency. *So, I like eleven o'clock Mass at St. Joseph's Cathedral in San Jose with the traditional choir and organist. It isn't torture for me like for other kids. Sometimes I lift out of my body and touch God. I don't like the drums and guitars played during other*

Masses. They hurt too much. Mom says my heart changes rhythm with loud music and it causes me pain. Anyway, there's nothing to be sorry about, Tessa. You cured me. If only I could convince Mom and Dad…

I willed Angelina to say more, to explain what was happening, why she wasn't back in school. I wanted a plot, a theme, a happy ending to her story. Then I realized, her story wasn't a box office hit full of action and climatic endings, but the story between; just as meaningful and exciting, if not more so, than the ones played out on a stage or Hollywood movie set.

We walked back to the classroom in silence, and in silence the students strapped on their backpacks and left for home. What this exercise had accomplished or where it might lead was uncertain, but at least the students had had their say and a chance to uplift one another; if only through their undivided attention.

🕷 🕷 🕷

Two days later marked the first day of spring, a full year since I'd entered the office of my psychologist, Dr. Tony Mendez, believing I'd lost my mind. How things had changed since then. Another two days until Spring Break, aka Easter vacation, a time of rebirth and regeneration, of resurrection into new life—of becoming. Yet I wasn't prepared for the students' enthusiasm when they entered class that day. I could have left the room for all it mattered. I was no more than a fly on the wall.

"I'm going to set up an information booth about marijuana and inhalants at Spring Faire," Luke announced. "And charge a couple of books for buttons with slogans like 'Grass and gas, not a laughing matter.' Then donate the profits for a special program here at school, maybe a drop-in center for troubled kids."

"Where they can escape their parents for a while," Codi said, passing her hand over the votive candle nearest her on the table.

"And we can be there for them like brothers and sisters," Luke said. His red hair wasn't spiked today but trimmed and combed into a soft, tousled style.

"Or friends," Tessa added.

Jason was digging into his backpack as usual, looking for his phantom pencil, no doubt. "I'll do a booth on cosmology and sell stardust for a buck. Pop will help me… If I ask."

"Where will you get stardust?" Cody wanted to know, while dripping candle wax onto a sheet of lined paper. "You could get slapped with a lawsuit for fraud."

"If you'd been paying attention at the Lick Observatory, you'd know," Jason said.

Codi rolled her eyes. "Like I really care."

The prospect of these kids taking on projects for Spring Faire with only two weeks to prepare worried me, but since thinking positive and expressing themselves was what I'd been encouraging them to do for the past eight weeks, there was little I could say or do to stop them.

"I'll make fortune cookies and sell them for fifty cents," Tessa said, her voice high-pitched and stutter-free. "With messages inside. They'll be upbeat and sound so real, people will believe them. I bet Granny Max will help me get started, and my mom will help, too."

"I'll make miniature Medicine Wheels out of beads and hoops and feathers and stuff," Codi said. Apparently, she'd forgotten about the votive candle, saving it from further abuse. I made a mental note to move it out of her reach first chance I got. "Kids can hang them in their bedrooms or from their backpacks like dream catchers, and I'll include URLs, where they can learn about the wheel's symbolism and how it represents the cycle of life. I'll make twenty of them for the cause and sell them for eight bucks."

Ethan looked up from the spot on the table that had absorbed his attention until now, his expression cookie-dough soft, his eyes like melted chocolate. "I'm going to make buffalo totems and put them in those mini zippered bags old people use for their pills. And I'll put cards inside explaining that the buffalo symbolizes survival. Since the buffalo is our school mascot, I know they'll sell."

"Tell them it's for good luck," Jason said. "It'll work better than explaining" —he glanced at Codi— "what the buffalo symbolizes."

Shawn leaned forward in his chair, his fingers working circles on the table. "I want to talk about Indigos, so kids quit thinking we're weird and work something like tarot cards into the conversation so they don't get bored."

"You mean tell people's fortunes," Tessa asked, looking like someone had just stolen her favorite toy. "Like my fortune cookies?"

"More like explaining what the cards mean. You know, take the mystery out of them, without destroying the mystery."

"How will that make any money?" Jason asked.

Shawn hesitated before answering. "It's not all about money, but I get what you mean. We'll need cash for the cause."

"You could sell the cards," Tessa said.

Shawn's brow wrinkled. "The best cards, like the Grim Reaper, would sell right away."

"How about making your own and laminating them?" I said, overstepping my new role as silent observer. "Make them colorful and mysterious, so their images help trigger the imagination like *SoulCards*."

I hesitated, half expecting Shawn to nix my suggestion. Instead he said, "Cool."

The more they planned, the more I worried. What if they were getting in over their heads? Only seven weeks ago, Jason had asked what would happen if this after-school class set them apart. Would their unique approaches to taking part in Spring Faire do just that? Maybe I should put a stop to this before it was too late; then again, maybe not. Before hiring me, Dr. Matt had said, "To see Shawn and kids like him happy again, to hear them ask questions and show enough interest to seek out the answers, would be the culmination of my career." But when push came to shove, would Dr. Matt again fail to back up his own words?

Next day the kids put their technological tools to the test, nearly frying them in the process. They brainstormed, argued, researched, and laughed. While I fretted.

"Thought equals form," Shawn reminded me while I hovered like a helicopter mom, "and mind manifests form."

"Think always and only about what you want," I said with the enthusiasm of a snail.

Shawn laughed. "I mean it, Ms. Veil. You're thinking negatively and that affects things."

"I know. But next week is Spring Break, and you'll be on your own."

"No, we won't," Jason said. "We're meeting at my house. Dad already called everyone's parents for their permission."

The news made my stomach burn. They were doing exactly what I'd been encouraging them to do, stepping into their own stories, walking their own paths, but it hurt that I hadn't been included.

Shawn looked at me and smiled.

I squinted at him. "You were supposed to teach me how to keep people out of my head."

His smile grew wider. "And deprive myself of access?"

"You dog," I said.

"Brown bear, remember?"

Symbol of wisdom, insight, introspection, protection. "Yeah, I remember…Will someone at least give me a call during Spring Break to let me know how things are going?"

"This will be a lesson in trust, Ms. Veil," Luke said.

"You do trust us, don't you?" Tessa asked.

I answered from my heart. "You guys are awesome, and I trust you."

But it didn't take long for my monkey brain to kick back in. No sooner had I gotten home that night than I started worrying again. What if this turned into a major fiasco? Not only would I get my ass kicked out of Dodge, but the kids would suffer. "Change sucks," I said. "Uncertainty sucks. The unknown sucks." I wanted to crawl back into my cocoon and hide.

Instead, I packed my bags and headed for the farm.

Chapter Thirty-six

THE KIDS RETURNED TO school on April first, heads hanging.

So much for positive thinking.

"Um, Ms. Veil…" Luke tilted his head to peer at me like a red-haired, bespectacled Einstein—minus the moustache. "We've changed our minds about Spring Fair."

I sat on the edge of my desk, the coward in me relieved, the teacher disappointed.

Tessa put both hands over her mouth and giggled, earning her a jab from Codi. Jason cleared his throat and stretched out his arms like an orchestra conductor, minus the baton. "A one, and a two, and a three…"

"April fools."

I pressed my hand to my chest to keep my heart from leaping out.

"For a minute there, you looked relieved," Shawn said, his brown eyes bright as glass beads. "You're trying to trust us, but we're only thirteen, compared to… How old are you Ms. V?"

"Twenty-nine and proud of it."

Codi grimaced. "Practically an old maid."

"She's getting married soon," Tessa announced. "A double wedding. Ms. Mask told me so. Is your fiancé as cute as Ben, Ms. Veil?"

I rolled my eyes. As cute as Ben? Hell yes. "They're practically twins."

"Will we be invited?" Ethan squinted at me as if memorizing my face for a future lineup. "Your sister said it would be okay with her, if it was okay with you."

My skin prickled. Was Ethan hearing Maya too? "Which sister?"

"Ms. Mask."

"Oh," I said, relieved. My students must have made quite an impression on my tight-lipped sister for her to share such personal news.

"Well?" Codi asked, a wary glint in her eyes, a pulling back, a suspicion that I'd forget them in June.

"We may be getting married at St. Mary's by-the-Sea Episcopal Church in Pacific Grove. Where Maya used to sing in the choir." *And where we held her funeral.*

"You could get married on the moon, and I'd be there," Tessa said.

These kids touched me in a way I would never have thought possible. Had Veronica felt the same? "I promise to send you all an invitation."

Luke cleared his throat. "Umm, back to Spring Faire. Our parents are coming tomorrow to help us set up."

🕷 🕷 🕷

Next afternoon, a BMW, an SUV, and two pickup trucks—one vintage red, the other a black king-cab towing a U-Haul trailer—pulled into the parking lot east of our classroom. A few teachers with rooms nearby used this area to park. Otherwise, it remained secluded from prying eyes. Ron Ardis dodged the bar sidestep of the king-cab on his way out the door. Luke's mom, however, planted both feet on the SUV's running board as though about to descend a steep mountain. I didn't recognize the two women getting out of the Beamer or the one driving the vintage truck.

"They're here!" Tessa dashed out the rear classroom door with five classmates in tow. I watched through the window to match parent with child. Codi ran to the vintage truck and pulled down the tailgate, ignoring the woman sliding from the driver's seat—a woman in sweats and running shoes, her brown hair twisted into a sloppy ponytail like someone waylaid after a workout at the gym. She walked to the back of the truck in slow, measured steps as if traversing a slippery slope instead of level blacktop.

Tessa and Ethan approached the two women leaning against the BMW. The petite blonde held up a set of keys. Tessa grabbed them and sprinted to the back of the car. The tall brunette frowned as Ethan followed Tessa without a backwards glance.

Ron waved me over when I approached the parking lot. I made a wide circle around the busy kids on my way to his side. Luke's mother rushed up and gave me a hug. "They're so excited."

"They've found a mission, that's for sure," I said into a mass of red hair.

Ron directed me toward the two women staring at me as if I were a celebrity. The brunette was taller than I'd estimated, had at least three inches on me. I found it hard not to cower under her intense brown-eyed stare. "This is Judge Stein, Ethan's mom," Ron said. "Your honor, meet Marjorie."

"Hello," I said.

Judge Stein reached for my hand and squeezed, conveying a positive message: *I'm on your side.* "Although my husband and I don't always agree with your methods, Ethan's attitude has improved beyond our expectations since enrolling in your class."

I smiled, cringing inside. Was she the one fueling Ethan's protests against discussing anything even hinting of God in the classroom?

The blonde I'd considered petite compared to Judge Stein, appeared about average in height when standing next to me. She wore jeans, a white T-shirt, and a turquoise windbreaker, neat and crisp, but nothing to write home about. In fact, none of the women were dressed to impress. "My name's Lisa," she said. "Tessa adores your class."

Barely had I responded with a "Nice to meet you," when Ron nudged me toward the woman in sweats and running shoes. "I'd like you to meet Blanche, Codi's mom."

Blanche? I didn't think women bore names like that anymore. Okay, so the name meant fair and white, but Blanche Baad? I opened my mouth to form a polite greeting but was spared from coming up with more than a simple "Hello" when Jenny drew our attention back to the kids. "They're really pumped up about Spring Faire."

"They're doing some serious hauling," Ron said. "Looks like the makings of a rummage sale."

I nodded on both counts. Tessa and Codi foraged materials from the BMW and red pickup like worker bees, while Ethan, Jason, and Shawn stood waiting for instructions, calling to mind drones kicked out of the hive. How had they accumulated all this stuff in two weeks? And how had they convinced their parents to lug it all over?

Ron read my face and laughed. "Worried?"

I wrapped my arms around myself to control a shiver. What if these kids—still fragile, still emerging—were mocked or, even worse, ignored?

"Oh, come on, teach. What've they got to lose?"

I raised my brows, as I often did with his son—*Wolf child, King of Hearts.*

"They're already accustomed to being ridiculed by their classmates," he reasoned. "So even if this project falls a bit flat, it won't be the end of their world." He paused, allowing his words to sink in, then added, "Anyway, seeing them this excited counts for something."

Ron's persuasive argument brought to mind one given by Granny Max during our cookie-baking therapy session. "You're helping me express and utilize my energies in altruistic love and service."

Shouldn't I help my students do the same?

Judge Stein murmured something that sounded like agreement; Jenny and Lisa voiced their unwavering enthusiasm for the Spring Fair projects; Blanche only blinked, apparently oblivious to the electricity in the air. Maybe her name fit after all.

"This is the kind of excitement I experience on making a new discovery in the cosmos," Ron said, his gaze wistful.

I found it hard to reconcile this man to the one Jason had described during our telepathic conversation in the nature area. Was this a case of Dr. Jekyll and Mr. Hyde, or just plain misunderstanding?

"It would be nice to experience that kind of excitement again," Lisa added, no doubt reliving some of her own fond memories of middle school.

"I have refreshments in the kitchen next to our classroom, if anyone's interested." Though I directed my offer to Blanche, she didn't meet my eyes or otherwise acknowledge my presence. Instead, she headed toward the building as if intuiting where comfort lay.

I glanced at the others for confirmation that something was off, but their expressions gave nothing away. "I assume you'll all be coming back tomorrow to witness the big event."

Judge Stein grimaced and put her hand to her hair. "Sorry. I have another commitment. Ethan assured me it's okay."

Don't even think about faulting her, I told myself, though I felt like giving her a good shake. *Of course, Ethan wants you to come. What can be more important than your child?*

"We'll be there," Lisa and Jenny said in unison, then broke into giggles.

I glanced at Ron. He winked. "Wouldn't miss it for the world."

"What about Blanche?" I tried to keep my voice neutral, but Ethan and Codi were about to be left out in the cold.

"I doubt it," Lisa said.

I shrugged before heading to the kitchen.

Halfway there, I heard the slap of sneakers on blacktop and turned to find Codi jogging to catch up with me. She wore a black T-shirt under her trench coat today, featuring a skull with a princess crown. I pictured my sister Veronica at her age, just as strong, just as brave, just as troubled, carrying a weight no child should be forced to bear. "I thought you should know," she said, sounding a bit breathless. "My mother's an alcoholic." She zeroed in on the open weave of my brown sweater, the kind of sweater one's grandmother would knit, the kind that makes you feel as though you're bundled in a chunky blanket. "I can get into people's heads and mess with their minds, but I can't help my own mother. Why's that?"

I thought of how Maya had chosen love over life, and there hadn't been a damn thing I could do about it. Followed by a reminder from Tessa next to James Lick's grave. "Maya's life wasn't yours to live."

"She walks her own path, Codi. All you can do is love and forgive her."

"Even when she hurts me?"

"Especially when she hurts you."

"Like Mr. Lacoste hurts you?"

And Cliff and my adoptive mother and the man who stole Maya from me. "When we hold back forgiveness, we block the flow of good in our lives."

She bit her lip.

"Uh, Codi. My dad quit drinking after Maya died."

"Does someone have to die first?"

I flinched. "Sometimes it takes something less drastic."

"Like what?"

Codi wasn't wiping her tears, so why should I wipe mine? *I wish I knew.* "Every case is different, so…"

Shawn walked by and waved, a reminder that no one was here for him either. "Codi, are Shawn's folks out of town?"

"I don't know…" Her forehead twitched. "Why don't you ask *him?*"

She had me there, but I preferred prying the information out of her rather than going directly to the source.

A knowing smile lit Codi's tear-streaked face. "Considering he reads your mind all the time."

The thought of him reading my mind still bothered me, but I returned Codi's smile. If she could find humor in the situation, so could I.

"Don't worry," she said. "He won't share." A wink. "But if he did, I bet he'd have some great stories to tell."

Chapter Thirty-seven

TALK ABOUT HAVING STORIES to tell. The kids outdid themselves. Luke's idea of adding a carnival-like atmosphere, via calliope music— *"Colonel Bogey," "That old Gang of Mine," "In the Good Old Summertime"* —with syncing lights and a rented aroma machine to give off a popcorn smell, brought in a crowd. "Being considered a bit weird can work to your advantage when it comes to carnival," he said, displaying his shrewd market savvy. "The peculiar attracts. Look at how many kids are showing up and buying our stuff, when usually they won't give us the time of day." He'd even talked Granny Max into the role of carnival barker, which she took to like a pro, tailoring her pitch to individual passers-by.

Soon students swarmed all six exhibits, not one booth more popular than the next. Lines formed, tapered off, and formed again, customers coming back a second time and a third, as if fearing they would miss out on the unusual items for sale—thereby increasing their value.

"We won't be selling products," Luke had said during one of their brainstorming sessions, "but solutions to problems people don't even know they have."

My throat hurt from holding back the tears, my chest from holding in the joy.

"I'm making a small fortune," Ethan whispered when I stopped by his display, consisting of two burlap-covered tables, four honey-scented candles, and piles of plastic pill pouches filled with mini ceramic buffaloes. "My totems are selling like... Well, you know."

"I get the point. Save one for me." I didn't mention my missing stone mouse. Not here. Not now.

He handed me a buffalo. "Better take one while they last."

I wondered if that meant I wasn't getting my mouse totem back. "Thanks, kiddo. You're doing an awesome job."

His smile didn't reach his eyes. "I know."

Moving on to Luke's booth, I noticed he'd almost run out of slogan buttons. "I should've made more," he said, counting out change. "They're practically biting my hands off to buy the ones I've got left. But no worries, I'll do rain checks." He'd gotten quite creative with his setup, using a small wooden storage shed spray painted with graffiti-type messages and slogans—*Grass and gas, not a laughing matter; Do dope, lose hope; Cope without Dope*—with multi-colored, bubble lettering of amazing quality.

I laughed when I got to Jason's black pop-up tent. With Joni Mitchell singing in the background about being stardust and an LED star ball projecting bright white beams on the inner walls, he was relating the story of man's origin. "Just think," he said to his spellbound audience, "we're all formed from stardust. Everything around us is crystallized mathematics."

Granny Max, aka Carnival Barker, who happened to be passing by, caught Jason's last words and smiled as if to say, *Math is God's language.*

On seeing me, Jason frowned. "I thought I'd ordered plenty of stardust but had to send Dad out for more." He was wearing white high-topped sneakers, white jeans, a white ribbed shirt, and a thin white headband. On anyone else, this getup would have looked ridiculous, but on Jason, well, he looked like a magician.

"Um, Jason. What's in those capsules?"

"Silicon dioxide." At my look of confusion, he added, "Everything in the physical universe is formed from stardust, Ms. V." He checked for eavesdroppers before whispering, "Which includes sand with some glitter mixed in."

Smiling as if I'd discovered the pot of gold at the end of the rainbow, I moved on to Tessa's booth. Fortune cookies gone, she'd resorted to writing messages—interspersed with tattoo-like symbols—on students' hands with fluorescent markers. I suspected each of her customers also received the benefit of her healing touch.

Codi, oh Codi. Her Medicine Wheel dream catchers were delicate yet sturdy like spider webs. Tiny colored beads and animal totems marked the four directions. I ran my fingers over a wheel decorated with faux buffalo skins and blew out my breath. "Codi, you've outdone yourself."

"They're a bit pricy, which hurts sales, but I doubt there'll be any left by the end of the day."

Each time someone stopped to inspect one of her Medicine Wheels, she stilled. *Calm as a clam*, I thought, and moved on.

Shawn's cards were selling like valuable pieces of art. I stepped in closer to inspect the ones displayed on a pegboard turntable. "I had to eliminate some of the cards I made as inappropriate for kids our age," he said. "The artist in me got carried away."

Maybe encouraging him to craft oracle-like cards hadn't been such a good idea. Like many works of art, they were open to interpretation. Depending on the viewer's state of mind, the free-flowing works could be seen as invitations to self-discovery or vessels of evil. What a relief he'd had the foresight to eliminate the ones he deemed inappropriate. It seemed everything I did with and for these kids involved risk and invited trouble.

"The ones I laminated sold right away," Shawn said. "As bookmarks and coasters."

I would have given a hearty whistle had I known how. "Good going, Shawn. Any luck with explaining about Indigos?"

"No time."

"I think they may be getting the idea."

Shawn picked up a card illustrating a man with his eyes closed and hands held out in front of him, palms up. It was hard telling if the sketched figure meant to draw in or ward off, invite or repel. "Most of the vibes I'm picking up are positive, Ms. Veil. But there's some bad energy floating around that's hard to shake off. Granny Max led a couple of rowdies out of here. The one she called 'Wyatt Earp' looked like he could cause some serious trouble. She gave him a hug and told him to shape up or there'd be more where that came from. Being cuddled by an old lady in front of a crowd probably spooked him more than threats of suspension."

Go Granny! I wondered if Shawn was reading his customers' minds.

"No time for that either," he said, his tone confidential. "The cards are a huge distraction to my original mission."

Kids pressed in like a crowd at a post-holiday sale. I met Shawn's gaze. "Are you okay with this?"

He nodded. "Good for business."

Throughout the day, I'd noticed teachers from other classes grudgingly checking out the Indigo's exhibits, but, so far, no sign of Charles Lacoste or Dr. Matt. I tried not to let this bother me. Dr. Matt, for one, had other duties on a day such as this; but darn it, offering these kids extra support had been his idea. So, where was he?

Shawn glanced over my shoulder and stilled. I turned to see the subject of my thoughts headed our way. And just like that, warmth crept into my heart. *About time.*

"I heard complaints about you stealing the show," he said.

My reaction, two thumbs up and a grin.

"Hi, Uncle Matt," Shawn called out. He looked like a kid who'd just hit a home run and wanted to share his victory with someone who cared.

Dr. Matt waved and gave him a tight smile.

Shawn's eyes lost their brilliance.

I wanted to grab Dr. Matt by the shoulders and tell him to shape up. His whole attitude was counterproductive to what he'd claimed he wanted to achieve with these kids. *Try putting yourself in his shoes*, I told myself. What could be causing his change of heart? I concentrated hard, but all I came up with was an image of Charles

Lacoste. *Oh, please, don't let it be something as petty as gossip from a fellow teacher.*

Keeping Dr. Matt in my sights, I took a deep breath and relaxed my mind. The result, a new picture, one of Angelina, smiling as if she knew something I didn't. Next came an image of Ethan. *Ethan?* I turned toward his booth and caught his eye. He looked worried— no, terrified. What was up?

Dr. Matt checked his watch— "I'll meet up with you later" — then walked away without a second glance at the exhibits the students had so painstakingly put together. Shawn followed his uncle's retreat with the blank expression of someone accustomed to such neglect.

"For crying out loud," Codi said from the booth next to Shawn's.

Yeah, I felt like doing just that. After experiencing what I had today, I realized for the second time that Dr. Matt had been right in hiring me. Too bad, on encountering a fork in the road, he'd taken a wrong turn. How long before he found his way back? For Shawn and the rest of the Indigos, I hoped it would be soon. For me, it hardly mattered. I'd lit a flame within my students, which wasn't about to be snuffed out by the likes of Charles Lacoste and Dr. Matt.

"Clean up time," I said.

Luke yelped. "We hit pay dirt."

Jason shut his cash box and shook it. "Enough to replace the projector bulb I blew. And then some."

I felt suddenly tired.

We faced a big cleanup ahead.

Chapter Thirty-eight

THE FOLLOWING MONDAY AND Tuesday just about ran themselves. I literally stepped back and watched. Right or wrong, good or bad, my efforts had sparked enthusiasm in my charges, which, according to Dr. Matt, was one measure of success at least. The kids had made a decent amount of money at Spring Faire: two hundred and fifty dollars; minus expenses, which didn't amount to much, since Luke had finagled financial sponsorship from most of their parents. They brainstormed on how best to spend the cash and planned to announce their decision during Open House, still eight weeks away.

Though he'd said he would meet up with me later, Dr. Matt continued to stay clear of our classroom—a relief. With his tight smiles and counterproductive attitude, I'd come to associate him with the bearer of bad news. I knew this wouldn't last but planned to keep that thought where it belonged, in the back of my mind, my priority to watch the students blossom and grow.

"Can you believe I'm getting paid for this?" I said at the end of Tuesday's class.

"And you deserve every dime," Jason said. "No other teacher would've stayed out of the picture this long."

"You mean kept my mouth shut."

"Your words, not mine."

On Wednesday, I broke some bad news. "Dr. Matt sent me a memo saying no more field trips, and this time, nothing and no one will persuade him otherwise."

"That leaves Dad out." Jason's light tone implied less concern about Dr. Matt's missive than whatever he was rummaging for in his backpack.

Codi tossed him a pencil. "That scraps our trip to the Winchester My-ster-y House."

Her end-of-sentence wail hardly registered before Luke drew our attention with a dramatic clearing of his throat. "Why not travel there by mind?"

Blank stares, as though he'd entered information, without pushing *Send*.

"It's called creative visualization."

No response. Luke had pushed *Send*, but the recipients weren't *Receiving*.

He trekked on. "Imagine what you want and then focus on it until it comes true."

"In your mind, anyway," Codi sneered. Message *Received* but treated as *Spam*.

Undaunted, though a bit red faced, Luke continued. "There's also astral travel, where your spirit and psyche transport to another place. Harder but more fun."

Codi rapped her fingers on the table. "And how would *you* know that, pray tell?"

Reconsidering; check *Spam* folder.

Luke hesitated just long enough to build up a smidgen of suspense, "Because I astral travel all the time."

Silence, a good kind of silence. *Not Spam, not Spam!*

"Me, too," Jason said, "and it works."

With Jason's admission, Luke's flush receded. "So, if the six of us put our heads together, we can travel as a team."

"Dream on," Ethan said. He looked uncomfortable in his own skin as if fighting the inevitable. He was an Indigo, therefore unique in unexpected ways. He could run with it or wallow in misery. Unfortunately, he seemed to be choosing the latter.

"Mind and astral travel are not imaginary," Luke said. "Scientists are researching out-of-body experiences at Stanford as we speak. So, do you want to give it a try?"

All turned to me, probably thinking I was about to freak out.

"Since you're already experiencing things beyond the norm and we're trying to stretch your abilities, I say go for it."

Eyes widened, jaws dropped, a sight so comical I had to exert every ounce of self-control not to laugh. "There's nothing wrong with being in one place physically and another mentally. People do so all the time."

Ethan chuckled. "Yeah, it's called daydreaming."

Ethan, who could look into the future, calling psychic teleportation daydreaming? Why are we so quick to downplay what we don't understand?

"No, silly," Tessa said. "What she means is, if we can't be someplace in person, we can still be there in spirit."

"You mean fantasize about it?" Codi shook her head. "Fantasy is for babies and wallflowers."

Tessa shot to her feet and waved her hands. "You still don't get it. It's like really being there."

"Yeah, right." Codi was familiar with the peculiar, so why the flippant attitude? Was she egging Tessa on?

"Angelina's been teleporting here every day since her parents pulled her out of school," Tessa said, her chest heaving like a skinny opera singer. "Haven't any of you noticed?"

Codi rolled her eyes. "Spirit walking."

"I can't believe none of you have noticed…" Tessa looked her fellow students up and down.

"I have," Jason said softly.

"I knew it!"

Shawn shifted in his chair, which drew Tessa's attention. "How about you, Shawn?"

He nodded but said nothing.

Tessa continued, "I bet when Angelina gets back, she'll know everything we've been saying and doing in this class."

"Yeah, after you tell her," Codi said.

Tessa's eyes widened. "Her parents won't even let her talk to me."

Codi glanced around as if seeking support, which came as a surprise. She normally disregarded anyone's yea or nay, something I respected her for and aimed to learn from. "I'll believe it when I hear it."

Luke pushed up his glasses and rubbed his eyes. "What makes you so skeptical all of a sudden, Codi? Either you don't get it or you don't want to."

"WHAT-ehv-err," she said with a toss of her head.

"About this astral travel stuff—" Jason turned to me. "You have no objections, right?"

"I'm here to encourage you to make the most of your gifts." I didn't add that I'd been there, done that. And it had scared the hell out of me. I'd been standing on a beach in Pacific Grove when I felt the sensation of lifting out of my body and floating above the wild, gray surf. Seagulls swooped around me. *Gah-gah-gah.* The ocean ebbed and receded, ebbed and receded. I floated down Lighthouse Avenue, past a car and a pedestrian, until I reached my friend Anne's Victorian. Tall. Stark. Ghostly. The front door was locked. No problem. I eased right through it. The crystal ball in the entry glistened and reflected my light. I drifted down the basement stairs with no fear of falling. How nice, to fly like an angel. A quick scan of the basement revealed Veronica lying on a round bed—crying. I reminded myself that this was only a dream. Veronica never cried. She was too strong, too controlled.

"Ms. V," Jason said. "Are you okay?"

I opened my eyes, rubbed my temples. "I think Luke would make a good guide."

"Since he's done astral travel before, right?" Tessa asked.

I nodded, tried to clear my head.

"Ms. Veil has done it, too," Shawn said.

The throb in my head turned into a drumbeat. "Thanks a lot, kid."

228

"Any time." He seemed pleased with himself, which was okay with me, as long as it drew him into the conversation. And the plan.

"I've never been to the Winchester Mystery House," Luke said, "but Shawn has. So, I elect him as guide."

Shawn looked down at his hands.

"You can do it." This from Tessa, a fellow chameleon urging her classmate on.

"You're in our heads half the time anyway," Codi added, "might as well make yourself useful."

Luke took off his glasses and balanced them in his hand. "Won't need these where we're going."

The clock ticked. Otherwise silence. No wind. No rain. No background music. "Someone has to stay behind," Ethan said, "to keep watch."

I caught my breath. I was about to be excluded from their journey.

"You've done this before, Ms. Veil," Shawn said, "so you can always do it on your own."

I nodded. Time to step aside. Again.

"Winchester Mystery House, here we come," Jason said.

"What if once we've projected our minds out of our bodies, we can't get back?" Codi asked, looking vulnerable—and scared.

"Once you've traveled by mind, you won't be afraid anymore," Luke said. "It's like riding a bike."

"No way. If my mom found me, she'd think I was dead and she'd do something stupid."

"She'd think you were sleeping," Jason said.

"You don't know my mother."

"Yes, I do."

"Great. Just great. You've been in my head, haven't you?"

"An invitation for investigation," Jason said. "I'm acquiring the skill."

Codi threw him a challenge. "Watch out. Revenge is sweet."

Jason shrugged. "I have nothing to hide."

She smiled in a way that implied otherwise.

"Codi's right," Ethan said. "If someone finds us, they'll think we're dead. Ms. Veil has to stand watch, or I won't go."

"What're you worried about," Luke asked, "that the bogeyman will steal our bodies while we're gone?"

"Just lock the door," Codi said.

Ethan jerked in her direction. "No! That'll make things worse."

"What in God's name are you talking about?" Codi asked, looking at him as if he were an annoying insect she'd swat if given half the chance.

"What if there's a fire drill or some kind of emergency and we don't get back in time?" Tessa asked, sounding less enthusiastic now that Codi and Ethan had expressed doubts.

I felt a prickle of apprehension, like a trick rabbit about to be yanked out of a hat by the ears. I looked at Jason. His wolf eyes shone back at me, compounding my sense of fear. Their questions were making me nervous, and I needed all the courage I could muster to allow this excursion to proceed. I reminded myself of what the priest had said about my sister at her funeral. "When Maya was stuck, when nothing seemed to be moving along, when people weren't doing what she wanted, she took herself out of the way, and miracle of miracles, things always seemed to work out fine."

"Just say the word, Ms. Veil," Shawn said into the breath-holding stillness.

As children, we'd called one another *chicken* when we needed a little help in the brave department. Sometimes bravery took a poke or a prod. Every decision came with a risk, a risk I'd never quite allowed myself to take, out of fear I'd choose wrong. What I needed now were some brave credits, like a PayPal account to draw from quickly and pay for later. Thank God, we weren't talking life or death here. What could possibly go wrong?

I leaned against the wall of bookshelves and locked my knees, feeling as ancient as the encyclopedias they held. "Okay, roll out your beach towels and go for it."

"Down on your backs," Luke ordered. "Arms at your sides, legs stretched out in front of you." He waited for everyone to comply before assuming the position himself. "Now close your eyes and take deep breaths. We want to lower our brainwave cycles into the alpha and theta state." He paused before continuing in a hypnotic voice. "You'll feel some tingling as your astral body leaves your physical body, but that's okay, just concentrate and breathe."

He allowed for a few minutes of silence before relinquishing the lead. "You're on, Shawn."

As their breathing slowed and their bodies stilled, the students appeared to be going into a deep, coma-like sleep. The wall clock ticked out the seconds, *tick tock, tick tock*. I slid into a sitting position on the floor and closed my eyes. *Tick tock, tick tock*. How long would they be gone? Minutes? Hours?

I'd read somewhere that the electrical impulses in the brain show up as squiggly lines on EEG machines and are given names such as delta, theta, alpha, and beta, depending on their waves per second. In altered states of mind, these electrical impulses heighten, and a person can experience sixty, seventy, even eighty conscious moments per second to the normal of thirty or forty. Time slowed. The outside world seemed to move half as fast. *Tick tock, tick tock*.

I felt a chill.

Tick tock.

Another wave of chills.

Too late, whatever happens, happens.

Bam!

The classroom door; I forgot to lock it.

"What the hell?"

Charles Lacoste!

My heart slammed against the wall of my chest as though someone had hit it with a bat.

"What have you done?" he cried.

Something in my head gave a painful pop. I glanced at the kids. Out cold. It looked bad, really bad.

"Oh God, oh God." Lacoste's anger spurt and crackled like fire catching hold of a patch of twigs previously too green to burn. Once the fire took hold, everything would melt and smolder until turned into ash.

The room swayed; my eyes burned. Why here? Why now?

Lacoste toed Ethan. "Wake up, buddy!"

No response.

He knelt, checked Ethan's pulse, pulled out his phone. "I'm calling for help."

I reached out to him. "They're fine. Trust me."

He bared his teeth, punched in three numbers, and charged out the back door.

I hardly had time to register that the fire station was only a five-minute drive away, Stanford University Medical Center about ten, before Charles Lacoste raced back into the room and knelt next to Ethan. "Hey, buddy, wake up."

Sirens? Already?

"You're history," he said without looking up.

A vehicle pulled into the parking lot.

Police? Ambulance? Fire truck? Never could tell their sirens apart.

Charles Lacoste stood. He was shaking. "On November eighteenth, nineteen seventy-eight, my grandparents died at Jonestown, Guyana, because of a whack job like you. Jim Jones, that crazy nut case, envisioned everyone living together in harmony and working for the common good. He had smart people like my grandparents, convinced they were living in fucking utopia. I swear, if anything happens to these kids, I'll kill you myself."

I waited for him to settle down, catch his breath. Instead, he clutched his stomach and exhaled as though he'd been punched by a log.

Then he rushed for the door.

I remembered seeing a documentary about the Jonestown tragedy and wondering how over 900 people could be gullible enough to follow someone like Jim Jones to the point of taking part in the largest mass murder/suicide in modern history. Yet, wasn't that what I expected Charles Lacoste to do? Believe the unbelievable, trust a stranger? From the rumors he'd probably heard, I, like Jim Jones, was securing the students' trust by making them feel special and providing them with a place to feel accepted for whom they were. How could I expect Lacoste to differentiate between Jones's intentions and mine? Especially after what he'd just seen.

I closed my eyes.

Another siren.

Another vehicle.

Any second now, medics would rush into the room.

Tick tock, tick tock. What was taking them so long?

I opened my eyes.

The kids were still journeying.

Commotion outside.

I walked to the bank of windows, using the tables along the way for support.

What the...?

Medics had strapped Charles Lacoste onto a stretcher and were wheeling him into the back of the ambulance. A police officer was headed for the classroom.

I stepped outside, closed the door behind me. "What happened?"

The officer frowned. "I was about to ask you the same."

"Everything's okay on this end. Charles...the guy they just put into the ambulance...made the call."

The police officer looked over my shoulder. "He said something about a mass suicide."

"He had the situation wrong."

A medic approached. "The patient has severe chest, upper back, and abdominal pain. Shortness of breath. Difficulty speaking. His blood pressure is two-sixty over one-forty. We're taking him to Stanford Hospital. Are the kids all right?"

"Kids?" I asked.

The medic pointed toward the classroom windows. I dared a peek. Six Indigos stood looking out.

I nodded, the words *Jonestown Massacre* stuck in my head. "They're fine, though probably worried about Mr. Lacoste. Will he be okay?"

"Not if we don't get his blood pressure under control." Another glance at the windows. "I must've misunderstood dispatch. Thought we were here for the kids."

The police officer and I stood in the parking lot until the ambulance and fire truck pulled onto Santa Cruz Avenue and disappeared from sight, ambulance siren blaring.

By calling 911, Charles Lacoste may have saved his own life.

After the kids had left for home, I locked all four doors leading to the classroom, hunched over my desk, and cried.

When the sobs subsided, I lifted my head and prayed, "Dear God, please embrace Charles Lacoste with your love and protection. Amen." To which I added, "I'm so sorry, Charles, that we couldn't find common ground."

Chapter Thirty-nine

IT WAS THURSDAY, APRIL eleventh, seven weeks before Open House. The votive candles were snuffed, the tables cleared, and the students' backpacks bulging for the trip home, when Dr. Matt entered the classroom without a greeting or smile. "I'd like to address the class."

I checked the time. Four forty-five. "Can it wait till Monday? There're about to head home."

He glanced at the students as they waited wide-eyed for him to continue, then focused on a spot above my head. "I prefer they get it straight from the source rather than second hand."

My heartbeat sounded like the hammer in a water pipe when the flow suddenly turns off.

Shawn came to stand next to me and took my hand, which did nothing to improve Dr. Matt's mood. His bland expression turned into a scowl. "Mr. Lacoste is in stable condition."

"I'm glad to hear that." I wished no harm to the man who so vehemently opposed me. His outburst and resulting injury were due to his concern for the kids. Too bad we disagreed on what was best for them. Too bad we were on different sides.

"He suffered a type B aortic dissection…" Dr. Matt turned to face the students as if the space above my head didn't offer the reprieve he sought "It's a tear in the inner wall of the aorta that causes blood to flow between the layers of the aortic wall, forcing them apart."

No response.

"It's amazing he survived."

Still no response.

Dr. Matt looked at me as if asking: *What have you done to these kids?* "I'm here to follow up on a situation Mr. Lacoste alerted me to before his illness." He cleared his throat and shifted his focus to Shawn. "Some of the teachers have petitioned for an end to this class, and I've also received negative feedback from Angelina's parents. I hesitated to take action because... Well, I'd hoped things would work out somehow. The lessons seemed to be going okay, but then veered off course."

"You mean, took a different path," Shawn said.

Dr. Matt's frown morphed into a press-on smile. "A member of this class has been keeping Mr. Lacoste informed."

I shot a look at Shawn, my heart feeling like an abused rubber toy.

"It wasn't me." He released my hand. "I'm no Judas."

Then who? The room seemed to heave in exhaustion, all energy sucked from its core.

Dr Matt smiled as if he'd just mastered the universe, when more likely it was about to implode. "Tell them, Ethan."

Ethan jerked to attention like a remote-controlled action figure with its power suddenly turned on. "You're asking us to conform, Ms. Veil, and I don't like it." His eyes appeared robotic in their unfocused stare, his words automated. "Greatness doesn't come from conformity."

Jeez, Ethan. He wasn't just turning on me but his classmates as well. Who had coached him? His mother? His father? Charles Lacoste? And why was Dr. Matt outing him in this way? Such exposure could have lasting effects on the poor, confused child. "That's a huge misinterpretation—"

"Yeah, sure," he said with a thin-lipped smile, the expressive lips of childhood stretched beyond recognition—along with his innocence. "You tell us not to be separate, but part of the whole. Isn't that conformity? Tell me, what's the right way?"

Talking to Ethan brought an emptiness beyond what I'd witnessed the previous day. All I'd hoped to accomplish by taking on this class was dying a slow death. From the beginning, Ethan had twisted my words and misinterpreted my messages. I longed to tell him not to worry, that everything would be okay, but didn't. Unlike Ethan, I couldn't see into the future. Why hadn't he prevented this, stepped out of the way? Did he believe the future was preordained, that he had no choice but to follow the rushing current over the jagged cliff?

"I don't know," I said, my throat clogged with tears.

"You sure say that a lot."

"Because it's true."

"You're our teacher. You're supposed to know things."

It looked like he might cry, which made holding back my emotions even harder. "I'm here to open some doors, that's all." Had my talks about thought molding reality fallen on deaf ears? "Pep talks," Jason had called them. Talk rather than action.

"No, you're supposed to tell us what to do, like Mr. Lacoste. He tells us what to do."

"He's about to flip," Shawn whispered, his hand cold as it touched mine.

"For God's sake, Ethan." Codi slapped her hand against the table, her skeleton ring hitting the surface with the hollow sound of a woodpecker hitting a knot in a tree. "Mr. Lacoste leads you by the nose. He'd make a good—"

"Drill sergeant," Jason finished for her.

Ethan's hands fisted on the table. "I like it when someone tells me what to do."

"Because you're scared," Codi said, her tone soothing as if a ventriloquist were throwing a caricature voice in her direction, dodging her usual razor-sharp tongue. "It's better to do what you think is right. In your heart, you know what's best."

"And that Mr. Lacoste is full of crap," Jason added.

Dr. Matt took a step in Jason's direction. "Now wait a minute. You're talking about a man who's fighting for his life."

"Mr. Lacoste is full of himself," Luke said, his hair looking even more tousled than usual as if he'd been running through it with frantic fingers.

Shawn shook his head and pulled in a long breath, his actions so adult, so forbearing they saddened me. I reminded myself that he could read minds and therefore knew far more than most about what was going on here. But still. What a burden. He had endorsed me for this job, and, unlike his uncle, had stood by me ever since. "It isn't right the way Mr. Lacoste has been messing with Ethan. He's one of us, and even if it doesn't seem like it, he's been trying his best."

Ethan's hands spread open on the table in front of him.

"It's okay, Ethan." Shawn smiled at his friend before turning back to his uncle. "I hoped you'd get the way things were on your own, instead of listening to Mr. Lacoste. That maybe after Spring Faire, you'd see that Ms. Veil was doing what you wanted her to." Shawn stopped, took another deep breath. "You screwed up, big time."

"Shawn," Dr. Matt said, his voice subdued. "I know drugs are hidden in this classroom."

Drugs? Dear God...

The students didn't appear surprised. Instead, their gazes veered to Ethan's owl locked behind the glass door.

"Noooo!" Ethan's cry blended with the sound of exploding glass in a way I equated with horror films and hoped never to hear again. Shards of glass burst like shrapnel from the trophy case and skittered across the floor to within inches of our feet.

Why on earth would anyone want to destroy Ethan's owl? Was this another case of uncontrolled energy?

Ethan leapt out of his chair and started forward, but Luke held him back. "No. You'll cut yourself."

"All forms return to the formless sooner or later," Ethan said, his voice so sad you'd think he was performing the eulogy at a friend's funeral. He looked at the remnants of his owl mixed in with

238

the wreckage on the floor. "You did a good job while you lasted, little buddy."

With the confidence of someone unaware he was walking through a minefield, Dr. Matt stepped over the debris. The fluorescent lights buzzed like bees in a jar as we watched him sort through the rubble with the tip of his shoe and bend to retrieve a cloth bag.

Ethan's face drained of color, his expression that of a lifeless corpse. "I'm sorry," he whispered. No thirteen-year-old should ever look like that, as if he had no reason to live.

"Mr. Lacoste and Dr. Matt are the ones who should be sorry," I said.

Dr. Matt's brows scrunched at me, but he said nothing.

"It's Xanax for anxiety and sleeplessness," Shawn said, "and Zoloft for depression." He paused and glanced at Ethan before continuing. "Some kids at West Coast are handing out the stuff for free. He was going to give it to Ms. Veil's sister, who knows a lot about drugs."

"Who's handing out the stuff for free?" Dr. Matt asked.

No response.

Why weren't the students sharing what they knew? Did they believe Dr. Matt would mishandle the information?

The name *Wyatt* floated from out of nowhere as if someone had spoken it out loud. *Wyatt?* There had been a student by that name in the remedial class I'd substituted for on my first day. I'd given him a plus for being in his seat and quiet when the tardy bell rang. Should I inform Dr. Matt? Or would doing so lead to further mistrust and misunderstanding? Best keep my ears open and mouth shut.

Dr. Matt gave Ethan a measured look as if noticing his stricken expression for the first time. "Who told Mr. Lacoste about the hidden drugs?"

"Not Ethan," Shawn said. "Someone ratted him out."

The space between us vibrated with tension, our nerve endings raw from over stimulation. The kids had known Ethan's secret without telling me. I should have been angry, or at least disappointed, but wasn't. They had used their powers to help rather than snitch on a friend. Plus, Ethan had planned to tell Veronica, which counted for something.

"And Mr. Lacoste messed up everything," Shawn said.

Dr. Matt spun to face his nephew, but Shawn held firm. "Ethan trusted him. And I trusted you."

The muscles of Dr. Matt's face seemed to pulverize like the glass from the trophy case, leaving no foundation for the skin on top. It was like watching a movie fast forward where he aged ten years right before our eyes. Shawn took a deep breath, reminding me that wisdom comes at a price. "Be thankful that Ms. Veil taught us not to judge, Uncle Matt, but to forgive."

Though pained at what I had just witnessed, I found relief knowing that no matter what, Shawn, for one, would be okay. By not passing judgment on his uncle, he had learned a valuable lesson about love and forgiveness.

Dr. Matt observed Shawn for what seemed a long time before addressing me. "I'll hold off on my decision until Open House." If he expected cheers of gratitude, he must have been disappointed. I ached for him as he stood facing an unappreciative audience. The clock clicked, a reminder that he had kept us after school. He checked his watch. "Want a ride home, Shawn?"

Shawn walked over to Ethan and put a hand on his shoulder. "We need to stay behind and give the owl a proper send off."

Dr. Matt glanced at the bag of psychotherapeutic drugs still clutched in his hand, then at the remnants of the owl on the floor. He picked up a rounded section of wing before looking at me. I didn't care that he'd caught me crying. "Can it be repaired?" he asked.

I shook my head no.

Ethan pulled in a deep breath, followed by Luke announcing, "But it can be resurrected."

Sweet Luke, not now.

"I've seen Mom do it," he said. "She crushes broken ceramic pieces and mixes them into glazes, then applies them to new projects with some amazing results."

Like desert seeds that burst open and spring to life only when activated by intense heat, Luke's slumbering powers had blossomed and sprung forth into action, resulting in new hope.

Chapter Forty

WHEN I GOT HOME, I emailed Morgan. Told him I wouldn't be driving out to the farm that weekend. Asked him to hold off on the questions, that I was okay and would explain when I could. Then I climbed the stairs to my bedroom, legs wobbly as a toddler's, and stripped off my blazer, slacks, and pumps for the unrestricted comfort of a robe and bare feet. Rather than give in to the lure of the weightless cloud of my bed's down comforter, I sought the refuge of my backyard, reclined onto the chaise lounge under the covered patio, and closed my eyes.

Birdsong. Cool breeze. Skin breathing…

🕷 🕷 🕷

I woke to a cat rubbing its face on mine. *Gabriel.* "Hey, buddy. What's up?" I would have liked to believe he was showing his love and affection by mingling his scent with mine, but no amount of wishful thinking would make that true. He'd claimed ownership of my backyard over a year and a half ago, awarding me with a *don't touch* attitude, hissing and bolting if I got too close. He consumed my food with what appeared to be ingratitude, eating each meal as if it were his last, only to demonstrate his appreciation and loyalty when I'd needed it most.

His current face rub served as a reminder that napping at dusk was not part of my daily routine. It also signaled time for his evening meal. Satisfied he'd gained my attention, he leapt onto the hardwood deck and padded to the sliding door separating him from the nourishment he needed to energize his play.

I sat up with the subtle understanding that the world wasn't what I had thought it should be. Neither, it seemed, was my life's purpose. But I didn't have the luxury of waiting for clarity about either. "Just show up," Shawn had advised during our chance meeting in Bayfront Park, along with his offer for help. Then I'd done the opposite. Took control, stopped the flow.

I needed to stop pushing my own agenda like some charismatic cult leader and allow my students to set their own course—butt out unless they required my help.

After filling Gabriel's water and food bowls, I checked my email. Morgan had replied to my gloomy message. Of course, he had. For him, love and trust came as naturally as the weather.

My Dear Marjorie. I'm here for you when you need me. Say the word and I'll drop everything to be at your side. Joshua says "Hi" and that he loves you. He also sends what he calls an important message. That he saw a barn owl last night. I figure you'll understand his meaning, as you have from the first day you met. I, on the other hand, continue to be baffled by his intuitiveness and insight. With all my love, Morgan.

Love you back, I typed. Then hesitated over "Send." *Give him more.*

I don't plan on hanging from the sagging bough of a towering fir for long, my colors concealed by closed wings. The wait is almost over. Thanks for not holding me too tightly.

SEND!

I opened a new tab in my browser and entered "barn owl symbolism" in the address bar. The first site in the search results read: *Call on the barn owl when you're going through confusing times. It's a reminder to pay attention to what usually goes below your radar, but is now of specific importance. Big changes lay ahead. Hold on. You are more powerful than you think.*

I turned off the computer. *Thanks for the warning, Joshua.*

Chapter Forty-one

LUKE, *MR. DETAIL,* THE most analytical minded and therefore mentally blocked among us, came to class on April 15 with a plan that concurred with my decision to step out of the way. "Remember when Jason said he felt like a test rat?" he asked after everyone had taken seats at their tables. "And you told him that in a way he was, that this class was an experiment and maybe we'd stumble onto something significant while fumbling around in the lab?"

I nodded, my mind fully attentive to his retrieval memory for a change. No more shaky breaths in response to his reflections and comments. No more "Good Luke. Hold that thought." Charitable, kind-hearted, companionable, *Nine of Diamonds* deserved respect, not tolerance. His ability to process incredible amounts of information should be embraced not ignored. Something told me this quality was about to pay off.

"And remember how you said that like Einstein or Ben Franklin, we should consider ourselves lucky volunteers?"

Another nod from a teacher who'd failed him with her determination to revise and edit the details of his story.

Luke took off his glasses and propped them on his head, his attention turning inward, where the precision of vision no longer depends on where light focuses on the retina but on the soul's inner essence, where perceptions come alive with razor sharpness. "Let's see what we can do with the molds we've been poured into."

Okay. So far, so good. A rerun of previous lessons—with a twist. I grabbed a chair and sat facing the students. Luke held center stage, and I meant to keep him there, beginning with a question: "Are you talking about experimenting on ourselves?"

"Sure, why not?" Luke rose from his seat and walked to my side at the top of the U. He glanced at me and some kind of understanding sparked between us. I nodded, and he took it from there. "We were all born with something special, or we wouldn't be here, right? So, let's quit making excuses for whatever makes us special and start putting it to use. No offense, but we've been acting like a bunch of half-conscious addicts. What we need to do is wake up and get to work." He peered at me with the myopic squint of someone trying to read the smallest line on a Snellen eye chart. "That is, if you give it a go, Ms. Veil."

Give it a go? Hell yes. The perfect opportunity to stop pushing my own agenda.

Before I could voice my reply, Jason broke in from the opposite end of the U. "Hey man, instead of a bunch of underachievers, we might be budding Einsteins."

"We already are," Luke said. "The biggest obstacle to this class's success is thinking things impossible."

Another dose of my own medicine but, evidently, easier for the students to swallow coming from Luke. No more fiddling with the contents of backpacks or staring at the animated vista outside the classroom window. No more peering into compacts or doodling on hands with black markers. The students appeared to be tuning in, and it took *Mr. Trivia* to point their receptors in the right direction.

I thought back to what Dr. Matt had said during my impromptu job interview. "I'm talking about kids who thought and spoke like adults at age nine, born with knowledge and wisdom independent of age or experience. They're way beyond what we're teaching them in school. Yet, they lack the keys to succeed. Which leads to confusion and restless impatience simmering just below the surface or, in a worst-case scenario, explosive anger and aggression." Maybe experimenting on their own terms was exactly what these kids needed. Before it was too late.

245

"I'm sick to death of looking for answers in books," Luke said. "So, before we experiment on ourselves, we'll experiment with water."

"What're we gonna do?" Ethan asked from his seat backing the east wall of windows. "Change water into wine?" I was glad to see Ethan come alive again, after the heartbreaking destruction of his owl. Luke had taken the pieces home to see if his mother could "resurrect" it. Via her talented and compassionate hands, it would no doubt turn out even better than before. A reminder that life is a series of births and resurrections, challenging us to grow, learn, love, and connect.

Luke took the glasses from the top of his head and slid them into place, bringing his external vision back into focus. "Actually, you're not that far off, Ethan. We're going to change water, but not the way Jesus did. More like the way Masaru Emoto did."

Squinted looks of confusion from his classmates.

"Apparently, you geniuses haven't heard of the guy. His experiments with water show the high likelihood that our thoughts aren't locked inside our heads and can actually change physical matter."

"Jason already proved that," Codi quipped. No votive candles on the table to help her de-stress today, though she didn't seem to notice. Twisting the skull ring on her right hand appeared to serve as her current fidgeting tool.

"Yeah, well, we need to prove it scientifically," Luke said, "or remain a laughing-stock."

"Scientific proof is a myth," Shawn mumbled.

The blades of Luke's thin shoulders rose and fell beneath his jersey T-shirt. "Okay then, at least we need to support the *theory* with evidence we can measure and observe, if not outright prove."

"Sorry to pop your bubble," Codi said, "but there's no convincing the skeptics. They're not ready to believe what we say or do. It freaks them out. They'd rather think of our gifts as misbehavior, mental illness, even scams. Sure, we got some positive vibes going during Spring Faire because of Luke's marketing skills. You know, lights and music and colorful props. And Jason gets by with pretending to be a trickster—"

"Magician," Jason inserted.

"Harry Potter, Harry Houdini, con artist, whatever. You know what I mean. And that gives people permission to clap for what you do like mindless rock fans instead of thinking you're one weird, crazy duck."

Luke's face reddened, and I wondered why. Then I remembered he'd chosen the duck mold to pour the slip of his thoughts into. The duck, symbolizing persistence and patience, a reminder to release one's intellect and embrace one's intuition, something difficult for Luke to do. "Maybe being considered a magician works for Jason," he admitted. "But, like Codi said, what we do...and I'm talking real magic here...scares the bejesus out of most people, including our parents. So, we need to explore it from an evidence-based, scientific perspective. Eyewitness testimony counts for zilch until measured in controlled experiments. What we see and do is taken no more seriously than an exaggerated good story."

"Lots of people think what we're doing here is evil," Ethan said.

"And dangerous," Tessa added from the seat to my right that she'd claimed in Angelina's absence.

Codi glared at Jason. "Which it can be, if treated like a joke."

"I hate the word evil." Ethan said. The heavy, soporific light entering the room through the windows behind him made him appear gray and out of focus, one more strike against a kid whose smoky white aura already cast him in shadow.

"I'm with Luke," Codi said, "if only to make ourselves feel less like freaks. So, what's the plan?"

Luke shoved his glasses back to the bridge of his nose, a gesture as distinctive as Codi's eye rolls. "We'll start by thinking in a focused way as a team."

Codi chuckled. "You mean, like the beam of a laser, powerful enough to—"

"Are we going to shoot laser beams from our eyes like Superman?" Jason asked.

"Quit messing around," Luke said. "This is serious. We'll all think the same thought at the same time and direct it toward water. And before you bombard me with more questions and wise-cracks, let me explain."

"Are you talking about how my thoughts find their way into other people's heads?" Codi asked, staring at the skull ring on her finger with the intensity of someone expecting it to speak.

Luke looked relieved that at least someone was taking him seriously. "Not just find their way in, but influence."

"Influence water. Cool," Jason said. "Like Moses parting the Red—"

"We're going to start with a simple test," Luke interjected. "We'll need matched controls of tap water. One to treat with our thoughts, the other to leave untreated."

"How do you prove the water has been affected by our thoughts?" Jason asked, getting serious at last.

"I'll explain tomorrow—"

Codi shifted in her seat in a way that suggested she was warming up to Luke's ideas and had input of her own. "Why not focus on something bigger, like a plant, and see how it reacts to our thoughts? Or seeds. Focus on seeds, then plant them and see what happens?"

Luke shot her a stern look like the ones I'd directed at him on many an occasion. "One experiment at a time, Codi. Anyway, I was thinking of calling our experimentation 'To the Eighth Power.'"

"But there are only six of us without Angelina," Tessa pointed out.

"You're not counting Ms. Veil and Granny Max," Luke said.

"But Granny Max doesn't have psychic abilities."

"We're all psychic to a degree. Plus, she's a mathematician, specializing in statistics. We can't just base our beliefs on anecdotes and personal experience."

"Are you saying, we're going to prove the power of prayer?" Tessa asked.

"In a way, except I'd rather call it the power of focused attention."

"Have you already talked to Granny Max about this?" Codi asked from her seat next to Tessa.

"No, but I'll bet she's in once I explain what we're doing."

"Shouldn't we okay this with Dr. Matt first?" she persisted, suddenly Miss-Play-By-The-Rules.

"Get real, Codi. We're talking about experimenting with water. Do you really think we need Dr. Matt's permission for that?"

The way things had been going, Dr. Matt would probably say no regardless of what we were doing, so I mentally sided with Luke. It was the students' turn to lead and time for well-intentioned outsiders like Dr. Matt and me to stop meddling and start practicing what we preached.

Luke turned to me with a small triumphant smile. "What do you say, Ms. Veil?"

"I say, go for it, with one stipulation…" I gave Ethan a warning look. *And this includes you.* "That we keep what we're doing in this classroom to ourselves for now. Depending on the outcome, you risk becoming sought-after school celebrities or shunned as wackos. And neither case scenario is something we should encourage or seek."

Chapter Forty-two

OKAY, SO WE AS a class already knew our thoughts weren't locked inside our heads. Thoughts, according to our experience, were trespassers, capable of traversing other people's minds and objects, even influencing them in some way. So, what if, as Luke had suggested, we sent our collective healing thoughts to a targeted substance? If a group of people thought the same thought at the same time, would that magnify the effect?

On Tuesday, Luke staged an experiment as a trial run to discover just that. He'd purchased a box of pH test strips, and, within minutes of everyone's arrival (minus Granny Max, who hadn't yet been pulled into the fray), he poured two glasses of water from the kitchen tap and labeled them "A" and "B." He selected the glass labeled "A" as the target for our group and the one marked "B" as the control. Then he dipped pH strips into both glasses and, after a few seconds, pulled them out and compared the color changes to the chart on the box. He recorded the results into a journal titled *To the Eighth Power* and placed the control glass of water in the kitchen.

"The pH of a liquid has to do with the concentration of hydrogen ions in water compared to a universal standard," Luke explained. "It measures the sample's acidity or alkalinity. The lower the pH measures below seven, the more acidic the substance; the higher, the more alkaline. The normal range for tap water is between six and eight-point-five. The water samples in both glasses I just tested registered seven-point-zero. So, our intention for this experiment is to raise the pH of the water by one full pH, to eight-point-zero.

Remember, this is only a quick test to see if we're onto something. We'll get to more complicated tests later. Got it?"

"Got it," we said in unison, undaunted that Luke had commandeered us into his investigative experimentation like seven docile test rats.

Luke placed the target glass of water on the floor and had us form a loose circle around it. "Consider this our power circle," he said, "held together by our purpose and intention."

The mention of a power circle reminded me of something I'd shared during our lesson on shifters. "When I feel the need to conquer some critical self-attacks or seek answers to seemingly unanswerable questions, I construct a big circle, sit inside, and meditate."

"A magic circle?" Luke had asked.

"Only if by magic circle you mean a place to bring about desired changes," was my reply.

Now, following Luke's lead, we breathed in and out as we'd done during our previous meditation sessions. "Focus your mind on the water," he directed, "then repeat after me: 'I'll do everything in my power to raise the water's pH by one full unit on the pH scale.'"

We focused and repeated as instructed.

"A full unit on the pH scale is a huge shift," Luke said, "so concentrate hard. If your body's pH went up that much, you'd be dead."

Jeez, Luke. Thanks for that vital piece of information.

"Okay," he said. "Keep your eyes on the water and visualize the pH rising to a darker green color on the test strip. Hold that thought for ten minutes. Believe in the desired outcome."

A stream of energy coursed over my arms and neck to the top of my head, producing a hair-standing-on-end sensation, as if I were part of a giant force field. I tore my gaze from our target long enough to glance at the students. They appeared relaxed, eyes focused on the glass of water in the center of our circle.

Just as my head started to ache and my limbs to feel heavy, Luke called an end to our session. We waited, eyes blinking, as if re-entering the classroom from a distance. Luke picked up the glass from the center of the circle and placed it on the counter below the wall of windows. He then headed for the kitchen to retrieve the control labeled "B." On his return, he placed the control water next to the target water and dipped a test strip into each.

One second, two seconds, three, four, five…

I felt a surge of excitement, as if waiting for the outcome of a Powerball lottery, where, considering the remote chance of winning, reason and logic are abandoned in favor of hope.

Luke lifted the test strips out of the solution— "A" in his right hand, "B" in his left—and waved them in the air to shake off excess moisture. Then he compared them to the color chart on the back of the pH strip package. "Only one of the test strips shows a marked change in color," he said. "The one dipped into glass 'A.' Not exactly a full unit rise in pH, but close."

Fist pumps all around. "Yes!"

🕷 🕷 🕷

"Now, don't get all excited," Luke warned as we gathered in the classroom the following afternoon. "Lots of people use pH strips to measure the chemistry of their pools and their body fluids, so we're not talking rocket science here. It was just a quick way to warm up our engines. We need to move on to more serious stuff, like making a prediction based on the hypothesis that our thoughts aren't locked inside our heads and can actually change physical matter. Then we need to test the prediction. Using lima bean seeds."

"Lima bean seeds?" Jason smirked. "Don't they have high levels of cyanogen?"

A small burst of air through Luke's nose. "We're going to experiment with them, not eat them."

"Good," Codi said. "I don't do the lima bean thing. They make me gag."

"We want to see if sending them our healing intention will affect

252

their growth and health. The prediction being that the answer will be yes."

"Instead of making them shrivel up and die, you mean," Jason said.

Luke ignored him. "We'll start with four sets of ten seeds. One for our target and three for our controls." He poured seeds from a paper bag onto the table in front of him and sorted them into four groups of ten. "I nabbed these from Mom's stash in what Dad calls her 'Fallout Shelter Pantry.' It's stocked full of canned food, powdered milk, jerky, and vacuum bags full of whatever else she thinks we'll need in case of a nuclear war. As far as I'm concerned, her hoarding is useless. If we don't get cremated by the initial blast, we probably won't survive the radioactive fallout."

Tessa shuddered. "So much violence. Can't we just make the world a better place?"

Luke paused from his monologue long enough to say, "Maybe someday. In the meantime, how about you choose one group of seeds so we can get started?"

Luke put the ten seeds Tessa had selected into a plastic bag and labeled it "A" with a black marker. The rest of the seeds went into three control bags, labeled "B," "C," and "D," which he placed in the kitchen.

On his return, Luke set bag "A" on the floor and instructed us to form a circle around it. "Now, close your eyes and do your meditative breathing. Clear your minds and hold the intention that the seeds will sprout and grow at least three centimeters by Monday. Picture them healthy and thriving. Connect with each other along with the target, like a psychic Internet, and hold the intention for ten minutes. Believe that these seeds will grow faster and be healthier than the untreated controls."

I found his instructions easier to follow this time around than during our previous experiment, as if I were improving with practice.

"Time's up," Luke said after what seemed like seconds instead of minutes. "Tomorrow, we're going to repeat what we did today and give the seeds another jolt of good intentions. Granny Max has agreed to be our lab technician. I won't tell her which set of seeds we selected as our target and which our controls. She'll plant and water the forty seeds tomorrow after we leave class. On Monday she'll harvest and measure them.

"I'll choose four more sets of seeds as a second-tier control. I'll label one set as our target, even though we won't be sending it our intention. I'll plant and water the seeds under the same conditions Granny Max uses. Then I'll harvest and measure them on Monday and have Granny Max record the results. Any questions?"

Chapter Forty-three

BETTER GET USED TO it," Linda, my future sister-in-law, warned over coffee and scones at the ranch-house kitchen table. Carla was getting groceries at the local supermarket, the boys practicing hockey on a roll-up shooting pad in the back yard, and the men prepping equipment for spring harvest. "Privacy doesn't come easily on a family farm. Everyone, mother, father, sons, daughters-in-law, grandchildren, cats, dogs, becomes part of your family. And your life. Which, let me tell you, takes some getting used to." She laughed and took a long, appreciative sip of coffee. "We van Dykes band together when times get tough. That's what we're good at, joining forces, protecting our own."

Protecting, or confining? I'd been there, done that, with Cliff and my mother—my protectors, my jailors. Would marrying into Morgan's family rob me of the freedom I sought so desperately? Would it mean surrendering my sense of worth, my newfound individuality? I didn't know Linda well enough to voice my concerns, so I kept silent.

"It's the small stuff that gets irritating," she said. "And frustrating. Small stuff that can take on monstrous proportions if you let it. Petty jealousies, grouchiness, bad crops, the constant need to pinch pennies. God, I get tired of hearing 'Next year things will be better.'"

Linda's sharing was personal. Another reason not to interrupt. Sometimes it's best to listen and allow things to play out. My students had taught me that at least. Plus, she was saying what I needed to hear. Morgan and I still had to set a wedding date. A double wedding with Veronica and Ben. I couldn't just leave them all hanging.

"Weigh the pluses and minuses before you opt in," Linda continued, as if I hadn't been doing that for months. "And when Pop and his two sons argue, stay clear."

I wiped my forehead with the back of my wrist. Carla wasn't the type to leave the thermostat set high, so the surge of heat I felt must have been coming from within.

"When he yells and calls his sons lazy asses, don't get pulled into the fray. They'll iron out their differences in no time and defend each other to the death. And you'll be glad you kept your ears plugged and mouth shut."

My coffee and blueberry scone stood untouched as I hung on to Linda's every word.

"Love Morgan, love his family with all its foibles, and expect us to do the same. But set your boundaries. I mean, from day one. You're marrying Morgan, not the whole clan, though at times it may feel like it. The van Dykes can drive you nuts, especially 'Old Leo,' whose bark is worse than his bite. But his bite still hurts. As it's meant to. It's his way of making sure we'll be ready to take over the reins when he's gone. Which, according to his calculation for the last five years, is 'any day now.'"

Linda halted and grabbed my mug. "You haven't even taken a sip." She emptied it in the sink and poured a refill. "Drink. You look like you could use the caffeine."

The warmth of the mug brought comfort as did the warmth in Linda's eyes. "Thanks."

"Drink," she said.

I took a sip. Hot and strong, just as I liked it. But getting the advice-laced liquid past the lump in my throat proved difficult. The family Linda described sounded formidable, though it was as clear as the untouched scone on my plate that she hadn't been brow beaten by joining their forces. Quite the opposite. She exuded confidence in the certainty that she'd found her place in the world. And liked it just fine. Was there hope for me?

"Momma Carla will smother you with love if you allow it, and so will my kids. I, on the other hand, will irritate you in ways yet unknown. My husband will be the first to testify that I'm infuriating as hell, a regular slave driver."

"Ha." I felt my spirits rise. "Someone I can learn from."

She chuckled. "And I from you."

I topped my scone with blueberry jam and took a bite, followed by another sip of coffee, both going down smoothly this time.

"Apologies to Morgan," Linda said with a grin, "but I'm sharing this up front. Draw the line...I mean, thick and bold, no wimpy squiggles...when it comes to what you will and will not tolerate as far as interference in your life. I, for one, will try to respect your wishes, as I hope you'll do for me."

I got up for coffee refills, an easy task, since we both drank ours black. I glanced at the clock. Twelve-thirty, nearly lunch time. Carla would show up soon, as well as the men. Lunch at one o'clock wavered only during emergencies, which seemed to occur exclusively at night and on weekends and holidays, as if some impish force were at work as a reminder that complete control on a farm is an illusion. From what I'd learned during my short visits thus far, Morgan took farm crises in stride, his attitude one of optimism and humor. He believed that true happiness came from watching his crops grow, his family thrive, and giving more to the world than he took from it. I couldn't wait to share with him—in private—the goings on at West Coast Middle School. Eight weeks and my stint there would be over. Eight weeks to prove that I had a talent worth sharing and the courage to share it. Eight weeks to help—and let go of—some of the smartest and most precious human beings I'd ever met.

"Boundary one," Linda said, as I handed her the last of the coffee. "Don't think for a minute that because I love, absolutely love, life as a stay-at-home mom, wife, and slave to the farm, you need to feel the same. Actually, I'd prefer you don't. We need a little balance here. Maybe you can bring something new to the table, something you and I can share over coffee between chores. I've heard how you helped Joshua speak again, something for which the van Dyke family will be forever grateful. I've also heard about the joy and pain you've experienced with the biological family you've only recently come to know. So, get this straight. I respect and admire you and want to get to know you better. Bring the outside world in for me, Marjorie. I could use a new friend, as well as a sister."

How much more of Linda's heart-felt revelations could I internalize before breaking into tears? She was too good to be true, and I wanted to respond accordingly, but…

"I know, this is a mouth full," she continued, "but once I shut up and get back to work, I may never get another chance to share what's on my mind. We could start on the wrong foot and build a wall of resentment and silence no less impenetrable because it's invisible to the eye. I've seen it happen on countless family farms, leading to years of silent hostility and the eventual break-up of the business. Because no one took the time to bare their thoughts, feelings, and love from the get-go."

She blew out her breath. "Sorry, but this last part's big, so bear with me. Morgan, that sweet brother-in-law of mine, is the type of person who loves because it's in his nature to do so. Once he's in, he's all in, no safety net, no holding back. You've captured his heart, big time. And his love for you increases every day. I don't know if I need to be telling you this, but he's someone you can depend on. I mean, he's rock-solid. Good thing I'm married to David, or I'd give you a run for your money."

After a long sigh signaling Linda's heartfelt monologue was over, she scooted out of the kitchen booth and rounded the table to give me a hug. "I'm not good at showing my affection, but, for you, I'm making an exception."

I stood and embraced her. "Thank you. I needed to hear what you had to say. Morgan and Joshua are either blind or too kind to admit that I suck at relationships. I mean, really, really, suck. One of my greatest fears is that I'll fail the van Dyke clan, let alone the two guys I love most in the world. I hope to learn from you how to give of myself without losing myself. From what I've seen, you've got that part down. Can we do this again soon? I want to share what's in my heart as you've just done, but right now, I'm not able to put into words how I feel."

"You bet, girl. We need to stick together. It'll be six to three in the van Dyke family, but though outnumbered, we're a force to be reckoned with. We're the fuel for the men's engines, and they're smart enough to know it. They can't run on empty."

🕷 🕷 🕷

Before I left for Menlo Park, Morgan, Joshua, and I spent two uninterrupted days and nights in our nearly completed home. The only things missing were some of the finishing touches and furniture, which we planned to choose together soon. When Morgan and I were alone, I explained the situation at West Coast Middle School and promised no more repetitions of last week, where I'd left him in the dark as to my mental state of health. I'd keep him informed and part of my world, if only from a distance.

Chapter Forty-four

THE STUDENTS AND I entered the classroom Monday afternoon eager to witness the results of Luke's germination-intention experiment. Granny Max arrived, folder in hand, no doubt holding photos, diagrams, and charts. Although the results would be observable without her research records—bean seeds being large and their sprouts easily viewed—her work would be invaluable in detailing the procedure used and subsequent findings.

After we'd taken our seats, Granny Max stepped into the U formation of tables. She explained that, after school on the previous Thursday, she'd planted and watered all the seeds in the same manner under standardized conditions—same soil temperature of sixty-eight degrees to a depth of one-inch; same containers on the kitchen counter below the east-facing wall of windows—which gave the seeds nearly four days to sprout though not fully emerge. Today at noon, she'd harvested and photographed the seeds she'd planted, then measured their length in centimeters and recorded the results. She did the same with the seeds Luke had planted as a second-tier control. "Thanks to my mathematical and statistical expertise," she said with a grin that implied she was putting us on, "and my basic understanding of the organization and conveyance of scientific thought, I was able to whip up some graphs and charts to display the factors for germination."

Codi released a hurry-up-and-give-it-to-me-straight sigh. "Did the experiment work or not?"

"Well, love, I can't tell you that, since I don't know which seeds were the target and which the controls."

Another sigh from Codi, which prompted Granny Max to add, "What I *can* tell you, however, is that one set of seeds outgrew the others by—"

"Which ones?" Codi blurted.

"Hold it." Luke reached for Granny Max's folder. "Let's see what our lab technician recorded before we divulge which seeds were which."

"Control freak," Codi said, though not unkindly.

Luke studied the photos, charts, and graphs with a dead-pan Botox brow. You'd think he was channeling his inner Spock the way he showed no reaction or feeling.

Okay, Luke, quit messing with us.

He glanced up at Granny Max and his frozen expression thawed into a smile. "Impressive work."

The depth of Granny Max's sigh equaled Codi's only minutes before, though it conveyed a different meaning. "Well! It's about time I receive a little recognition for my mathematical abilities, which are totally unappreciated teaching a bunch of" —she glanced at me— "students with empty mental gas tanks, who aren't amicable to the fun and excitement of math."

Before Granny Max could start a math exposé worthy of a TED Talk, Jason interjected. "Well, said, Granny Max. The results, please."

Luke held up what appeared to be a bar chart. "The plant embryo of the target bean seeds marked 'A' grew five point six centimeters compared to four point eight centimeters for the non-targeted seeds. Which means, not only did our target seeds outgrow our intention of three centimeters by two point six centimeters, but they also grew about a third of an inch taller than the controls. The seeds I planted as a second-tier control grew four point eight centimeters and less. Which means" —Luke hesitated, an obvious tactic to build suspense— "our intention had a big effect on the results."

A silence descended over the room.

"Well," Luke said, while I tried to think of something insightful to say.

"We did it," Tessa whispered as though witnessing a miracle.

"Soooo…" Codi's cheek rested on her palm; her expression boringly blank. "Now that we've proved what we already knew, where do we go from here?"

"We move on to another experiment," Luke offered.

Codi's eyes orbited in their sockets. "What the hell for?"

"We need to take it to the next level."

"Like what?" Ethan asked.

"See if we can affect human health."

"You mean, like Tessa did with Angelina?" Codi asked, straightening in her chair.

"We have no proof that Tessa affected Angelina's health," Luke said. "Angelina says so, which in my book is evidence enough, but we have to back something like that up with facts and figures."

Another eye roll from Codi. "How? Angelina's not here."

"We'll send our intention to someone in this room. And before you ask 'Who'? I want Codi to repeat what she told me yesterday after school."

"I told you that in confidence, Luke."

"Drastic times call for drastic measures."

"But—"

Luke glanced at Granny Max. "I don't think the person we were talking about will mind."

Granny Max's face turned a paler shade than usual. Come to think of it, she'd been looking rather ashen lately. Her upbeat attitude, however, had erased any thoughts of a cause from my mind. As with one of Jason's slight-of-hand tricks, she'd only allowed me to see and believe what she wanted me to see and believe. She grimaced, then wiped her eyes with the back of her hand. "Holy Toledo, nothing's private around here."

Codi looked like she wanted to leap over the table and give her a hug. "Sorry."

"I'd like to ask your permission, Granny Max" —Luke took a deep breath and released it slowly as if the request he was about to make affected him more than he was letting on— "to send our intentions for your recovery and good health."

Recovery? Dear God, was Granny Max sick, too?

It took a few moments for Granny Max to answer, which she prefaced with a what-the-heck shrug. "They'll perform my breast cancer surgery in sixty days, followed by chemotherapy and/or radiation. The call from my doctor came as quite a shock, if you must know, but it is what it is. Breast cancer. Treatment in June. After school's out, so not to abandon my students. And...well...my oncologist and care family need time to develop a personalized treatment plan and consider all my options. You know, lots of tests and procedures and workups and... Anyway, I trust my doctors completely. You bet I do.

"That said, you have my permission to send your intentions for my speedy recovery on one condition, that you call it prayer to the great Lord above. I realize prayer doesn't sound as scientific as intention, but since I'll be serving as a human guinea pig...not only for you, but for the team of doctors who'll be attempting to save my life...let an old fuddy-duddy call the shots on how you approach the Divine Universal Energy, or whatever you call *It.* And, allow me to add another two cents of wisdom that I've gained from being on this earth five times longer than you have. I've witnessed and therefore believe in the abilities the good Lord gave you. And I believe He gave them to you to use for the good of your fellow man. But you are not God. If it's not His will for me to become well, nothing you do or say, no matter how focused your intentions, will change that. Your powers may be great, but God's are greater."

Granny Max eyed us one by one. "I love you. I love what you're trying to do. And that's what matters here. Love. Do you understand? Love. If for some reason, your prayers and the best efforts of my doctors fail to cure my cancer, it's God's will and I'm okay with that. He gave me sixty-nine years of reasonably good health to pursue a career that brought me more joy than I ever believed I'd experience on this earth. A career so good, in fact, that it's hard to believe Heaven can offer anything better. But I'm ready to find out if and when the time comes. If you guys are okay with that, go for it. I'll help in any way I can. But no charts, graphs, and photos on your part until June when the doctors take over. I'll keep a daily journal on how I feel until then, which I'll share with you, and I'll provide you with the results of all blood tests and x-rays the doctors have performed and will perform over the months to come, which should give you some good before-and-after visuals of my progress. But that's all you're going to get from me. Got it?"

At our silent nods, she added. "And one last thing, probably the most important of all. You don't need to prove anything to the world, only to yourselves. Because, my dears, I've seen other students like you pass through West Coast Middle School. You may be happy to know that they've done quite well in the medical field, as teachers, and in many other occupations, without broadcasting their gifts. Learning how to use your powers is just the beginning. Using them for the common good should be your goal. Now, I've got to go. I'm tired, though my heart feels young and healthy due to your kindness and love.

"Toodeloo, my friends."

🕷 🕷 🕷

Granny Max sat behind her desk, three hours after the closing bell, sorting through a stack of papers and singing the lyrics to Celine Dion's "That's the Way It Is," as though she didn't have a care in the world. *I can read your mind and I know your story…* I stood amazed at how much time she spent at school after her classes ended for the day. Did she have a husband? Kids? Grandkids? I'd never thought to ask. For now, I just wanted to offer my help and support. She must have been going through hell since learning she had breast cancer, and she'd never let on.

She hadn't heard me enter, so I took a few minutes to look around. Where I'd expected a room as drab and uninspiring as the math classes of my youth—with posters of fractions, decimals, and equations on walls the color of hospital rooms that inspired more gut-sliding than flying—my gaze instead locked onto a mural of a ten-foot lightbulb splattered with kaleidoscopic colors. Blues, greens, yellows, purples, pinks, oranges, and whites struck it from all directions and ricocheted onto the surrounding surface like gun shots, displaying tints and hues of an imagination gone wild. The heart-stopping mural fortified my conviction that—though still small and wet due to the tight space of my metamorphosis—with a little more flapping and pumping, my wings would soon harden for flight.

Posters of math wit and wisdom covered the remaining walls— *The essence of mathematics lies in its freedom. ~Georg Cantor; Mathematics is the most beautiful and most powerful creation of the human spirit. ~Stefan Banach.* Pentagons, hexagons, pyramids, and trapezoids hung from the ceiling like jeweled piñatas. I imagined taking this all in as a teen, and realized that, yes, in such an environment, math could be exciting and fun, the language of the soul.

"What are you still doing here, Granny Max? I thought you were tired."

She looked up and her whole face smiled. *Trickster sage, presenter of wild wisdom.* "Do you have a beau, Marjorie?"

Now, where did *that* come from? "Yes, I do."

"Then why aren't you with him instead of here?"

"He lives in Elk Grove, a three-hour drive away."

"So, I repeat. Why aren't you with him instead of *here?*"

She raised her brows at my slow response.

"I took on this job to find myself." I felt silly saying it out loud. Still searching at twenty-nine years old? "And contribute to the world in a meaningful way. Until then marriage is out."

"Which, more or less, answers the question you asked me. Except I'm not trying to find out how I can contribute to the world. I've already discovered that, and I've been doing it for forty-six years."

At my silence, she shook her head. "Marjorie, dear, I plan on teaching as long as possible and go out kicking and screaming. Most instructors my age have been retired four to ten years, but I'm not budging. I gave up marriage and a family of my own for my career, and I don't regret it for one minute. Teaching is my life. The students are my children." She chuckled. "Actually, my grandchildren by now. Anyway, I don't own a pet. I don't have a garden. I have no hobbies, besides baking cookies when I see the need. I'm independent and free, just how I like it." Another smile. "Yes, I know, freedom comes at a price, a price I was willing to pay to do what I love. So, my dear, don't worry about me. There's nothing like grading my students' work and helping them improve to relieve any distress I might feel at the sliders that life throws my way. If you get what I mean."

She'd given up marriage and a family of her own for the freedom to do what she loved to do. Was that the kind of freedom I sought? "Yes, I believe I do, my friend."

"And if you're here to talk about the cancer…"

"I think I'm getting the picture. You plan to live each day with a positive attitude and not dwell on what might or might not happen. But please let me offer my support, as you've done for me."

"Having no family to provide for means I've built up quite a nest egg," she said, "which means I can afford to hire out most of what I need. Lawn service, house cleaning, grocery shopping. I'm a totally independent woman."

"How about emotional support?" I asked.

"I have God for that."

I stepped up to her desk and hugged her. "Bet He can't do this." Then I kissed her cheek. "Or this."

Granny Max seemed to deflate in my arms, not due to loss of self-assurance or good cheer, but in recognition that no one is totally independent in this world. "I wouldn't be so sure about that, although to be quite honest, He has neglected that means of support until now. So, I do appreciate the hug and kiss, I really do."

"And there's more where that came from," I said, recalling her words to the rowdy kid she'd nicknamed Wyatt Earp during Spring Faire after spooking him with an embarrassing hug.

"Tell you what," Granny Max said, her voice a bit slurred. "I'd love to meet your beau sometime. Bet he's really something if he's claimed your heart."

"Yes, he is. How about I take you to meet him after school's out? I'd also like you to meet my soon-to-be adoptive son, Joshua. He, too, might be an Indigo."

"Sounds heavenly. Now leave me to my work so I can get home before dark."

I'd come to offer my support and ended up receiving something I needed to hear. I cast her a parting glance. "See you tomorrow for our intention experiment."

"Prayer experiment," she said as I headed out the door.

Chapter Forty-five

PRAYER OR INTENTION. WHAT distinguished the two? Weren't they both ways of using the mind to manifest a desire or cause things to happen? Or was intention only meant to be used for things that lay within our power to control; and prayer, as Granny Max had suggested, reserved for what lay beyond our power to control? If prayer was a way to address God, then whom were we addressing through intention? Our own source of power? Should intention, then, be limited to the mundane, like influencing the growth of seeds and plants and affecting the pH of water; and prayer be reserved for the imperative, like curing Granny Max and Angelina of cancer? Either way, weren't we projecting our own energy into the Universe for a particular outcome? Such thoughts plagued me all night and during my drive back to school on Tuesday.

Today we would send out our intentions for Granny Max's good health in the form of prayer. But who would lead us? Science-minded Luke? Jason, dealer in magic? Codi or Shawn, readers of minds? Tessa, our reluctant healer?

Angelina would have been my choice, since she regularly attended Mass at St. Joseph's Cathedral in San Jose and claimed to feel a special connection to God. But she hadn't attended class since our field trip to the James Lick Observatory.

That left Ethan, twister of words, mis-interpreter of messages.

Stumped, I decided to leave it up to Granny Max to choose. She'd know who would be the right choice.

🕷 🕷 🕷

After her students had left for the day, Granny Max arrived at our classroom to take part in the "prayer" experiment. When I asked her who should lead us, she immediately chose Ethan.

Jason ducked his head. "*Sheesh*, that's a relief. The only prayer I know by heart is the Serenity Prayer. Great for funeral cards and cremation urns, but not for what we're about to do."

"I wouldn't be so sure about that," Granny Max said softly.

Ethan rose from his chair with the confidence of someone accustomed to talking to God. He motioned for us to form a circle then placed a chair in the center for Granny Max. "I'm probably no better at this than Jason, but I'll lead the prayer because you asked me to, Granny Max." He moved to a spot on the rim of the circle between Shawn and Luke. "If anyone has a problem with the words I use, go ahead and pray on your own. The thing to remember is we're asking for God's help in making Granny Max better and we need to believe, really, really believe, He'll answer our prayer. Now, close your eyes and clear your minds the way we did during Luke's intention experiment. Then hook up, not like smooching or anything, but mentally, like we've been practicing. Then connect with Granny Max, and, together, we'll reach out to God."

I opened my eyes—yes, I cheated, my prerogative as a teacher— and saw Ethan bend his knees and upper body and take a deep breath as if he'd done this hundreds of times before. "May the Blessed Holy One be filled with compassion for Granny Max's health. May He send complete renewal of her body, mind, and spirit. Amen."

Repeating Ethan's prayer with all the belief I could muster, I wondered how Granny Max had known to choose Ethan to lead us. *Ace of Spaces, source of illumination for others, key to the profound secrets of life.* The perfect emissary between us and God.

Apparently, I didn't know my students as well as I'd thought. One thing for certain, though, I had seven arguments to prove it possible for thirteen-year-olds to be perceptive and wise beyond what was conceivable for their age.

Chapter Forty-six

OVER THE FOLLOWING SIX class sessions the experiments continued, each with positive results. Luke replanted the sprouted lima bean seeds, and with the daily treatment of our intentions, the target seeds continued to outpace the controls.

"The treated seeds will need a trellis soon," Codi said on the fifth day while inspecting the foliage about to flop over the rim of the planter. "You'd think they were enchanted or something like the ones in 'Jack and the Beanstalk.'"

Luke glanced at the ceiling and shook his head. "We're only interested in their health and how fast they grow. That means no assistance besides our good intentions."

After we'd "healed" targeted water in one of Luke's experiments, he used it to irrigate one of two identical plants—maidenhair ferns that had so far subsisted on benign neglect. He irrigated the other with untreated water.

"Is 'healed' water like holy water?" Ethan wanted to know after entering class on day six and taking a seat next to Shawn at their table.

"Sort of," Luke said from his new position at the head of the U as class leader. "After the tap water receives our healing intentions, I guess you could call it holy water."

Codi gave him a snarky grin. "How do we prove the water changed at all? Check its pH?"

"We'll check it with a Raman Spectrometer."

Her grin turned into a frown. "A what?"

"An instrument that can measure changes in water's molecular structure via a probe connected to a CCD camera."

"Hold it, boy genius." Codi ran the tips of her fingers through her hair as though taming it with pomade. "What the hell is a CCD camera, and doesn't that kind of equipment cost like thousands of dollars? What are you, King Midas?"

Jason stood and placed his foot on the seat of his chair as if it were the rear bumper of his father's pickup truck. "Over the weekend, Dad borrowed the modular Raman Spectrometer used for undergraduate and graduate experiments and research at UC Berkeley. As far as the CCD camera goes, he's got dibs on one that costs only like forty-thousand, used in astronomy for photographing the faintest light from distant galaxies."

Codi slid from her chair in a display of shock that could have earned her a coveted spot in West Coast's drama club. "Forty-thousand!"

My less embellished contribution to the conversation was, "You and Luke sure work fast." Followed by the thought: *Ron Ardis better have good insurance coverage for all that valuable equipment.*

Codi rose from the floor without injury, ignoring the dust clinging to the back of the trench coat she now considered her own. "Okay, so how does your dad get that stuff here?"

The sudden straightening of Jason's back embodied pride at his father's continued contribution to the class. "The equipment is compact and portable and can operate on batteries. Perfect for field measurements."

🕷 🕷 🕷

On May 6, Ron showed up with the spectrometer, CCD camera, and computer as promised. With that, the measures Luke and the students used in their experiments became ever more sophisticated.

I didn't know what to say, besides "Thank you." After that, I kept my mouth shut.

Over the following three days, the fledgling scientists continued to experiment, becoming more and more comfortable with their scientific inquiry. Practice didn't make perfect, but they were getting better at what they aimed to do—prove that a group of people thinking the same thought at the same time could magnify its affect.

The only trial over which they had no control or conclusive results was their prayer experiment to cure Granny Max of cancer.

"Maybe we should have her drink some of our treated water," Codi suggested after we'd completed another prayer circle. Besides praying on Granny Max's behalf, we'd envisioned each of her cells smiling at each other, offering their love and gratitude. "Or maybe we could have Tessa heal her."

"That would make it a different experiment," Luke said with the patience of someone who'd given up trying to explain scientific methods to the technologically inept. "It takes time for cancer to grow, so it'll take time for it to go away. Anyway, Granny Max will share her journal and test results with us soon. Until then, all we can go by is how she feels."

"She looked kind of pale and tired when she left today," Tessa said.

Codi nodded. "I can see into her head, at least most of the time, but my findings are inconclusive."

"Talk about findings." Luke held up the journal containing all their test results. "Who do we share our research with?"

"No one just yet," I cautioned from the seat behind my desk in my new role as advisor rather than teacher. "Not that you need to keep a lid on it forever…" A warning look at Ethan, though after the destruction of his owl, I suspected thoughts of betrayal no longer entered his mind. "Only until you have proof of the experimental significance of your theory. How, for instance, can you apply your findings to the world?"

"Are you saying we need to show ways our findings can help others?" Tessa asked.

"Yes, and after that, the first person you should notify is Dr. Matt. He started this class because he cared, really cared, about you and wanted you to use your abilities to advance yourselves and the world. Something's bothering him at the moment. Not about you, but me. So, we need to handle the situation with care. Being teased or made fun of is the least of your worries. It's the people who'll take your findings seriously" —another glance at Ethan— "that you need to guard against. The ones who might use, even hurt, you."

Shawn came to a slow stand from his seat next to Ethan. "I've been trying to keep my opinion to myself, but..." He started to pace the room as if working off, or through, something nagging at him. The rest of students remained silent, possibly relieved that he was providing them with a reprieve from opinions they, too, harbored and were unable, or unwilling, to voice. "I get where Luke's leading with his experiments. But, as I see it, science can't prove or disprove what goes on in our heads. Especially when it comes to the gifts we're caught up in, mostly against our will." Shawn's grin emerged like a break in a cloud. "In Luke's case, it's called genius." His comment drew chuckles, but the sparkle of his wit faded as quickly as his smile. "So, how are we supposed to make claims about the world—our world—when they can't be supported by first-hand evidence? How, for instance, do we prove that what we're doing during our experiments is responsible for the outcome? We've seen what happened, and Luke and Granny Max took lots of notes, but how can we *prove* what *actually* happened?"

My eyes stung, touched by the sincerity and concern in Shawn's voice. And the brilliance of the workings of his mind.

"And even if we could prove that our so-called magical powers are real," Shawn continued, "it could lead to disaster. Look what happened with nuclear power... Anyway, I agree with Ms. Veil that we should keep what we're learning to ourselves for now. Uncle Matt is pretty upset with us because of Mr. Lacoste—"

"You mean pissed," Jason said.

"Yeah," Shawn concurred.

"So, we need to shut up about it," Jason said.

Shawn returned to his table and slumped onto his chair. "Uncle Matt will come around. It's just that...I'm staying out of it for now."

Chapter Forty-seven

"DID YOU KNOW TODAY is Ascension Thursday?" Granny Max asked when I stopped by her classroom after my students had left for the day.

Ascension Thursday? Jeez, I'd forgotten. I checked my watch. Quarter past five. My mother was probably already headed for Mass.

Granny Max pushed aside the stack of worksheets she'd been correcting. "I've given a lot of thought to the meaning and significance of the Ascension since my cancer diagnosis and your students started beseeching God on my behalf. What, for instance, is the likelihood that Jesus ascended into heaven physically and the Apostles were able to witness it? Is there a scientific way to prove this biblical account as true? Or, did the Apostles experience Jesus' rising while in an altered state of consciousness or a group trance?"

I moved a student's chair to the foot of Granny Max's desk and sat, figuring the best I could do for her at the moment was lend her a listening ear.

She swiveled her chair toward the ten-foot lightbulb painted on the wall to her right. I followed her gaze, taken in once again by the mural's capacity to jolt the senses. "Science functions by reproducible experiments and observations," she said. "Miracles, however, are non-reproducible, so they can't be proven by scientific means. And if science can't find defeating evidence of a reported event such as the Ascension, it can't say one way or another whether it truly happened or is a miracle." She wheeled her chair back to her desk and eyed me as though she'd caught me drifting. No chance of that; except for the powerful magnetism of all those colors ricocheting off the wall to my left. "Do you get where I'm going with this?"

Her argument touched on the concerns Shawn had voiced in class only a short while ago. "Yes, I think so."

"That's good, because I'm not sure I do. Anyway, science is best at describing normal workings of the world. Miracles like the resurrection are not normal. If science, then, can't say if Jesus' resurrection happened or not, should we give up the plausibility of the claim?"

I thought of my students' attempts to prove scientifically that the mind's range was beyond the brain and could change physical matter. "Well—"

"Hell, no!" she said with a fist to her thigh. "Because science isn't our only means for accessing truth."

"I agree, but…"

She folded her hands on the desk and leaned forward. "I don't have a physical explanation for what happened with Jesus or, for that matter, what's happening with your students, but I do have rational ground to believe it did and does happen. Luke and his cohorts can spend the rest of their lives investigating whether we are more than our physical brains and never come up with a scientific explanation. The trick is to keep an open mind. There's more to consciousness than we'll ever understand."

"No argument there," I squeezed in.

"I think of heaven and earth as two interacting and interpenetrating fields of force, so, I don't see a sharp dichotomy between the material and the spiritual." Granny Max's gaze sharpened and she laughed. "I can tell by the way your face is wrinkling like a Shar-Pei pup that you're wondering how a mathematician and closet quantum physicist, who revels in facts, figures, and the stretching boundaries, can also be a Christian."

"*Pfft.* The thought never crossed my mind."

The quick lift of Granny Max's brows indicated she knew I was pulling her leg. "A mathematician and physicist, more qualified than

I once said, 'Science without religion is lame, religion without science is blind.' Validation that science and religion depend on each other, don't you think? Especially coming from Einstein, who claimed neither faith nor disbelief in the existence of God."

I nodded. When this self-proclaimed fuddy-duddy got going, she never failed to intrigue.

"*Hmph*. Quantum physics and its application of mathematics isn't only compatible with God's existence, but makes it more likely, by illuminating some of His most creative work."

Impressed at her ability to reconcile science and theology, I released a long breath.

"Okay, okay, I get the hint," she said, "better rein in this one-sided conversation before your sighs turn into yawns and you start searching for an excuse to hightail it out of here." She shot me a smile that prompted no other interpretation than mischievous. "Like joining your mother for Ascension Thursday Mass."

"Too late for that. Though I plan to join her for Mass on Mother's Day."

Granny Max slumped over her desk and cradled her chin in upraised hands, something I'd seen my students do at the end of a long day. Venting for so long had tuckered her out. "As far as your students' prayer experiment is concerned, tell them it's okay to ask for guidance from the wisdom that surrounds and informs us. I feel a divine presence whenever I'm in their healing circle, and for me that's enough. But also... Please tell them not to beg for a specific outcome, such as praying away my cancer. No one but God knows what's best for me. He's providing me with the opportunity to discover something about myself and redirect my life in some way. A 'give her comfort and strength' or 'thy will be done,' is far more effective."

My eyes started to tear, and I visually searched Granny Max's desk for the box of tissues I knew would be there. Nothing, it seemed, escaped her when it came to the comfort of others. She pulled a couple of tissues from the box bookending her letter tray and handed them to me, then pulled out a couple for herself.

"Granny Max—"

"Let me finish, dear. Somehow, I get the feeling you need to hear what I've got to say."

I reminded myself that I'd come to offer my support by listening. With both ears.

"Tell the kids I'm feeling fine. Okay? If it weren't for the doctors saying different, I'd insist I was healthy as a horse. Problem is, I have difficulty accepting help from others... It opens up a whole bag of issues and anxieties I'd rather ignore. The thought of being dependent on someone else overwhelms me, literally knocks me to my knees. I'm trying to convince myself that allowing you and the kids to express your love and support is a form of giving on my part, you know, providing you the gift of meaning and purpose."

I wanted to say that, yes, helping her was giving the students and me a sense of meaning and purpose, but I could see by the impatient flutter of her hands that she wasn't done.

"Where was I going with this...?" Granny Max tapped her temple. "Forgive me for a brief mental lapse. Oh yeah, here we go... The messages that need to come through to us have a passageway, and sometimes it takes an *enemy* to break it open. In my case, that enemy is cancer. And you can be darn sure I'll find meaning in the teachable moments ahead. Otherwise, I refuse to give the situation more power. As the saying goes, 'What we resist persists.' The students at West Coast will remain my number one priority with every precious breath left to me. There's no finish line, Marjorie. Many of the changes that may or may not take place as a result of my teaching will do so after my death. Until then, I hope to touch as many students as I can."

"It's the ultimate sacrifice," I said.

"Sacrifice? Are you kidding? What I do is no sacrifice. The students are my window to the sacred, and when the window swings open, love rushes in."

Chapter Forty-eight

MOTHER AND I WALKED from my house to the Church of the Nativity for Sunday Mass as we had thirteen and a half months ago. This time, however, it was at my suggestion not hers, a Mother's Day gift but so much more. After my conversation with Granny Max on Thursday, I wanted to reopen to the church's message from the perspective of an adult rather than a child. But as we neared the Gothic Revival building with its spired steeple ablaze in sunlight—so white, so pure it appeared illuminated from within—I feared the fabric of my religiosity had grown so thin I'd never again experience the sense of community, solidarity, and unity I once did.

My mother—normally so rigid and controlling—took my hand as we ascended the brick steps to the church threshold. My heart raced as I recalled my last visit here, the shock of finding my ex-fiancé waiting in the vestibule and my mother's betrayal in inviting him. Instead, it felt as though I'd been transported to a place as soothing and sacrosanct as Granny Max's classroom. I dropped Mother's hand, blessed myself with holy water from the entry font, and headed for the pew next to the Sixth-Station-of-the-Cross. Of the fourteen carvings representing the slow and painful journey from Jesus's condemnation by Pilate to His crucifixion and burial, the one picturing Veronica wiping the blood and sweat from His face affected me most. Little had I known when I first sighted this plaque, that I had a sister named Veronica, a woman, who like the Veronica of biblical times, would step out of the crowd and offer her help.

As the pipe organ burst into the first, deep notes of "How Great Thou Art," I knelt and brought my hands together in thanks for Morgan, Joshua, and my soon-to-be van Dyke family; for my adoptive parents, Truus and Gerardo; for my birth family, Antonia, Bob, Veronica, and Maya; and for Granny Max and my seven students at West Coast Middle School.

"You haven't lost your faith," my mother whispered from where she knelt next to me. "And that's the best Mother's Day gift ever."

Lost my faith?

If by faith she meant turning off the brain and relying solely on the heart, if she meant squashing reason in favor of emotion, then her definition of faith differed from mine. My understanding of the universe and my place in it, even my concept of God, contrasted with hers and likely with the rest of the congregants currently expressing their devotion. Acceptance of the big bang theory, in my opinion, didn't exclude me from being a Christian. I saw no contradiction between belief in God and belief in scientific theories regarding the evolution and the expansion of our universe. God and science could, and did, work together.

While I focused on the stained-glass windows that sparkled like translucent marbles, Granny Max's words merged with those of the choir expressing wonder at all the worlds God's hands had made. "If science can't find defeating evidence of a reported event such as the Ascension, then it can't say one way or another whether it truly happened or is miraculous." I found comfort in visualizing science and religion as two sides of the same coin, one side representing the realm of the physical, the other the realm of the spiritual, the boundary between signifying the intersection occupied by my students and me.

The steeple bell rang, announcing Mass was about to begin, and my thoughts continued to whirl. Until science came up with a testable theory of the laws of the universe, how could it claim to be free of faith? According to Granny Max, quantum physics and its application of mathematics was not only compatible with God's existence but even made it more likely, by illuminating some of His most creative work. As far as I could tell, religion and science were both founded on faith.

I belong to the religion of love.

My loyalties, my aspirations, and my faith were my own. I squeezed my mother's hand. "No, I haven't lost my faith."

The priest entered, paused in front of the altar, and made the Sign of the Cross. "In the name of the Father and of the Son and of the Holy Spirit…"

I belong to the religion of love; I belong to the religion of love; I belong to the religion of love, I repeated between the hymns and prayers leading to the part of Mass I'd been waiting for: The Homily.

The priest stepped from the altar and opened his commentary with a question that, as far as I could tell, bore no relationship to the day's scripture readings. "Do you reflect the glory of God out of limitation and fear? Or do you reflect His glory out of love?"

The priest scanned the congregates as if expecting one of us to raise a hand and blurt out an answer. Though I intended to follow the upcoming sermon with the same focused attention I'd offered Granny Max three days before, I, along with the rest of the parishioners, kept my hand down and mouth shut.

Limitation and fear? Hell, yes. Love causes pain. It takes away the freedom to do what I want. Choosing love is illogical, yet… I belong to the religion of love.

"If the answer is fear," the priest said, "don't resist it or try to overcome it. Instead, see through it with the eyes of love."

Was love the only way to get what I wanted? Was it that simple? That hard?

"Be love and act from love in alignment with your faith."

There it was again, the question of faith.

"Spiritual power comes from faith in a power greater than yourself, a power that can be used for the good of the world."

That sounded like what we'd been discussing in class. I could hear Tessa now. "So much violence. Can't we just make the world a better place?"

"You are better than you know and more than you believe."

Wow. I should share this with my students.

Just as I was getting into what the priest was saying, I mean, really getting it and feeling it, he concluded with, "Happy Mother's Day to all the mothers in attendance today. You are the very embodiment of God's limitless and fearless love." Then he stepped back onto the altar, the missive of his sermon impressive, its brevity disappointing.

I stood and joined the rest of the congregation in praying the Nicene Creed— "We believe in one God, the Father, the Almighty, maker of heaven and earth..." —all reciting the same Christian truths from different perspectives. How could I align this statement of belief with my concept of faith, a faith that was fluid instead of concrete and observable, unsolidified by the mold of tradition? My students and I had experienced, and continued to experience, the impossible. How did God fit into this?

"God is love," I whispered. *The answer science can't provide.*

A nudge to my side. "What did you say?"

I glanced at my mother and smiled. There was so much about her I didn't and would never know. She, like God, transcended my thoughts.

"I love you," I said.

Chapter Forty-nine

O N MONDAY, SHAWN—*JACK of Diamonds, perceptive, shrewd, original thinker*—once again took the floor. I settled behind my desk to listen, which, I'd come to discover, beat trying to figure out everything on my own. He paused near the center of our power circle, the perimeter of which existed only in our minds. "The results of our experiments have so far been positive. No surprise, right? We pretty much knew all along how they'd turn out. Except for our prayers for Granny Max. Which shouldn't be considered an experiment, anyway. As she said, her recovery depends on God's will, not our good intentions. No matter how powerful."

No one responded to what sounded like the prologue to a one-man discourse by an exceptionally intelligent and insightful thirteen-year-old. Shawn was opening up for the second time in a matter of days, as if the bedrock of his resistance to our united cause had loosened due to our talk about teamwork and using our God-given skills. Maybe his silent opposition had already been prone to dissolution, but my guess was that we'd worn him down with a stream of discussion too large to ignore, yet too insignificant, until recently, to take firm hold in the riverbed of his conviction. By assuming center stage, he'd finally been dragged into the flow. The attack of wind-driven twigs and debris against the windows failed to distract us from what he had to say. "My vote is for no more experiments. We need to move on."

Move on to what? was my first question. The second: *Who'll be in charge?*

"We don't know enough and will never know enough to figure out who we are and what makes us different," Shawn said. Followed by a pause which the wind filled with distorted street sounds and its continued battering of the windowed wall, as if cautioning us to allow for the opposite of our desired understanding. "Why not just live life instead of trying to explain it? Admit that we all want the same thing. To be safe, to belong, and to matter. Right Ms. Veil?"

I nodded. That about summed it up, especially the part about wanting to matter.

"Maybe, someday, we'll know what to do with our gifts," Shawn continued, "but I doubt all these experiments will get us there. Let's focus on our next step instead of trying to map the whole road."

Not good enough, was my unvoiced response and, apparently, that of the rest of the students. Our silence was one of resistance as strong, if not stronger, than that of the single-paned windows battling the impact of the wind. Shawn's sigh hardly registered compared to the tumultuous display outside, but on the Richter scale of inner turmoil, it probably measured a magnitude of six points or higher. "We might not like the way some people treat us," he said. "But you know what? It depends on the stories they've been told. Our stories tell us they're wrong, even evil, but we'd probably do the same in their shoes. How about we accept that their stories are different from ours and use that as a start in making the world a better place?"

"I don't follow you," Codi said, honesty one of her best, and most irritating, traits.

"How do we make the world a better place?" was Tessa's gentler response.

Shawn glanced at Luke. "By using our combined intentions to actually do some good."

"How do we know if our intentions are doing any good?" Tessa asked.

"We don't. But we've done enough experiments to know we're onto something. Guess, it's just time to believe."

Codi fingered the skull medallion hanging from the chain around her neck, a chunk of steel so large and heavy it could serve as a hood ornament. "Since we know we're onto something, I agree, let's give it a rest."

"The experiments, but not our intentions," Shawn said. "We still need lots of practice."

The medallion slid from Codi's hand and hit the table with a clang loud enough to make one's teeth ache. "What for?"

Ethan popped in as if he knew something the rest of us didn't. "In case we need it."

For some reason, I shivered.

"We're still not very good at what we do," Tessa admitted.

"Actually, that might be for the best," Luke said, not as upset about Shawn's suggestion to drop the experiments as I thought he'd be. "It keeps us from accidently blowing something up." He smiled at Tessa's startled expression, acknowledging he'd hit his mark. "Like unleashing a genie from a bottle and not being able to put it back."

"Or opening a pandora's box," Jason added.

Tessa's intake of breath suggested dismay at Jason's analogy. She glanced at the bracelet she'd worn on her right wrist since Angelina had tossed it to her during our trip to the Lick Observatory. "The box was filled with special gifts from the gods. Pandora got curious, and I don't blame her. I would've opened it too. Then all kinds of nasty stuff came out, and when she shut it, hope got locked inside. It reminds me of us…"

"Pandora gets blamed for everything," Codi snapped. "Why give her a box full of gifts and not let her open it?"

Luke frowned as if regretting his contribution to the conversation, opening his own Pandora's box. "I've read that our intentions can warp the universe in some way."

"Good God," Codi said.

"That somewhere else a distortion appears and something…or someone…will push back to restore things to the way they were."

"I swear, this discussion's getting spookier and spookier." Apparently, Codi was in no mood to go where Luke was leading. "How about an early dismissal, Ms. Veil?"

I, too, was having difficulty following the conversation, from no more experiments to practicing our good intentions to unwise interference causing warps in the universe.

"Like the Butterfly Effect," Luke said, unwilling to let go of a subject once he got started, "the idea that a butterfly flapping its wings in Brazil can cause a twister to touch down in Texas."

"Like a punishment," Tessa said, inserting more weirdness into the conversation.

Luke grinned as though delighted to have regained a prominent role in the workings of the classroom. "More like consequences, which can be good and bad. We need to decide once and for all if our gifts were meant to be used or kept hidden.

"Or you could call the Butterfly Effect a form of balancing," Jason added. *Good ol' Jason.* "And then there's the theory of the Hundredth Monkey. Spread good and other people might start copying our behavior."

Codi zipped up her backpack as if preparing for a quick escape. "Can we change the subject, puh-leeze? My head is spinning."

"Why don't we form a circle and use our intention for world peace?" Tessa suggested.

The skull medallion Codi had been twisting in her hands like a coping tool slammed against her chest with enough force to cause whiplash. "Oh Lord."

Luke shot Tessa a look that wavered between compassion and exasperation. "How about we start on a smaller scale, like peace in our school?" He paused as if googling his mind for a way to put his suggestion into practice. "Remember, how back in January we had 'School Violence Awareness Week,' and no one seemed to be listening? A few assemblies and guest speakers and then all the talk of violence prevention stopped as if it never happened."

"Okay, then we'll set an intention to stop school violence," Tessa said with a spark of determination I hadn't noticed in her before.

And from that moment and throughout the next five class sessions, my six students had the motivational willpower to kick into what Luke called "Intention Training," sensitizing themselves to undercurrents lying beyond language and external appearances.

As homework, they applied what they'd practiced in class to their daily lives, tuning into the thoughts and emotions of family and friends, and whenever possible, defusing explosive situations.

"Notice more and judge less" became their catchphrase as they continued to train their brains and supersize their powers. Day after day, their confidence grew.

Until, of course, disaster struck.

Chapter Fifty

IT'S CALLED RUG RAT Rage, this anger epidemic in preteens and teens, where dead-eyed kids beat up siblings and classmates, attack opponents in sports, and yell profanities at anyone who sets them off. Circumventing such rage was one reason Dr. Matt had instigated our after-school class, an antidote to aggression and despair.

On May 22, one week before Open House, a young man burst into our classroom, shoving the door with such force it slammed against the book-shelved wall with the boom of a cannon. "You're evil, the Antichrist," he screamed at no one in particular. He looked like an avenging angel—an angry, angel-faced innocent. The intruder stood silhouetted inside the entrance with what appeared to be a red-tinted halo. He waved a handgun as if it were a pennant flag instead of a lethal weapon, causing my heart to hit the wall of my chest with the force of a baseball hitting a catcher's mitt. "You're promoting paganism, reverting to the primitive." Though the revolver shook in the teen's hand, he appeared determined, self-righteous, and secure in his mission. "Mr. Lacoste said you need to be stopped."

Bits of previous conversations with my students floated up from memory like scrolling text on a brokerage wall: warps in the universe; distortions; push backs; consequences; balancing; punishment. I felt a crawling sensation on my arms, my face, my scalp. *Dear God, help us. This is so wrong.* Then it struck me. This was Wyatt, the young man I'd given a plus for good behavior on my first day substituting at

West Coast. Could he be an Indigo—invisible, ignored, explosive, expressing a messed-up call for help?

"Shut up and put down the gun," Ethan said, jolting Wyatt's focus to the kids.

He glared at Ethan. "What's your problem? I thought we were friends."

"Me, too," Ethan said. "Guess I was wrong."

"Fuck off," Wyatt said. "You're one of them. A bunch of hand-picked, spoiled, have-it-alls, living on easy street." He hesitated on noticing our circular formation. "What're you doing? Playing ring around the rosy?" He had a powerful grasp on everyone's attention; I felt the pull. Had our actions drawn him to us like a homing device? Too late to worry about that now.

"Don't be stupid," Ethan said.

A thousand needles pricked my cheeks and arms. *We're isolated from the rest of the school. No one can see us. No one can hear us. No way of negotiating our way out of this.* The world narrowed to a pinpoint. Everything before this moment ceased to matter. *Stay safe, stay small.* I didn't need to map out the whole damn road, just focus on the next step.

"Who's calling who stupid?" Wyatt asked. "I'm the one with the gun, not you."

"Exactly," Ethan said.

The pain of delay was agonizing, but I had to do something equally agonizing. Send my students a silent message. *Pop quiz. Final exam. Grade: live or die.*

Now? came their silent response.

Yes. We live only if we unite.

A shaft of white light angled at the edge of my vision. I tried to ignore it. *No time for this now.* It began to swirl, then move toward me like a mini twister. *Maya?* The rotating column of light superimposed over me, filling me with a powerful sense of self I didn't own or control.

You are better than you know and more than you believe.

Wyatt focused on me. I met his feverish gaze. This was someone's child, a miracle, a whirling mass of atoms, fluid, dynamic, filled with possibility. Had he lived thirteen years to prepare for this? What a waste. What a pitiful waste.

I heard a hiss, followed by a tiger-cub growl before a cat launched from out of nowhere and wrapped himself around Wyatt's leg.

"Whose damn cat," he yelled. He couldn't shoot it without shooting himself or detach the cat without putting down his weapon. He tried to kick it loose, but it clung to his leg like a furry boot.

The students drew into a wide circle around him.

I had to make a move or risk them getting shot.

Maya—or was it me? —rushed forward.

Wyatt saw her coming but froze for the seconds it took her to bend at the knees and bring her extended forearms up and under the revolver as if redirecting a volleyball spike. The room rippled and for a moment, time stopped, reversed, and started again.

A bang, an ear-splitting crack. Hot, liquid metal flew across the left side of my head, then hit the tiled ceiling. Old and accumulated dust filtered into the room like tears.

Wyatt cried, "What the fuck?"

Maya grabbed the butt of the pistol and yanked it from his grasp.

In the eerie silence that followed, I reached up to wipe something warm running down the side of my face. The tip of cool metal touched my skin. I lowered my hand. I was holding the gun, its tip covered with blood. I looked for my sister and found myself standing in my own light—face-to-face with Wyatt.

"Good going, Ms. V," Jason said.

I shook my head, not trusting myself to speak.

"You're bleeding," Tessa said. "We need to call for help."

I raised my free hand. "Not yet."

We had opened a Pandora's box and wouldn't be able to put back what we'd unleashed. But, by God, we could provide the oxygen of hope to the good flickering in this confused man-child before handing him over to the authorities. "Get me a towel from the kitchen to stop the bleeding, Tessa. Then we'll treat Wyatt with our healing intentions"

"Are you sure? It looks like you're missing a little skin and hair."

I felt a dull burning, followed by a wave of nausea. "That's what happens when a piece of metal uses your scalp for a landing strip."

Wyatt was shaking. Aftershock, I assumed. Quite a transformation from the wild-eyed kid who'd entered the room only minutes before, living proof that anyone can become an instrument of evil given the right motivation. Is this what happens when hope dies and despair takes over, when facts and competition alone occupy our classrooms, minds, and hearts? "How'd you know my name?" he asked.

"You were in my class when I substituted for Ms. Goldsberry."

He squinted at me as if seeing me for the first time, not as an evil Antichrist reverting to the primitive, but as the teacher who'd recognized something worthwhile in him and given him a plus for good behavior. "I didn't know the gun was loaded."

I staggered back, groping for the table behind me for support. Dear God, if Wyatt had thought the revolver wasn't loaded, then so had my students. I bowed my throbbing head, realizing that with each outbreath I was releasing a low, pitiful moan. Codi and Shawn had no doubt read Wyatt's mind and shared the information telepathically with Shawn, Ethan, Luke and Tessa, which meant they'd all known—or thought they'd known—that the weapon wasn't loaded. I wanted to kneel in thanksgiving and bawl my eyes out for an outcome that could have been disastrous. Instead, I sat on the table and whispered a thank you to Maya and the cat—my cat, Gabriel—for coming to our aid. How either of them had known to be here and accomplished what they did was likely not meant to be understood.

Wyatt kicked his leg in another attempt to shake my cat loose, but Gabriel maintained a firm grip on the fabric of his jeans. Most cats would have run at the commotion. But not this one. Not my Gabriel.

Tessa pressed a kitchen towel to my grazed scalp. "Are you okay?"

"A bit dizzy, but I'll live."

"You're losing a lot of blood. You may need stitches."

Release. Reveal. Go with the flow. "Facial wounds are notorious for excessive bleeding."

She wiped my face and neck with a second towel she'd brought from the kitchen and pressed it on top of the first. Bless her. Then she cupped the fingers of her left hand over my wound. The throbbing pain eased. I didn't ask how, just said, "Thank you."

Her response, a smile.

I motioned for Shawn to join me.

He left Codi, Luke, Jason, and Ethan standing in a circle around Wyatt. "Sorry, Ms. Veil, Codi and I thought—"

"That the revolver wasn't loaded. Yeah, I figured as much."

"You could've been killed…"

"Exactly. So, why wasn't I?"

Shawn bowed his head and took a ragged breath, affirming that he was as disturbed by the incident as I was. "Even though Codi said the gun wasn't loaded, Ethan had a vision of it going off. And Jason said he'd been trained to never, ever, point a firearm at anyone, that you never know for sure if there's a live round of ammo inside."

"So, you put your heads together and decided not to take the chance."

"It all happened so fast… Wyatt had his finger on the trigger and…at the last minute… Jason did his thing. You know, like he did when you substituted in Ms. Goldsberry's class. Except this time, the rest of us helped instead of getting in the way. We focused all our energy on moving the gun—"

"Just enough to save my life," I said.

Shawn looked up with tear-filled eyes. "We used our gifts to do some good for a change."

"Whose cat?" Jason asked, pointing at Gabriel, who'd let go of Wyatt's pant leg and now sat next to him with what appeared to be bored contentment.

291

"It's the cat from the nature area," Luke said before I could answer. "It looked cold and lonely when I checked on it before class, so I let it in. The way it went after Wyatt, you'd think it was trying to protect us. We should give it a name."

"He already has one," I said. "He's Gabriel, my backyard stray. How he managed to trek so far from home is beyond me, but nothing about him surprises me anymore."

Jason shrugged, then pointed at my hand. "Put the gun on the table, Ms. V, before you accidently shoot someone. No offense, but you're holding a semi-automatic pistol, a Glock 19, and I'd rather pick it off the table than have you hand it to me."

The Glock felt cold and heavy and seemed glued to my palm. Someone as inexperienced as me shouldn't be holding a killing machine, but I hesitated. Would it be any safer on the table or with Jason?

As if sensing my doubt, he said, "I do regular dry-firing training at the shooting range in Cupertino, so, I know how to handle a weapon."

I put the revolver on the table, then relieved Tessa of the bloody towels she still held to my head. "There's a first aid kit in right-hand bottom drawer of my desk," I said, hoping her nursing skills would hold until I had time to assess the damage.

Jason left the circle and picked up the Glock with his finger outside the trigger chamber, his gaze fixed on Wyatt. "Is your dad a cop?"

Wyatt nodded, his pupils dilated, as if comprehension of what he'd done was sinking in.

"Looks like you need a reminder of the first two rules of weapon safety," Jason said with a shake of his head. "Treat every gun as if it's loaded and never, ever, point it at something you don't want to shoot." Jason eyed the revolver. "The slide isn't locked back, so there might still be a round in the chamber." He pointed it at the ceiling, then pressed a button on the grip behind the trigger. A curved black box dropped free. He set it on the table and glanced my way. "I'm going to release the thumb safety and pull back the slide to eject the cartridge." A metal casing popped free. After one last inspection, Jason put the Glock on the table. Then he flicked his fingers, and, where he'd been holding the revolver only moments before, he now held a pencil. He walked up to Wyatt and handing it to him. "Use this next time you want to express yourself."

"Holy shit," Wyatt said, emerging from what appeared to be a moment of genuine regret. "How'd you do that?"

Before Jason could answer, Ethan cut in from the circle he, Luke, and Codi still held around his disarmed friend. "What do you want, Wyatt?"

Wyatt's eyes—too wide, too intense—darted from student to student, finding no place to settle. "To put a stop to this nonsense."

Ethan barely batted an eye, though he'd believed pretty much the same only six weeks ago. "Why?"

Wyatt's gaze settled on Ethan. "You're messing with the unholy."

"Says who?"

"Mr. Lacoste, and he knows what he's talking about."

"How do you know?"

"Because he's my teacher."

"What do *you* think?"

"I agree."

"Did you research Indigos?"

"Mr. Lacoste did."

"So, you're taking Mr. Lacoste's word for it."

Wyatt shot me a look that felt like it pierced my skin. "He's my teacher, and he takes me into his confidence."

This didn't sound like a thirteen-year-old talking, more like Charles Lacoste putting words into his mouth. Then again, if Wyatt was an Indigo, he'd be advanced for his age.

"Mr. Lacoste took me into his confidence, too," Ethan said. "I was free to choose, and I chose not to be free."

Ethan's words burned into my brain as if melted there by a branding iron. *I was free to choose, and I chose not to be free.*

293

For the past year, I'd been *willing* a finish line that lay beyond my power and control, when I should have *surrendered* to the meaningful moments at the starting line of every second of every day. I'd just experienced the most lived moment of my life, where I'd claimed the freedom to live each unpredictable moment with genuine concern for others, without presuming to know how it all worked or would work out.

"You're bull shitting me," Wyatt said. "He told me it was between the two of us."

Ethan said nothing.

I felt a drain of energy as Tessa removed the blood-soaked towels and pressed wads of antibacterial gauze to my injury. She wrapped medical tape around my head like a bandana to hold the gauze in place. "Girl Scout training to the rescue," she said, then treated me to another healing touch.

"So, what did *you* do?" Wyatt asked Ethan.

"Attacked this class, like you did. Minus the gun. Then I fell apart."

"Where?"

"Right here. I freaked out big time."

"What happened?"

Ethan closed, then opened his eyes. "My friends helped me."

"And now you're going to help me?"

"If you want us to. But we'll need your permission first."

I thought I saw Wyatt's shoulders shake, but it could have been my imagination. "Permission? Fuck yes. What've I got to lose?"

Emphatic listening, that's what was going on, listening without dispensing judgment or solutions. I couldn't have been prouder of Ethan for stepping forward with compassion and forgiveness, or the rest of my students for allowing him to take charge—something he desperately needed to regain his sense of worth after his breakdown six weeks ago.

While doing my own emphatic listening, previous conversations with Morgan started making more sense. He'd known all along that we can't be totally free from all that binds us. The key to the lock of our cells starts turning the moment we commit to love, family—and a job. But he'd allowed me to discover this for myself. When I'd told him that I needed to discover who I was and what I could give, he'd replied, "Which sometimes means being acted upon and giving in to a higher power."

I'm coming home, Morgan. Playing solo is no longer an option.

"We still have to report you," Shawn said. "School rules."

Shawn was right, the incident was too serious to ignore.

I motioned for the students to restore our circle.

"So, what's *your* special talent?" Codi asked.

Wyatt looked startled as if no one had ever asked him this before.

"Your power," she said. "What you do besides threaten people."

He hung his head."

"It's okay," she said. "You're safe here."

He massaged his right shoulder, likely injured by *my* strike to his arm. "You'll think I'm schizoid."

Codi laughed. "Pots calling the kettle black. I don't think so."

"I hear voices. I mean for real. When no one's around."

"No biggie. So does Ms. Veil."

Wyatt looked at me as if about to pass out with relief. "When you came at me for my gun, I saw two of you." He shivered. "It gave me the willies."

Codi saved me from responding by tossing her skull necklace into the circle. It landed at Wyatt's feet with a clang.

"What's this?" he asked.

"A gift."

He picked up the necklace and weighed it in his hand.

"In exchange for teaching me that I can't choose when I die," Codi said. "But I *can* choose how to live."

Dared I hope she'd just given him a key to recovery?

Tessa—*shadow, Eight of Spades, healer*—walked into the circle and touched Wyatt's right arm with raised fingers, creating a spherical basket over a spot above his elbow. An orb of blue light flared, then disappeared when she lifted her hand and drew it into a fist.

Wyatt reached up and touched his arm. "What'd you just do?"

She tilted her head but said nothing.

"It feels like you filled me full of Novocain," he said, flexing his bicep.

"Her hands are like low-level lasers," Jason said.

Wyatt put his hands to his face. The skull medallion—morbid, disturbing, fascinating—slid from his fingers and dangled from his arm. "The gun wasn't supposed to go off. I only meant to scare you, make you do what's right."

I remembered what Shawn had said in class the day before. "We might not like the way some people treat us. But you know what? It depends on the stories they've been told. Our stories tell us they're wrong, even evil, but we'd probably do the same in their shoes. How about we accept that their stories are different from ours and use that as a start in making the world a better place?"

"Let's apply what we've learned in class and send Wyatt our good intentions," I said.

"A scientific prayer treatment," Luke clarified. "Works like a charm."

"Except we're not going for a set result," Ethan added. "This is your mess, Wyatt, and you might need juvie to help you know how to get back up."

"Ethan's right," I said. "You have a right to your own choices, and the right to grow as the result of those choices. We'll focus our creative energy on a positive outcome to what lies ahead for you. Then we'll call in Dr. Matt."

"He's going to be okay," Tessa said.

And I believed her.

Chapter Fifty-one

JUDGE STEIN ARRIVED FIFTEEN minutes early; Open House didn't start until six. She wore pumps with two-inch heels, which gave her another two inches on me. "I can't stay," she said. "Duty calls." She must have noticed the telltale lift of my brows, because she added, "I know it looks bad, but it can't be helped. I serve as a trustee on the school board. During tonight's closed session, we'll be discussing school violence and deciding whether to add metal detectors, surveillance cameras, and extra security guards to our schools. We need a quorum for a decision, so my vote is crucial."

I managed not to shake my head. For one thing, I understood too well the struggle of choosing between duty to one's vocation and one's loved ones. For another, I believed the school board was going about this all wrong. A majority of students already considered school a prison, let alone adding "Checkpoint Charlie" and cops to the mix. The most effective way to find out about weapons and drugs on campus is to encourage students to tell. Which means forming bonds of trust between them and school authorities. More after-school classes like this one, where kids and faculty could learn to communicate, seemed the way to go. But I was talking to an expert—a judge—who knew more about school violence and its prevention than I.

"Ethan may have found an extended family here," I ventured.

"That's what I wanted to tell you before the rest of the parents arrive," she said, "although they probably feel the same. With you,

Ethan has found something he doesn't receive at home." She grimaced, rubbed her forehead. "Don't get me wrong. My husband and I love our son, but he needs more than we provide." Her intense brown eyes softened under a haze of tears. "He says he betrayed you."

I thought back to all his scowls and sneers and looks of suspicion; his theft of my mouse totem and his friendship with Wyatt and Charles Lacoste. *Ace of Spades: solves problems through doubtful means, source of illumination for others, key to the profound secret of life.* "Betrayal is too harsh a word for what happened."

Her eyes pinned me like a juror in the juror's box. "I'm a judge, remember? By the time I got through interrogating Ethan, he revealed all. I know that his misguided veneration of Charles Lacoste led to his disdain for you. And how, despite that, you provided a safe space for him to grow and apply that growth in helping to deflate the encounter with Wyatt. The situation was a dangerous one, Ms. Veil, and I commend you for the way you handled it."

Before I could tell her that forces beyond my control had come to our aid she said, "Ethan claims that Wyatt suffers from severe depression and needs people to watch over and out for him. A sure sign that we need more after-school options such as this."

Numb and dumb, I waited for further revelations and was not disappointed.

"Charles Lacoste has learned a valuable lesson about what happens when you interfere in situations you don't understand. It took near disaster for him to realize that we must manage our own stress and anger before offering advice to someone facing a similar situation. Wyatt caught on to Lacoste's disapproval of you with consequences that will extend far into the future."

We must manage our stress and anger before offering advice to those facing a similar situation. How could I criticize Charles Lacoste when I was guilty of doing the same? He'd done what he had in concern for his students. And, yes, the consequences would extend far into the future.

"What will happen to Wyatt?" I asked, praying the positive intentions we'd sent his way would help him endure the severe consequences to his actions.

"He's currently in secure detainment at Hillcrest Juvenile Hall awaiting a trial hearing and further placement decisions."

The track of stitches on the side of my head started to throb like short-circuiting relay coils detecting an oncoming train. "Will he be okay?"

"A crisis responder at the detainment facility will examine and evaluate him. The results are then sent to juvenile court, which will determine the final outcome of his arrest. The overriding aim of the court is to rehabilitate youthful offenders and get them back on track. So, I have high hopes the presiding judge will defer prosecution until Wyatt has successfully completed a treatment program. After which charges could be dismissed."

"That would be a relief."

"His parents have hired a lawyer because of the seriousness of his offenses. Not only did he bring a loaded gun to school, but prescription drugs as well."

"Darn."

"Which he was distributing to his classmates at no charge. The gun, his father's service revolver, came from a locked closet safe purchased by the sheriff's department. Considering how easy it was for Wyatt to pry the safe open with a wire hanger and a bit of doorknob juggling, I expect it will soon be pulled from the market." Judge Stein paused to eye the ten stitches on my scalp. "Since the gun came from a locked safe, Wyatt's parents won't be criminally liable. And since you aren't pressing charges, they won't be required to pay the substantial sum you're entitled to for injuries and resulting trauma."

The loud click of the wall clock reminded me that Open House was about to begin. "One last thing. Ethan led us in prayer on Granny Max's behalf…"

"Yes, something else I meant to thank you for. He'd been

working with our rabbi for months in preparation for his Bar Mitzvah. You should've heard his speech, all about what's important, like family, community, and a relationship with God. He talked about moral awareness and learning to take responsibility for one's actions. Having the opportunity to put his words into practice" — Judge Stein paused and cleared her throat— "has made a big difference in his world. And my husband's and mine as well." She glanced at her watch and stepped toward the door. "Now, I really must go."

"Thanks for coming by," I said. "The school violence issue you'll be discussing tonight is an important one. I understand why your vote is crucial."

No sooner had Judge Stein left than Codi rushed in. "Ms. Veil, Mom's not coming."

"I'm so sorry—"

"No, don't be sorry. She's in rehab. Tessa healed her."

Oh Lord, not again. "There may be other reasons," I cautioned.

"Of course, there are. My attitude's better since we started talking about *stuff* in class, but Mom changed, too. When she picked me up at the Ardis's during Spring Break, Tessa touched her."

"Just touched her?"

"She gave Mom a hug and *then* did whatever she does. She said it's like kissing with your hands."

"What about your father?"

"I'm hoping he'll come back once Mom stops drinking. He says he still loves her but can't stand watching her kill herself."

"He left *you* behind."

"I couldn't leave Mom. She needed me. And because of me…because of us…she's going to be okay."

What happened next, I can only describe as the opening of floodgates. Jason, Luke, Tessa, and their parents walked in, followed by Granny Max carrying a platter of cookies. As promised, she'd provided our class with her journals and the results of tests her doctors had performed, all amazingly positive. Her cancer had shrunk. Which she attributed to meditation, journaling, music therapy—and our healing prayers—rather than relying solely on her doctors for a cure. "I may have to reduce my workload next year," she'd informed us, "but I'll be back, no question about it."

After that, I only recognized one of the other thirty people who crowded into the room—Dr. Matt. His neck craned forward and his head turned right, then left, reminding me of a periscope searching for threats in enemy waters. He caught me watching and gave a slight nod. "What's with all the people?"

I shrugged, equally amazed at the big turnout, but not about to admit it. It was Open House for *all* at West Coast Middle School. Why *shouldn't* people visit our classroom? "Don't have a clue."

He frowned.

Okay, so my answer implied that I didn't care, but darn it, this after-school class was his idea and, as far as I could tell, a great success. The creative energy and enthusiasm circulating the room were impossible to ignore. He tugged at his ear and opened his mouth to speak when Tessa skipped through the open door, bright as tinsel and as hard to ignore. "Angelina's back!"

No sooner had the news filtered my mind than Angelina entered, accompanied by a couple I assumed to be her parents. My clue? The tears in their eyes. They'd attracted a crowd of well-wishers, who clapped as if at a revival. Weak-kneed, I sank onto the edge of my desk.

Angelina walked toward me with her parents in tow. "Ms. Veil, I'd like you to meet my mom and dad."

I stood and held out my hand.

"Oh no, you don't." Mr. Sousa pulled me into a victory hug, like the hug players give one another after a big win; not quite the running toward each other and leaping into the air kind of hug, but a pre-hug invitation and a quick pull and release. "Name's Greg."

Mrs. Sousa nudged him aside. "And I'm Marci." She kissed one of my cheeks then the other. "Sorry we took so long to get back to you, but we didn't believe at first that—"

"She was cured," Greg said, his voice wobbly.

Cured or healed? Cured meant Angelina's illness was in remission and her symptoms gone, a miracle by medical standards. If healed, Angelina would recognize that her physical condition didn't change who she was. And that would be the true miracle.

"We can't thank you enough," Marci said.

I'd done little more than lead the students—and myself—to the edge, where our imaginations could breathe, grow wings, and soar. The kids had taken it from there. Imagine that, a bunch of indulged, troublesome, impatient, resistant, tuned-out brats accomplishing the extraordinary.

"The doctors said the cancer's gone," Angelina said, "and there's no scientific explanation. So, I told them the explanation is spiritual."

"They couldn't refute the test results," Greg said.

Angelina grabbed Tessa's hand and pulled her close. "Tessa is the healer I told you about, Mom and Dad. She heals with her hands. I asked her how, and she said she didn't know, so I looked it up on the Internet. It's called Reiki. Tessa even sends Reiki through her eyes."

Tessa beamed at Angelina, the way a younger sister beams at an older sister who can do no wrong. Members of the crowd whispered and gathered close.

"Anyone interested in checking out our Open House projects?" Jason asked, a glib reminder of the reason for our gathering. "Shawn calls his project 'First Light.'"

Warmth crept over me. *First Light?* The name Maya had given our class.

Shawn motioned for his Uncle Matt to follow him and then launched into his rehearsed presentation. "'First Light,' refers to the first light emission, billions of years ago moments after the big bang."

"My project is out in the nature area," Codi said to those within hearing. "It's getting dark, but you don't need light to appreciate what I'm going to show you. If you like drumming and music that gets you shaking, this demonstration is for you."

I laughed, having gotten a taste of Codi's presentation earlier in the day, an effective opening to divine connection and healing.

"My project is about nonviolent communication," Ethan said. "I modeled it after Marshall Rosenberg's Nonviolent Communication Training Course, which tells you how to connect with others through empathy, integrity, and peace."

He didn't look very peaceful to me, but his scowl was now one of concentration instead of disapproval, which came as a relief. It was hard to imagine thirteen-year-olds talking about light emissions, the big bang, shaking, and nonviolent communication, the smartest teens I'd ever known.

The crowd was thinning when Charles Lacoste walked in. I experienced a defibrillator-type kick to my chest and sat back down. Not only was he walking unassisted, he had a smile on his face. Tessa touched my arm and signaled with a glance. *Don't worry. I'll divert his attention.*

"Mr. Lacoste, we're so glad you're back," she said, her voice gentle, her face luminous. I wondered if she was sending him Reiki through her eyes. "Would you like to see my epigenetics project?"

He nodded a greeting to our little group and followed Tessa to the southeast corner of the classroom.

"Let's listen in," Angelina said to her parents. "Tessa's project is about the wisdom of your cells."

"I'm glad Mr. Lacoste is okay," Luke said. "Did you know Ethan invited him to our classroom the day we teleported to the Winchester Mystery House?"

"Why on earth did he do that?" I asked.

"Beats me," Luke said.

"Ms. Veil?" It was Brad, *Brave Puppy*, with his mother in tow. "Can we take a look around?"

"Of course." I enjoyed seeing him again, despite his visit during our mask-making session, which had precipitated a tongue-lashing from Dr. Matt. Maybe he, too, was an Indigo. He was certainly drawn to the class, as was his mother.

"I pray they'll come up with something like this for kids like Brad," Vicki said. "He would benefit. All kids would."

I agreed but didn't say so. It's all about living in the *now* anyway and, at that moment, Brad was one of us.

"Marjorie?" It was Charles Lacoste. Tessa's epigenetic demo must have been a short one. "I owe you my deepest apology and need to tell you something I've told no one." He pulled in a breath so deep his chest expanded like the diaphragmatic breathing of yoga meditation. "What no one around here knows is that I died on the way to the hospital."

He closed his eyes for several seconds, giving me time to absorb what he'd just said. The word "died" pierced like a sting.

"My experience was a carbon copy of what you hear about in all those near-death accounts," Charles Lacoste said. "The light-at-the-end-of-the-tunnel thing. And the sense of peace, love, and well-being on the other side. What differed was that Ethan and the rest of your students joined me in my out-of-body travel. Crazy, but true. Ethan told me I was the best teacher he'd ever had and that he needed me. Can you believe it? Then he and the others pulled me back. I haven't shared this with anyone, because I'm afraid they'll think I'm a nutcase like…"

"Like me," I said, not the least bit offended.

Lacoste's eyes widened for a moment, as if to let more of me in or more of himself out. Then he smiled with such kindness and understanding I knew he'd changed in a life-altering way. "Yes, a nutcase like you."

"Um, Ms. Veil." It was Angelina. "Dr. Matt wants to talk to you."

I looked at the clock. Eight-thirty. Already?

"The presentations were amazing," Dr. Matt said to the crowd gathered around him.

Shawn beamed at me like the Big Sur lighthouse. I accepted his light with gratitude, feeling rather shipwrecked and glad for the solid ground beneath my feet.

"I've witnessed a group of nonconformists tonight," Dr. Matt continued, "independent and self-reliant beyond imagination, yet united as one."

So, what else is new?

"The danger of nonconformity is that children can feel different, isolated, and lonely," Dr. Matt said. "They risk losing friends, losing interest, and turning to drugs and alcohol."

Nothing I haven't heard before.

"But what I witnessed eight weeks ago at Spring Faire and again tonight shows none of these negatives. To put it in a nutshell, I'm quite impressed."

The clapping sounded strange to my ears, too loud—too much. My cheeks burned. My belly hurt. What now?

Angelina motioned for me to come forward. "Ms. Veil, we'd like to present you with a small token of our appreciation."

More clapping.

Oh dear.

Ethan held out what appeared to be a small jeweler's box. "You answered a lot of my questions with, 'I don't know,' and it really bugged me."

Applause. Hooting. I cringed. How could anything good come from this?

"But now, I know it's okay not to have all the answers," Ethan said. "It's the questions that are important." He glanced at Charles Lacoste, then back at me. "When you believe you know all the answers, you stop asking questions, and then the learning stops." He handed me the box in a quick, jerking motion. "This is from us…your students, Ms. Veil."

My hands shook as I opened the lid. Inside rested a silver chain. I lifted it out of the box and held it to the light. An exquisite pendant in the shape of a question mark swayed in front of my eyes like Chevreul's pendulum.

"We had it specially made," Tessa said.

I couldn't speak.

"Out of platinum," Jason added. "Our parents and Granny Max chipped in."

I shook my head, couldn't get a word past the humungous lump in my throat.

"Do you like it?" Angelina asked.

"Of course, she does," Shawn said. "That's why she's crying."

"You were courageous to take on an impossible task," Dr. Matt said, "and, miraculously, the after-school class worked."

Courage had played little part in my decision to take on the task, but I didn't have time to explain. "Ignorant might be a better word."

"A little ignorance plus unconditional love," Dr. Matt said, "works every time."

"She took us to the edge," Shawn said.

"Here, here," Jason cheered. "As in edge-ucation."

I pressed my hand to my heart, unsure how much more I could take without bawling my eyes out. Shawn laughed. He was reading my mind again. And for once, I didn't care.

"One more announcement," Codi said, which drew the attention away from me, thank God. I needed a tissue and time to regroup. "We made two hundred and fifty bucks at Spring Faire and decided to put it toward extending our after-school class into a program open to many. It's not much, but it's a start. We're calling it *First Flight,* and" —she held up Ethan's new owl, which had dimension, texture, and character that the original had lacked— "the owl will be its mascot to symbolize intuition, independence, and freedom."

The applause hurt my ears, warmed my heart.

The line between ecstasy and pain is a thin one.

Chapter Fifty-two

"NEXT THURSDAY WILL BE your last day," Dr. Matt said when I arrived at school on June 5—as if this were groundbreaking news. He'd caught me in the hallway next to the attendance office sorting through my mail. "I wanted to let you know..." He started to reach for his ear, then dropped his hand as if about to pledge to the flag.

Now that I knew him better, I found his ear tugging habit endearing rather than a signal to get my dander up. I waited to see where this conversation would lead.

"Starting August, I'm extending our after-school class program threefold and opening it to students other than Indigos. Thanks to Judge Stein, the school board has given me its full backing. All we're missing is the funding and" —he paused, his gaze expectant, almost clinging, as if trying to drag something out of me— "qualified teachers."

I didn't know what to say. Well, actually I did, but wasn't about to say it. Two additional after-school classes wouldn't be enough for all the students with latent, possibly dying, talents that needed to flower and grow. But Dr. Matt would have to discover that for himself. "For funding, I'd contact Ron Ardis," I said, recalling his promise to provide moral and financial support for the addition of more classes to the after-school program if I helped his son. "I'm sure he'll do everything within his power to promote your project. As for teachers... How about Granny Max and" —*what the hell*— "Charles Lacoste?"

His mouth dropped.

"These kids don't need teachers with psychic abilities to help them re-imagine themselves," I said. "They need teachers with love and compassion. And, believe me, Granny Max has both in spades. As far as Charles Lacoste is concerned…" I inhaled and took the plunge. "In his tough-love way and relentless attack on me, he revealed his concern for these kids. As for understanding their unique abilities, I believe he received a demonstration he'll never forget."

While Dr. Matt absorbed my suggestion—which going by the attack on his ear lobe, promised to take a while—I approached a subject I'd wanted to address for some time. "I have a question about Shawn…"

Dr. Matt blinked and dropped his hand. Apparently, this wasn't what he'd wanted—or expected—from me. Which suited me just fine. I planned on undertaking a lot in the future that challenged the expectations of others. Like marrying Morgan.

I had found my true north, using love as my honing device.

"What's with his parents?" I asked. "They haven't made a single appearance at school or shown the slightest interest in their son."

"They're afraid of him," Dr. Matt said, his voice a bell tolling.

We were still standing in the hallway. Backpacked and jean-clad students jostled in front of the attendance desk all talking at once, waving notes from their parents and late slips from myriad sources for myriad reasons. The school secretary looked harried as if this were something new instead of a common occurrence. An announcement came over the intercom about permission slips for the end-of-year dance.

"Come to my office and I'll explain," Dr. Matt said.

He signaled for me to take the chair in front of his desk and then, right on cue, walked to the window and looked out. This brought up another question: What was so darn interesting about the front parking lot? But that would have to wait; Shawn first.

Dr. Matt turned and looked at me, yet through me, making me feel like a window with a view to the past. "Even as a baby, Shawn would stop what he was doing and stare with the eyes of a wise old soul. You'd sense him probing your mind, which was not only eerie, but downright uncomfortable."

"I get what you mean," I said, then wished I hadn't. He focused on me with liquid eyes that seemed to ask, *Do you? Do you really?* To which my answer would be, *No, probably not. But I come close, closer than most.*

Dr. Matt perched on the edge of his desk rather than taking the chair next to mine as he had on my first visit to his office. This implied calm, though his downcast eyes and tight-lipped frown suggested otherwise. "When Shawn started to talk, he'd repeat people's most private thoughts. And as time went on, he stumbled onto family secrets without lifting a finger or opening a door. Nothing was private. Imagine how this affected his parents."

I'd experienced what Dr. Matt was referring to, not only with Shawn but also my birth mother, sister Maya, and future son, Joshua. All four had the ability to communicate between minds. Fortunately, I'd learned to accept this as a blessing rather than a curse. I was no longer afraid.

"I can't blame Shawn's parents for distancing themselves," Dr. Matt continued, "but they went too far. They unintentionally punished him for exposing things they wanted no one, including themselves, to see. Shawn didn't understand what he'd done wrong or why his parents treated him as though he had a contagious disease, hardly able to touch him, let alone show him their love. Over time, Shawn believed he didn't exist."

Imagining the pain Shawn must have suffered closed my throat. Swallowing became an effort instead of an unconscious act. Knowing what I did now, his progress in our class seemed extraordinary.

Dr. Matt rubbed his hands together, fingers outstretched and laced. "Later, after Shawn had aired so many closets that it brought healing instead of pain, it was too late to go back. The die had been cast, the wounds set. His parents had shamed him so many times, he'd learned to live without and in spite of them. One reason he turned to me."

As Dr. Matt paused to clear his throat, his words hung in the air, canceling out the voices on the other side of the door, the blare of the intercom, the ringing of phones.

He turned to me.

"I helped him the best I could, and, in all honesty, it was easier for me than for his parents. Like a grandparent, I was able to indulge Shawn to my heart's content, then send him home when things got tough. But it wasn't enough. Shawn struggled."

"Thus, the plan for an after-school class for Indigos."

My comment propelled Dr. Matt to his feet, his arms opening as if about to wrap me in a hug. "And then you came along. Just in time."

"The perfect solution until Charles Lacoste filled your head with nonsense about my instability. And rather than learn a lesson from what Shawn's parents did to him, you did the same to me. Penalize me for exposing things you wanted no one, including yourself, to see."

"I thought I'd put Shawn into—"

"The clutches of an incompetent teacher," I finished for him.

"No, Marjorie." Dr. Matt sat back on his desk and rubbed his eyes. "Shawn was already accustomed to incompetence. What I feared was putting Shawn into the hands of a beautiful, well intentioned, and misguided young woman, just the person to win his heart and destroy his soul. Something I'd never have forgiven myself for."

"So, any good news about the class's progress only confirmed what you feared."

"I'm afraid so."

I stared at his suit, wondering why he wore such ridiculously expensive clothes to school, then chastised myself. What business was it of mine, anyway?

He ran his hands down the sharp creases of his slacks. "Like my suit?"

I nodded, bit my lip.

He drummed his fingers on his knees; then, finally, a smile. "A hand-me-down from my brother. As are most of the clothes I wear. Shawn insists I have them, says it's the least his dad can do in exchange for taking over his duty as a father. I'm not sure how I'll survive when Rick retires and stops replacing his dozen suits every year. I'm spoiled. Armani is out of my league."

"Which probably explains the Mont Blanc, too," I said.

"A gift from Shawn."

I reminded myself that this is what happens when people judge without knowing all the facts. I'd done him a disservice. "One more thing…" Might as well go for the gold. "Why are you always looking out the window?"

He turned a fierce shade of red, then laughed. "Sure. Why not? Come take a look."

I joined him at the window and saw the usual: a parking lot jammed with vehicles picking up students after school.

"It's a wolf spider," he said.

I nearly disjointed my neck in my rush to face him. "A what?"

"A member of the Lycosidae family, wolf spiders live a solitary life and hunt alone."

I glanced at the disturbing paperweight on his desk. "You're talking about a spider?"

"What did you think I was talking about?"

"A sports car." I shifted my search to the windowsill for a cobweb instead of the parking lot for a convertible with the word "spider" tacked to its name.

He chuckled. "If it's a web you're looking for, you're out of luck. Wolf spiders are wanderers and burrow into the ground or under rocks. They're great at camouflage, so they're hard to detect."

"Don't see a spider," I said.

"There's one down there all right. I've been tracking it for some time."

At least he hadn't brought it inside like the one preserved in his paperweight.

"Do they remind you of something?" he asked.

I checked the flowerbed below the windowsill for a rock or burrow hole. "Not really."

"Think, Marjorie. Solitary. Great at camouflage."

"Give me a hint," I said, though I was beginning to get the picture.

"Shawn."

"That's an answer, not a hint." Actually, he had described all the Indigos as they'd been when I first met them: solitary, hiding behind protective walls, blocking the information stream.

"Yes," he said, "that's the answer."

Actually, that *was* the answer. My students didn't resemble wolf spiders anymore. They'd taken the personal responsibility to accept freedom. And I hoped they'd step up as leaders as well, to upset the consensus and change the world. As far as spinning webs was concerned, they'd done a topnotch job of weaving the finest of silken lines around my heart.

Chapter Fifty-three

I'LL NEVER FORGET OUR last day together. The students sat at their tables still arranged in horseshoe fashion—Shawn and Ethan to the east, the place for self-renewal; Angelina, Tessa, and Codi to the west, the look-within place; Luke and Jason to the south, where you find your true self.

And I stood at the top of the U, in the position of the north, where you put an end to the conditioning that prevents you from relating to the world.

Although the wall of windows faced east, the room absorbed enough afternoon heat to give it a stuffy feel. The air conditioner, probably installed back in the eighties, made a lot of rattling sounds, but did little to cool the air. As I observed the group of seven, now as familiar as family, I didn't know what to say, where to begin. An unnerving expectancy filled the room as though our fragile sense of strength and accomplishment would retreat into confusion if we dared talk or breathe.

"Let's crack open some windows," Codi said, and I teared up with gratitude. Without makeup, she looked like she'd just stepped out of a cool primordial rain forest, dark brown eyes, Doris Day freckles.

"Sure, why not?" I said. "This place could use a little airing."

We all watched Codi struggle with the ancient windows, using the rod with a bronze hook designed for that purpose. You'd think we were watching a juggler with five plates in the air, the way we concentrated on her efforts—a respite from the conversation to come, the questions in the air. *What now? What's to become of us?*

"Hey, Ethan," Angelina said, digging in her backpack. "Tell Ms. Veil about the mouse totem you brought me."

Ethan rounded his shoulders as though trying to compress into his former hard shell.

When Angelina held up the mouse totem, my first urge was to snatch it out of her hands, but I forced myself to remain still and wait this out.

"When I was sick, Ethan came to visit me," she said. "He borrowed your mouse totem to help him get over a few problems he was having, but figured I needed it more." She paused at the look on my face, then turned to Ethan. "You did get Ms. Veil's permission, didn't you?"

He shook his head.

"Oops."

"I figured the little mouse would find its way home," I said, though, in truth, I'd had my doubts. "It always does."

"This class is about forgiveness, right?" Jason said. "So—"

"All's well that ends well," Luke finished for him.

Jason slapped his palm against his forehead.

"The mouse totem helped me, "Angelina said before placing it on the table and sliding it in my direction. "Which counts for something."

I picked up the totem and put it in the pouch containing my marker stones. "Did my totem help you too, Ethan?"

He looked me straight in the eye for what seemed the first time. "Yes."

"Are you going to tell us your story now, Ms. Veil?" Tessa asked. "You promised."

My vote was to forget the past, not rehash it, but Tessa was right, I'd promised to share. Maybe experiencing the events of the previous year through the eyes and ears of my students would force me to look beyond the narrative, to the story behind the story. A story I could embrace.

"Forgive your past," I said, surprising myself. "We can't go back and start over, but we *can* start today and create a new ending."

"You mean give up our old stories?" Jason asked.

"Our *smaller* stories, so we can wake up to larger ones."

"She means release the dead hand of the past," Codi said.

We all turned to look at her, and right on cue, she rolled her eyes. "Dad's an attorney, okay?" At our silent stare, she shrugged. "I've heard him use that phrase like a zillion times to describe a negative capability."

A negative capability. Maybe by telling them my story, I could do just that. Release the dead hand of the past, and break its hold on my future. I pulled the chair from the front of my desk and sat; decision made. "Let me tell you about change…"

The trees beyond the window, heavy with leaves, seemed to heave a massive sigh. Class was almost over for the day, then four more days until summer break and the end of my tenure here. "Let me tell you about being different. Let me tell you about my walk through *the between.*"

"Cool," Ethan said, prepared to like my story. But it wasn't that kind of story. Its sole purpose wasn't to entertain.

I continued, my voice matching the soft rhythm of music playing in the background, "Memory," from *Cats* this time. "In his book, *Megatrends*, John Naisbitt says, 'We are living in the time of parenthesis, the time between eras…clinging to the known past, in fear of the unknown future.' He called this transition period, 'a great and yeasty time, a time filled with opportunity.' Unfortunately, during the story I'm about to tell you, I wasn't aware of Naisbitt's hopeful portrayal of what appeared to me as a big black hole. And I probably wouldn't have cared if I had. You see, I thought I was losing my mind."

No one said a word. Were they hoping that somewhere in my story, they'd find a clue to their own stories, or did they, in their wisdom, realize that the telling would be curative for me; their gift, rather than the other way around?

"You're now gazing into the between, except you have an advantage. You're not alone, and you know you're not losing your mind. So, listen carefully. Take notes if you like. Because after my story, I hope you'll discover a way through the dark wood and step forward with confidence into your own life stories."

The kids sat, silent, their eyes fixed on mine as I began.

"Sometimes, quite suddenly, we are caught unaware, and a door opens, offering a new insight, a new path, and we hesitate at the threshold, reluctant to go through, because we know if we do, life will never be the same..."

Acknowledgments

MY DEEPEST THANKS TO: my husband, John, who has been patient with me over all the years I've been writing and promising, "I'm almost done, just one more revision, this is it." Well, sweetie, it's finally true; my first reader, Kathy Simoes, whose praise and encouragement gave me the confidence to continue writing to the end; my readers, Jo Chandler, Natalia Orfanos, Christine van Steyn, Brock Kaiser, and Theresa Adrian; my long time writing buddies Dorothy Skarles and Lee Lopez, and members of *Amherst Writers and Artists' Group* directed by Gini Grossenbacher; my line and content editors: Judith Reveal, Melanie Rigney, and Moira Warmerdam, for their helpful input and encouragement; Coby Vink for giving me a tour of San Jose and the surrounding area for the setting of my story; all my students at Joseph Kerr Middle School for showing me that teaching can be fun and inspiring and can bring a great deal of meaning into one's life; my cover artist, Clarissa Yeo of *Yocla Designs* and Jonnee Bardo of *Gluskin's Photo Lab and Studio* for my author photo; my sons, Todd and Jon, and daughter-in-law, Martina, for not complaining about the countless hours I've spent at my computer writing, writing, writing; and my granddaughters, Angelina and Tessa, for demonstrating how smart and visionary today's youth truly are.

Many books were helpful in researching this novel, particularly *The Indigo Children,* by Lee Carroll and Jan Tober; *Beyond the Indigo Children,* by P.M.H. Atwater; *The Children of Now,* by Meg Blackburn Losey; *The A.W.E. Project, Reinventing Education,* by Matthew Fox, *The Last Dropout, Stop the Epidemic!,* by Bill Milliken; *Earth Medicine* and *The Medicine Way,* by Kenneth Meadows.

About the Author

Margaret Duarte, the daughter of Dutch immigrants and a former middle school teacher, lives on a California dairy farm. She earned her creative writing certificate through UC Davis Extension. A twenty-year fascination with the remarkable parallels between science and spirituality led to her four-book "Enter the Between" visionary fiction series.

For links to Margaret and her work, visit her at: www.margaretduarte.com.

Book one of the "Enter the Between"

Visionary Fiction series

Silicon Valley resident Marjorie Veil has been conditioned to ignore her own truth, to give away her power, to subjugate in relationships with others, and to settle for the path of least resistance. But she has many surprises in store, for there are synchronistic forces at work in her life that, if she listens, will lead her to her authentic heart and happiness. The seemingly impossible happens in the wild of the Los Padres National Forest where Marjorie goes on retreat to make sense of her life when she thinks she has gone insane. The innocence of the Native American orphan Marjorie befriends, as well as more mystery and adventure than she bargained for, show her how love can heal in what turns out to be a transformative spiritual quest.

Book two of the "Enter-the-Between"

Visionary Fiction series

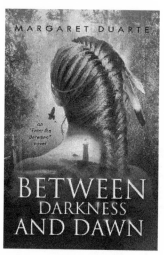

Marjorie Veil is running again. But this time, she's not running from herself. She's running to embrace her past so she may move on with her future. A future that includes a man and an orphaned boy who both love her. But in order to build a life with them, she must have the strength to defy the expectations of her over-protective adoptive mother, and she must be steadfast in deciphering the veiled messages coming from the Native American woman who died giving her birth. Marjorie's quest is the story of the soul trying to break free of its conditioned restraints to live a life of freedom, courage, and authenticity, and focus on what is really important in her precious present moments.